ALSO BY JUDITH A. BARRETT

RILEY MALLOY THRILLER SERIES

MAGGIE SLOAN THRILLER SERIES

GRID DOWN SURVIVAL SERIES

DONUT LADY MYSTERY SERIES

TAGGED BY DEATH

RILEY MALLOY THRILLER

BOOK 1

Judith A. Barrett

TAGGED BY DEATH

RILEY MALLOY THRILLER, BOOK 1

Published in the United States of America by Wobbly Creek, LLC

2021 Georgia

wobblycreek.com

TAGGED BY DEATH is a work of fiction. Names, characters, businesses, places, events, locales, and incidents either are the products of the author's imagination or used in a fictitious manner. Any resemblance to actual persons, living or dead, or actual events is purely coincidental.

Edited by Judith Euen Davis

Cover by Wobbly Creek, LLC

ISBN 978-1-953-87005-6

DEDICATION

TAGGED BY DEATH is dedicated to the color red and to all those who love and care for animals, especially strays.

CHAPTER ONE

As Riley Malloy, vet tech, eased her SUV into a spot in the last row of staff parking, she shuddered at how full the lot was. *I have a bad feeling about today.* As the sun cleared the horizon, she dashed to the back door of the Truman & Truman Veterinary Clinic and hurried inside. Her friend, Marcy, stood in the hall alone; her hands were shaking, and her face was pale.

"What's wrong?" Riley asked.

"I'm not sure, but it's not good. Big staff meeting in the lobby and everybody's here, even Dotty, the bookkeeper; in fact, Doctor Allen Truman, Senior, is making a rare appearance this morning. I peeked into the breakroom, and Doc Senior is there with two other men and a sheriff's deputy, but I haven't seen Doctor Truman, Junior, yet. I sure hope they aren't planning on cutting our hours again or laying off any more people. I know at least three vet techs will give notice today. Some of the girls have been crying—everybody's scared."

Riley frowned. *Marcy's right. A surprise staff meeting on a Wednesday? I'm scared too.*

Riley and Marcy stood next to the receptionist's counter. The remaining staff members were seated or standing in small groups. Dotty had moved the receptionist's rolling chair into position in front of the lobby door and had a clipboard in her hand. When the last two vet assistants arrived, Dotty recorded two checkmarks on the paper with a flourish.

Doctor Truman, Senior, and two other men stepped into the lobby. When a sheriff's deputy followed them, Marcy elbowed Riley. "Just like I said," Marcy whispered.

"Everyone here?' Doctor Truman asked.

"Yes, sir." Dotty scanned the paper on her clipboard.

Doc Truman motioned toward the men who stood next to him. "This is my lawyer and my—um—accountant."

Riley narrowed her eyes as she examined the two men. The middle-aged lawyer wore a brown suit and black shoes, and the other man's broken nose and clenched fists reminded her more of a has-been boxer than an accountant. *Maybe the lawyer dressed in a hurry; at least his shoes match each other.* Riley shook her head as she remembered the time she wore one black shoe and a blue shoe to work, and Marcy teased her the entire day and still mentioned it months later.

The lawyer glared at the staff, and the accountant crossed his massive arms as Doc cleared his throat. "You may have heard. It's very tragic news. My son passed away last night." Doc side-glanced at the accountant. "I think he was murdered."

Doc held up his hand at the uproar. "I don't want to talk about it. I'm closing the business. Gather your things, and leave your keys. We hired the deputy to be a witness when we inventory the controlled substances."

When Doctor Truman turned and walked toward the breakroom, the accountant and deputy followed him.

The lawyer opened his briefcase and removed a large manila envelope and a stack of folded papers that he handed to Dotty. While she shuffled the papers then stuffed each envelope with a folded sheet, he spoke to the group. "Your severance checks are in the envelopes with your names on them, and we'll include your letters for professional recommendations. Exchange your keys for your envelope."

"Written by a lawyer? No, thanks," one of the girls behind Riley muttered.

Marcy clutched Riley's arm and whispered, "Are you okay? Doc Junior always said you were his favorite vet tech. Everybody said he had a crush on you."

Riley's eyes widened. "I didn't know that. He never said anything to me."

Marcy and the other vet techs hurried to gather personal items while the vet assistants and receptionists lined up to exchange their keys for their paychecks. The lawyer snapped his briefcase closed before he hurried to the breakroom.

Riley watched as one by one, each staff member gave Dotty a key and received an envelope.

A vet assistant who stood near Riley elbowed her friend and whispered, "Did you know Doc Senior had an accountant?"

"No, and I've been here fifteen years," her friend whispered. "From the look on Miss High-and-Mighty's face, she didn't either."

The two giggled as they moved along with the line.

I have one more thing that's mine. Riley strode to the kennels and opened the door for Toby, a five-year-old, black and brown German Shepherd-Lab mix. All the staff recognized him as Riley's dog after a new client dropped off Toby for an exam but never returned. Truman, Senior, said Toby's arthritis was what scared people away from adopting him, but Marcy claimed Toby played up his limp when people were around because he didn't want to go home with anyone but Riley.

"Toby goes with me." Riley narrowed her eyes as she stood in the doorway with her arms crossed and Toby at her side.

"He's a mutt—not worth anything." Dr. Truman handed the lawyer a file folder but didn't look up from the paperwork he was reviewing.

The lawyer flipped through the folder before he placed it into his briefcase then glared at Riley. "Okay. You can take the dog."

"Good answer," the deputy growled. "Let's do the drug inventory, so I can leave."

"Medication room is this way." Dr. Truman led the other three men to the hallway.

While Dr. Truman and his lawyer counted the controlled substances in the presence of the accountant and the deputy, Riley loaded Toby's crate into her car then returned. She dropped her stethoscope and bandage shears into her purse and gathered Toby's records and his arthritis and flea and tick medicines into a sack before she picked up his partial bag of dog food. "Let's go, boy."

When Riley and Toby reached the bookkeeper at the front door, Dotty nodded, and her smile was weak. "I knew you wouldn't leave without Toby. You two belong together."

Riley handed the key to Dotty and accepted the envelope with *Malloy* inscribed on the front in Doc Senior's tight handwriting. Before Riley reached the door, Dotty rose and headed to the breakroom as a small, crumpled slip of yellow of paper fluttered from her lap to the floor. Riley picked up the scrap of trash and said, "Dotty—"

Dotty grimaced as she turned. "You should get away from here as fast and far as you can."

Riley stuck the piece of paper into her scrubs pants pocket and hurried outside. After she and Toby were in her SUV, Riley opened the envelope and slammed her palm on the steering wheel. *Two weeks' pay. I can't live in the car; it's impossible to apply for a job with no address.*

"We're meant to be together, Toby, just like Dotty said." Riley drove away from the vet's clinic. "My apartment doesn't allow animals, but we'll find a cheaper one that allows dogs. We'll need a little more money than this." A tear slid down Riley's cheek. "I can dip into my savings, but there's not much there."

Riley sniffed back the tears as she shoved the check, the envelope, and the sack of medications into her purse then pulled into a parking lot to call the apartment owner, who was a longtime friend of her Aunt Millie.

"I lost my job because the vet closed his business. How soon can I move out and still get my security deposit back?" Riley bit her lip.

"Sorry to hear that, Riley. We'll chalk it up to extenuating circumstances. Is this Friday okay? I'll advise the apartment manager to release your deposit."

Two days. I'll need to scramble, but I can do this.

She called her Aunt Millie. "Dr. Allen Truman, Senior, closed the practice today; he told us that Dr. Truman, Junior, died last night."

"Oh no. How tragic, but what a drastic reaction on his part. I can understand closing for a few weeks to mourn the loss of his son, but why would he shut down his business with no notice? Didn't he think about the impact on the staff? That's not right," Aunt Millie said.

"No argument from me," Riley said. "Do you know of any vet tech openings? And I need to find an inexpensive apartment that allows dogs."

"Everybody knew many of the Truman clients changed to a different veterinarian because Senior had become erratic in showing up for appointments. Junior didn't have the charisma his father did, and their business has been in a slump for the past six months. What did you say? You don't have a dog."

"Toby's mine now."

"Of course. I should have known Toby would be with you. You always were a dog whisperer, even when you were a toddler. I have an idea—why don't you stay at Grandma's cabin? It would be perfect, and the new vet in town needs help. You remember how to get to Grandma's? It's easy to find. Take the state road or the interstate to Barton, but before you get to town, look for the white house with a red barn. Grandma's driveway is next to that. Key's under the mat."

Riley scribbled down Aunt Millie's directions then she and Toby visited the farm store that allowed dogs. Riley and Toby selected a collar and a leash then Riley picked out food and water dishes before they examined the items in each aisle.

A woman with her hair tied up with a bandana stopped to talk to Toby. After he licked her hand, she rubbed his ears. "Your dog is so well behaved. The big box hardware store allows dogs on leashes too. I stalk stores looking for dogs to talk to. I'm the caregiver for my mother, and she's allergic to them. I get my dog time in when I can." She chuckled as she strolled to the carousel of seed packets.

After another hour of browsing, Riley stood in line to pay for her items and the package of flashlights that were on sale. The cashier gave Toby a treat and added two treats when she handed Riley her change. "We love all our customers," the cashier said.

Riley ordered a sandwich at a drive-through and ate in the parking lot at the hardware store the woman had recommended. As they strolled the aisles, Riley said, "We're going to need packing boxes, Toby."

A hardware clerk, who was shelving paint, said, "Two aisles over."

Riley snickered as she and Toby strolled to pick up boxes.

Riley fed Toby at the park then picked up a taco at a fast-food restaurant. After dark, when Riley decided most people would be in bed, she and Toby hurried to her apartment. She packed two of the boxes before she fell into bed.

* * *

The next morning, Riley carried the two boxes to her SUV in the dark then she and Toby left the apartment long before daylight. They ate at the park, visited the big box store, and strolled through downtown until after dark. Riley cruised the parking lot, and when she didn't see anyone around, they scooted into the apartment.

She packed the rest of her things then carried the boxes to her SUV. When she returned to the apartment, she sat on the floor next to Toby and hugged him as tears slipped down her face. "I'm scared. What if I can't find a job?"

Toby whimpered and licked her face.

"Thank you, Toby. I love you too."

* * *

"Friday, finally," Riley muttered as she brushed her hair then packed her toiletries into a backpack. She stared at her sunken eyes in the mirror. "I look as exhausted as I feel, Toby. Let's go." They slipped out to her SUV in the dark with the last of her things from her apartment.

After they had breakfast, Riley called the apartment manager to confirm her nine o'clock appointment then called the groomer that bathed dogs in partnership with the Truman veterinary clinic.

"I'll drop you off for a bath at eight then pick you up as soon as the apartment manager inspects the apartment, Toby."

By ten o'clock, the manager had inspected and returned her deposit. Riley picked up Toby and swung by the bank before she left her hometown, Pomeroy, Georgia, for Grandma's cabin near Barton, Georgia, three hours away.

After Riley passed the fifth white farmhouse with a red barn that she'd seen in the past hour, she slowed as she lifted her sunglasses to read a sign on the left side of the road. The once-black lettering burnt into the brown wooden sign that hung cockeyed on the fence was faded and almost unreadable—*Malloy Tree Farm*. In contrast, the sign on the gate, *No Trespassing*, was more prominent with its bright red letters against the faded black background.

"We finally found the Malloy Tree Farm, Toby. Aunt Millie saved us from living in the car, but we sure burned the gas when we traveled south for three hours on the highway then crisscrossed two counties only to find every white farmhouse with a red barn behind it."

After Riley climbed out of her SUV to open the tree farm gate, she pulled her sticky shirt away from her back and lifted the damp, golden copper ponytail off her neck. *Fixing the car's air conditioning is officially higher on my list of priorities.*

Riley peered down the lane that led through rows of towering pines and frowned. *I don't remember going past tall trees when Mom and I visited Grandma.*

Toby sniffed the air, and his low growl was guttural.

Riley wrinkled her nose. "I agree—it's the distinctive, pungent odor of a dead animal. The buzzards will be busy before long." She closed the gate behind her then eased her four-wheel-drive vehicle down the dirt path that led to a dip in the road and up a small hill.

At the top of the hill, she turned right onto a wider lane. After they reached a clearing, she exhaled in relief at the sight of a chimney.

She parked next to the weather-beaten dwelling then hurried to the door that faced the wide lane, but there was no welcome mat. A moment of panic intensified the throbbing pain in her head. *Cabin's smaller than I remember.*

Her voice squeaked. "What if this is somebody else's cabin?"

Toby nuzzled her hand, and she scratched his ears. She pulled out the used envelope with her notes from Aunt Millie's instructions. *Key under the welcome mat by the front door.*

The call of a hawk silenced the singing birds while the twitch of a rabbit's ear in the grass across the lane caught Riley's attention. The hawk dived toward the terrified, motionless rabbit trying to hide in the grass. At the last minute, the rabbit broke out of its trance of terror and dashed into the blackberry briars. The hawk scraped the dirt with its talons as it swooped the now-vacant spot then soared away.

"Let's walk around the cabin, Toby."

As they rounded the side of the cabin, Riley said, "I should have parked here; there's plenty of room, and I wouldn't be blocking the way in case Aunt Millie decides to check on us."

When they turned the corner to the other side of the house, Riley smiled in recognition of her old friend, the porch swing, and hurried to the doormat on the wide porch.

"Here's the key—in the first place any self-respecting burglar would check." Riley snorted as she opened the door and paused when the familiar aroma swirled around her. *Cinnamon. Grandma's signature scent.*

She flipped the light switch, and a flood of memories almost overwhelmed her as she gazed at the well-worn wooden floors, the old blue sofa with Grandma's favorite quilt thrown across the back, the soft rocking chair, and the four chairs around the small, hand-hewn wooden dining table with a cinnamon candle in the middle.

Toby investigated the cabin while Riley hurried to unload the dog crate, four boxes, and two suitcases. After she brought in her last box, she locked her SUV and sent Aunt Millie a text: "Here."

All of Grandma's things were gone from the bedroom, and Riley's eyes widened at the transformation to a vet tech's dream décor. A large dog bed lay on the wooden floor near the foot of the bed. A sage-green and brown tree quilt covered the bed, and the pillow shams were a scene at a dog park. A lidded glass jar filled with dog biscuits sat on the five-drawer dresser, and a small jar of pine-scented candle melts was next to it.

She carried her suitcases into the bedroom and opened the closet with spare sheets and blankets on the top shelf and a row of empty hangers. A built-in cabinet with shelves stood in one corner, and in the other corner were Grandma's deer rifle and shotgun. Riley backed up and stood on her tiptoes to peer at the top shelf and spotted Grandma's pistol and holster. *I'm five-two; Grandma was five-nine. I'll need a chair to get those down.*

She and Toby padded to the kitchen. The old bench and the boot tray for muddy shoes were next to the kitchen door, and the windshield scraper and brush hung on their pegs. Riley smiled at the elevated dog dishes for food and water. *Thank you, Aunt Millie.*

After she opened the refrigerator, she stared in wonder. "Aunt Millie left eggs, bacon, cheese, milk, and a covered casserole—no way will I go hungry this week."

She smiled as she opened the pantry door. "Dog food and treats. Guess you aren't going to bed hungry either."

After Riley lit the oven and popped in her casserole, she wandered into the living area and gazed at the fireplace. "I never understood Grandma's rule to lay a fire for the next person until now."

Toby whined.

"Oh, sorry. You don't have any water, and it's past your suppertime." Riley hurried to the kitchen and filled the dog water bowl.

While Toby drank his fill, she lifted the sack of dog food and read the label. "Not what you're used to, but it's close." She turned the bag to the front. "Fancy label. I'll bet it costs extra." Riley chuckled.

Toby furrowed his brow and pressed together his expressive eyebrows as he peered at the food bowl while she measured his food. When she placed his bowl on the mat, he licked her hand.

"You're welcome. Bon Appétit, my friend."

Toby sat and grinned, and Riley smiled as she waved her finger like a wand at the bowl.

"Okay." She pointed at the bowl, and Toby tasted his food then gobbled it down.

While Toby ate, Riley removed his medications from her backpack and set them near the kitchen sink before she pulled out a week's worth of laundry from her suitcase. "My own personal washer and dryer is a luxury. My apartment had a laundry room."

Before she dropped the clothes into the washer, she went through the pockets. When she found the scrap of paper in her scrubs pocket, she jammed it into her jeans pocket. After she returned to the living room and lit the kindling in the fireplace, she examined the books on the bookcase and snickered. "Aunt Millie arranged these. They're in alphabetical order by author."

She picked out a book of poetry, sat on the hearth, and read the first twenty pages. When Toby nudged her hand, she stuck her envelope with Aunt Millie's directions into the book to mark her place before she set it down on the coffee table.

"Break time?" She grabbed her sweatshirt and stepped out to the front porch. Toby stopped at the edge of the porch and growled as a gust of wind blew from the south.

Riley frowned. "I caught a whiff too. I'll bet the dead animal is close to the road. We'll investigate in the morning. I sure hope it isn't a dog."

While Toby wandered around the yard, Riley moved her car to the parking area on the east side of the cabin then returned to the porch. When Toby bounded to her, they went inside.

She hung up her coat on the peg by the door. "Homey fragrance of garlic and onion—my supper's ready." She placed two logs on the fire and grabbed her book.

After she served herself a plate of casserole, she sat at the dining table with her supper and her book. Toby flopped on the floor at her feet. When Riley finished eating, she wrapped the casserole dish for the refrigerator. "There's enough here for three more meals." She placed her dishes in the dishwasher and moved her laundry from the washer to the dryer before she hurried to the sofa with her book. Toby jumped up and joined her.

Riley woke when Toby nudged her elbow. She yawned as she picked up the book that had fallen to the floor and returned the book to the bookcase. "Outside, boy?"

Toby rushed to the door and nosed it. Riley put on her sweatshirt, and the two of them went outside to the porch. The nippy night air made her nose run, and she shivered. "Brr. Hurry up, Toby. It's cold."

Toby trotted to the yard then disappeared around the side of the house. When Riley sat on the porch swing, it creaked. *Just like it always did.*

After Toby wandered back to the porch, they went inside and to bed.

* * *

It was daylight when Riley woke, and her heart raced as she leapt out of bed in a panic. Toby raised his head and whined. Riley blinked. "Sorry. I forgot we're at the cabin. How did you sleep? I slept great until I scared myself."

Riley padded to the front door to let Toby out before she started a pot of coffee.

After her breakfast of bacon, eggs, and toast, Riley wiggled into her jeans then slipped on her favorite pink shirt before she stepped into her boots. *I need to either get new jeans or lose a few pesky pounds.*

She brushed her long copper hair then pulled it into a ponytail and hurried to her car while Toby investigated the yard. Riley started the engine then shivered and dashed back into the cabin for her sweatshirt before she opened the car's back door.

"Ready, Toby? I know, whenever I am, right?"

Toby leapt into the seat and grinned.

"Pretty agile for a guy with arthritis." Riley smiled as she headed down the driveway to the road. After she opened the gate, she pulled up the collar of her T-shirt to cover her nose. "Whatever died is close. Let's see if we can find it."

Toby jumped out of the car and trotted ten yards along the side of the road then stopped and stared at the woods. He took a few steps toward the ditch before he barked with a sound of urgency.

Riley frowned as she hurried to see what he'd found. "What is it, Toby?"

Her eyes burned and teared from the intensity of the pungent odor when she reached Toby, and she gagged at the sight of the body that was face down on the other side of the ditch. She slapped a gloved hand over her nose. *That man is dead.*

"Toby, come." She jogged to her car and grabbed her phone.

"State Police. What's your emergency?"

Riley slowed her breathing to calm herself. "There's a dead man in the woods near the road. I'm at the Malloy Tree Farm on the county road south of town."

"Someone will be there soon. How did you find the body?"

"The odor is awful. Last night I thought it was a dead animal, and it is even stronger today. I checked because I thought it might be a dog."

"Do you see a cruiser yet?"

Riley listened to the wail of a siren as it came closer and peered up the road. "I see it."

"If you're okay, I'll hang up."

"Yes, thank you."

The cruiser slowed then pulled onto the shoulder next to the driveway. The side of the car read *Sheriff*. A lean, middle-aged man in a tan uniform climbed out of the car. After he closed his door, he removed his sunglasses. "Riley Malloy—all grown up—and who's your friend?"

"This is Toby."

Toby trotted to him, and the sheriff held out his hand for Toby to sniff. When Toby nudged his hand, the sheriff absently scratched Toby's ear while he spoke. "I'm not going to ask you to show me where the body is. Ripe, isn't it? Just point." As he strode in the direction of the body, he said, "Don't leave. I'll be back in a minute."

When Toby followed him, the sheriff asked, "You got my back? Thanks, Toby."

The sheriff crossed the ditch and approached the body then spoke on his handheld radio. When he and Toby returned, the sheriff said. "The Georgia Bureau of Investigation is sending a team. No need for you to wait around for them. You staying at the cabin? I heard you're looking for work. They need help at the new veterinary hospital."

When Riley raised her eyebrows, the sheriff chuckled. "Millie's an old friend." He handed her a business card. "That's my cell phone. Call me if you need anything, but if it's urgent, call nine-one-one. Dispatch will send someone to you right away, and I'll be notified too."

After Riley opened the door to the back seat, she rolled her eyes at Toby who remained at the sheriff's side and watched her. "I'd rather stay too, but we've got things to do. Let's go."

The sheriff chuckled and waved to her as Toby dashed to the car and hopped in. The drive to Barton, the nearest town, took only fifteen minutes.

She smiled at the busy gas station. "Nice to see their business is still thriving. Grandma always said they had the best coffee and the best gossip in town."

When Riley reached the edge of town, she passed a small strip mall with five shops, but three of the shops were vacant with plywood over their front windows. The laundromat in the middle unit had a neon sign in the window, and a barbershop on the end had a brightly painted barber pole. She slowed to peer at the building next to the strip mall that had a faded sign near the road, *Small Animal Clinic, Edward Witmer, DVM*, and an empty parking lot. *The name's familiar, but I don't remember why. This doesn't look like a new vet's office.* Riley pulled in to check their hours of operation then frowned at the paper taped to the door.

"We didn't know for sure that Doc Truman, Senior, planned to retire, but the rumors sure flew when Doc Junior closed on Saturdays except for emergencies. I'm not ready to go through all the drama again so soon, but I'll see what the sign on the door says."

After she stepped closer to the door, she read the sign: *Gone Fishing. Be back on Monday.*

When she returned to the warmth of her SUV, she said, "Everybody's entitled to a vacation. We'll come back next week. Let's check out the town. Wonder if it's grown?"

She slowed to rubberneck as a crew paved the parking lot for a new, two-story building with a large sign near the road: *TWR, Termaine & Witmer Research.*

"Looks like a new business with the potential of jobs for people."

She passed a new housing development and the combined elementary-middle school campus. "That's another good sign, Toby. There are new houses, and the school has updated the old building and added at least two new wings of classrooms."

As Riley neared what she knew as the historic section of town, she marveled at the freshly painted and updated homes with neatly landscaped lawns. "I remember how rundown those houses were when we visited Grandma. I think the small town of Barton is thriving."

When she reached the downtown section, she gawked at the renewed storefronts and chuckled when she passed the contrasting hardware store. "Good to see the old hardware store looks exactly the same in spite of all the fancy boutiques and cafés that surround it."

Riley stared at the houses on the north side of town that were converted to business use: hair salons, barbershop, computer repair, and auto parts. Her eyes widened at the white clapboard house with the sign: *Barton Veterinary Hospital.*

She parked in the spacious, graveled area on the side of the building then led Toby to the grassy, designated dog walk. He sniffed and explored before he made his mark. When they went inside the building, a young woman behind the desk was on the phone. She had tied her blond curls away from her face with a pink bandana. Riley smiled at the dog and cat dishes with appropriate treats on the counter and selected a dog treat.

"Sit, Toby."

Toby dropped into his best sit, and she gave him his treat then rubbed his face. "Good boy."

The young woman hung up, and her eyes twinkled as she pointed her pencil. "You're Riley Malloy. Hi, I'm Amanda."

Riley raised her eyebrows, and Amanda giggled. "Your aunt said you'd be here, but we didn't expect you until Monday. We know all the dogs in town and their people. I'll let Doc know you're here."

Riley smiled. "Aunt Millie missed her calling. She should be a publicist."

Toby put his paws on the counter and rose to see Amanda.

"Who's this cutie? Toby, right?" Amanda asked as she offered Toby a treat.

"Just one more." Amanda gave Toby another treat before she left the receptionist area and hurried to the back hallway.

A few minutes later, Amanda came out a door on the other side of the reception desk. Her blaze orange scrub top stretched across her baby bump. "Come with me, Riley."

Amanda led Riley and Toby to an office in the hallway. "Doc will be here in a second. Like now." Amanda grinned, and Riley turned.

"Riley, how nice to see you. I'm Julie Rae Sorensen." A slender woman in her thirties, who wore a white lab coat over her jeans, held out her hand, and they shook. She was three inches taller than Riley, her black hair was clipped short, and her skin was a dark brown.

"Let's go into my office to chat for a minute or two." Julie Rae's smile crinkled the corners of her hazel eyes. "Who's this handsome fellow?"

A phone rang, and Amanda hurried away as Riley said, "This is Toby."

Toby dropped to his best sit position, and Julie Rae chuckled and pulled a treat out of her pocket then offered it to him. When Toby eased the treat from her hand, Julie Rae said, "Nice manners, Toby."

Julie Rae pointed to a small round table with two chairs. "Make yourself comfortable, Riley."

After Julie Rae rubbed Toby's ears, she joined Riley at the table. "Toby's welcome to come to work with you, but I warn you that he might put on a few pounds. Your aunt said you're a vet tech and one of the best. I respect an unbiased opinion, don't you?" Julie Rae raised her eyebrows and smiled.

Riley returned the warm smile. "I came here because Aunt Millie said you needed help; I need a job."

"Good, because I do need help. Pia is my other vet tech; she's been with me for two years. Our business continues to grow, but so far, we haven't turned away any clients. I have a new veterinary graduate that will start next week; he'll give me some relief, but the two of us will swamp Pia even more. I'll show you around, and you can tell me about your old job."

After a quick tour of the exam rooms and the kennel, Julie Rae said, "Talented vets aren't necessarily suited to be business owners. Sad, don't you think? I'm lucky. My husband takes care of the business side, and I play with dogs, cats, and the occasional horse. Did you ever work with horses?"

"I did," Riley said. "I was lucky enough to be the only vet tech who was willing to go to a farm. I don't know what the rest of them were afraid of."

"City folks." Julie Rae shrugged. "What color are your uniforms?"

"I have two colors: blue and gray."

"Wear whatever color you like. I like our diversity. We all wear jeans because they are sturdier than scrub pants. I hate to run, but I have to check on my patients. Be here Monday at seven. We've learned to reserve Mondays for the problems that popped up over the weekend." Julie Rae hurried out of her office, and Riley and Toby made their way to Amanda's desk.

"See you Monday." Amanda waved before she answered the phone.

"What do you think, Toby?" Riley asked on their drive back to the cabin. "I'm not sure you'd be happy left by yourself. They've got a kennel area just like we're used to. We can try it out."

Toby yipped.

"Good. It's settled."

When they reached the cabin's driveway, Riley shuddered as she peered at the four black cars parked along the side of the road and a large white tent that covered the location of the body.

After lunch, Toby followed her to the front porch then romped in the grass and explored the nearby woods while Riley read her book.

She was startled when her phone rang. *Marcy.*

"How are you doing, Riley? I have a new job. I start on Monday. I'm really excited because my friends say this is the liveliest clinic in town. It'll be a great change after the boring job at the Trumans'. I'm glad I'm not there anymore, aren't you? If you haven't found anything, I'll put a word in for you. You're the best vet tech I've ever known. You'd be a shoo-in."

"That's great news. I have a new job that begins on Monday too."

"We'll do lunch sometime—our version. I'll call you, and we can munch our sandwiches and crunch chips while we talk. It'll be just like old times." Marcy laughed, and Riley joined her.

"Thanks for calling. Have a great week."

After she hung up, Toby dashed to the front porch and turned to point as he quietly whined. Riley looked in the direction he was facing, and they watched in silence as a bobcat kit stalked a squirrel. The squirrel glanced at the kit and swished its tail in defiance. The tiny bobcat poised in the attack position and twitched its bottom before it pounced for the kill and grabbed the squirrel.

Riley's eyes were wide as the proud kit pranced away with its prey in its mouth. "That was awesome, Toby. Thanks for showing me. I can't believe how brazen that squirrel was. Do you suppose it has been watching that little bobcat since it was hunting grasshoppers?"

Riley closed her book and stretched. "Let's go for a walk." They strolled down the wide lane then continued on the long driveway to the road. When they reached the road, they turned back, and Riley stared at the hill. "I wasn't thinking. We have to go uphill to get back."

Toby raced to the top of the hill then sat to wait for her. A crumpled piece of lined yellow paper along the driveway caught her attention, and she picked it up. *Somebody's trash.*

She smoothed out the torn remnant and read: "Cooperate or die. Your choice." The handwriting was a scrawl that reminded her of a child trying to imitate cursive writing. *Must be part of a game.*

Riley snapped a picture of the note then stuck the paper into her pocket before she trudged up the slight incline. As they continued on the wide lane, Toby raced into the grass and flushed two quail. One of the birds feigned a wing injury and chirped a distress cry as it flew over the field. "She's distracting you from her nest, Toby."

Toby grinned and trotted toward the cabin. When Riley reached the porch, she picked up her book as Toby nosed the door. After they were inside, Toby rushed to his water bowl, and Riley flopped onto the sofa and pulled off her boots. "Your job for the rest of the day is to relax; I'll finish unpacking."

She hung her coats, shirts, and pants on hangers, and placed her underwear, socks, and pajamas on the cabinet shelves. After her suitcases were empty, she slid the luggage under the bed. She opened her boxes and placed her dressy pair of boots and the pair of sneakers in the closet. After she sorted through her text and reference books, she selected four she'd like to have handy then stacked the boxes of her remaining books and kitchen items in the closet.

Riley selected the first book in a series and propped up her feet to read. She woke with a start when the book dropped onto the hardwood floor with a thud. The deepening shadows of dusk replaced the bright sunlight in the cabin, and she shivered in the cooler temperature.

She disturbed Toby's nap when she turned on a lamp. He yawned and stretched before he plodded to the door; Riley threw on her sweatshirt as they headed outside. Toby dashed to the woods, and Riley gazed at the orange and red on the horizon and smiled at the memory of watching the sunset with Grandma. A single gunshot off in the distance reminded her of Grandma, who always said, "Last shot of the day. Hope it was a big 'un."

* * *

The next morning, Riley woke to the early light of dawn. She listened to a nearby barred owl and the return call of its mate before she pulled on warm socks and dressed for the chilly morning then rushed to the living room to light the kindling for a fire. After Toby followed her to the living room, she threw on her warm coat to go outside.

"Ready for a walk?" Riley headed to the door, and Toby trotted to join her.

When she stepped off the porch and crunched on the frozen dew on the grass, she shivered at the sight of the shimmering, icy frost on her car's windshield.

"Let's wait until it warms up a bit." She stomped her feet and clapped her gloved hands while Toby hurried to complete his business then dashed to the porch. When they were inside, she put more logs on her fire and sat on the hearth to warm up.

After the toasty fire chased away her chills, she went to the kitchen and flipped through Grandma's recipe box. "Here we are. Grandma's cinnamon roll recipe. I'll make these to take to the Barton Veterinary Hospital for my first day of work."

She lined up the ingredients on the counter and referred to the cookbook for the next step as she mixed, kneaded, and baked her cinnamon rolls. While the rolls cooled, she made a small pot of coffee to go with her obligatory sample taste. She examined the cinnamon rolls in the pan. "They don't look as nice as Grandma's did. I may need more practice."

She placed one on a plate and carried it and her coffee to the living room to enjoy her roll next to the fire.

After breakfast, she put on a warm jacket and the frayed pair of work gloves she found on the wooden bench next to the back door before she split kindling and carried wood from the woodshed to the porch. "Grandma always said, *she who cuts her own wood is warmed twice*, and when I was six, she told me carrying kindling to the cabin counted."

Riley hugged Toby. "I miss Grandma. Let's try again for that walk."

Toby dashed ahead to clear the way, and Riley trudged along then slowly picked up her pace as she fast-walked to the road and back up the hill. After she topped the hill, Riley jogged to the cabin.

"Thanks, Toby. I might lose my extra twenty pounds after all with your help as my exercise partner and the extra motivation of the cold air to move faster."

She hung her coat on the hook by the front door and backed up to the fireplace to warm herself before she scooped Toby's food into his bowl. After she twirled her finger and pointed with their usual, "Okay," Toby chowed down.

She poured a cup of coffee and placed another log on the fire before she sat on the hearth to enjoy the crackles of the fire and plan her day. When the heat drove her back, she sat on the well-worn braided rug, and Toby planted himself next to her.

When she finished her list, Riley rose. "Let's go exploring to see if we can find the hunting stand."

Riley sauntered down the wide lane while Toby investigated both sides along the way. When they came to the driveway, Toby stopped and glanced back with his head cocked.

"To the right, Toby."

. As they continued on their walk, Riley dragged branches out of the path but stepped over the downed trees and branches too large for her to manage. "I'll bet Grandma has a chainsaw somewhere, but I'd have to learn how to operate it."

Toby leapt over the downed tree trunks. "Very impressive, Toby. You jumped like a professional show dog."

When they came to a tree with branches that held it off the ground, Toby crawled under it before Riley climbed over the tree. "Were you trained before you came to the clinic?"

Toby grinned, and Riley nodded. "Thought so."

Riley smiled as they continued on the path. "I've always been able to interpret what dogs were telling me, but I never had a companion before. It's nice to have someone to talk to. Did you ever have a person who understood you?"

Toby gazed at Riley with adoration.

"I'm sorry you didn't, but I'm glad we're together too."

When they reached the wooden hunting stand, Riley examined the ladder. "This bottom rung's broken. I'll have to replace it before I can climb up because I can't reach the next step. I'll bet that key by the back door is to the shed where Grandma kept her tools."

As they neared the cabin, Riley hit her stride and kept up her pace except when she slowed to climb over trees. "Good walk." She flopped onto the porch swing and relaxed while she listened to the birds sing before she and Toby went inside.

Riley spent the rest of the morning watching videos on chainsaw upkeep, how to cut wood with a chainsaw, chainsaw safety, and chainsaw killers, but when the videos shifted to chainsaw injuries, Riley stretched and closed the link.

"I got lost in a maze of videos, Toby, but I have a better understanding of chainsaws and could probably tell a decent story around a campfire about a chainsaw murder."

She refilled Toby's water bowl then grilled a cheese sandwich and turned on the tea kettle for hot water. While Riley ate lunch, her phone rang. She smiled. *Marcy.*

"I just got a call from one of the girls in the office. Everyone is freaking out. Dotty was killed last night. I don't have any details at all. I don't know how or anything else about the circumstances."

"Whoa. That's horrible."

After they hung up, Riley shuddered as she finished her lunch. *First Doc Junior then Dotty.*

She cleared ashes out of the fireplace and laid the kindling and logs for her evening fire. When Riley examined her work, she furrowed her brow at the placement of the kindling and logs in the fireplace. After she rearranged them, she grabbed the key at the back door and hurried to the shed.

When she opened the shed door, she smiled at the slightly warped, wooden worktable with a garden wagon underneath it. *I remember when I stood on my tiptoes to see what was on that table.*

After she rolled out the wagon, she examined the boxes of nails, screws, nuts, and bolts on a small shelf over the table. A leather work apron, hammer, screwdrivers, chainsaw, and replacement chains hung above the shelf on a pegboard; an ax, maul, and splitting wedge sat in the corner of the shed, and scrap wood was stacked on a pallet. *I've got some learning to do.*

She shrugged. "At least I know what everything is, right, Toby?"

Toby grinned as he raised his expressive eyebrows. Riley selected a piece of wood from the stack of two-by-fours that she estimated was the same size as the broken step. She tied on the work apron, hung the hammer on one of the loops, and dropped a box of nails into a pocket.

After Riley spied a pair of leather work gloves, she shook them to remove any spiders or other occupants, just like Grandma showed her, and popped them into another pocket.

"Let's go. If I forgot something, we'll do what we can." Riley closed the shed door then she and Toby headed for the hunting stand.

After she pulled off the pieces of the broken step, she nailed the board onto the supports close to where the original board had been. She stood back to admire her handiwork. "Four nails on each side might be overkill, but I'm a beginner." She grabbed onto the board and pulled with all her weight, and it remained tight. She untied her work apron and laid it on the ground. *No sense in trying to haul any extra weight up that ladder.*

"Here goes nothing." After she climbed onto the first board and it didn't collapse, she tested each rung on her way to the top.

Riley felt along the side and top for a handle. "There's nothing here for me to pull myself up." She flopped onto her belly and scooted to the middle of the stand. When she arose, she gazed in awe at the view. "This is beautiful. I'm sure Grandma had binoculars. I'd love to sit up here and read and watch birds."

When she was ready to climb down, she couldn't reach the top rung with her foot; beads of sweat broke out on her forehead and trickled into her eyes as she clung to the side wall in her effort to reach the step. *Don't fall. Don't fall.*

After both feet were on the top rung, she clung to the floor with her fingertips as she felt for her next step with her foot. When she reached the ground, she exhaled in relief, and Toby nudged her hand.

"Grandma was a lot taller than me. I need to install a handle or something to hold onto going up but especially for coming down."

She dropped the scraps of wood, her tools, and the work apron into the wagon before she returned to the cabin with Toby alongside. Riley placed her tools in their respective places and added the wood to the small stack in the shed before she locked the door.

After they returned to the cabin, Riley pulled a chair to the closet and climbed on it to retrieve Grandma's pistol, holster, ammunition, and some paper targets. "I haven't fired a pistol in a year. Does the sound of gunfire bother you, Toby?"

After she put on her jacket, she opened the door, and Toby flopped down on the rug. "Not going?" she asked.

Toby closed his eyes, and she headed outside to set up her targets.

After forty-five minutes of target shooting, she hurried inside to show Toby. "I started off rough while I learned the idiosyncrasies of the pistol, but you can see here on this target that my aim improved."

Toby whimpered, and Riley shrugged. "I thought it was good. Guess I need more practice."

When he padded to the door, Riley took her latest book outside and read while Toby enjoyed his freedom. She had left her phone on the table. When it rang, she dashed inside to answer it. *Aunt Millie.*

"Glad you got to the cabin okay. How are you doing?" Aunt Millie asked.

"Tomorrow is my first day at Doctor Sorensen's veterinary hospital. I think I'm going to like it there."

"I'm sure you will. Julie Rae is awesome. She opened her business five years ago, but people still call her the new vet. Did you meet Amanda and Pia? They are really sweet girls, not like at your old place where everybody was snippy, but that was probably the stress of not knowing how long their jobs would last."

"I met Amanda but not Pia. She was busy. Thanks for the dog bed for Toby. He loves it, and thank you for the food for both of us. I appreciate all you've done."

"Good. You deserved a little pampering. I look forward to meeting Toby. I may be in Barton in a couple of weeks."

After she hung up, Riley opened the front door, and Toby trotted in for a drink then the two of them went back outside again to relax on the porch. At the sound of a rifle shot, Riley said, "Hope it was a big 'un," and kept reading.

CHAPTER TWO

As the sun hovered at the horizon, Riley kept the swing moving with a push of her toe on the porch as she enjoyed the impressive reds of the sunset. "It looks like a fire, Toby. Grandma said the sunset burned away any harshness of the day and left only peace. Mom said Grandma was the wisest woman she knew."

After their evening meal, Riley and Toby took a short walk then hurried back to the cabin. Riley lit a fire before she put her stethoscope and bandage scissors into her small work tote then picked up her book; Toby hopped up on the sofa with her. She rose to stoke the fire and placed another log on the hot embers before she returned to the sofa. When she'd read the same paragraph four times, she took Toby out for a quick break before bed.

It was dark when Riley peeked at the clock next to her bed. *Four thirty*. When she stirred, Toby padded to her bedside, and she rubbed his ears then hopped out of bed. "I think I'm excited."

After she served Toby his breakfast, she said, "I'll wear a blue top today; I haven't worn one in ages. It used to be my favorite before the clinic staff voted to switch to gray."

She rushed to the bedroom to dress. When she pulled her blue top over her head, she grunted when she couldn't get her arms through the sleeves. "I'm stuck."

Riley bent over and tugged at her top until she yanked it off and tossed it aside as she muttered, "At least I have three gray tops. The bad news is that I need more tops to get me through the week; the good news is that I can get my tops in different colors."

She scrambled an egg and toasted a single piece of toast. She stared at her dry toast then buttered it. "I'm pretty sure butter is good for you. Grandma always said it was."

After breakfast, she popped the cinnamon rolls into the oven that she had set at low heat to take off the chill from the refrigerator. While they warmed, she put on her long-sleeved, cotton jacket with pockets and packed her lunch and treats for Toby. She placed the warmed rolls on an aluminum pie plate and covered it with foil before they left.

"I'm glad you'll be at work with me, Toby," she said as they drove into town. When she passed the Witmer animal clinic, she peered at the empty parking lot. *Sign's still on the door.* She shrugged. *Not everybody has early hours.*

Amanda was on the phone when Riley and Toby tapped on the locked door.

As Riley waved, a young woman who wore a red scrub top rushed to answer the door. She was the same height as Doc Sorensen, but similar to Riley in body build; Aunt Millie said *curvy* ran in their family.

"Hi, I'm Pia." Her Puerto Rican accent was distinctive; her grin was infectious, and Riley smiled.

"Amanda will give you a key to the back door. This is Toby?"

Toby sat when she said his name, and she gave him a treat. Riley furrowed her brow, and Pia laughed. "It's just our way to get acquainted. We'll all adjust in a day or two."

"I brought cinnamon rolls." Riley bit her lip. "It's our way to get acquainted too."

Pia chortled. "I like how you think, girl. I'll show you where the breakroom is. Doc and I brought treats to celebrate your first day at work. It's our new tradition. Doc brought a box of vanilla coffee this morning, and I brought pound cake for lunch. Amanda has two babies to get ready for daycare in the mornings and has an automatic pass. Doc told her she can make it up after the babies are in college."

On the way to the breakroom, Pia said, "We have a scrub top stash. Sometimes things happen. It's handy to grab a fresh shirt that may or not fit, but at least it's clean. Toby can hang out with Amanda, you, or in our kennel area. Whatever he likes."

After Pia showed Riley the scrub stash, she said, "Follow me this morning to catch our routine. You'll be ready to solo after lunch. Kicked out of the nest first day. How's that for kid glove treatment?"

Doc came out of her office. "You pampering our new hire, Pia?" Julie Rae chuckled. "Seriously, if you have any questions, Riley, grab one of us and ask. I'm on my way to the breakroom. Anyone else?"

Riley and Pia followed Doc. Doc put a cinnamon roll on a paper plate and brewed a cup of tea for Amanda. After she returned from the receptionist's desk, she served herself a cinnamon roll and a cup of coffee then sat at the break table.

When a buzzer sounded, Doc and Pia dashed to the reception area.

"We've got an emergency," Pia called out over her shoulder.

"Stay, Toby." Riley raced to catch up with Pia.

When Riley reached the reception area, an overweight man in a suit with blood on the front of his shirt and suit coat stood near a dog that was wrapped in a ripped blanket on the floor. Amanda had knelt next to the old black dog; she stroked its neck and cooed as the dog whimpered.

"He darted out in front of my car. I didn't see him," the man said. "I threw him into my car and stopped at the gas station; they told me you'd be open."

"It's Dr. Witmer's Labrador retriever, Jordy," Julie Rae said. "Let's get him to an exam room."

Pia and Riley grabbed the blanket in a two-person lift, carried the dog to their trauma room, exam room six, and placed him on the table.

Julie Rae pulled back the blanket, ran her hands over his body in a quick survey then peered at his head laceration and his gums. "Poor guy. His left front leg is deformed. Let's take some x-rays to see what we have. The lac over his eyebrow doesn't look like it needs stitches. No blood around his mouth or belly distension."

After she listened to his chest with her stethoscope, she stroked his neck. "Heart's good. Both lungs sound fine. The head wound was the major source of all that blood. Let's get the x-rays then clean him up a bit."

Amanda opened the exam room door. "The man wants to know if Jordy will be okay. I can tell him yes, right? It's curious that the dog was on the road south of town, at least twenty-five or so miles away from Dr. Witmer's house in the country north of town.

I've never known Jordy to wander. I'll call Dr. Witmer's office and leave a message. They open at ten."

Amanda eased the door closed then returned a few minutes later. "I gave the driver a cup of coffee for the road, and he left his cell phone number, so I can call him with a report. Really nice man. He wanted to write a check for Jordy's care. I told him it was covered. Am I fired?" Amanda chuckled as she hurried to the receptionist's desk when the phone rang.

Riley helped Pia load Jordy onto the rolling table they used as a gurney while Doc wrote up her notes.

After the x-rays, Toby followed the gurney as Riley and Pia rolled Jordy back to the exam room. Riley sat at Jordy's head, and Toby stood next to her while Pia prepped to set his leg.

"I'm going to clean that cut, Jordy," Riley said. "I'll be easy."

Jordy whimpered, and Toby's soft moan in response sounded like a purr.

"See, Toby says you can relax."

Jordy yipped.

"Thank you. Now, let me know if I need to stop a minute."

Riley hummed a soft tune as she cleaned, and Jordy relaxed.

"All done," she said, and Jordy licked her hand.

"You're welcome." Riley beamed.

"We have another patient, Doc," Amanda said. "Run in with a skunk. I asked them to wait outside."

"Riley, are you up to doing the work up on a stinky patient?" Doc asked.

"I'd love to say no because this isn't my first skunk encounter patient," Riley said. "Shall I bathe him with vinegar?"

"Perfect. Let me know if you need me; otherwise, it's all yours."

"We have a room out back that we use for doggy baths," Amanda said. "I'll show you."

Toby followed Amanda as she showed Riley the washing station then Amanda and Toby returned to the reception area while Riley went outside to the front parking lot where a woman stood next to a golden retriever who lay in the grass.

"Whew. You got the full dose, didn't you, boy?" Riley asked as the dog looked up at her with sad eyes.

The woman shook her head. "This isn't the first time either. I'm not sure if he was protecting the house or playing with a new friend. I think he was still a little damp from the spray because he felt wet when I grabbed him before he ran into the house. I'll need to wash my clothes and take a shower when I get home."

Riley led the dog to the inside dog bath, and he whined as he trudged up the ramp to the tub with his head down.

"You won't be stinky after we get rid of the skunk odor," Riley said. "You must have been trying to get away because your eyes didn't get sprayed at all, did they?"

The dog yipped, and Riley chuckled. "They can spray a lot farther than I thought too. You had the bad luck to run across an ornery skunk."

Riley towel-dried him after his bath then led him back to the parking lot where the woman waited.

"Tell Amanda to call me if Doc wants us to come back for a checkup, but I have to get home to take a shower and clean this truck." The woman opened the passenger's door, and the retriever jumped inside.

Riley hurried inside to the stack of scrubs and found a top that fit her. After she changed to the new, hot pink scrub top, she dropped her smelly shirt into a sack and stuck it outside at the back door. She joined Toby and Amanda at the receptionist's desk and completed the paperwork for her patient.

"Toby's smart, isn't he?" Amanda smiled. "I'm not much into hanging around skunk baths either."

At eleven o'clock, a purple-haired woman in black scrubs burst through the front door and plopped her backpack onto Amanda's desk with a thud. "I'm here!"

Toby uttered a low growl, and Amanda reached down and scratched his ear before she glanced at the woman. "That's nice, Daphne. What can I do for you?"

"You're so funny, Amanda. I'm reporting to work." Daphne sniffed. "And since when does the doctor allow dogs in the office? Dr. Witmer's practice closed, so here I am, of course."

Daphne drummed her fingers on the counter and scowled. "Don't tell me that hussy, Alyse, beat me to you. Whatever she said about me, it isn't true."

Amanda removed a form from her bottom desk drawer and snapped it onto a clipboard. "We're a veterinary hospital. There are any number of dogs around here at any one time. Doctor Sorensen is a licensed veterinarian, and this is a business. We require an application for employment. Don't leave any blanks. If something doesn't pertain to you, indicate *not applicable* in the space." Amanda tilted her head. "What do you mean, Dr. Witmer's practice is closed?"

Daphne rolled her eyes. "Don't tell me you didn't know. Some out-of-town woman murdered him over the weekend. I heard she was the one who called the sheriff and told him where the body was. Ghoulish, if you ask me. We can just skip that little old application, right?"

Amanda turned in her chair, opened a file cabinet, and thumbed through files.

Doc walked out of an exam room. "If you're serious about working here, you're welcome to complete an application, and I'll review it for our next opening."

Daphne snorted. "Everybody knows you need help. Pia can't keep up with her work as it is, and no one can understand—"

"You can stop right there." Doc snatched the clipboard out of her hand. "Interview's over. You're welcome to leave."

Doc stormed into an empty exam room and slammed the door.

Daphne stared at the door and muttered, "I should have known that ignorant quack would stand up for her incompe—"

"You still here, Daphne? I'll be happy to walk you out." Amanda glared as she whirled her chair around and rose.

Daphne lifted her chin and growled at Riley. "I should have known you'd be behind all this. You're just like her."

When Amanda took a step toward her, Daphne scurried to the door and slammed it as she left. Amanda grabbed Riley's sleeve and pulled her to the breakroom.

"I need a cinnamon roll to calm my boiling blood," Amanda said. "Want to split one?"

She cut a pastry in half before she handed Riley her half on a napkin. "Daphne spews so much nonsense," Amanda continued. "I don't understand why her brother moved back here, but he was always big on family. Dylan's a really nice guy; maybe Daphne will sweeten up a bit with her brother's influence, but I doubt it because Daphne's so spiteful when she talks about his wife. The thing about Daphne is that sometimes there's a drop of truth somewhere in all her rantings. Do you suppose Dr. Witmer really was murdered?"

Riley bit into her cinnamon roll. "I don't know. Toby and I found a body close to my grandma's cabin this weekend, and I called the sheriff. Now that I think about it, I should let him know about Jordy. Sounds like the truck hit Dr. Witmer's dog not far from the cabin too. Who's Alyse?"

"She is—was Dr. Witmer's business partner. I don't think she was at his clinic very often. I've never met her. I think she managed the finances for the business, but she's not a vet or a vet tech."

Amanda returned to her desk while Riley left a voice mail about Jordy for the sheriff.

Doc joined Riley in the breakroom. "Sorry I lost my temper with Daphne. I know it was unprofessional, but I couldn't listen to any more of her hateful talk. I'll apologize to Amanda too."

Doc stepped toward the door then stopped. "If you and Amanda forgive me, I won't have to apologize to Daphne. It's a business rule."

Riley nodded. "You're right. It was unprofessional because you missed Amanda's threat to toss her out."

Doc laughed. "I knew you were one of us. Whatever that is."

The rest of the morning was a steady stream of sick and injured patients. Amanda showed Riley how the systems worked for making appointments, checking in patients, and accepting payments. Riley and Toby staffed the desk, and Pia took care of patients while Doc and Amanda ate lunch. When Amanda returned to her desk, Riley and Toby joined Pia in the breakroom.

"Sure glad you're here," Pia said. "We've always eaten lunch solo because we don't stop seeing patients at lunchtime." After they ate their sandwiches, Pia and Riley helped themselves to slices of pound cake.

"Are you familiar with our x-ray machine?" Pia asked.

Riley's mouth was full, so she shook her head. After she swallowed, she said, "The machine we used was a different manufacturer and an older model. Similar, but the one here seems to have some newer features."

After they finished eating, Pia walked Riley through the steps of operating the machine.

"I like this machine; it's more straightforward than the older ones," Riley said.

Not long after lunch, Amanda stopped Riley in the hallway. "Sheriff's here. I gave him the driver's cell number and told him what the driver told me. He'd like to talk to you when you're free."

When Riley went into the reception area, the sheriff was writing in his notebook. She sat next to him, and he looked at her and smiled. "Thanks for calling me. It was Dr. Witmer's body that you found; his car was close to where Jordy was hit. We think Dr. Witmer left Jordy in the car with the windows down. Jordy jumped out but must have waited for Dr. Witmer to return. Too bad Jordy can't tell us what happened. I'm waiting for Dr. Julie Rae and her report of Jordy's injuries."

Doc came out of an exam room. "Come to my office, Sheriff. I'll give you the latest on Jordy in return for the latest gossip." Her laugh was infectious; Sheriff guffawed.

At the end of the work day, Amanda switched the phone to voicemail, and Pia and Riley locked up the medications after Doc made her final calls to check on the day's patients. Doc met Riley in the hallway. "Our retired county animal control officer, George, is a widower and is happy to stay overnight with our sick or injured animals. Amanda called him after Jordy's leg was set."

"I love how organized you all are," Riley said. "See you in the morning."

"You have your key to the back door, right?"

"Sure do."

After Riley and Toby went out the front door, Pia locked it. When Riley reached her car, she narrowed her eyes at the torn sheet of lined, yellow paper under the windshield wiper. She shuddered as the removed the paper. *Just like the paper I found alongside the road.* When she unfolded the note, her eyes widened. The handwriting was the same childlike scrawl as the first one. She read the note: "Cooperate or die. Your choice."

She called the sheriff and left a voicemail before she snapped a photo with her phone then stuffed the note into her pocket and opened the back door for Toby.

"I don't know how I'm supposed to cooperate," she muttered as she drove home. "This note was obviously directed to me, but I don't know who the target for the first note was."

After Riley parked beside the cabin, she said, "I'll put my things inside and throw that stinky top into the laundry then we can go for a walk."

While Riley strolled, Toby dashed ahead then back to her. Riley said, "I need a warm-up before I can pick up the pace."

By the time Riley and Toby reached the hill going down, she was jogging. After they reached the road, she turned to face the hill and said, "Okay, hill. I can do this." She put her head down and walk-jogged up the hill. When she reached the top, she danced, and Toby howled.

When Riley reached the cabin, the sun had dipped below the horizon, and she gazed at the soft, glowing pink light in the west then shivered. "Turned cold when the sun went down, Toby."

She hurried to the front door, but before she was inside, the loud sound of a gunshot startled her. After a pause, there was a second shot then another.

"Target practice," she said. "Let's get the fire going."

After she and Toby ate, her phone rang. *Sheriff.*

"Got your call, Riley. Tell me about the notes."

Riley told him about finding the first then the second note.

"I can't make any sense of it," he said. "They sound threatening, don't they? Are you home?"

"Yes, Toby and I are at Grandma's cabin."

"We'll add your road to our night deputy's patrol route. Call nine-one-one any time, and he'll be there within ten minutes. I'll see you in the morning at Dr. Julie Rae's office. Bring the notes."

"Thank you."

Riley settled on the sofa to read, and Toby jumped up with her and placed his head on her leg. When Riley yawned later, she and Toby went to bed.

* * *

When Riley and Toby arrived at the vet's the next morning, the sheriff's cruiser sat in the front parking lot. Riley parked in the back then went inside the building with Toby.

Amanda was checking the day's calendar at her desk. "It wasn't supposed to be this cold." She shivered as she tugged at her crimson sweater in her futile attempt to wrap it over her neon yellow top and her round belly. "Did you see the sheriff? He's waiting for you."

As Toby padded to Amanda's desk then flopped down next to her, she asked, "Too cold for you too, Toby?"

"My dog's smarter than I am." Riley rolled her eyes. "I'll tell Sheriff I'm here."

When Riley hurried outside to the parking lot, the sheriff stepped out of his car. "Let's go inside. Dr. Julie Rae won't mind if we use an exam room."

When the two of them entered the building, Amanda was on the phone but waved two fingers.

"Exam room two?" Riley asked, and Amanda nodded.

After they were in the exam room, Riley removed the two notes from her pocket and placed them on the table.

Sheriff pulled a pair of exam gloves out of his pocket and inspected the two notes. "You're right. The paper, the handwriting, and the text look identical. I'll send these to a lab."

He pulled out two small plastic sacks from his top pocket and dropped the notes into the sacks then sealed them before he completed the evidence tags. As he headed to the door, his brow furrowed. "I'd tell you to be careful, but I don't know what to warn you about. My best advice would be to use your instincts and pay attention to Toby."

"How's Jordy?" Riley asked after the sheriff left.

"Doing well. The housekeeper called; Alyse expects Dr. Witmer's daughter to pick up Jordy soon."

Riley hurried to put her lunch in the refrigerator. When she returned, Amanda was on the phone.

After a quick conversation, Amanda asked, "You ready for today's emergency? I just got a call that a curious six-month-old Mastiff puppy tangled with a porcupine. Let Pia and Dr. Julie Rae know, would you? The puppy will be here in twenty minutes."

"Six months old? That puppy will weigh at least a hundred pounds," Riley said.

"You got it, girlfriend." Amanda answered the ringing phone.

Riley stuck her head into the exam room where Pia was administering the annual shots for an old Yorkie. Pia glanced at Riley and nodded. Riley stopped Doc before she went into the next exam room. "Six-month-old Mastiff puppy coming in with porcupine quills."

"Oh, boy," Doc said. "Prep exam room five. It's the largest we've got. Do we have an ETA?"

"Twenty minutes," Riley said.

"Good. I can see my patient that is waiting in an exam room. Have you told Pia?"

"She was busy, but she knows we've got something coming in."

Doc nodded as she rushed to her patient. Riley reviewed the quill removal checklist that Pia had showed her during her orientation and collected the supplies for room five.

Riley returned to the reception area to watch for the puppy. When a truck screeched to a stop in front of the building, Amanda said, "Here we go."

Two young men hopped out of the truck and lifted out the blanket that served as a stretcher for the large, injured dog. The driver hurried to catch up then walked alongside as she stroked the puppy.

Amanda pushed the alert button while Riley opened the front door.

"We'll go to room five—last room on your right." Riley followed them.

When the puppy whimpered and wiggled in its makeshift carrier, the woman stroked his back and cooed, and the dog settled down. "I can't stay and watch," the woman said. "Is that okay?"

As the family left the exam room, Riley whispered to the puppy as she stroked his side with a light touch. "I'll be right here."

While Pia placed a pad under their patient's face, the puppy shook as it whimpered.

"You're not in trouble," Riley said. "You're a good boy—just trying to protect your family. But now you know to stay away from porcupines, right?"

The puppy yipped.

"Yes, the porcupine knows to stay away from you too." Riley rolled her eyes, and Pia and Doc smiled.

After Doc made the dog comfortable enough to remove quills, she released Pia to care for the other patients that waited to be seen. When Doc removed the final quill, the puppy sighed, and Riley nodded. "That was the last one. All done."

"I'll talk to the family and let them know he's ready to go home," Doc said.

Doc escorted the woman and her sons into the exam room then they left with their puppy.

Doc's eyes twinkled as she and Riley inventoried the supplies they used. "Ready for a nap? Please say yes, so I don't feel old."

Riley chuckled. "That's the biggest puppy I've treated."

"Can you believe the morning's gone?" Doc asked. "Sure am glad I'm on first rotation for lunch today. I'm starved."

After Riley straightened the room, she went to Amanda's desk to check in.

"While you all were in there playing with a puppy, Dr. Witmer's daughter in Columbus called. She hopes to be here tomorrow to take Jordy home with her," Amanda said. "Aren't you glad that's over? Now you know why I'm happy to work the desk."

Amanda handed Riley a patient history folder. "Room four."

When Riley finished the preliminaries with the patient in room four, Pia sat at the receptionist's desk. After Pia hung up the phone and double-checked the appointment she had entered, she said, "Look over my shoulder. Did I schedule the appointment right?"

Riley peered at the screen. "Ten-thirty on Monday. It's there."

Pia exhaled. "Good. After Doc checks your patient, she'll meet Amanda in the breakroom. Do you mind straightening room one? I can't remember if I put everything away."

"Not at all." Riley cleaned room one and checked all the other exam rooms. When she finished, Amanda and Julie Rae were returning from lunch.

"Our turn." Pia jumped up from Amanda's chair.

While they ate, Pia said, "If I had my choice between quills or the front desk, I'd take quills every time. Scheduling appointments rattles me, and I don't know why."

"The credit card thing throws me," Riley said. "I'm always afraid I'm going to double charge somebody."

Pia smirked. "I feel better knowing you're only kind of perfect, just like me."

After lunch, Riley and Pia stopped to peek at Jordy who opened an eye before he resumed his nap; they chatted on their way to Amanda's desk.

Riley stared at Amanda's pale face and red-rimmed eyes.

"What's wrong?" Pia hurried to Amanda's side.

"I just got a call. Daphne died sometime last night. No details."

"Do you want to go to the breakroom for a bit? We can handle this," Pia said.

"No." Amanda blew her nose. "It's not like we were friends or anything. It was just such a shock. I already told Doc."

Riley shuddered. *Dr. Witmer then Daphne.* She frowned. *Just like Dr Truman, Junior, then Dotty.*

* * *

The next morning, Riley woke up at four thirty. When she pulled back the covers, she shivered. "Got colder than I expected."

She dashed to the fireplace and rekindled her fire. Toby padded into the living room and cocked his head. "I know. Too early to get up, but I couldn't sleep."

She warmed herself by the fire then raced to the bedroom and grabbed her clothes, so she could dress in front of the fire.

"I should set out my work clothes the night before, so they warm up with me next to the fire." She fed Toby then ate her breakfast. "I don't want to go for a walk this morning. Let's go into work. I can clean or reorganize or something."

When Riley and Toby arrived at the veterinary hospital at five thirty, Julie Rae's truck was in the parking lot. Riley and Toby hurried into the building, and Doc met them at the door.

"What are you doing here so early? I sure am glad to see you. I got a call from the sheriff's dispatcher. A woman was traveling to Atlanta and crashed after she hit a patch of ice. They flew her by helicopter to the trauma center. She had two Yorkies and a cat with her. The cat was in a carrier and is mostly angry, according to the on-scene deputies, and one Yorkie's badly injured; the other one may be okay because it took them a while to catch that wily girl. The crash was in the county north of us, but we're their closest veterinary hospital. A county deputy will be here with all three animals in a few minutes. Pia takes her son to school at six forty-five then comes to work. I need to put you in my cell phone contacts."

Doc hurried to the front to watch for the deputy while Riley placed food and water in two small dog kennels then water and cat food in a kennel with a cat box before she prepped the trauma room. After Riley and Toby joined Julie Rae at the front door, a deputy pulled up to the building. Doc and Riley rushed to the cruiser as a lanky deputy, whose nametag read *Carter,* stepped out then removed the small dog that was wrapped in a blue absorbent pad. Doc took the whimpering dog, and the deputy handed the cat carrier to Riley then picked up the other Yorkie and followed Riley inside.

"I'm handy with animals," Deputy Carter said. "I'll hang around for a little while. Where do you want this little girl?"

"Take her into the first room on the right. I'll see if Doc needs me then be right back."

Riley dropped off the carrier in the first room then hurried to join Julie Rae in exam room three.

Doc glanced at Riley when she came into the room. "Toby's calmed her down. He's amazing, isn't he? She's got a bad gash over her ribs. I'll need x-rays. Can you do that? Where's the other dog?"

"I can do the x-rays. The other two animals are with the deputy in room one."

"Ooo. You captured the cute deputy." Julie Rae chuckled as she left the room.

"Where do you hurt?" Riley removed the Yorkie's collar and read the attached tag as she touched the dog lightly and watched its sad eyes.

When the Yorkie whimpered and winced, Riley said, "You have a bad cut, Carlie. Let's see if you have any broken ribs. It won't hurt and won't take long."

Toby padded alongside as Riley rolled the dog into the hallway to the x-ray room but stopped at the door. The Yorkie yipped, and when Toby yipped in return, the little dog relaxed. Riley said, "He'll stay close."

After Riley took the x-rays, Julie Rae waited for them in the hallway. "I'll take over this little girl. The other dog is fine; she can go into a kennel. The cat's just irritated. Put him in a cat kennel. Maybe he'll be happier after he uses a cat box, but I doubt it."

When Riley went into exam room one, the deputy grinned. "Doc said both of these are fine. I'm Ben."

"Riley. Thanks for staying with them. I'll take them to their kennels." *Nice eyes. His hazel eyes are greenish. Mine are more golden.*

"I'll help then I have information about the driver of the car for you. This is Bella, according to the tag on her collar. I don't know what the orange cat's name is. I called him Psycho, but he turned his back on me." Ben side-glanced at Riley, and she fake-coughed to keep from smiling.

"That's a terrible name," she said. "After the cat's in his kennel, I'd like to take Bella outside for a walk. We won't be long."

"I'll tag along," Ben said.

CHAPTER THREE

Riley put a leash on Bella, and Ben followed them to the kennels with the orange tabby cat. Riley handed the leash to Ben then placed the carrier opening inside the kennel. "There you go, cat. Food and water."

The cat yowled, and Riley said in a quiet voice, "She's fine. Go on in."

The cat flipped its tail then marched into the kennel and growled.

Riley laughed. "Your secret's safe." She closed the kennel door and reached for Bella's leash.

Ben's eyes were wide. "Did you just talk to the psycho cat? Who's fine?"

The cat hissed.

"He heard you. Carlie's fine." Riley led Bella to the back door.

When they were outside, Riley dropped the leash.

"Make it fast, Bella," Riley said. "It's cold."

The little dog squatted then raced to the door. When Bella pranced to her kennel, Jordy whined, and Bella yipped.

"That was nice, Jordy," Riley said as she put Bella inside her kennel. The small dog drank her fill then flopped down and closed her eyes.

Riley hung up the leash. "She's settled. I need to see if Dr. Julie Rae needs any help."

"What did Jordy do that was nice?" Ben asked.

"He told Bella she'd be safe here."

Ben shook his head as he followed Riley to exam room three.

Julie Rae smiled. "Good news. No broken bones and no internal injuries. I stitched up her laceration. She'll need a bandage and a cone."

"I can do that, and the deputy has information for us about the woman who crashed."

"I'll wait while you take care of Carlie," Ben said.

"That works. I'll do my paperwork." Julie Rae winked at Riley before she left.

"What do you need me to do?" Ben asked while Riley scrubbed her hands.

"Wash your hands if you're going to help me."

After Ben dried his hands, Riley pointed. "Slip your hands under here and lift. A wrapped bandage will be more secure, and I won't need to shave her for the tape."

Ben lifted, and Riley placed a four-inch square gauze pad over the laceration before she deftly wrapped the bandaging material around the dog's abdomen. She nodded, and Ben lowered the dog to the table with care.

Riley selected a cone and handed it to Ben. "I'll put this on her after she's settled in her kennel. I suspect she'll sleep the rest of the afternoon."

"Who looks after the animals at night?" Ben asked as Riley eased Carlie to the cart to move her to the kennel.

After Riley explained, Ben said, "That's great Doc has around the clock expert care for her patients."

As they walked to the receptionist's desk, Ben said, "You're the best vet tech I've ever worked with. I've volunteered at our county animal shelter, and I've worked with a lot of different people with different levels of skills."

Riley tilted her head and peered at him, and Ben said, "I'm serious. I've never known anyone who understood their patients like you do."

"Thank you." Riley swallowed and felt her cheeks grow warm.

"Sorry." Ben cleared his throat and pulled his notebook out of his pocket as they reached the desk.

After Ben gave her the woman's name and address, he asked, "Is it okay if the dispatcher gives the family the veterinary hospital's phone number in case they want to make arrangements to pick up the animals?"

"We won't release them without authorization. It might be better if the dispatcher calls us first and gives us their names."

"Makes sense." Ben tapped his pen on his notebook then reached for a card. "Is this the number I can call to talk to you about how they are doing?"

"Sure," Riley said.

Julie Rae sauntered into the reception area from the hallway and raised her eyebrows at Riley.

Ben sighed. "Okay, then. I'll go." He stood with his hand on the door. "I might drop by the sheriff's office. Courtesy visit."

"How long have you been working nights?" Julie Rae asked.

Ben relaxed his hand as he stepped away from the door. "Two years—my last shift was supposed to be last Friday, but the sergeant asked me to work three more shifts this week because the department has two new hires that needed field orientation. Everybody starts on the night shift. I was on the day shift waiting list for a year and finally made it. I start on days tomorrow."

"Congratulations. We appreciate all your help, Deputy," Doc said.

"Thanks. I'm glad I could help." Ben smiled at Riley then left.

Julie Rae scowled at Riley. "He won't be able to make personal calls during business hours."

Riley's eyes widened. "I wasn't thinking. I'll give him my cell number." Riley ran outside. "Ben, wait."

He turned. "Did I forget something?"

"I need to give you my cell phone number. You can call me after your shift, and I'll tell you how our patients are doing."

"I'm glad you thought about that." He strode to her and handed her his notebook. She shivered as she wrote her cell number.

"Thanks. You need to go inside. It's freezing out here." Ben grinned as he opened the cruiser's door.

Riley ran back inside and blew on her hands. "It's cold."

"Certainly is. While we're thinking about cell phones, here's my cell phone number." Julie Rae handed Riley a card. "Send me a text, so I'll have yours. Amanda called. She has a doctor appointment this morning at eight thirty. It's on the calendar, but she knew she had to remind us."

"I'll straighten the rooms then make coffee," Riley said.

"Coffee. I haven't had my coffee yet. It's been a busy morning. I'll get the pot going while you work on the rooms."

After Riley cleaned the rooms, she found a steaming cup of coffee waiting for her at the receptionist's desk. As she sipped her coffee, she wrote her cell phone number on a sheet of paper for Amanda then checked the day's appointments. When her coffee had cooled to her preferred tepid temperature, she downed it and carried along her empty cup while she and Toby checked the kennels.

The sound of Jordy's tail thumping against the crate greeted them. When Toby yawned, so did Jordy, and Riley giggled. "Catching, isn't it?"

Carlie still slept, Bella wagged her greeting, and the cat swished its tail while it watched Bella and Carlie. Riley refilled her coffee then unlocked the front door and returned to the desk.

Pia burst through the door. "Sorry I'm late. The parent drop-off loop was a zoo. There was a car crash in the county north of us early this morning, and parents whose children normally ride the bus drove them to school instead because the roads might be icy. We need a drop-off line for experienced parents and another one for bus-kid parents. We have a patient in ten minutes, right?"

Pia dashed to the breakroom to hang up her coat and put her lunch in the refrigerator. She returned with a cup of coffee. "I started another pot. Like I need more coffee." She chuckled. "I guess I've completely adjusted to small-town living when I get all riled up by extra cars in the parent loop."

"Where did you live before Barton?"

"We lived in New Jersey. My husband's family is here, so when the new distribution center opened, he put in for a position and was promoted. It took some fancy talking on his part to get me away from my friends, but I love it here, and I'm closer to my family because my mother and sister live in Orlando. The school is small, the teachers are excellent, people in Georgia are nice, and I sure don't miss the traffic. My old friends tell me I've lost my edge." She laughed. "What about you?"

"I was south of Atlanta. Most of my family that lived here moved away or passed on, but my dad's sister kept my grandmother's cabin as a vacation rental. It was vacant, so that's where I'm living. I'm like you; I don't miss the fast pace and the traffic at all."

As a car pulled into the parking lot, Pia said, "First patient. Are you staffing the desk until after Amanda's appointment, or are we switching off?"

"I don't mind covering the desk." Riley smacked her forehead. "Almost forgot to tell you, we have a patient and two visitors in our kennels from the crash that your newbies talked about. Oh, and we have Jordy too."

Pia squealed. "Dr. Witmer's Jordy? I've always loved that sweet dog. I'll tell him hello as soon as we get a quiet minute."

As Pia and Riley headed toward the desk, Pia said, "I'm sure glad nobody's heard about the pets being here with us. I'd be stuck at school for the rest of the morning. You owe me details later."

"One more thing—here's my cell phone number."

"I'll text you later." Pia walked to the door and opened it for the new arrivals.

When Amanda came into the lobby later, she said, "I heard about the crash at the doctor's office. Tell me about the dogs."

"Go take a peek. They're in the kennel."

Amanda hurried to the breakroom and the kennel then returned. "Jordy's resting, and so is Carlie. Those little dogs are so cute. The cat's tag says *Mr. P*—unusual name, don't you think? What do you suppose the P stands for?"

Riley snorted. "No telling. The county dispatch office will call us before they give anyone our name or contact information. A deputy brought the animals here early this morning. You may get a call from him asking about the animals too. His name is Ben."

Pia strolled to the desk from the back. "According to Doc, Deputy Ben is a hottie. You left that part out, Riley."

Riley shrugged as she rose to greet their next patient.

Toward the end of their busy day, Amanda caught up with Riley, Julie Rae, and Pia who were in the hallway on their way to their next patients. "Just got a call from our county dispatcher who heard from the sheriff north of us. The woman's sister called him. She wants to pick up the dogs and cat in the morning around eleven. Is that okay?"

"It is if the sister will take Carlie to her vet to examine then take out the stitches later in the week. I'll need to know the name and phone number of the vet, so I can transfer care," Julie Rae said.

"Got it," Amanda said. "Thanks."

When Riley stepped into the hallway later to take out the trash from an exam room, Julie Rae called her into her office. Pia stood near Doc's desk with her arms crossed. Her face was red, and her lips were tight.

"Amanda asked me to call Dr. Witmer's daughter. The daughter told Amanda she wasn't sure when she could pick up Jordy. Amanda gave me the daughter's number, and I called her. She wants Jordy to be fostered."

"What? I don't understand people like that. Why wouldn't she want to have her dad's closest friend at her house?" Riley fumed.

Julie Rae shook her head. "I don't know, but it might be best for Jordy that she admitted she couldn't care for him rather than take him and not keep him."

"I have no words." Pia stormed out.

"He'll stay with us at least until he's well," Doc said.

Riley paused before she left Doc's office. "Thank you."

At the end of the day, Julie Rae said, "I talked to Carlie's regular vet. She's happy to take over Carlie's care, and she told me what Mr. P stands for. Any guesses? If anybody gets it right, I'll pick up bagels in the morning."

"Persnickety," Pia said.

"I'll bet you're right." Amanda giggled. "I'll guess Personality."

Riley grinned. "Perfect."

"Is that what he told you?" Pia raised her eyebrows, and Riley shrugged.

"Riley's right." Julie Rae stared at Riley. "Guess I'm buying bagels."

* * *

After Riley and Toby were home, Riley said, "It's not as cold as yesterday. I'll be brave, and we can take our walk."

Riley walked while Toby ran ahead until they reached the hill. She jogged to the road then back up the hill and on to the cabin.

When they reached the cabin, Riley dropped onto the top step and leaned against the post. "A little more every day."

Toby growled then pointed toward the tree line as he bared his teeth and growled louder.

"A bear?" Riley asked. Toby barked, "Yes."

Riley stood tall on the porch and raised her arms up over her head as she growled. "Go away, bear. Not safe here. Go away." Toby snarled and barked.

Riley listened to the sounds of an animal as it crashed through the woods and barreled away from the cabin. Riley stomped her feet on the cabin porch and shouted, "Don't come back, bear. Not safe."

As they went inside the cabin, Riley said, "I think it got the message."

Riley fed Toby then started the fire before she warmed her casserole.

Her phone buzzed notifications of texts. "Most activity my phone's seen in a while." Riley added Doc, Pia, and Amanda to her contacts. "I didn't do much other than work and take classes before we came here."

After she ate, Riley fluffed a sofa pillow before she settled down with her half-read book. "It's been a long time since I could relax in the evening. No money worries and no classes. Just a book and the best dog in the world."

Toby grinned as he jumped up next to her. When the fire died down, she stoked it and threw on another log. She was deep into her book when her phone buzzed again. After she finished reading the last page of the chapter, she picked up her phone and read the text: "It's Ben. Now you have my cell phone number."

Riley smiled as she added him to her contacts then texted back. "Thanks."

When her phone rang, Toby raised his head to glance at Riley. Before she answered, she whispered, "You knew he'd call, didn't you?"

"I've been wondering about Carlie. How's she doing?" Ben asked.

"She's comfortable. The injured woman's sister will pick her up tomorrow."

"Good news. I'm not sure I could have slept until I knew about Carlie. I think I told you I go to days tomorrow after two years of night shift."

"Yes."

"Yeah, well, I'm worried I can't get to sleep and afraid I won't wake up when my alarm goes off. I might drag tomorrow, but I don't think it will take me more than a couple of days to get back into a routine for the dayshift."

"That's good." Riley furrowed her brow and glanced at Toby who cocked his head at her. *Not a very sparkling comment, was it?*

Toby shook his head then put his head on her knee.

"What about you? How are you doing? You had a long day too," he said.

"I'm tired."

"Talk to you later then."

"Okay."

After they hung up, Riley bit her lip as she put another log on the fire. "Did I sound as awkward as I felt? I'm out of practice with this small talk thing." She stared at her phone. "Should I call him back?"

Toby rolled his eyes.

"Fine. I won't," she said. "It's a lot easier to talk to dogs than people sometimes." She rose and headed to her bedroom. "Almost forgot. It's Wednesday." She grabbed her scrub tops and tossed them into the washer. When the washer buzzed to indicate it had reached the end of the cycle, she placed her scrubs in the dryer.

After she finished her book, Riley rubbed Toby's ears. "Dryer's done."

As she hung up her scrub tops, she said, "I need to track which books I read and whether I'd want to read them again. Wonder how long it will take me to work my way through all the books? Wonder if there's a book on how not to be boring on the phone."

She yawned. "Time for bed, Toby."

* * *

While Toby ate his breakfast the next morning, Riley stared at her phone. When Toby stopped eating and yipped, she texted Ben: "Happy first day on dayshift."

When her phone rang, Toby growled.

"Don't nag. I'll be upbeat," she said before she answered.

"I was on my way to my truck when I got your text. You took away my jitters."

"Oh, good. I'm glad I could help."

"It's bright out here. I have to go back for my sunglasses."

Riley chuckled. "I never thought about that. I know you need to get on the road. Be safe. Talk to you later."

"Thanks."

Riley dropped into her chair and gulped her coffee. "You were right, Toby. It wasn't so bad."

After Riley and Toby arrived, Riley put her lunch in the refrigerator before she hurried to the kennels to check on their overnight visitors. Bella danced in her crate, and Carlie stood and wagged her tail as Mr. P cleaned his paws.

"You're going home today," Riley said.

"Don't let Bella tell you a sad story." Pia joined Riley at the kennels. "She just got back from a long walk; Carlie went outside for a few minutes too. Even Jordy got out for a few minutes. Did you know we have a dog wagon? It's like a people wheelchair, except it has a sling for the dog's torso. I'm not describing it very well. I'll show you when we take Jordy for his walk later this morning. Our first patients will be here at seven thirty. We'll be busy again today."

When they went to Amanda's desk, Amanda smiled. "Doc's at the bagel shop and will be here in a few minutes. Thanks for covering for me yesterday."

"You're welcome. As far as I'm concerned, your job is safe. Besides, Riley covered your desk." Pia smirked.

Riley laughed. "New girl here. You've got desk seniority, Amanda."

Doc called from the breakroom. "Bagels back here. I'll bring you yours, Amanda, along with some tea."

"Rank has its privileges." Amanda patted her hair.

A car pulled into the parking lot.

"Get your bagel, Riley. I'll take this patient; you can have the sweet cat with the irascible mama." Pia wiggled her eyebrows before she ambled to the front door to meet the arriving patient.

"Help yourself to a bagel," Doc said as Riley entered the breakroom. "How did our overnight guests do?"

"Carlie was on her feet and wagged her tail. Pia took both of the girls out for a walk, and Mr. P has settled down a bit. Jordy is happy to relax in his kennel and listen to Mr. P"

"Good. I hoped they'd have a good night. What's our schedule like today?"

"Busy, but I didn't see anything extraordinary on the calendar."

After she ate half a bagel, Riley hurried to see if her patient had arrived. When she reached the reception area, Amanda stood at the file cabinet.

"Here's your patient's history." Amanda held out a file as a blast wave from an explosion rocked the building. When Amanda screamed and lost her balance, Riley and Toby rushed to her. Toby leaned against Amanda to keep her from falling, and Riley grabbed Amanda in a bear hug to hold her steady. Amanda clutched Riley when their building shook with a second then a third blast.

Amanda breathed in short, gasping breaths. "What was that?"

"It's okay. Slow down your breathing." Riley cooed in a quiet voice, and Amanda took a deep breath and relaxed.

"Thanks," Amanda said as Riley helped her to the desk chair. "You two are an awesome rescue team."

Pia and Doc ran to the desk. "I got a text from the school. Their buildings weren't impacted, but they are under lockdown," Pia said.

Doc nodded. "Proactive on their part to go into lockdown; otherwise, they'd be bombarded by parents pulling their kids out of school."

"I'd be first one in." Pia's dark eyes flashed. Her phone buzzed a text. "My husband. The explosion wasn't at the distribution center," Pia said as she responded to his text.

Amanda's phone buzzed. "My husband just got home. He's okay." She replied to his text.

"I'd better text my husband too," Doc said.

Riley and Pia dashed outside then returned.

"Billows of black smoke south of town," Pia said.

Riley hurried back to her exam room, and Doc followed her.

"Did you hear that?" The cat's mama rushed inside. She carried her black cat with white-tipped ears and paws in her arms. "I think it came from the south. It wasn't the school, was it?"

"No." Amanda checked her in.

Riley walked around the desk to the woman. "I'm Riley. We can go into room two."

"Well, I'm glad it isn't the school," the woman said. "We'll wait for Pia. She has lots of experience."

Riley smiled. "I'm an experienced vet tech; I'm only new in town."

The woman frowned. "I don't know. How long will Pia be?"

Amanda glanced at the woman. "Pia has a complex case. You might want to sit. It may be an hour."

The woman huffed. "You might be okay, but I'll keep my eye on you, Reba. We'll see how you do with my little snookums."

"Riley." She led the way to exam room two.

When the woman set the cat down on the examining table, the cat arched its back and growled at Riley.

The woman's face tightened. "She doesn't like you."

Riley moved to the side of the table and held out her hand for the cat to smell. "Just girl smells, right? What do you think?"

The cat lay down on the table and purred. "Thank you. You're a pretty girl too."

While the woman gave a litany of the cat's symptoms, Riley stroked the cat's back then said, "I'd like to weigh her. We'll be right back."

Riley picked up the cat who snuggled in her arms. When she placed the cat on the scale, Riley said, "You and I need to lose a few pounds then we'll feel better."

The cat meowed.

"You're right. A little more exercise and a little less food might help both of us."

Riley returned the cat to the exam room and placed her on the table. "Doc will be here in a minute."

Doc met Riley in the hallway and nodded toward the exam room. "What do you think?"

"Poor cat's overweight. She needs a little more exercise and a little less food. I suspect fewer treats."

"I agree. I hadn't thought about exercise. That gives our client a reason to shop—she'll like that. I'll ask her to write down every time the cat gets a snack and drop off the list next Friday. That'll slow the snacks." Julie Rae chuckled.

After the cat's human paid her bill and left, Amanda said, "Our eight thirty appointment called and canceled. She lives south of town, and the road is blocked at the city limits. She'll either come in this afternoon or tomorrow morning. I made two appointments for her. It helps me to pull the patient's record before they get here."

"That's really smart," Riley said.

Amanda shrugged. "I don't know about smart, but I've discovered it's a great way to keep down the wait time. I'd rather avoid a backup, so we can all go home on time."

"South of town, you said?" Doc asked. "Riley, if you can't get home at the end of the day, you and Toby can go home with me. We have a guest bedroom, and I'd love for you to meet my family. My husband homeschools our eight-year-old and five-year-old boys, Kenny and Freddy, and runs our business from home. He'd enjoy seeing another live adult."

Riley smiled. "Thank you. So far, Toby and I have managed to avoid sleeping in my SUV."

"Ugh." Amanda shivered. "It's too cold to sleep in a car, at least tonight. Have you ever spent the night in your SUV?"

"No, and I sure am glad. I can't believe how cold it turned this week."

Pia had joined them. "My husband, son, and I spent the night in our moving truck when we came here, but it was a mild night. My husband claimed he was worried about our furniture being stolen, but we both knew we didn't have enough money for a motel. We splurged on breakfast, though."

A slight, gray-haired man parked in front of the building. As he stepped out of his car, a Boston terrier hopped out with him.

When they came into the lobby, the man said, "Did you hear about the big explosion? Dr. Witmer's building is gone, and the strip mall burned."

Doc's eyes widened. Pia snatched up the dog's file before she escorted the man and his dog to an exam room.

"I'll call the gas station," Amanda said.

"I've got some calls to make too." Julie Rae rushed to her office.

"This is Amanda. Is anyone hurt?"

She sighed in relief. "Okay, thanks."

After she hung up, she said, "My husband's brother works at the gas station. Their front glass shattered, but everyone's okay."

A car pulled into the parking lot, and Amanda handed Riley a file from her drawer. "Here you go."

At eleven thirty, a woman and a teenaged boy, who carried a small carrier, came inside.

"We're here to pick up Bella, Carlie, and Mr. P. I'd like to settle their bill too," the woman said. "My sister's still in the hospital but expects to be released tomorrow. She's been anxious about her pets."

"We'll send her a photo before we leave," the teenager said.

"Is that a carrier for Carlie?" Pia asked.

"Yes, we picked one up last night after the vet suggested it might make travel easier for her," the woman said.

Riley peered inside. "That's a nice pad. Bella's fine to go to your car on her leash."

The teenager grinned. "We have a carrier for her too. It's green. Mom vetoed the camouflage one I picked out."

"Bella is not a camouflage kind of girl," the woman said.

Pia chuckled. "We'll get the girls and Mr. P for you."

"Can I see where they are?" the teen asked.

"Of course," Pia said. "Bring the carrier and follow us."

When Bella saw the teenager, she danced and whined. Riley smiled. "She missed you. I'll snap on her leash, and you can walk her to the front parking lot, so she can have some time for a break and to explore before another car ride."

The boy and Bella left as Pia took Carlie outside for her break before her trip.

Riley opened Mr. P's cage and stroked his back. "Are you ready to go home?" she asked, and Mr. P purred.

"Here's your carrier." She held the carrier opening near the kennel door, and Mr. P marched into it.

When Pia and Bella returned, Riley said, "We have a new carrier for you, Carlie. You'll be more comfortable with the long ride ahead. Bella has one to ride in too."

Pia lifted Carlie into the carrier, and Carlie yipped.

"Is she okay?" Pia furrowed her brow.

Riley nodded. "You're welcome, Carlie, and you're right—Pia's good."

Pia tilted her head. "She was just saying thank you?"

"Yes, and you have a gentle touch."

"Thank you, Carlie." Pia bit her lip and blushed. "That was okay, right? I mean, to talk to Carlie like she'll understand me."

"Oh, she understands you." Riley smiled.

Pia carried Carlie, Riley brought Mr. P, and Toby followed as they paraded to the reception area.

After their overnight guests left, Riley and Pia relaxed at the break table with their lunches.

Riley smeared cream cheese on a bagel. "I haven't heard of anyone hurt. You?"

"No. A woman who brought in her sweet cat said the laundromat people don't open until ten, so no one was there. I'd heard the laundromat and the barbershop keep the same hours because they're the only two businesses that are out that far." Pia pointed at Riley's bagel. "That's a good idea. I have one of those microwave dinners that always leaves me hungry. I'll have a side of bagel too."

Riley's phone buzzed a text. When she picked it up, her eyes widened. *Ben.*

"r u ok?"

She felt her cheeks grow hot as she responded. "Yes. Not our clinic."

"Thanks."

Pia raised her eyebrows and cleared her throat.

Riley narrowed her eyes. "It was Ben."

Pia grinned. "Knew it."

Riley tore a piece of bagel, smeared extra cream cheese on it, and scowled. "He was being nice. I'm sure he heard a vet's clinic in Barton had an explosion."

"Of course. Everybody knows people in Georgia are nice." Pia covered her mouth as she dabbed her lips with a napkin, but her eyes crinkled, and Riley crammed the large piece of bagel into her mouth and glared.

Julie Rae hurried into the breakroom to refill her cup. "According to the grapevine, no one was hurt in the explosion. At least there's that."

Before Riley and Pia left the breakroom, Pia said, "I'm sorry if my teasing is heavy-handed sometimes."

"I'm not used to being treated like a real person. I'll adjust." Riley smiled.

Pia laughed. "You're about as real as they get, and I'm not joking."

While Riley relieved Amanda for lunch, Pia ushered the next patient into an examination room. After Pia closed the door, their next scheduled patient came in thirty minutes early. Riley weighed the patient before she showed them to an exam room then took over Pia's paperwork while Pia examined the other patient. After the two families and their pets left, Pia flopped across the counter in an exaggerated collapse. "Couldn't have done it without you, Shorty."

Riley crumpled a piece of paper and threw it at Pia as Amanda strolled back to her desk.

"I can't be gone for thirty minutes?" Amanda put her hands on her hips, and the three women chortled.

"Did I miss something?" Julie Rae handed a file to Amanda.

Before Amanda answered the phone, she said, "Just the usual paper fight."

Julie Rae shook her head. "Riley, I came to tell you the sheriff called me, and the road is clear for you to go home. I still owe you a dinner sometime though. My husband thinks we need to have everyone over for no reason at all before it gets much colder."

After the day's last scheduled appointment, Riley cleaned the kennels while Pia took Jordy out for his later afternoon walk. Toby padded to the kennels to inspect Riley's work.

After Pia and Jordy returned from outside, she said, "I'm so glad you're here. Amanda would have tried to help me, and she's got plenty to do."

"This job was a lifesaver for me," Riley said. "There aren't many vet tech positions open with good vets."

"I've heard that. Doc is a relatively new vet in a small town. It's hard to find good people that are able to relocate."

"Toby and I were definitely relocatable." Riley rubbed Toby's ears before he returned to Amanda.

"I've noticed Toby guards Amanda," Pia said. "Amanda says he checks out everyone who comes in the door."

"It's his job," Riley said.

"How long have you and Toby been together?" Pia asked.

"Eight months. A man brought him in for a checkup then disappeared. The phone number associated with Toby's chip was out of order. Dr. Truman had a lot of faults, but he had a kind heart. He didn't declare Toby a stray or abandoned dog and claimed Toby was the night watch dog. He didn't have a boarding license, so we didn't keep dogs or cats more than one night."

"Except for Toby."

Amanda and Toby joined them. "We've got a visitor," she whispered. "He's in Julie Rae's office. I think it might be the new vet. He's cute—dark blond hair and dimples. Want to peek at him? We can go to my desk by way of Julie Rae's office."

"You go first," Pia whispered as she pushed Riley.

Riley sauntered down the hall toward Doc's office, and Toby walked alongside her. When Toby whined, she whispered, "What do you mean, too awkward? This is my casual walk."

"Riley," Julie Rae called to her. "Come on in."

Riley stubbed her toe on the floor and stumbled but kept from falling by grabbing onto the doorknob. When the door swung back from her weight, she slammed into it and hit her face against the edge before the young man could reach her in his effort to stop her fall. He helped her up then held onto her as she walked to a chair at Doc's conference table.

After she dropped onto the seat, she felt her cheek below her left eye. "Ouch. Sorry, I tripped."

Doc blinked. "Yes, you did. You may end up with a black eye. Riley, this is Special Agent Reeves. He's from the Georgia Bureau of Investigation."

CHAPTER FOUR

"I have some questions about Edward Witmer, Ms. Malloy," Agent Reeves said. "I understand you found his body."

Doc rushed out of her office then returned with an ice pack and gave it to Riley. "I have patients to see."

Agent Reeves nodded as she left then he pulled out the other conference room chair to sit with Riley. Riley told him about the odor she noticed on Friday evening, how she and Toby found the body on Saturday, and the two notes that she gave to the sheriff.

Agent Reeves flipped open his pocket-sized notebook. "Tell me more about the notes."

"I found the first note Saturday afternoon. I picked up the crumpled paper in the driveway because I thought it was litter and read it only on a whim. It was such a strange message, and the handwriting was so childish that I didn't think it was as ominous as it sounded. I stuck it into my pocket to throw away. I found the second note on my windshield on Monday after work. I thought Daphne had left the second note because she was so angry that I was hired."

"Why was that?" Agent Reeves asked.

"When she confronted Amanda on Monday morning, it was obvious from her tone that Daphne assumed she already had a position here, but Doc hired me on Saturday. You can ask Doc more about it, but Doc didn't seem interested at all in hiring her, whether I was here or not."

"Where did you work before you came here?"

Riley told him about Dr. Truman laying off all his staff and closing his business, Toby, and moving to her grandmother's cabin.

"Allen Truman? Did you have free access to the entire building?"

"Of course," Riley said. "Well, except for his office. He kept it locked."

"Is that unusual?" He glanced around Doc's office. "Seems like Dr. Sorensen doesn't mind us in her office."

"He was the only vet I'd ever worked for. Seemed normal at the time," Riley said. *Why the interest in Dr. Truman?*

Agent Reeves pulled out a sealed, clear plastic bag from his top pocket and handed it to Riley. She stared at it then tilted her head. "This is a different note than the other two even though it has the same scrawl and same words: *Cooperate or die. Your choice.*"

"Are you sure? Look again," he said.

Riley pulled her phone out of her pocket and showed him the photos she had taken of the other two notes. "None of them are torn exactly the same."

He narrowed his eyes. "Why did you take pictures of them?"

She furrowed her brow. "I always document anomalies. Is that unusual?"

"Yes, it is."

He closed his notebook and returned it to his pocket before he stared at her face. His mouth quivered. "You'll need a photo of your cheek. I'll take your advice and find Dr. Sorensen. I'll be in touch."

He printed a number on a business card then gave it to her as he rose. "My cell number. If you think of anything else or come across any more anomalies, text me."

After he left, Pia rushed into the room. "That fall was astounding. You were a regular ballerina, and I thought you were going to recover. Too bad you hit your face. Do you need more ice? What happened?"

Riley glowered. "Have you ever tried to be casual so hard that your feet got confused? I fell into the deep pits of awkwardness."

"You totally owned it," Pia said. "The good news is Agent Hunk will never forget you."

"Don't tell me that. I'm hoping for amnesia. You don't happen to have a magic wand on you, do you?" Riley pulled out her phone and gave it to Pia. "Snap a photo of my face. Agent Reeves was right—I need to document it. I'm just hoping it is an anomaly."

Pia snapped the photo then squinted at it. "We'll need another picture after your eye blackens. Are you going to text him? He practically begged you to. Do you think I need another hobby besides managing your dating life?" Pia chuckled.

Riley grinned. "You'd be really good at crocheting, you know."

"I need an afghan." Doc came into her office. "I'll buy the yarn."

"Riley is pulling my leg. She's such a tease," Pia said.

Doc snorted. "I still like the idea of an afghan."

"You having a party without me?" Amanda stood in the doorway with her coat on. "I'm ready to go home, y'all. The latest speculation is that the Witmer building explosion was caused by chemicals, and someone was in the building when it blew."

"This is a lot of excitement for a small town. By next week, we'll hear from all our homegrown experts on crime investigation." Pia followed Amanda to the back door.

Doc frowned at her desk. "I'll organize this mess of paperwork before I leave."

Riley and Toby took Jordy outside for a break. When they returned to Jordy's kennel, he whined.

"No, I'm sorry, but Dr. Witmer won't be coming to get you," Riley said.

When Jordy howled, Riley and Toby sat on the floor next to him. Jordy laid his head on Riley's leg, and she hugged his neck then stroked his back and hummed a soft tune.

"Is Jordy okay?" Doc asked.

"He's sad that Dr. Witmer died." Riley patted Jordy's neck then rose.

"I'm so sorry, Jordy," Doc said.

Jordy scooted into his kennel and relaxed.

As Doc, Riley, and Toby left, Doc said, "I'm glad you were able to comfort Jordy. When he howled, it was so mournful that I thought something was wrong. I guess I was almost right, except he wasn't in physical pain. Thank you, Riley."

On the way home, Riley slowed when they passed Dr. Witmer's lot; the building had been reduced to rubble, and yellow crime scene tape closed off access to any of the property.

When Riley and Toby arrived at the cabin, Toby wandered as he investigated the yard. Riley zipped up her jacket. "Sure cools off fast in the country when the sun goes down. I guess all the pavement in the city holds the heat longer." She inhaled. "Fresh air with no city smells. Nice."

Toby trotted to the corner of the house and whined.

"A walk? That's a good idea. I'll take my things inside and be right back."

After Toby raced to the end of the lane, Riley broke into a jog and maintained her speed down the hill and back then on to the cabin. When she reached the front porch, she dropped to sit on the top step.

"Good run, Toby. Today was a stressful day. Ready for supper?"

Toby barked and ran to the door. After Riley fed Toby, she opened the pantry door and stared. "I need to plan my meals," she said as she surveyed the shelves. "Home canned chicken soup, and a bag of wide noodles. I can have chicken noodle soup and crackers. Perfect for a chilly night in a cabin."

While the soup heated and the noodles boiled, Riley glanced at her phone. "I have a voice mail."

She listened. "This is Doctor Truman. I have some paperwork you have to sign. I can bring it to you, if that's more convenient for you. I went to your address we had on file, but the manager said you moved. Call me back, or text me your address, and I'll be right there."

Riley frowned. "It's kind of creepy that he went to my old apartment without calling first, Toby."

Riley heated water for a cup of tea and stirred her soup before the timer went off for the noodles. She strained the noodles then mixed them with the soup and smiled. "Looks like there's two meals here. I love leftovers."

She took her soup, crackers, and hot tea to the dining table and frowned at her phone while she ate. After she cleared her dishes and packaged the extra soup for the next day, she pulled out Agent Reeves's card. *This is an anomaly.*

She sent a text: "This is Riley Malloy. Dr. Truman left VM wants my address/location. Okay?"

While she waited, she cleaned the firebox then laid a fire. When her kindling caught right away, she smiled and added a larger log to the fire. As she rose from the hearth to go to the bookcase, her phone buzzed a text.

Agent Reeves: "Not okay. Will talk tomorrow."

Riley stared at her cell. *Not the answer I expected.* She grabbed her book and propped up her feet, and Toby joined her on the sofa.

She was deep into her book when her phone rang and startled her. *Ben.*

"Hope it was okay to call," he said.

"I'm glad you did. How was your first day?"

"Day calls are completely different from night calls. Nobody told me that. The sergeant assigned me to traffic. Traffic is where everybody starts. There's a lot of people out in the daytime. I sound like a rookie, don't I?" Ben chuckled. "But I want to hear about you. How was your day? What do you know about the explosion?"

"Dr. Witmer's office building is south of town. Nowhere near us. I don't really know anything. There are rumors galore, but most of them border on unbelievable. One thing about a vet's office is that we hear them all. Bella, Carlie, and Mr. P went home with the injured woman's sister. Remember Jordy? He's going to be with us for a while. Pia rigged a dog cart for him so he can explore outside."

Ben yawned. "Excuse me. My trainer told me it would be four or five days before I'll adjust to the change to days. What are your days off?"

Riley's eyes widened. "I don't know. I'll have to ask Doc. I know we're closed on Sundays, but I don't see how the office could operate at less than full staff."

"I work on Sundays. I thought maybe you and Toby might want to go to a park some afternoon."

"That sounds great. I'll ask Doc about days off tomorrow. Get some rest."

"You too."

After they hung up, Riley put another log on the fire and opened her book. When Toby whined, she said, "Just four more pages."

At the end of the book, Riley slowly closed it then hugged the book before she replaced it on the bookshelf. "That was a really good story. Now, I need to find the second book."

Toby yipped.

"Right, tomorrow. It's time for bed."

* * *

When Riley and Toby arrived at the veterinary hospital early the next morning, Julie Rae's truck and the sheriff's cruiser were in the parking lot.

As Riley stored her lunch in the refrigerator, Julie Rae and the sheriff came into the breakroom.

Julie Rae poured two cups of coffee and refilled hers. "Your eye blackened from your fall yesterday just like I thought it would. How does it feel?"

"My cheek is sore." Riley touched her cheek. "How bad does it look?"

"Like you got the last beer." Julie Rae snorted then returned the pot to the coffee maker. "The sheriff and I have been talking, and he wanted to talk to you too. I told him you usually arrive early, so he was waiting for you."

Julie Rae carried her cup to the door. "I'll be in my office if you have any more questions, Sheriff."

After they sat at the table, the sheriff said, "I have a few questions to update my notes." Sheriff peered at her face. "This isn't on my list. How'd you get the black eye?"

"I fell and hit my cheek just right yesterday."

Sheriff shook his head. "That's too bad. Back to my list—when did you come to your grandmother's cabin?"

Riley smiled. "On Friday, a week ago. Toby and I drove here after my apartment manager gave me my deposit."

Sheriff sipped his coffee. "What was your last day of work at your previous employer?"

"On the Wednesday of the week that we moved here. At the time, it seemed like the worst possible thing that could happen, but it turned out to be the best."

"I know Doc is glad you're here," the sheriff said. "What did you do until you left?"

"During the day, Toby and I went shopping and hung out at a park. Dogs weren't allowed in my apartment complex, so we left before daylight and returned at night."

"What did you do about lunch? Did you go to any of your favorite places? What about the bank? Didn't you deposit your check?"

"I deposited my paycheck online on Wednesday and my apartment security deposit at the bank on Friday. I talked to a woman at the farm store, but I didn't know her. I never had any special lunch place because I always packed a sandwich or a salad for work, so I picked up sandwiches at a drive-through." Riley rose to refill their cups and started a fresh pot before she rejoined the sheriff at the table. "Sounds boring, but I've always been careful with my money."

"Did you run into anyone you knew or see any of your friends that week?"

"My only friends were people at work, and we were all busy trying to find new jobs." Riley furrowed her brow.

The sheriff raised his eyebrows. "The entire office was out of work?"

Riley nodded. "Dr. Truman, Senior, told us that morning that Dr. Truman, Junior, was murdered, and Senior was closing the business. We left our keys with the bookkeeper in exchange for two weeks' pay." Riley furrowed her brow. "My friend from work called me on Sunday and told me that the bookkeeper was killed Saturday night."

The sheriff set his cup down with a thud on the table, and his eyes widened. "Witmer then Daphne aren't the only vet and staff person combination to be murdered this month? Too much of a coincidence for me. We need to let GBI know about this. I'd heard a vet from Pomeroy was missing, but I didn't know he was murdered. They may have different teams working on the murders without realizing they may be related."

"Special Agent Reeves will be here later to talk to me," Riley said.

"That's good. All of this is out of my jurisdiction. I'll give him a call as a heads up. Thanks for the coffee. Be careful." Sheriff stopped at Doc's office before he left.

Pia and Amanda were going over the day's schedule when Riley arrived at the receptionist's desk. "We've got another busy day today." Amanda said. "Ooo. You have a black eye."

"I fell, but my cover story is that I got the last beer."

Pia and Amanda snort-laughed.

Doc joined them. "I assume you've noticed Riley's eye and are showering her with your usual level of supportive. Our new vet starts on Monday. He may come by today or tomorrow. Be nice."

Riley, Amanda, and Pia glanced at each other.

"Define *nice*," Pia said, and Riley and Amanda laughed.

Doc threw her hands into the air. "You three are impossible. We need another vet tech—one that knows how to be nice."

"Are you serious about another vet tech?" Amanda asked. "My cousin graduates next week and hasn't found a job yet."

"Would you want to work with your cousin?" Doc asked.

"He's a sweet kid. Hard worker, but really quiet. I wouldn't mind working with him."

"I vote we hire Amanda's cousin," Pia said.

Doc chuckled. "Amanda, ask your cousin to submit an application, and we'll go from there. I'd like to talk to a couple of his instructors too. Maybe we can schedule some regular days off if we can get our office staffed properly."

"Days off?" Riley asked, and Amanda and Pia smirked as they elbowed each other.

Doc sighed. "We close the office every Saturday, officially at noon, but it's sometimes one. Wretched, I know. When we first started, we were closed on Saturday and Sunday then over time, our scheduled appointments were getting later and later in the day. The business has grown."

"I suggested the Saturday mornings because the later times during the week caused problems at home for all of us. Dumbest idea I've ever had, but at least now, our latest scheduled

appointment every day is at four, and we go home at five o'clock."
Amanda glanced at the front parking lot. "Speaking of
appointments, here's our first patient."

"Would you take the first patient, Riley? I want to take Jordy
out for his morning constitutional and some fresh air," Pia asked.

"Sure will," Riley said.

Their second patient arrived as the first one approached the
door.

"Don't worry, Pia," Riley said. "I can handle both of them;
take your time."

"Thanks."

* * *

As Riley cleaned an exam room at eleven, her phone buzzed a text.
Aunt Millie.

"Call when you have a break."

Pia came into the room while Riley stared at her phone.

"You okay?" Pia asked.

"I think I might be in trouble. Aunt Millie texted me to call
her." Riley frowned. "I'm pretty sure the principal didn't call her,
but that's kind of what I felt at first."

Pia helped Riley finish up. "I remember those days. The
principal told my mother he had our home number on speed dial.

Go ahead—call her. There's only one more patient scheduled before lunch, and they haven't arrived yet."

When Riley went into the breakroom, Toby followed her. "Here for moral support, Toby? Thanks."

Riley sat at the table; Aunt Millie answered immediately.

"I just heard about Dr. Witmer and Daphne this morning. It worries me to death you're so far out of town and isolated at Grandma's cabin. A friend of mine has a small rental house that she has been renovating. It's close to Dr. Julie Rae's office in an old neighborhood. Helen said it will be ready for you to move in tomorrow, and she'll drop off the key this afternoon at your office. Your first month's rent is gratis, and Toby is welcome. She says it isn't fancy, but I'm sure it's nice. It's furnished. You'll have to provide your own linens, dishes, and pots and pans. If you need anything, borrow it from the cabin. Take a nice quilt with you. Nobody uses the cabin except for you and me. Please don't say no."

"I love the cabin." Riley bit her lip in thought.

"So do I."

"It does seem like the best thing to do, and it would be more convenient for me and for Doc if I were closer to the office."

"Thank you. I can breathe easier knowing that you're close in." Aunt Millie hung up.

Pia peeked into the breakroom. "Good you're off the phone, and you aren't crying."

"Maybe I should be because it was actually kind of sweet, now that I think about it," Riley said. "Aunt Millie was worried about me being so isolated, so she found a house in town. I guess I'm moving tomorrow."

"I hope you're not unhappy because it sounds awesome to me," Pia said. "Will you need any help moving?"

"Most of my stuff is still packed. Toby and I can move our things in one carload."

"I overheard. I'm excited you'll be closer." Amanda smiled as she stood at the doorway. "Our patient is in the parking lot, and I'll be ready for lunch after they leave."

While Riley staffed the receptionist's desk, a woman and a mixed breed miniature poodle came inside. "I'm so sorry," the woman said. "I just checked my calendar, and we were supposed to be here yesterday. I got day-confused. Can you squeeze us in?"

"We can. I'll get her weight then we'll go into exam room three."

A client, who carried a cat carrier with a Siamese cat inside, followed Pia out of exam room one. "Riley will schedule your next appointment." Pia ushered the unscheduled client and poodle into exam room three.

While Riley took the client's credit card, the woman said, "Welcome to Barton. You and Pia work so well together; it's like you've been a team for ages."

"Thank you." Riley returned the woman's card. As she scheduled the feline's next appointment, Agent Reeves carried two sacks as he came inside.

After the woman and the Siamese cat left, Agent Reeves said, "I usually eat lunch in my car. I was hoping to trade some cookies for a cup of coffee while we talk." He frowned. "You have a black eye from your fall yesterday. Does it hurt? Did you already have lunch plans? I should have checked first."

Riley smiled. "After Amanda returns to her desk, Pia and I have lunch in the breakroom. You're welcome to join us. Is it okay if we talk in front of Pia? And I feel better than my eye looks."

"Maybe we can eat lunch before we talk? I have a few questions about Dr. Truman."

"That would work," Riley said.

"Especially since you brought cookies." Pia grinned as she stepped out of the exam room. "Doc's with the patient now."

"And I'm back," Amanda said. "Sneak me a cookie later, okay, Riley?"

Agent Reeves chuckled. "I should have known I'd get caught." He handed the sack to Amanda. "Help yourself."

Amanda pulled out two milk-chocolate chip cookies and two snickerdoodles. "Two for me, and two for Doc."

Agent Reeves followed Riley and Pia to the breakroom.

As they ate, Pia said, "I'm glad you're here, Agent Reeves. I have a call to make, and now I won't be abandoning Riley. Doc told me I could use her office."

After Pia tossed her trash into the can, she said, "Two cookies, please."

Agent Reeves chuckled as he handed her the sack. She peered inside then selected a macadamia nut white-chocolate chip cookie and a sugar cookie with pink sprinkles.

"You have a remarkable variety of cookies, or is that a magic sack of cookies?" Riley giggled.

"I cheated. I bought these at the cookie shop in town and asked them to load me up with the favorite cookies of Dr. Sorensen's staff."

"Brilliant." Riley peered into the sack and raised her eyebrows. "You still have cookies left."

"I also have two éclairs in my lunch sack. I couldn't pass them up. Care for one?"

Riley accepted an éclair then bit into it. "This is wonderful. What a great find."

Agent Reeves bit into his éclair. "Tell me about the voicemail from Dr. Truman."

"He said he had paperwork for me to sign and that he'd gone to my apartment, and the manager told him I had moved. He asked for my address, so he could bring me the paperwork. I thought it was creepy that he went to my apartment before he called."

"Your instincts are good." Agent Reeves gave her a card. "This is my office address. Give it to him, and tell him it's your brother Eli's address. The office staff will watch for any mail addressed to you, but I have a feeling there isn't anything for you to sign. If he becomes more insistent about needing to meet with you, tell him you're staying at your brother's, and text me right away."

Riley nodded as she finished off her pastry. "Thanks."

She sent a text to Dr. Truman. "That's done, now I need to get back to work."

"So do I. Thanks for the company," he said.

Riley followed Agent Reeves as he headed to the door and smiled when he set the sack with the remaining cookies on Amanda's desk.

Amanda said, "You're welcome to join Riley for lunch anytime you like."

Agent Reeves grinned then waved as he climbed into his car.

"Nice guy. I need a glass of milk," Amanda said.

"I'll bring you a cup of hot tea," Riley said.

After Riley delivered Amanda's tea, the next patient arrived, and the rest of the day was a steady stream of scheduled patients.

At four o'clock, a woman with silver hair and thick glasses came inside without a pet. Toby slipped close to her, and she rubbed his ears and cooed, "What a sweet boy."

"Hello, Ms. Helen. That's Toby," Amanda said. "It's nice to see you. How is Petey doing?"

"That rascal is fine. I'm here to drop off the key for Riley."

"Ms. Helen, this is Riley. Riley, Ms. Helen," Amanda said.

Helen grabbed Riley's hand. "It is so nice to see you. I'm sure you don't remember me, but I would never forget you. Your eye is blackened. Are you okay? Are you still sassy?"

"Yes, ma'am, I'm fine. I tripped and fell. I think I might still be sassy," Riley said.

Helen placed a white envelope on the counter. "Well, good for you. The key is in the envelope. I wrote down the address of the house and my cell number. Now you call me anytime something isn't right. I can fix almost anything. Isn't that right, Amanda?"

"Yes, ma'am. You sure can. My mama used to say if you want something fixed right, invite Ms. Helen to dinner."

Helen threw her head back and laughed. "She always was such a wit, but I'll tell you, that woman could cook."

After Helen left, Amanda said, "You'll love that house, Riley. Did Pia tell you about the housewarming party at your place? We haven't planned it yet. We'll let you know."

After their last patient for the day left at four forty-five, Riley's phone buzzed a text as she and Pia cleaned the last exam room. Pia peered at Riley's phone. "It's from Ben. I'll read it to you. *I have tomorrow afternoon off. You have plans?*"

Riley and Pia laughed. After she caught her breath, Pia wiped her eyes. "Now, wait. Maybe we're being a little hasty. Ben can help you move then you two can go to Doc's for dinner. Doc's husband is a wonderful chef. I'll be right back."

Pia rushed to Doc's office and returned with Doc in tow.

Doc smiled. "Riley, Pia's a pest sometimes, but only because she jumps to an obvious solution more quickly than the rest of us. I am formally inviting you and Ben to dinner at my house tomorrow night after you finish moving. I have to warn you, though. If you dress fancy, Charlie won't feed you."

Riley smiled. "Sounds wonderful. Thank you."

"I am not a pest," Pia said.

"Matter of opinion," Amanda called out from her desk.

Riley picked up her phone and sent a text. "Plans include you. Call me after six?"

Ben: "Okay."

"Thank you, Doc. I'm formally accepting," Riley said.

"I am so glad you'll be moving to town," Doc said. "All the rooms clean?"

"Ready for tomorrow," Pia said.

"Let's go home. I've got paperwork to do, but it can wait."

"I'll lock up. I want to take Jordy out for our evening stroll," Pia said.

After Toby jumped into the SUV, Riley said, "Let's check out the new house to see what we might want to take with us."

When she pulled into the empty driveway, Riley's eyes widened at the white house that was surrounded by a black chain link fence. "It's so cute. I love the hanging geraniums on the covered front stoop."

She unlocked the door and squealed as she walked inside. "This is perfect."

The great room on her left had a gas fireplace in the corner, and the sofa, two chairs, and three end tables were arranged in a semi-circle around the fireplace; on her right was the dining area: a wooden dining table and four chairs and a small bookcase against the wall. The gleaming hardwood floor was covered with a sage-green area rug on the living room side. She picked up the controller that was on top of the fireplace mantle. When she pressed the on button, the gas logs in the fireplace ignited. "Wow. This is awesome. We still have the cabin fireplace when I need the satisfaction of cutting my own firewood." She pressed the off button. "We're going to love this when we come home from work on a cold day."

The kitchen and dining area were divided by a tall breakfast bar with three barstools. She continued through the living area to the hallway on her left. The bathroom and a bedroom were on the right side of the wide hallway. She peeked into the bathroom. "It has a tub and a shower curtain. Good."

She hurried to the bedroom and smiled at the oval braided rug on the floor, the dark gray curtains, and the new queen-sized mattress and box springs. "One of Grandma's quilts would be perfect in here, and my sheets are queen-sized, so we're good."

Riley and Toby returned to examine the kitchen, and she opened the kitchen drawers and cabinet doors before she peered into the small pantry. "Plenty of storage."

The washer and dryer were in a small alcove between the pantry and the back door. When she opened the back door, Toby dashed outside.

"Nice wide porch—it's perfect for reading and relaxing—and we have two chairs and a little table. We'll spend a lot of time out here, won't we, Toby?" She sat on the padded seat of a patio chair. "This is comfortable."

She sighed as she rose. "Time to lock up; I need to organize my packing."

As Riley drove to the cabin, she said, "I planned to do my cleaning right after work tomorrow afternoon, but the little house is spotless. The best thing that ever happened to us is when Doc Senior laid me off, and you went home with me."

Toby yipped, and Riley's eyes crinkled as she smiled. "I like it in Barton too."

After they arrived at the cabin, Riley surveyed her belongings in the closet. "Most of my stuff is still packed. I have sheets, and a few dishes and pans. I'll inventory what I have so I can take Aunt Millie's advice and borrow what I'd need from the cabin."

While Toby ate his supper, Riley's phone rang. *Ben.*

"So, what are my plans?" Ben asked.

Riley snickered. *I hear the smile in his voice.* "I'm moving into a house in Barton tomorrow after work. You feel like helping?"

"Sounds great to me. I can be there by two."

"Meet me at my new house then we can go to Grandma's cabin to pick up the rest of my things. I'll text you the address."

"Anything I need to bring? I can borrow a dolly to move furniture."

"I don't have anything heavy to move, and the house has everything I'd need as far as furniture is concerned. After we move everything to the new house, I may have enough time to unpack at least the kitchen, but it isn't critical because we're invited to Doc's for dinner."

"Oh, no. I planned to wear jeans. Will I have time to run home and change?" Ben asked.

"I don't think that's a good idea. Doc said we're supposed to go straight to their house after we move my things, and if we're dressed too fancy, her husband, Charlie, won't allow us to eat. Pia said he's a chef."

Ben chuckled. "We wouldn't want to miss out. Jeans, it is."

"I should tell you that I tripped and fell yesterday. I have a black eye."

"Did everybody who saw you today tell you that?"

Riley laughed. "They sure did. You don't know how bad I wanted to be shocked and say I didn't know that my eye was black."

Ben laughed with her. "I ran into a pole my first week at the police academy. The next day, at least two hundred people told me that my eye was black. Might not have been two hundred, but it sure seemed like it."

"It's nice to talk to a kindred klutz," Riley said.

"I agree—see you tomorrow."

After she ate her quick meal of toast and jam and scrambled eggs with cheese, Riley grabbed a pen and pad and went through her boxes. She sighed. "Toby, let's go outside for some fresh air. You can run around, and I'll work on my list."

When Toby trotted to the door to go back inside after his break, Riley rose from her patio chair. "Good timing. I'm ready to start packing."

Riley opened one of her boxes and added kitchen items. "Toaster, cast iron skillet, coffee maker." She ticked items off her list; Toby fell asleep on the rug. After she filled her first box, she marked it with the contents then carried it out to her car with a quilt folded on top of the box.

"Might be smart to do my laundry now. I won't have time tomorrow, and I'll be busy unpacking on Sunday."

Toby opened one eye then rolled onto his back. Riley picked up her dirty clothesbasket. Toby followed her from the bedroom but stopped for a long drink at his water bowl. As she removed items, she checked pockets then tossed the clothes into the washer. When she pulled out her jeans from the bottom of the basket, Riley checked the pockets and frowned at a scrap of yellow paper. "Where'd this come from?"

CHAPTER FIVE

She shuddered as she unfolded the paper. *Same scrawl.* She furrowed her brow as she read: "Good choice."

"This is the paper that Dotty dropped. How did it survive being washed?"

Toby yipped.

Riley bit her lip. "You're right. I was wearing these jeans last Friday when I did laundry and found the paper in my scrub pants pocket. I washed the skunk-smell top on Monday then washed all the scrub tops including rewashing the skunk top on Wednesday." Riley rolled her eyes. "I haven't actually washed clothes except for tops since last Friday even though it seemed like I've done laundry every other day for the past week. I'll text Agent Reeves."

After Riley sent the text, she hurried to the bedroom to resume her packing.

When Riley opened her second box, Toby stuck his nose into the box and peered at the contents. She frowned as she scratched his ears. "It's full, and I have more kitchen items that I need to pack. Because I was so focused on my classes and stressed about work, I didn't realize how much I relied on frozen dinners and pizza for my meals. I forgot how much I love to cook. I need to borrow more kitchen basics from the cabin."

Toby backed away from the box when she sealed it then followed her as she loaded it into her SUV. After they were back inside, Riley sat at the dining table and added *pick up two packing boxes* to her list then started another list that began with the extra items she had packed in her first box: *Return to cabin.*

Her phone rang. *Agent Reeves.*

"Tell me about this latest note," he said.

After she explained how and when she found the note, he said, "Sounds like a follow up note, doesn't it?"

"Isn't finding a note a little more intimidating than a phone call?"

"Maybe. The person who is writing the notes can get physically close enough to the person to leave them a slip of paper, but a phone call adds the intimacy of speaking into their victim's ear.

Now, I need to research the intimidation factor." Agent Reeves chuckled. "Do you work tomorrow?"

"In the morning," Riley said.

"I'll be by in the morning or ask the sheriff to pick up the note from you. Are you sure you're safe? Isn't the cabin where you're staying isolated from any neighbors?"

Riley rolled her eyes. "My aunt is way ahead of you. She asked me to move into a house her friend owns in Barton. I'm moving tomorrow."

"And she didn't know about this latest note?" Agent Reeves asked. "I like your aunt. What's your new address?"

Riley gave him the address of the new house then after she hung up, she heated water for a cup of tea, and added *tea kettle* to both of her lists. She stacked the items that were on her list on the counter before she settled down to read. Toby snored until bedtime.

*　*　*

While she and Toby ate breakfast the next morning, Riley said, "I love the cabin, but I'm excited about moving into town. Isn't that strange?"

Toby glanced up then resumed eating. After they went outside for a bit, Riley packed her clothes in her two suitcases then loaded the luggage, the rifle and shotgun she had wrapped in a quilt, and the other two full boxes into her SUV.

"Let's go, Toby," Riley said after she locked the cabin. When they reached the office, Riley was the first one there.

"Maybe we should wait a few minutes. Doc usually comes early too." When Doc parked next to her, they hurried into the building.

"I'll make coffee if you'll check for any messages," Doc said. "There usually are on Saturday morning. Amanda will be here soon. If you'll make her a list of who to call, she'll work them into our schedule. Saturdays are sometimes frantic because it's the one day that we double-book to make sure we get out of here in time."

"Six messages." Riley hurried into the breakroom for coffee. "Only two sounded like they couldn't wait until next week."

"Amanda's brilliant at working with our clients," Doc said. "I'd have them all come in at eight because I like to get things done and out of the way."

"What are we going to do when Amanda has her baby?" Riley poured two cups of coffee.

"My plan is to get an office cell phone and a tablet so she can answer calls and book appointments from the delivery room." Doc's eyes twinkled.

"Very logical plan. Let Pia tell her," Riley said.

"Tell who what?" Pia asked as she poured a cup of coffee.

Riley explained Doc's plan, and Pia snorted. "I'd love to tell Amanda, but I'll be busy with patients."

"Tell Amanda what?" Amanda asked as she came into the breakroom.

"My brilliant maternity plan." Doc beamed.

While Riley and Pia peered into their coffee cups, Amanda said, "It's a logical plan except we can't get my husband to approve it."

"Dang it, Doc," Pia growled. "You got us with that one."

Doc snort-laughed. "We've been planning that for a while. Didn't know we needed Riley to trigger it." Doc and Amanda smacked a high five and continued laughing when Pia grabbed Riley by the arm, and they marched out of the breakroom.

When Amanda returned to her desk, Riley and Pia joined her while she reviewed the list that Riley had left for her and made phone calls.

"We'll have two urgent cases show up as soon as they can get here; one's a trauma—dog versus bicycle—boy is unhurt, and the other one is a face-to-face raccoon encounter. Raccoon isn't our patient; it got away," Amanda said.

"Good news about the boy," Pia said. "I'll take the trauma."

"I'll set up the two rooms for our scheduled appointment and the patient with raccoon injuries," Riley added. The dog with facial injuries came in fifteen minutes before the dog that was hit by the bike.

After the patient who tangled with the raccoon left and while Doc cared for the dog injured by the bicycle, a woman held the door open for a large brown dog that followed her inside. As the woman approached the counter, the dog stayed close to her.

"Can you scan for a microchip?" she asked. "He showed up at our house last night and slept under my husband's truck. Even though he doesn't have a collar, I don't think he's a stray, but he's very nervous about a leash. He's a sweet boy and welcome to stay with us, but we'd like to reunite him with his people."

"Come with me," Riley said.

The woman followed Riley, and the dog followed the woman. When they went into the exam room, the woman chuckled. "We're quite the parade, aren't we? He panicked when we put a leash on him, but he has stayed right with me, so I skipped it. When I opened the car door, he jumped right in."

Riley scanned the dog but didn't find a chip.

"Thanks," the woman said. "My children are posting pictures of him. I'm sure he belongs to someone, but the kids think he's been lost for a while. I'll feed him and treat his fleas when we get home then call the county Monday morning."

After the woman and dog left, Amanda said, "I think that dog found his real people."

When Toby yipped, Riley smiled. "Toby agrees."

"I'm going to take Jordy out for a walk. We missed it earlier," Pia said.

"Take your time," Amanda said. "We're in our mid-morning lull."

After all the clients left, Riley finished cleaning the last exam room as Agent Reeves came inside. "Don't throw me out, Amanda, but I didn't bring cookies."

"I'll let you slide this one time." Amanda giggled.

"Can we talk, Riley?" he asked.

"Sure. Let's go to the breakroom."

As they headed to the breakroom, Amanda called out, "Talk loud."

Riley snickered, and Agent Reeves smiled.

"Did you hear from Dr. Truman?" he asked after they were in the breakroom.

"I didn't. I really thought I would, Agent—"

"Do me a favor and call me Eli; otherwise, I'd have to call you Ms. Malloy."

Riley smiled. "Okay, Eli."

"Do you have the note?" he asked as he removed a clear plastic bag from his front shirt pocket.

Riley nodded and pulled out the note from her pocket then dropped it into Eli's plastic bag.

Eli examined the note before he completed the evidence tag. "Looks like the same scrawl to me too. Have you thought of anything else?"

"I haven't, although I wish I knew why I've become a note magnet."

"I've wondered that too." Eli shook his head.

As they strolled to the front door, Eli asked, "Do you need any help moving?"

"No. I don't have much to move, and a friend's going to help me."

"That's good. I'll breathe easier knowing you're in town. I have a meeting in town on Tuesday morning. Do you suppose I could invite myself to lunch with you and Pia?"

"Sure can," Amanda said, and Riley laughed. "Amanda does all our scheduling."

Eli grinned. "Good to know. See you Tuesday."

"Well, Ms. Riley," Amanda said after he left, "Not only are you a note magnet, whatever that is, you're a hunk magnet."

"What's up?" Doc asked as she came out of the exam room.

"Agent Reeves told Riley to call him *Eli*." Amanda wiggled her eyebrows. "I'm a champion at jumping to conclusions."

"Yes, you are." Doc rolled her eyes. "Riley, would you show our client how to change the patient's dressings?"

"Love to." Riley hurried to the exam room.

By noon, they'd seen and treated all of the patients. After the exam rooms were cleaned and all the supplies were put away, Pia asked, "Does anyone have any objections if Jordy goes home with me? He's healed enough to be out of his crate, and my family and I would love to foster him."

"It's fine with me," Doc said. "He's ready to be in a home that will care for him. I'll give George a call to let him know Jordy will be with you."

"Same way I felt about Toby," Riley said.

"It's awesome," Amanda said.

On the way out, Doc said, "Be at our house by six at the latest. If you come at five, the boys will have a chance to harass you before we sit down at the table. Will that give you enough time to get everything done?"

"Sure will. I packed almost everything last night except staples and nonperishables and loaded the boxes into my SUV. I may need another box or two for some items. We should have everything in the new house by five."

"My plan when I move is to make the beds first. Everything else except the coffee maker and coffee cups can wait until the next day," Doc said.

"I like that," Riley said as she opened the door for Toby.

Riley stopped at the hardware store to pick up boxes, and Toby accompanied her inside. A half hour and a few dog treats later, they were on their way to the house.

"I should know you and I can't just run into the hardware store and leave, but I'm happy with the screwdriver set that was on sale. I appreciated it when you reminded me to get the two boxes before we left, but did you notice the clerk laughed the third time you went through the checkout line by yourself for another treat?" Riley asked.

After she parked at the new house, Riley opened Toby's door. "Can you believe how quickly we got here except for our little stop at the store, that is. We can walk to work if we plan ahead."

Toby bounded to the front door, and Riley carried her suitcases as she followed him. When she opened the door, her eyes widened at the vase of assorted white and peach-colored flowers on the dining table. She read the note next to the vase: "I was doing a last-minute check & these arrived as I was leaving at ten thirty. Beautiful flowers. Housewarming gift from your Aunt Millie and me in the refrigerator and pantry. Enjoy your new home. *Helen.*"

Riley pulled the florist's card out of the flowers and read it: "Best wishes as you settle in your new place. Be safe, *Eli*."

Riley opened the refrigerator door and stared. "It's full, Toby. Can you believe it?" She opened the freezer, and it was full too.

She hurried to the pantry, and the shelves were filled with all the staples she would need, and on the counter next to the sink was a cookbook. She sat at the table and thumbed through the cookbook then dropped in the florist card to save her place. "This is awesome. We're really spoiled, aren't we, Toby?"

She sent a text to Eli: "Thanks for the surprise. The flowers are beautiful."

Eli: "Glad you like them. They're double duty. Heal fast & happy housewarming."

Riley smiled. "Brilliant."

She texted her thanks to Helen and Aunt Millie and added *thank you cards* to her shopping list. "They really went above and beyond, don't you agree, Toby? I'll follow up with a note in a thank you card. Aunt Millie will be pleased."

Riley took her suitcases to the bedroom and quickly unpacked and hung up her clothes then carried in the boxes from the SUV. She opened the box with sheets and made her bed then tossed the quilt onto the bed. Next, she unpacked her coffee machine, coffee, and coffee filters and set up her coffee for the morning. "Doc's right, Toby. My bed's made, and the coffee machine is ready to go. Everything else can wait until tomorrow."

Riley opened the back door, and Toby trotted to the yard to investigate his new territory. Riley sat on a patio chair and put up her feet. "This is relaxing. I just realized I don't have to stay out here with you or ask you to come inside when I'm ready to go in just because I'm nervous and we don't know the neighborhood."

Toby yipped.

"I agree. A nice fence is another bonus to being in our house in town. Break's over. I'll see how much I can unpack before Ben gets here. Maybe I can empty my boxes then I won't need to buy any more."

After Riley finished unpacking the last box, she added to her list of items to purchase as Ben knocked on the door.

"Come in," Riley said as she hurried to the door.

Ben checked the front door as he entered. "Good, you've got a deadbolt."

He smiled at Riley before he surveyed the interior. "Thanks for telling me about your black eye. What's your official story?"

"Doc said I look like I got the last beer."

"Best possible answer." Ben chuckled before he furrowed his brow. "Is that a gas fireplace? You'll be comfortable here, don't you think?"

"I've never had a gas fireplace. It seems fancy to me, but I know Toby and I will appreciate it."

He nodded at the dining table. "Nice flowers. Good kitchen layout too. You've got a washer and dryer? Now, that's fancy as far as I'm concerned. My apartment has a laundry room for the tenants."

"My last apartment had a laundry room. Half the time all the washers were busy, and I'd have to go back later—made washing and drying clothes a real chore. Come see the backyard." Riley and Toby led the way; when Riley opened the door, Toby bounded to the yard.

"Great porch for relaxing," Ben said, "and a fenced yard. Perfect."

When they returned inside, Riley rolled her eyes as Ben examined the back door and nodded at the deadbolt. He strolled down the hallway and peeked into the bathroom and walked into the bedroom. "Nice size room. How's the closet space?"

After he opened the closet, he asked, "Are the rifle and shotgun yours? They look a little big for you." He pointed to the pistol on the top shelf. "Nice pistol. You stay in practice?"

"The rifle and shotgun were Grandma's, but she taught me how to shoot them when I was a kid. I never thought they were too big because I got used to them. It's been a while, but I did shoot the pistol at the cabin last week. I was rusty, and a little slow, but I had a tight circle on the target after a few rounds."

"Sounds good. Do you have a carry permit?"

"I've had one for a long time and kept it up."

Ben nodded as they strolled back to the living room. "Sounds like you've got a good place to practice your skills. Do we need to pick up packing boxes?"

"I have four. I don't think I'll need all of them though," Riley said.

"I'm ready when you are. Toby's going too, right?" Ben asked as he picked up the flattened boxes, and Toby pranced to the front door.

"If you don't mind your truck getting doggified," Riley said.

As Riley locked the house, Ben opened the truck passenger's door. "Okay, Toby."

Toby leapt into the truck's front seat, and Riley scooted him over after she climbed in.

On the way to the cabin, Riley asked, "How was your first week?"

She leaned back and listened as he talked about new procedures, a new trainer, and the more rapid pace of a day shift.

"My trainer said not everyone who goes from nights to days can take the pace," Ben said. "He said over half of the deputies ask to go back to nights in the first three months. I told him I'd adjust, and he agreed."

"I know you will," Riley said.

"Tell me about your week."

Riley told him about Dr. Truman, Junior, Dotty, Dr. Truman, Senior's voice mail message, Agent Reeves, all the notes, Pia and Jordy, and the stray dog.

"What's your theory about these notes that keep appearing and the deaths?" Ben frowned. "Isn't all this wearing you down? Where do you think you fit in?"

"I'm not sure. It seems like I'm a note-finder and that's about it."

"The note on your windshield makes it more than just note-finding. You'll call me if you need me, right? I may be an hour away, but I'll show up."

"I know you will. Thanks."

As they neared the cabin, she said, "The driveway to the cabin is about a half mile ahead. Turn left after the white house with the red barn. There's a sign that says Malloy Tree Farm, but it's so faded it's hard to see."

After he pulled into the driveway, Riley said, "I left the gate open this morning, but I'll close it when we leave. Go up the hill then turn right at the lane. The cabin's at the end of the lane."

When Riley unlocked the cabin door, Ben peered over her head. "This is a great cabin. I can see why it would be hard to leave it for any other place except your perfect house in town. I suppose I'm not the first to tell you this, but I'm glad you won't be so far away from people."

Riley nodded as they stepped inside. "You'd be right."

After Ben put the boxes together, they packed the items Riley had set on the counter while Toby wandered in the yard.

"I think that's it except for the refrigerator and freezer," Riley said.

"I have a cooler in the back of my truck. We'll load into it what we can and box up the rest of the food."

They packed the cooler then took one last look through the rooms, closets, and cabinets.

"What about books?" Ben asked. "Don't you want to take a few books to the house in town?"

Riley raised her eyebrows. "That's an outstanding idea. I read every evening. What gave me away?"

"You've got a quilt and a pillow on the sofa on the side closest to the table, and the lamp on the table is set in the perfect spot for reading."

"I need my pillow, quilt, and the lamp too. There's an end table for the lamp at the new house but no lamp."

Ben packed the lamp and cushioned it with the pillow and quilt while Riley packed a box of books.

"You have your own lending library. You can return a stack of books and pick out more." Ben carried the books to the truck and placed the box next to the rest of the boxes and the cooler.

"Is that it?" Ben asked.

"Sure is. I'll lock up," Riley said.

Before they left, Ben said, "What about the shed? Anything in there you want? Should you lock the padlock?"

"Good catch. It needs to be locked."

Ben strolled with Riley to the shed and examined the contents. "Great tools. Let me know when you want to come out here to stack some firewood, and I'll help."

After Riley closed the door, Ben clicked the padlock then called out, "We're going, Toby."

Toby beat them to the truck, and after everyone was inside, Ben drove to the end of the driveway and hopped out to close the gate.

"How's our timing?" Ben asked on the way back.

"We're doing great. Doc would like for us to be there at five. It's three thirty now, so we can unload your truck and probably unpack most if not all the boxes. After I feed Toby, he'll need a little time outside before we leave."

"I can put the food in the refrigerator and freezer and set up your table and lamp while you unpack your boxes."

"It's okay if I don't get everything put away. I still have tomorrow. This is a real luxury to have so much time off and not be stressing because I'm out of work or worried that someone will see Toby."

Toby yipped, and Riley chuckled.

"What did he say?" Ben asked.

"Their loss."

Ben grinned as he rubbed Toby's neck. "You're right about that, Toby."

While Riley placed her books on the bookcase then rearranged them, Ben and Toby went outside.

"We'll be back soon," Ben said after he opened the back door.

"Fine," Riley muttered as she moved a book from the second shelf to the first then frowned before she moved it back.

She sat back on her heels and glared at the bookcase. "Alphabetical by title has the sizes and colors all wrong." She rearranged the books by series then rubbed her forehead and rose. "I have to stop."

When she stepped onto the porch, she frowned. *Where are Ben and Toby?*

She walked around the house to the front. *Truck's gone. They've gone on a quest.* She smiled. *I've only known Ben for three days, and he's my best friend.*

Riley strolled to the back porch and sighed as she dropped onto a patio chair. *Ben's right. The notes are wearing me down.*

When Riley heard the truck pull into her driveway, she hurried to the front.

Ben grinned. "We checked your propane tank, and it was almost empty. We got you a bigger propane tank and a padlock so your tank isn't stolen, and a gun locker for your long guns. It won't keep them from being stolen if someone breaks into your house, but they'll be more secure than sitting in your closet. Happy housewarming from me and Toby."

"You two are awesome." Riley grinned as Toby yipped.

"What did Toby say?" Ben carried the tank to the side of the house and knelt to connect it.

"You're a great friend," Riley said. "He's right, you know."

Ben rose, brushed off his jeans, and raised his eyebrows. "Really?"

"Yes. Thank you for the tank and the gun locker—perfect housewarming gifts. I wouldn't have known my propane was low until the fireplace wouldn't light, and I was worried about leaving the guns at the cabin but didn't think about how secure they'd be in the house."

"It's what friends are for," Ben mumbled as he locked the tank into place.

After Ben carried the locker inside and placed it in the closet, Riley set her rifle and shotgun inside then locked it.

"I feel better. Thanks," she said.

Ben smiled. "Ready to go?"

After Riley locked the house and climbed into the truck, she said, "I'm totally out of touch with the social graces. Do you think it makes sense to stop by the grocery store and pick up a small vase of flowers? I think it's customary to take a bottle of wine to a friend's house for dinner, but I don't know what Doc and her husband might like. What do you think?"

Ben snorted. "I think I'm in the same boat. The last time I was invited to anyone's house was in college when we'd gather at a friend's house with the largest TV to watch football, eat pizza, and drink beer. Can you imagine someone showing up with anything other than wings?"

Riley smiled. "The good old days, right?"

Ben chuckled. "No way could we take wings to a chef's home. Flowers, it is."

On the way to the grocery store, Riley said, "Drop me off at the front, and I'll run in. Won't take me long."

When Riley returned to the truck, Ben said, "I like the yellow daisies in the yellow pitcher. Very cheerful."

"I can't take full credit." Riley closed her door. "An elderly shopper asked me what I was looking for. When I told her I needed flowers to take to my boss's house for dinner, she told me about the first dinner party she and her husband hosted. She forgot to turn on the oven, and the turkey was raw. She burnt the potatoes, and her fancy souffle fell. She flopped down on the kitchen floor and was crying when her husband came to see how she was doing."

"What a disaster. What did they do?" Ben asked.

Riley chuckled. "They made peanut butter and jelly sandwiches and cut them into fancy shapes. She opened five cans of tomato soup and six cans of tuna then added every spice she had to the tomato soup while he ran to the store and picked up a case of wine and some crackers. She served the PB and J appetizers while he kept everyone's glasses full then she served the spicy tomato soup in shot glasses and the tuna, which she called tuna tartare, on crackers. She said one person brought yellow flowers, and she always had a small vase of yellow flowers at their dinner parties to commemorate their most unforgettable party."

Ben laughed. "What a great way to bounce back."

"I know. If I'm ever brave enough to have a dinner party, I'll definitely have yellow flowers."

"Here we are." Ben parked in front of Doc's house. "Wonder if we're having hand-thrown, stone-baked pizza, craft beer, and peanut butter appetizers?"

Riley chuckled as she opened her door, and Toby slipped past her feet to jump out. "That would definitely deserve yellow flowers and actually sounds good to me."

When Ben knocked, two boys opened the door. The eight-year-old looked like Doc, except he was tall for his age. The younger one's skin was much darker than his brother's, but he was short for a five-year-old.

The older one said, "Mama said we should open the door and be polite. I'm Kenny. You like dragons or dinosaurs?"

"I'm Freddy. I like dinosaurs," the younger boy said. "Sissies like unicorns. Do you like unicorns?"

"It's a trap," Ben whispered, and Riley laughed.

"I like dogs. This is Toby," she said.

Toby remained still while the boys approached him then petted him.

"You can come in," Kenny said.

"I like Ms. Riley, Toby, dinosaurs, and dragons. I've never had much use for unicorns," Ben said.

"You can come in too," Freddy said. "I like Toby."

Doc hurried to the door. "Come in, come in."

"We were being polite, Mama," Freddy said.

"I heard," Doc said. "These are my friends, Ms. Riley and Mr. Ben."

"Nice to meetcha," the boys said in unison as they followed Toby toward the back of the house.

"Hey, Dad," Kenny shouted. "Ms. Riley brought Mama yellow flowers."

"We're working on our manners." Doc hugged Ben and Riley. "I'm so glad that you could come. Let's go to the great room, and I'll introduce you to Charlie. Those flowers are beautiful." Doc smiled as she accepted the flowers when Riley handed them to her. "I'll put them on the dining table."

"Welcome to our home." Charlie rinsed then dried his hands to greet them. His booming voice had the pleasing Bahamian dialect of mixed British and African language. He was tall like Kenny with dark skin tones like Freddy and wore black-framed glasses. He shook Ben's hand and hugged Riley.

"Did I forget to warn you we're huggers?" Doc chuckled.

"Dat's why my Julie Rae became a vet. So she could hug her patients." Charlie guffawed.

Kenny opened the sliding glass door to the backyard, and Toby joined the boys as they rushed outside.

Doc beamed. "I knew Toby would be a hit. I should have warned you about unicorns, though. You would have gotten a long lecture about unicorns being imaginary animals that aren't real. Somehow, dragons and dinosaurs are real and not only still roam the earth but visit our house regularly."

Charlie stood at the glass door and peered at the boys and Toby. "Toby may have joined in their imaginary world. Maybe I'm changing my mind about a dog."

"You're the one who's home with the boys," Julie Rae said. "If it was up to me, Riley, we'd have a houseful of animals. Come sit at the bar; it's where I sit to watch Charlie cook. He's a maestro in the kitchen. We have wine, sweet tea, and ice water, and Charlie prepared snacks for us."

Charlie strode back to the kitchen. "Julie Rae, I make snacks for the boys. For the adults, I prepared hors d'oeuvres."

Doc winked at Riley, who snickered.

"I'd enjoy a glass of wine," Riley said.

"Iced tea sounds good," Ben said.

While Julie Rae poured the tea then opened a bottle of wine and poured wine into three glasses, Riley sat at the bar that overlooked Charlie's prep counter, and Ben sat on her left.

"This is like sitting at the chef's table at a restaurant, except I've only read about it. Is that really a thing?" Riley asked.

"It is inconvenient from a chef's standpoint." Charlie filleted a fish then paused and waved his knife. "No swearing about what the diner ordered."

Riley and Ben chuckled, and Julie Rae smiled. "Charlie's been waiting for someone to bring up the chef's table, so he could complain about no swearing, and you're the first one to mention it."

"That's true. It's not often a stay-at-home dad with two boys gets the chance to complain about no swearing," Charlie said.

As Riley sipped her wine, she glanced at the far end of the bar, and her eyes widened. *A yellow note?*

"What's that?" Riley asked.

"What's what?" Julie Rae asked.

Ben peered over Riley's head. "Yellow something?"

Julie Rae set down her wine glass then picked up the paper. "Oh, yes. This paper was on my car when I left work today. I think it blew onto my windshield. It's part of a note or something." Julie Rae handed it to Riley. "It didn't make sense to me."

Riley opened the note and read it. *Same scrawl. Different words.* "You haven't learned yet."

"Okay if I snap a picture of it? It's similar to others I've seen," Riley said.

"Go right ahead." Julie Rae placed crackers and cheese on two small superhero plates for the boys.

Riley showed Ben before she took a photo and sent it to the sheriff and to Eli with the text: "Doc found this on her car today. I'm at her house."

"Did you see any other notes before this?" Ben asked.

"No." Julie Rae tilted her head. "Should I have?"

"Something is wrong, isn't it?" Charlie narrowed his eyes and stepped closer to Julie Rae.

CHAPTER SIX

"I don't understand what the note means," Ben said, "but others who are associated with a veterinary practice received notes with the same handwriting and on paper like this."

"I sent the picture to Sheriff and Agent Reeves. They're keeping track of the notes," Riley said. "If they have any questions, they have my number."

Charlie set two white rectangular plates on the bar. "Spicy shrimp in phyllo cups and hot crab pinwheels."

"I'll call the boys in," Julie Rae said. "They love their pinwheels."

While Julie Rae took the boys to wash their faces and hands, Charlie said, "I made pinwheels for the boys too. Peanut butter and strawberry jam—it's their favorite."

Ben glanced at Riley and smirked. Riley tried to turn her giggle into a cough.

"You've met Mrs. Smythe then." Charlie grinned and his eyes crinkled. "Her story about her first dinner party is a classic around here."

Julie Rae and the boys came into the great room, and the boys sat at the dining table. Charlie poured their milk, and Julie set their milk, pinwheels, and cracker and cheese snack in front of them.

"They know?" she asked. When Charlie chuckled, she laughed, and Riley and Ben joined in. Julie Rae wiped her eyes. "I wondered if Mrs. Smythe was behind the yellow flowers. She loves to find a newcomer looking for flowers in the grocery store."

Charlie reached under the counter and pulled out a small vase with a yellow zinnia. "We always have a yellow flower on the table when we have a dinner party. When the boys told me you brought yellow flowers, I set ours out of sight."

"It would have ruined the surprise of the boys' special pinwheels." Julie Rae chuckled.

Charlie handed Julie Rae macaroni and cheese for Kenny and Freddy. After the boys ate their dinner, they cleared their plates, and Charlie gave each of them an ice cream bar. They dashed out the back door with Toby.

"Our turn," Julie Rae said.

"We'll eat family style." Charlie set a bowl of rice with peas and a platter with cornbread on the bar, and Riley and Ben set the food on the table while Julie Rae set silverware and placemats at four seats. "Is sweet tea okay for everyone?" she asked. She poured tea while Charlie dished up the fish stew. "Charlie sits at the head of the table, and I sit on his left." Julie Rae pointed to the chair opposite Charlie and the chair next to it. "Those are your seats."

Riley sat at the place across from Julie Rae, and Ben stood next to the chair across from Charlie's seat. Julie Rae picked up a bowl of fish stew and set it in front of Riley; Charlie brought two bowls to the table while Julie Rae picked up the last one. Ben sat after Julie Rae took her seat.

After he took his seat, Charlie waved his hand over the table. "For your dinner tonight, we present Bahamian fish stew with snapper fish, johnny cakes that are very similar to your Georgia cornbread, baked crab, rice, and pigeon peas, a legume like beans. You have been transported to The Islands. Enjoy."

As Charlie explained that he lived in Nassau with his grandmother who taught him to cook, his Bahamian accent deepened as he spoke. "When I was t'ree years old, Grammy put me on a stool in front of a pot on da stove and told me to stir dat stew. She tole me cookin' would be my superpower, and as long as

I could cook, I'd never go hungry. I went on to college and earned a degree in accounting, but I never forgot my superpower."

"Charlie's superpower got us through graduate school. If it hadn't been for him, I would have barely survived on ramen noodles," Julie Rae said. "I lived with my grandparents on their farm from the time I was two. Grandma and I raised chickens for eggs and meat. She had a stand out near the road and would sell produce, eggs, and chickens. She'd tell me stories about her childhood, and I'd read farm pamphlets and books to her while we sat in the shade and waited for customers. What about your childhood, Riley?"

Riley smiled. "I spent summers with my grandmother at her cabin. Grandma taught me to read novels the first summer I spent with her and later taught me to shoot. She had a small garden, and the farm was covered with wild blackberries. We spent most of the summer picking and canning vegetables and jams. She always had at least two dogs, usually strays, and they were my best friends. Grandma said she knew I was a natural born dog whisperer when I was three because I'd tell Grandma what the dogs told me while she cooked supper. Grandma fed feral cats but told me I shouldn't repeat what the cats said when I used some words she called *not polite*."

Riley smiled at Charlie's deep chuckle. "My grammy would like you, Riley," he said. "What about you, Ben?"

"I was raised on a farm, and all my dad's relatives lived nearby. When I was six, my uncle, a veterinarian, asked if I wanted to go with him while he visited farms to care for cows, horses, goats, and mules. Every summer and during school breaks, I'd travel with him until I graduated from high school. After I left for college, I still worked with him a couple of times a year."

"Sounds like you were on track to be a vet," Julie Rae said.

"That's what all the family thought except for my uncle. He knew I wanted to be a cop, and I earned my degree in biochemistry at his suggestion in case I wanted to go the forensic route. He said it was good to have options."

When they finished dinner, Charlie said, "We're having guava duff for dessert. The traditional duff has a rum sauce, but I make a nonalcoholic sauce for the boys. There's plenty if you'd rather skip the alcohol. It's the island way to be heavy-handed with the rum."

"The boys can come inside for their duff, and we can take ours out to the patio," Julie Rae said.

Riley and Ben helped Riley clear the dishes while Charlie slid the glass door open. "Anyone for duff?"

Kenny, Freddy, and Toby rushed into the house. "Wash those hands," Charlie said as he slid the door closed.

After Kenny and Freddy showed their dad their clean hands and plopped at their places at the table, Charlie served their duff then poured on the sauce with a flourish. The boys polished off their dessert and cleared their places.

"We're going to the patio," Charlie said. "You can have a little inside time to cool down."

"TV?" Freddy asked.

"As long as you don't fight," Julie Rae said.

"Non-rum sauce for Ben. Riley?" Charlie asked.

"I'd like to try the rum sauce."

The four adults took their desserts outside. Charlie and Julie Rae's chairs were so close that the arms touched. When Ben scooted his chair closer to Riley, Charlie smiled. "Good to stay close to da woman." Ben's face reddened, and he poked at the duff with his fork.

Riley's phone buzzed a text from the sheriff. "Tell Doc will see her Monday morning unless you say otherwise."

Riley read the text aloud.

"I'm happy the sheriff didn't think it was necessary to show up with lights and sirens and is okay with waiting until Monday," Julie Rae said.

Riley examined the duff on her plate. "It reminds me of a cinnamon roll or a fancy pinwheel, in a way."

She took a bite. "The pastry is light and spongy. I think this is my new favorite dessert, and no way would I drive after one mouthful of sauce."

Julie Rae laughed. "I understand completely. The guava pastry is awesome, but sometimes I think it's just a vehicle to deliver copious amounts of rum."

"Do dinners get raucous after dessert?" Ben asked. "Your rum sauce smells like a party on a plate."

Julie Rae took a bite. "Mmm. We only have duff when we have company. What are y'all doing next Saturday?"

Julie Rae smiled when Ben and Riley laughed, and Charlie nodded.

After they finished dessert and chatted a while, Riley rose. "Thank you so much for the wonderful meal and the relaxing evening. I don't mean to rush off, but we need to finish unpacking."

As Ben rose, Julie Rae said, "I was serious about getting together again. We don't entertain very often because the boys are sometimes a handful, but Toby is a perfect babysitter."

"Yes," Charlie smiled. "I need for the boys to have a dog."

Toby joined Riley and Ben as Julie Rae and Charlie accompanied them to the door.

"Bye, Toby," Freddy said.

"See you soon, Toby," Kenny added.

Julie Rae chuckled, "I'm sure you're included, but that was from their hearts, wasn't it?"

"I'd be the last person to complain," Riley said. "When people told Grandma she needed to work on my manners because I ignored them to listen to the dogs, she told them they needed to work on their own manners."

Charlie grinned. "My grammy and your grandma went to the same school."

On their way back to Riley's house, Ben asked, "Are you too tired for company?"

"Not at all. I need to kick off my boots and my polite face though. Is that okay?"

Ben nodded. "You were smooth when you saw that note."

"So were you, but I knew you would be," Riley said, and Ben beamed.

When Riley unlocked her door, her phone buzzed a text from Eli: "Where are you?" Ben peered over her shoulder.

Riley replied: "At home."

"See you Monday. Text sheriff or call 911 if problem."

Ben locked the front door, and Riley pulled off her boots before she, Ben, and Toby went outside through the back door.

Riley and Ben sat in silence while Toby ran from one end of the yard to the other. When Toby returned to the porch and flopped next to Riley, Ben asked, "What are you thinking?"

"I was thinking about all the notes. The first one, the one to Dotty, was directed to her, but whatever her good choice was, I think she changed her mind."

Toby growled and yipped, and Riley stared at him. "Toby agrees because she shredded some documents while Doc Senior watched before we left the office."

Ben frowned. "Could those shredded documents have anything to do with why Dr. Truman wanted to see you?"

"I'd almost forgotten about that," Riley said. Toby yipped, and Riley rubbed his chest. "Toby thinks so."

"I have every confidence you'll figure out a way to let Agent Reeves know Dotty shredded some documents and that's why Truman needed to see you." Ben snickered when Riley snorted.

"Sometimes I feel like I'm saying the dog ate my homework." Riley rolled her eyes, and Toby hung out his tongue and grinned.

"The next three notes were in Barton," Ben said.

Riley frowned. "You're right. What's the connection between the two veterinary offices in Pomeroy and Barton?"

Ben raised his eyebrows, and Riley furrowed her brow as she asked, "Me? What if it's coincidental?"

She rose and strolled to the fence, and Ben followed her then put his hand on her shoulder.

"I have no answers, but even the timing points to you," he said. "Text or call me any time you want to talk. I need to head back."

"Do you work tomorrow?" Riley asked as they walked to the front door.

"Yes, but you can text. It might be a while before I answer unless you say it's urgent. Today was a great day overall." He paused to gaze at her face. "Be safe."

"You too, Ben. I thoroughly enjoyed today, and thank you for your help and for listening."

He smiled. "It's what friends do."

Riley waved from the door as Ben pulled out of the driveway then she and Toby went back inside before she double-locked her front door.

"Shall we read or go to bed, Toby?"

He yawned then padded to the hallway.

* * *

When dog whiskers tickled her cheek the next morning, she opened one eye, and Toby kissed her nose. She giggled as she sat up, and sunlight streamed through her partially open blinds.

"I slept late. Must have needed the rest is what Grandma always said." She swung her feet to the floor and threw on her robe as she padded to the back door and let Toby out.

After she fed Toby and finished her second cup of coffee, Riley dressed then sat at the table to list her meals for the week. Before she finished, her phone rang. *Marcy.*

"How's your new job? I love mine. We're busy, the clients are nice, and the people I work with are smart and super helpful. I'm even being paid more than I made at the Truman vet office. Some girls from the old office are going together to get some flowers or something for Doc Junior's memorial service. I told them to include you and me. You don't mind, do you? But it's odd because there hasn't been any news about anything planned. How you are you doing? If you aren't happy, I'll put a word in here for you. I know they'd be happy to have you. How's Toby?"

Riley smiled as she listened to Marcy. *So full of energy.* "I love my job too. Isn't it great that both of us found a place where we're happy? Toby loves being outside, and he has the run of the office. He's the best when it comes to calming our patients."

"He would be. I miss you both. Have you met anybody? I don't think I told you the latest about Todd. I ran into this nice woman at the gym yesterday, and we were talking as we paced each other on the treadmill. She asked me if I had a boyfriend, and I told her I'd been dating a guy for four months. She told me about her husband, Todd, who was an engineer. While we had a juice together after the spin class, she asked me more about my boyfriend, and I laughed and told her his name was Todd, and he was an engineer too. She seemed a little upset, but when she showed me a picture of her husband, I guess my surprise told her everything she wanted to know because she stormed out of the gym. Not that I blame her."

"What a shock. I'm so sorry," Riley said.

"I was super upset at first then I realized how lucky I was that I ran into his wife. He obviously wasn't for me."

"You're right. Your type has never been jerk," Riley said, and Marcy giggled.

Riley continued, "My big news is I moved again. I was staying at my grandma's cabin before I moved to town into a house that's smaller than grandma's cabin, but it's a perfect size for Toby and me. The biggest advantage is we can walk to work, which we'll do when the weather warms up a little."

"How exciting. I meant to tell you, Dr. Truman, Senior, left me a text asking me if I had your address. It was so weird; I ignored it. Did he get in touch with you?"

"No, and thanks for not saying anything. Sounds creepy to me."

"Speaking of creepy, I got an email from Dotty. She sent it last Saturday not long before she was killed, but I didn't see it until Sunday night because I don't check my email very often. She and I used to have coffee together once in a while. Didn't seem to me that she had many friends, and I've never minded talking to people that are a little lonely. Anyway, the email said she'd gotten herself into something that she needed to get out of, and that my friend from work had the key and needed to be careful. That's you because everybody knew we ate lunch together. So, did she give you a key or something?"

"No, and I can't imagine what she's talking about. I wonder if she meant the answer to something or a physical key. Forward the email to me, would you?"

"Sure. This guy told my cousin about a barbeque and folk music festival in Carson next Saturday and Sunday, and my cousin told him I'd like it too. My cousin's going with her boyfriend. My cousin and I had lunch last week. Can you imagine me going away from the office for lunch? It was the only way to get my cousin off my back, but she bought lunch. She said I was becoming too morose. I said she does too many crossword puzzles. According to my cousin, the guy is kind of quiet, but she said he would never get a chance to talk when he's around me anyway, so what do I care?" Marcy giggled, and Riley smiled. *It's nice to hear her happy again.*

Marcy continued, "Carson isn't far from you, right? You might like it. We could meet there."

"It's only an hour north of me. I have a friend who lives in Carson who might like to go too. Which day?"

"I don't know yet," Marcy said. "See if she'd like to come too. The more, the merrier. I've always enjoyed doing things with lots of friends. I have to see the schedule that comes out on Monday. If I work Saturday morning, we wouldn't have much time. Might have to be Sunday."

"I work every Saturday morning. I could go Saturday afternoon or on Sunday."

"I'll send you a link then call you back next Thursday or Friday. Is that too late?"

"Are you kidding? With my social calendar? I'll squeeze you in." Riley giggled.

"I'll have my people call your people." Marcy snort-laughed.

After Marcy hung up, Riley furrowed her brow. "When I mentioned I had a friend in Carson, I just realized Marcy said *she*. I forgot to tell her about Ben. Would it be too awkward to call her right back? Or should I see what Ben's weekend schedule is before I get Marcy all stirred up."

Toby yipped.

"I agree—waiting until I have some facts won't hurt. I'll check with Ben first. Let's go for a walk."

Riley and Toby walked to the park then Riley jogged and Toby trotted on the path around the park. After one time around, Riley said, "No hills. I like it."

Toby barked, and they ran the path one more time. As they walked home, Riley said, "That was fun. I can't remember that I ever thought I'd have the energy to jog around a park. Twice."

When they reached home, Riley checked her email; Marcy had forwarded Dotty's email and the link to the festival in a separate email.

She sent Ben a text with the link to the festival included: "Here's a link for you to look at later."

She read the email from Dotty to Marcy. "This email is longer and more disjointed than I expected, Toby. Dotty said she's sorry she gave the key to Marcy's friend from work because she never dreamed the friend would end up where the pot would boil over. What does that mean?" She squinted at the screen. "There's a lot of rambling about falling into a trap when she thought she was helping a friend, and Marcy's friend needs to know that people aren't what they seem. And then toward the end Dotty said it was never about the money and for that she was a total fool." Riley leaned back in her chair. "I sure hope Agent Reeves can make sense of this because I can't."

She sent a text to Eli: "Do you have email? I have one to forward to you."

Riley was relaxing on her back porch with her lunch while Toby lay in the grass when she heard back from Eli. Not long after she forwarded the email from Dotty to him, her phone rang.

When she answered, Eli asked, "Is this the Dotty from the Truman veterinary practice? Who's Marcy?"

"Yes, Dotty was the bookkeeper for Dr. Truman. Marcy and I ate lunch together every day; everyone in the office knew we were friends. Marcy called me today and told me about the email she received from Dotty, and I asked her to forward it to me. She also said that Dr. Truman sent her a text asking if she knew my address. She ignored it."

"What key did Dotty give you?"

"The only thing Dotty gave me was an envelope with my last paycheck enclosed when I turned in my key to the office." Riley frowned. "The lawyer said there was a reference letter enclosed in our envelopes, but I didn't pay any attention to it. I pulled out the paycheck and deposited it."

"Do you still have the envelope?"

"I'll have to hunt for it."

"Let me know if you find it. I'll turn over the email to the team working on Dotty's death."

After she hung up, Riley sat on the sofa, and Toby jumped up with her. "How do we retrace our steps to find the envelope, Toby? I put the envelope and the sack with your medicine in my purse, and when we moved into the cabin, I put your medicine on the kitchen counter, but what did I do with the envelope?"

Toby snuggled close to her, and she stroked his back. After a half hour, she said, "This isn't very productive, is it? I need to pick up some thank you cards and stamps. I can do that at the grocery store then we can go clean the cabin. It would be like laying a fresh fire for the next person, wouldn't it? Grandma would approve."

When they reached the driveway for the cabin, Toby whined, and Riley chuckled. "I'm excited to be here again too. It's like we're visiting our vacation home, isn't it?"

After Riley parked, Toby bounded out and scoured the area around the cabin for interesting scents. Riley poured a bowl of water for him and set it on the porch before she began her cleaning. She put her sheets in the washer and pulled out the smaller area rugs to air before she dusted and swept. After she moved the linens to the dryer, she mopped. While the floors dried, she and Toby jogged to the road and back then relaxed on the front porch.

"I suppose the floors are dry by now, Toby, but I'm enjoying watching the clouds and listening to the birds."

After she gathered the airing rugs, she went inside the cabin and placed the rugs on the floor before she made the bed with the freshly washed sheets. She scrubbed the bathroom and kitchen sinks, and as she wiped down the kitchen countertops, she paused. "Wonder if I stuck the envelope in a kitchen drawer?"

She searched the drawers and cabinets and the space between the counter and the refrigerator. "Nothing."

After she locked the cabin, she and Toby headed for town.

"I feel good about giving the cabin a thorough cleaning in case Aunt Millie decides to take a weekend break, Toby. Good walk too."

She glanced in the back of the SUV and smiled at her sleeping dog. *Always the sign of a successful day when the dog's worn out.*

When they reached the house, Toby growled as Riley pulled into the driveway. "What is it, boy?"

She opened her car door and smelled the distinctive propane gas additive. Toby stayed in the SUV when she walked to the side of the house. Her eyes widened at the severed pipe between the propane tank and the house and the folded slip of yellow paper that lay close to the pipe.

She snatched up the paper and backed out of her driveway as she called nine-one-one.

After she parked across the street from her house and spoke to the dispatcher, she opened the folded slip and read it— *Leave now. Last warning.*

She furrowed her brow. *Why do I have to leave? Where am I supposed to go?*

She glanced in her rearview mirror then stuffed the paper into her pocket as the sheriff pulled in behind her before the fire engine parked in front of her house.

"Do you have a key to your padlock with you?" Sheriff asked.

Riley removed the key from her keyring and gave it to him.

"Thanks," he said. "The firefighters will be sad, but this will save your padlock."

The officer on the fire engine climbed out of the passenger's side and met the sheriff in the driveway. After the sheriff spoke to him, the officer motioned to a firefighter to return the bolt cutter to its compartment.

The officer unlocked the padlock and turned off the gas bottle then returned the key to the sheriff before he climbed back into the vehicle.

"The fire crew turned off the propane bottle. They'll document the source of the leak in their report," the sheriff said after he returned to Riley's SUV. "I understand you found a note. It's safe to go inside your house. Let's go talk."

Riley coaxed Toby out of the SUV, and they went inside the house.

"What does the note say?" Sheriff asked.

Riley handed the sheet of paper to the sheriff.

"Nothing ambiguous about this note." Sheriff narrowed his eyes. "Take your photo and send a copy to Agent Reeves. I'll take the original."

After Riley snapped the photo and sent a text to Eli, Sheriff pulled a plastic sack out of his pocket, and Riley dropped in the note.

The sheriff snorted. "I've learned to always carry an evidence bag and extra tags with me since you've moved to town. Did you hear or see anybody? Didn't Toby alert to someone near the house?"

"Toby and I have been at Grandma's cabin for the past two or three hours. I wanted to clean it, and we spent some time enjoying the property too."

Sheriff nodded. "All they had to do was see you leave town to know you'd be gone a while. It wouldn't take long or any special skills to snip that pipe, and the tool is cheap at any hardware store. I'll have a deputy talk to the neighbors—maybe somebody saw something, but I doubt it because nobody came outside to watch the fire truck. Speaking of people watching, one of our dispatchers overheard a woman in the grocery store tell a friend that Daphne must have dinged your car in the vet parking lot last Monday because the woman saw Daphne put a note on your windshield. Our eyewitness is coming to my office tomorrow morning for coffee, and we'll take her statement."

Riley's phone buzzed a response from Eli. *See you at lunch tomorrow.*

Sheriff chuckled. "You and Eli seem to have this standing weekly lunch date."

Riley rolled her eyes. "Is it my charming personality, or is his favorite color yellow?"

The sheriff snort-laughed then wiped his eyes. "That was great, Riley. Charming or yellow?" His chuckle turned into another bout of laughter. "It's a tossup, isn't it?" The sheriff's shoulders shook as he headed out to his cruiser.

"The sheriff has a strange sense of humor, Toby. He thinks I'm funnier than I do, and I think I'm pretty funny."

Toby grinned.

Riley tittered. "Thank you, Toby."

When Riley's phone rang, she smiled as she answered. *Ben.*

"Thanks for the link, Riley. I knew the festival was coming up, but my head must still be stuck on nights. I've never been able to go before, so it wasn't on my radar. Are you planning to go? It's only twenty minutes from my apartment, and I have next Sunday afternoon off. Can I pick you up? Would you want to meet there?"

"I have a friend from Pomeroy that wants to meet me there, and—"

"Oh. Maybe I'll see you there or something. Not to intrude on your personal time or anything like that. I could wave. You know. Not bother you or anything. So, guess that's about it. Not much else to talk about, is there? See you next week. At the festival." Ben hung up, and Riley stared at her phone then called him back.

"Was there something else?" he asked.

"You big dope, why did you hang up on me?" Riley asked.

"I didn't want to intrude on your date," he said.

"Marcy is my friend, not my date."

"Oh." As Ben's voice brightened, Riley rolled her eyes. "Well, in that case, I have a neighbor in my apartment building who doesn't know many people. He's new to town and kind of fun. Maybe we could meet there?"

I don't know…" Riley smirked. "Wouldn't want to intrude on your personal time."

Ben cleared his throat. "Okay, I'm sorry I'm a big dope."

Riley chuckled. "Apology accepted. Marcy is already riding to the festival with someone, but we're not sure which day yet. I'll get back to you."

"That's great. I hear it's a lot of fun," Ben said. "My day was busy, but it was nothing unusual—just work stuff. How was yours?"

"Toby and I cleaned Grandma's cabin, and while we were gone, somebody cut the pipe from the propane tank to the house and left a yellow note." Riley bit her lip as she waited for Ben's reaction.

When he was quiet for a while, she asked, "Are you still there?"

"Yes. Move here—my uncle will hire you. The apartment next door to me is vacant, and they allow dogs."

Riley put her hand on her heart. "That's very sweet of you, but I couldn't leave Julie Rae, at least not right now."

Ben sighed. "Call a plumber to fix the pipe, and ask if he can bury it and bring it up through the floor."

Ben likes to fix things. Riley smiled. "That's a good idea. I'll do that. So, do you get alternating Saturday and Sunday afternoons off?"

"Yes. It's nice, isn't it? My partner said this is new. A lot of the deputies like it because the schedule gives them a chance to spend time with their families."

"That's important," Riley said. "Julie Rae hopes to hire another vet tech so we can work five days a week. Did I tell you we have a new vet that will start on Monday?"

"Man or woman?" Ben asked. "I have to ask, so I won't embarrass myself again."

Riley chuckled. "A man. I hadn't thought about it before, but I hope he isn't too serious because he'll never last." Riley glanced at the clock. "It's time for Toby's supper. I'll let you know what Marcy says."

After they hung up, Riley fed Toby then sent Helen a text asking her to recommend a plumber for the propane.

While Toby ate, Riley said, "I didn't want to alarm Ben, but I'm officially scared. Do you think we should consider Ben's offer?"

Toby yipped.

"Right. We love it here, but Ben's suggestion would be the smart thing to do. I'll think about it." After Riley ate, she wrote her thank you notes.

"Our new vet starts tomorrow. Let's make cinnamon rolls. I'll bake them in the morning."

When she reached the point where it was time for the rolls to go into the oven, she placed them in the refrigerator then read until bedtime.

* * *

When her alarm sounded the next morning at five, Riley swung her feet to the floor and touched something furry. She jerked her feet up then peeked down. *Toby.*

Toby stretched after she climbed over him then followed her to the kitchen.

"You didn't sleep on your soft pad last night because you were guarding me, weren't you?"

Toby grinned then after she opened the door, dashed out to clear the backyard of squirrels. While he was outside, Riley placed the cinnamon rolls in the oven. When Toby returned to the house, Riley fed him then stood in front of her closet. *The only scrub top I like is the pink one.* She slipped on a gray top and placed the blue tops that were too small and the pink one she had borrowed into a sack for the stash.

While the cinnamon rolls baked, she buttered a piece of toast then slathered strawberry jam on it. After she pulled the rolls out of the oven, she wrapped the sweet pastry in foil then she and Toby left.

CHAPTER SEVEN

When she reached the veterinary hospital, only Julie Rae's truck was in the staff parking lot. After Riley and Toby hurried inside, Riley set the wrapped cinnamon rolls on the counter next to a plate of scones.

After she set her lunch inside the refrigerator, Doc joined them in the breakroom. "Good morning, early birds. I like to sneak into the office extra early to catch up on my paperwork then I can go home on time in the evening. Before I forget, Charlie made cranberry-orange scones, my favorite, for us today. Help yourself. They're on the counter, and the coffee should be done soon."

"The scones look great. I made cinnamon rolls to celebrate our new vet's first day too."

"That's great. I thought I smelled cinnamon rolls but decided it was wishful thinking," Doc said. "I have to tell you how much we enjoyed your company on Saturday, and Ben is a delight. I assume you have no plans to let that man get away."

Riley chuckled. "We are becoming good friends."

"I agree that good friends is the best way to go. Charlie has been my best friend for ages. We heard about the problem at your house yesterday. Charlie ran into Mrs. Smythe at the drug store." Doc smiled. "One of the features of living in a small town is that everyone knows your business. Charlie and I want you to know if you're ever scared or need a place to stay, we have a guest bedroom, and you and Toby are welcome anytime. Charlie also wanted me to tell you so you could tell Ben—"

Toby yipped. "Amanda's here," Riley said.

"Toby told you? You and Toby are spooky sometimes. By the way, thanks for bringing Toby to our house. Charlie saw how much energy a dog can help the boys run off. He worries about the amount of time they spend inside."

Toby whined, and Riley said, "You'll know when you've found the right dog."

"Thanks, Toby. I think you're right." Doc sighed as she poured a cup of coffee. "I have to get a jump on that paperwork, but I'll take a cinnamon roll and a scone along to fortify me."

Riley took a plate with a cinnamon roll and a scone and a cup of coffee to Amanda's desk to check the messages while Amanda put her lunch in the refrigerator.

When Amanda arrived at her desk, Riley was listening to the first message.

"I just got started," Riley said, "so I don't have a list for you. I need some scrub tops. Do I order them, or is there somewhere I could go?"

Amanda pulled a catalog out of her bottom desk drawer. "Pia and I order ours through this catalog. We like the way they fit, and they're sturdy. If you place your order this morning, you'll have your new scrubs on Thursday. We have ours delivered here. You'll get a discount if you do the same."

"Thanks." Riley thumbed through the catalog. "These do look nice. I brought back the pink top and the blue scrubs that don't fit me for the stash. I'm ready for a little color."

"That pink was so cute on you. Take it and wear it to work. No reason to have it sit on the shelf. After you get your new ones, you can bring in a few gray tops for you to change into, if you get your shirt messy."

"It's nice to have the backup scrubs here. Would you like a cinnamon roll and a scone? I'll get you one of each while you listen to the messages from the weekend."

As Riley returned with Amanda's plate, a slender young man with a receding hairline tapped on the front door. He was taller than Doc and Pia, but not as tall as Ben. Toby yipped, and Amanda said, "Did Toby say it's our new vet? He's right. Want to let him in, Riley?"

Riley opened the door, and the young man strode inside. "Hi, let me guess. You're Riley. I'm Thad Faraday." He waved at a car in the parking lot, and the young woman returned his wave then drove away. "That was my wife, Claire. She's a teacher, but since it's the middle of the school year, she's going to apply for a substitute position at the school."

Amanda rose and smiled. "Come on in, Thad, and I'll take you to Dr. Julie Rae's office. I'm Amanda."

"You don't have to get up," Thad said, but Amanda stretched her back. "I don't mind stretching my legs once in a while, and it's just around the corner to the hallway."

When Amanda returned, Riley was reviewing the day's schedule.

"He's super smart," Amanda whispered. "Doc and I are hoping our clients don't eat him alive because he's nice too."

"We could charge them extra," Riley spoke in the same quiet voice as Amanda. "Anyone who is testy with Dr. Thad has to pay a fine."

Amanda giggled. "I like that. I'll work up a crochety payment schedule. Speaking of schedules, we've got two semi-urgent cases that we'll work in when they show up. The urgency is for the nervous clients with new companions; the patients are actually fine. Everyone else has an appointment sometime this week."

Dr. Julie Rae rushed to Amanda's desk and whispered, "I need your help. I didn't even think about an office for Dr. Thad."

"We'll take care of it, Doc. Riley can clear out our spare storeroom—there's not much in there, anyway, and we'll set it up. I'll order a proper desk and chair and call our techie guy to set up a phone. We'll make do with a folding table and chair for now. Why don't you and Dr. Thad discuss what supplies he'll need in his office and give me a list. I have a new laptop for him, and I've already set it up on our system."

Dr. Julie Rae hugged Amanda. "You are awesome." As she hurried back to her office, she called out over her shoulder, "You too, Riley."

Riley stacked items for Thad's new office on top of a rolling cart then unloaded them in the breakroom. When Pia came into the breakroom to put away her lunch, she said, "I have so many questions, but most importantly, are the scones fair game?"

"Help yourself," Doc said as she and Thad strolled into the breakroom. "Pia, this is Thad Faraday."

"We're glad you're here, Dr. Thad," Pia said. "Are you setting up his office, Riley? I'll help, but coffee and pastries first."

"Bring them with you, and I'll show you what I've done so far."

While Pia tore her cinnamon roll apart and ate it piece by piece, Riley said, "There wasn't as much stuff in here as I thought at first. It shouldn't be hard to fit the extra supplies in the storeroom after we organize it."

"I heard about your propane tank. What did Ben say? You told him, didn't you?"

"I've asked Ms. Helen for the name of a plumber to fix it, and Ben suggested the pipe be placed underground where it won't be so accessible."

"That's a good idea. Wonder why it wasn't done in the first place? Of course, I wouldn't have thought about it," Pia said.

"We've got patients," Amanda shouted from her desk.

Pia chuckled. "We probably could use an intercom system or something,"

"That's actually a good idea. Wonder if it could be part of our phone system." Riley stacked the last few items onto the cart before she and Pia hurried to examine their patients.

While they were cleaning Pia's room together before lunch, Pia said, "I'm sorry about Dr. Witmer, but I really regret that all his records were lost. We don't have any history on Jordy. I'm being completely selfish, but it bothers me. "

"Would the records be stored electronically? Maybe on a laptop or cloud?"

"Dr. Witmer was pretty old school." Pia gathered their cleaning supplies. "Maybe he kept copies at home. He had a housekeeper, but I'm not sure if she'd still be there."

"I'll ask Amanda to call Dr. Witmer's house after lunch to ask if anyone has access to his records. If not all his patients, at least Jordy," Riley said.

While Riley staffed the receptionist's desk, Amanda ate lunch, and Eli Reeves parked in front of the building. He carried a white box and two sacks. Riley hurried to open the door for him.

He set the box on the counter and smiled. "It's a home baked cheesecake, but don't tell anybody I can bake. I'm trying to preserve my tough guy image."

Pia came out of the first examination room and hurried to the desk. "What's in the box?" She peeked. "This is not store-bought, Agent Reeves. You have a talented friend who bakes, don't you?"

"You're right. I do." He glanced at Riley, who smirked.

"Your secret's safe with me, but you might have to share her name sometime. I need to impress my mother-in-law. I'll take this to the back for Amanda and the docs. Did you come to interrogate our sketchy pal, Riley, or to have lunch with us?"

"This sack has small plates and forks." Eli smiled as he placed the white sack on top of the box. "Can I choose both?"

"If I get to take the leftover cheesecake home to impress my family."

Pia hurried to the breakroom with the box and sack and returned as Dr. Thad went into the first room to examine the patient.

"Gotta go." Pia rushed to join Thad.

Amanda returned to her desk with a piece of cheesecake on a plate. "The docs deserted me. My cousin emailed his resume and transcripts, and I forwarded the documents to Julie Rae to review. She went into her office with her cheesecake, and Thad gobbled his down then left to see a patient. I'll enjoy mine in peace. Go ahead and have lunch. I've got a call to make between bites."

"Thanks, Amanda." Riley said before she and Eli strolled to the breakroom.

While Eli unwrapped his sandwich, he said, "So, what do I not know?"

Toby padded into the breakroom and lay under the table near Riley's feet. "Quick version: I went to my grandma's cabin to clean, and when I returned to the house in town, I smelled the propane leak. The pipe had been cut, and the note was on the ground next to the pipe. I gave the sheriff my padlock key, and the fire department turned off the gas."

"According to the fire department, the potential for an explosion or even a fire was low, so what was the point? Intimidation?"

"I suppose. It worked because I'm scared, but I don't know why I'm supposed to leave Barton. The best I can come up with is that if I stayed, I would see something that no one else would notice."

Eli finished off his sandwich. "That's more than I had. So, are you going to leave?" Eli cut two generous slices of cheesecake and placed them on plates.

"I thought about it, but what guarantee do I have that would end the threats?"

"None. I see your point."

Riley handed him a fork then took a small bite with hers. "Mmm. This is heavenly, Eli."

His eyes crinkled as he toasted her with a large bite of cheesecake on his fork. "I'll let the baker know you appreciated the culinary skills."

"I sure do talk fancy." Riley took another bite.

"Hey, you two had better have left some for me." Pia grinned as she stood in the doorway with her hands on her hips.

"Just barely. You need to eat your lunch before it's all gone," Riley said.

Pia rushed through her sandwich then took her time to enjoy each bite of cheesecake. "This is excellent, Agent Reeves. I was kind of kidding about taking the leftovers home, but now I'm not. Is that okay?"

Eli laughed. "Of course."

"I'm going to put my cheesecake in the refrigerator. Y'all can have a little privacy for your meeting. Just don't close the door because Amanda will have to come listen with a glass, and she always leaves out the interesting parts." Pia tossed her hair and sashayed out of the breakroom while Riley and Eli laughed.

"So, for the super-secret part, what's my next step?" Riley asked.

"I don't know. I'm not convinced that staying is the best idea."

"Yes, it is," Amanda called from her desk.

"You'll have to admit, I have a good support system here." Riley snickered.

"I'll give you that." Eli rose. "Time to get back to the office. Call or text if anything else comes up. It would be nice if I came to town to have an entertaining lunch with friends not because someone is trying to terrify you. What really bothers me is how rapidly the threats are escalating."

After Eli left, a client parked in the lot near the dog walk. She followed a black cocker spaniel puppy as he marked his territory.

"That's one ambitious puppy." Riley snickered.

"No kidding," Amanda said. "I left a message on Dr. Witmer's home phone, and his housekeeper called me back almost immediately. She said Dr. Witmer's sister has access to his veterinary records, and she is contacting all his customers. Jordy's records are at Dr. Witmer's house, and the housekeeper said she'd leave a copy in an envelope on the porch if someone could drop by and pick them up. She was picking up her personal things when I called and will be leaving town. Do you want to go by after work? I'll give you the address."

"Toby and I could do that," Riley said.

Amanda wrote down the address. "Here you go. It's north of town. It's actually a nice drive. I think it's about twenty minutes or so away."

Riley read the address then folded the paper and stuck it in her back pocket as the woman and puppy came into the building. Toby sniffed the puppy, and the woman laughed as the cocker wagged its tail so hard that it slipped and fell to the floor.

Amanda handed Riley a patient folder, and Riley stooped. "Hello, Jack."

Jack wiggled and wagged to her then flopped onto his back for a belly rub. After a good rub, he rolled over and followed Riley and his person to the exam room.

"I'm a little worried about Jack's hearing," the woman said as they went into the exam room.

After Riley weighed him, Dr. Julie Rae came into the room and examined the puppy. "His ears are clean, and there's some signs he's been scratching his right ear, but I see what you mean about his hearing." She pulled out a squeak toy from a drawer, and when she pressed it, he cocked his head but didn't look in the direction of the sound.

"He heard the squeak. I'm suspicious that he's not hearing in both ears. Let's start with an antibiotic to see if there's an infection I can't see."

Dr. Julie Rae recorded her findings and placed the order for the medicine.

Riley rubbed Jack's right ear, and he laid his head on her hand. "I'll meet you at the front desk with your medicine."

When Riley arrived at the counter, the woman was putting her checkbook and receipt into her purse; Jack had crawled under Amanda's feet and was asleep. Riley rattled a plastic bag then lifted the lid of their treat jar, but when Jack didn't react to the plastic or the clink of the lid against the glass jar, she stooped under

Amanda's feet and stroked Jack's head. After he sat up, Riley gave him a treat, and he trotted to the door.

"Thanks, Riley." Amanda rose after they left and leaned from one foot to the other while she held onto her desk, "I got a cramp in my foot, but I didn't want to disturb the little guy."

"We'll try the crinkling plastic and treat jar tests when he comes back for a checkup," Dr. Julie Rae said. "That was brilliant, Riley."

"Toby taught me that a while ago," Riley said. "A family brought a willful boxer to our office for his annual and told the doc he couldn't hear. They'd taken him to every specialist they could find. I had a lingering cough, and Toby told me to take my medicine. I unwrapped a lozenge, and the boxer was busted."

Toby grinned, Jordy howled, and Doc and Amanda laughed.

Pia came out of an examination room with a client who carried a cat carrier. She narrowed her eyes as she passed Riley. "You'll tell me what was funny later, right?" Pia whispered.

After her next patient left, Riley checked her phone, and she had a text from Ms. Helen. "Gas pipe and connection fixed and made more secure."

Riley exhaled a long slow breath, and Amanda asked, "What?"

"Ms. Helen fixed the pipe and connection for the propane. I don't know why this makes me feel better."

"Too much of a reminder until it was fixed," Amanda said.

At the end of the day, as Riley and Pia sanitized the exam rooms together while Toby and Jordy sat with Amanda, Riley recounted the story of the boxer who had selective hearing.

"And Toby told you to take your medicine? The sad part is I believe this fantastical tale of yours."

When they returned files to Amanda's desk, she had already left. Riley filed the folders, and Pia locked the file cabinets.

"How was your first day, Thad?" Julie Rae asked as they strolled to Amanda's desk.

"It was good," he said as Claire parked near the door. "See you tomorrow."

After he left, Pia said, "He might be weak in the small talk department, but he's amazing with our patients. He leaves the chatting with the clients to me."

"You two did work well together," Julie Rae said. "I'm sure you'll get an opportunity to work with Dr. Thad tomorrow, Riley. I want to be sure we're all relatively compatible. Now, you two go home, so I can too."

Jordy followed Pia, and Toby followed Riley as Julie Rae locked the door.

Riley entered Dr. Witmer's address in her phone before she and Toby left the parking lot. After they left town, the large homes on well-manicured lawns surrounded by wrought iron fences with ornate gates looked like modern day plantations. "Out of our price range, Toby, but aren't they beautiful?"

Toby yipped and grinned, and Riley laughed. "You're right. We couldn't afford the heating bill."

When they passed a large pecan orchard, Riley said, "I have always loved pecan trees. It's so amazing to me how bare they are in the winter. It's like they died long ago and only their skeletons remain. Then in the spring, they explode with green leaves. Maybe someday we can live next door to a pecan orchard."

As she turned at the long, circular driveway that led to a renovated nineteenth century Victorian-style mansion with three towers and turrets and a wide, wraparound porch with decorative railings, her eyes widened. "A person would have to have a housekeeper with a home like this. The rose garden on the side of the house is beautiful. I don't know anything about growing roses, but I guess we could learn. Let's check Grandma's books for gardening and roses the next time we go to the cabin."

After Riley parked the SUV, she peered at the house. "I think the housekeeper heard us coming up the driveway. I thought I saw her set something outside, but she's gone back in."

When Toby hopped out, he growled a low guttural snarl.

"We're fine, Toby. It's just the housekeeper."

His growl intensified as she stepped up to the porch. *Front door isn't quite closed.*

Toby dashed past her and pushed aggressively into the house as he snarled and barked.

"Wait, Toby," she shouted as she followed him inside. She froze at the sight of a woman on her back in the foyer with a single bullet wound in the middle of her forehead. The woman's lifeless eyes stared at the ceiling. Riley's knees weakened, and her head was swimming. She grabbed onto the door to keep from falling.

Toby barked and scrambled until he gained traction on the slick hardware floor then he dashed toward the back of the house. Toby snarled with the ferocity of an attacking tiger; a man screamed then a door slammed. Toby trotted back with a bloody remnant in his mouth and assumed a guard position at the front door. Riley removed her phone from her back pocket and called nine-one-one.

She backed out of the house and picked up the envelope on the chair nearest to the door and shoved it into her back pocket. As she dropped into the chair, a yellow piece of paper fluttered onto her lap, and she gasped. "A note."

"They will be right there, ma'am. Are you safe?"

"I think the murderer left by the back door when I got here. My dog is calm. I'm safe. I need to talk to the sheriff."

Riley sent a text to the sheriff. "Found a dead woman and a note at Dr. Witmer's house."

"Be right there. What does note say?"

Riley opened the folded note then gagged and rushed to the railing and retched until she was overcome with dry heaves. When her stomach spasms slowed, she picked up her phone, snapped a photo of the note, and replied: "It's on you."

When Riley dropped to sit on the porch and lean against Toby, the sound of a wailing siren comforted her. *Sheriff will be here first.*

Sheriff tore up the driveway, slammed on his brakes, and rushed to Riley. "Are you hurt?"

Riley shook her head, and the sheriff helped her to her feet then supported her as they walked to his cruiser. After he helped her into the passenger's seat, he lowered her window before he closed the door. Toby guarded her while the sheriff went into the house.

When the first state police car arrived, the trooper jumped out with his weapon drawn as he eased toward the back of the house. The sheriff walked to Riley's side of his cruiser. "There's a torn piece of blood-saturated cloth near the body."

"Toby chased a man to the back of the house, and returned with the cloth in his mouth. He must have dropped it."

"Good boy, Toby." Sheriff reached down and scratched Toby's head. "You got us our first piece of evidence. So, Riley, why were you here?"

Riley told him about the call Amanda made about Jordy's records then what happened after they arrived. "Here's the envelope. Do you mind looking in it? I need to take it to work if it is Jordy's record."

Sheriff opened the envelope and pulled out four sheets and glanced through them. "Looks like records to me." He placed the sheets inside the envelope.

"Did you see anyone?" he asked as he gave the envelope to Riley.

"No." She shivered.

"You took a picture of the note, didn't you?" Sheriff asked. "Send a copy to Agent Reeves. He's got all the best working on this. I'm convinced you know the killer, but his people don't agree with me."

Riley frowned. "I can't imagine who it could be. It's not like I even know a lot of people. Maybe a client?"

Sheriff shrugged. "I don't know. Just feels more personal than a casual acquaintance to me, but I'm an old school cop not a profiler. Speaking of personal, I talked to the woman who saw Daphne leave the note on your car. The complete story is that the woman stopped at the corner to watch when she saw Daphne take the note off her own car. After Daphne read it, she put it on your car, which means the note was not intended for you."

"Why did she stop to watch?"

"It's what nosy people do." Sheriff chuckled as he strode to meet the state trooper who pulled in behind the sheriff's cruiser.

After the two men talked, the sheriff motioned for Riley to join them, and the state trooper took notes while Riley repeated her story about finding the housekeeper.

"There's a piece of cloth that the dog had after he returned from chasing off the man," Sheriff added. "Toby may have provided us with our first break."

As he walked Riley and Toby to the SUV, Sheriff said, "Deputy Ben Carter asked me to keep an eye on you. Okay if I give him a call?"

Riley furrowed her brow. *I should call him myself.*

"I'll wait until you get home." Sheriff smiled.

"Thanks. I'd like to talk to Ben, but I don't think I could go over what I found a third time quite yet."

Riley jumped when her phone buzzed a text from Eli. "Got it."

She showed the text to the sheriff who nodded. "He'll be here tomorrow."

After Riley and Toby arrived home, her phone rang. *Ben.*

"Sheriff called me. Are you okay?"

Riley's eyes welled up at the gentleness in his voice. She dropped onto the sofa, and Toby jumped up next to her.

"I'm okay. It really shook me up."

"You have every reason to be shook up. I am too. Sheriff told me he's concerned because he thinks you might know the man. We know Toby does because he got a good whiff when he bit him, right?"

Riley hugged Toby. "Yes."

"I wish I were there. Start carrying your pistol on you. Get an inside the waistband holster at the pawn shop. They'll help you pick out the right one for your pistol."

I knew I'd get practical advice from Ben.

"Toby and I will go right after we hang up."

"Call me after you get back. I want to hear about your normal day and tell you about mine."

After she hung up, Riley asked, "Want to go to the pawn shop, Toby?"

Toby jumped off the sofa and trotted to the door.

When they arrived at the pawn shop, Riley unloaded her pistol before they went inside.

"Looking for anything special?" The woman behind the counter smiled as Riley and Toby walked inside the shop.

Riley scanned the shop and smiled. *They have everything.* "I need a waistband holster for my pistol. Can I show it to you? It's unloaded, and the slide is open."

"Set it on the counter." After the woman looked at the pistol, she said, "I know what you need. You can put it back into your purse."

The woman had Riley try on different styles of new holsters while she gave Toby a treat.

"I like the inside the waistband one best," Riley said. "I thought it would be uncomfortable, but it isn't. This is perfect."

"Us girls have the advantage of a little extra cushion for the holster and pistol to snuggle against and leave no imprint. Do you normally wear your shirt tucked or untucked?"

"I rarely tuck in a shirt," Riley said.

"Then the inside the waistband is right for you. I'll have it for you at the register if you want to look around. We just got in a few shirts," she said.

Riley and Toby wandered to the section with women's clothes, and Riley looked through the shirts. "They're all so pretty, Toby, but I like these three. Which one do I choose?"

Toby yipped.

"You're right—all three."

When they reached the cash register, the woman sneaked another treat to Toby. "He sure is a sweet dog. I'll bet he's really protective though."

"He is."

After they were home, Riley loaded her pistol and put it into her waistband holster before she called Ben.

"We got a holster that fits inside the waistband. I was surprised how comfortable it was."

"Are you wearing it now?"

"I knew you'd ask." Riley giggled. "Of course, I am."

"Am I that big of a nag?" Ben asked.

"Yes. So, how was your day?"

"Three speeders, a fender bender in front of the school, and a gas station robbery. We caught the robber. All in all, a successful day of work. What about you?"

Riley told him about Jack and her story about the boxer, and he chuckled.

"Toby is really smart. Actually, so are you because you pay attention to him."

Riley smiled. "I loved the pawn shop. I have to go back again and browse. I saw all kinds of things that I didn't know I was lacking in my life and even more things that I had no idea what they were."

Ben chuckled. "That's how I feel about pawn shops. What about your new vet? Do you like him?"

"He's kind of quiet, but Pia said he's good with animals, and she likes working with him. Doc said I'd work with him tomorrow. We're all hoping he can survive the week. Amanda's working on setting up Doc Thad's office for him. We didn't think of it until today. His wife is a school teacher and applied for a job as a substitute."

"Has a dog found Doc Julie Rae?"

"Not yet, but I'll bet it won't be long."

"My partner has a Chihuahua and a Great Dane. He said his Chihuahua is fierce and protects the bigger dog from spiders and shadows."

Riley smiled. "Grandma told me about a friend of hers who had a Chihuahua on his horse farm. When a big storm hit, the little dog ran out to the horse barn to comfort her friends."

"What are you doing for supper?" Ben asked. "I bought a loaf of herb bread from the bakery to make a grilled cheese to go with my can of soup."

"That sounds good. I planned to throw a potato into the oven and make a salad to go with it."

"We should swap recipes," Ben said, and Riley snickered.

"One of the things the sheriff told me was that he thought I know the killer."

"What do you think?"

"It makes sense, but I don't really know that many people. Could they be a client?"

"I don't know. Are you likely to recognize a client that you only met a few times?"

"No. I'd recognize any dog or cat that I've seen, but not a client. Has to be someone I've worked with then."

"What about a class?" Ben asked.

"Maybe, but it would have been a while ago because the last couple years the only classes I took were online."

"I guess it's suppertime for Toby," Ben said. "Wear your weapon even in the house and keep it close at hand when you go to bed. I'm glad you have Toby."

"I am too. Talk to you tomorrow."

"Be safe."

After they hung up, Riley put a potato in the oven to bake then fed Toby before she scanned her book shelves. "I found a book on gardening, Toby. Do we want to grow flowers or vegetables?"

Toby yipped.

"Both, it is."

Riley turned on her gas fireplace and prepared her salad to go with her potato.

"Did you hear that?" She tiptoed to the front window and peeked out between the slats of the blind. Toby rose and padded to her.

"I don't see anything." She rubbed his ear.

She read her gardening book until time to pull out her potato then ate her supper while she read. After she ate, she carried her dishes to the sink and paused. "Is there something on the back porch?" She set her dishes in the sink without making a sound then eased to the back door. She opened the door to peek out, but Toby barreled past her and dashed outside. Riley held her breath while Toby sniffed the grass, relieved himself then returned.

"I'm making myself nervous," she said.

Toby licked her hand before they went inside. She stopped in the kitchen to open the envelope from Dr. Witmer's house. "I'm glad we have this. We'll need to check Jordy's ears to be sure his infection is cleared up."

At bedtime, she stretched and returned the book to the bookcase. "A garden sounds too much like actual work. We'll just visit the farmers market and pick blackberries at the cabin."

* * *

Riley woke before five the next morning. After she and Toby ate breakfast, they went to the office. When they parked in the employee lot in the back, Julia Rae's truck and Thad's car were parked near the door.

After Riley and Toby went into the breakroom, Julie Rae joined them. "I heard about the murder at Dr. Witmer's. The offer for you to stay with us is still open. Same goes for Ben. If he decides he needs to stay close, he's welcome at our home. I won't pester you if you promise you'll tell me when I can help."

"I will." Riley smiled.

"I suppose we'll have company for lunch again today." Julie Rae's eyes crinkled.

"It would be a safe bet, wouldn't it? Agent Reeves said he had a meeting in town today, and I suspect he'll have things to say about yesterday." Riley put her lunch in the refrigerator before she headed to Amanda's desk.

Riley handed Amanda Jordy's records. "Doc needs to see these. She might want to recheck Jordy's ears."

Amanda's brow furrowed when she saw Riley. "I'll make sure she does. Doc told me to leave the front door locked in the mornings until someone else was in the front with me. I think all of us are shook up. I am so sorry I sent you to Dr. Witmer's house alone."

"Don't be. I'm glad it was me and Toby and not Pia; I wasn't alone because I had Toby, and the sheriff was there right away. He's been remarkably responsive."

Amanda nodded. "He's brilliant. I got into some trouble when I was a kid. When he found me where I had no business being because I was trying to fit in with the wrong crowd, he told me everybody was allowed one mistake, and I had picked a doozy. I don't know why I thought that was so funny, but when I laughed, I was absolutely liberated from trying to be like others and could be myself."

Riley nodded. "That's it. He understands. He asked me if he could call Ben. He knew I'd want Ben to know what had happened, but I wasn't ready to go into the details again quite yet."

"Speaking of the sheriff, he's here." Amanda pointed to the sheriff's cruiser as it pulled in front.

When the sheriff came inside, he said, "Got a few minutes, Riley? Can you come out to my rolling office?"

After they were seated, the sheriff said, "Did you go any farther into the house than the foyer?"

"No, the housekeeper was in the foyer, and I didn't go past her."

Sheriff nodded. "Just verifying. The killer must have ransacked the house. The investigative team thinks the housekeeper confronted him. Pure conjecture."

"So, I saw the killer put the note on the envelope?"

"That's what I think. He took advantage of the opportunity to terrorize you but didn't consider the fact that you'd have Toby with you."

As the first client parked in the lot, Thad came in the back door, but before he reached the breakroom, Pia and Jordy rushed in behind him.

"Every morning when our first patient arrives, I want to say *Show time.*" Amanda giggled.

"Now, you've done it. I'll hear *show time* first thing every morning when you say we've got a patient." Riley hurried to unlock the front door.

"My work here is done." Amanda smirked. "But don't tell Doc I said that."

The wide-eyed client rushed inside with a listless English Springer Spaniel puppy wrapped in a soiled sheet in her arms. "I don't have an appointment, but she's vomited several times and had diarrhea all night. I tried to give her a little water by an eye dropper, but it came right back up."

"Get Doc, Amanda. Room one." Riley took the puppy from the woman and hurried to the examination room. Doc came into the room behind her.

"What do we have, Riley?"

"Dehydrated. Gray mucous membranes. Listless. Vomiting and diarrhea all night."

"Set up an IV, and get Dr. Thad."

Riley dashed to Dr. Thad's office. "Dehydrated puppy. Doc wants you to join her in room one."

"IV?" he asked as he hurried down the hall.

"Getting it set up." Riley rushed to their back treatment room. When Julie Rae and Thad joined her with the puppy, she had the IV solution hung and treatment table ready. Doc nodded, and Riley left to talk to the pale and shaking client in the exam room.

"What's your puppy's name?" Riley asked.

"Holly," the woman whispered.

"Doc Julie Rae and Doc Thad will give Holly some fluids by IV. Do you know if she ate anything that could have made her sick?"

"Somehow she got into this and opened it." The client pulled out a plastic butter tub that was chewed and cracked and handed it to Riley.

"How full was it?" Riley asked.

"It didn't have butter in it. It was gravy, and it was about half full. I didn't find it until this morning. I don't know how she got it. I thought I'd put it in the refrigerator."

"When was the last time she vomited or had a bout of diarrhea?"

"About an hour ago. I thought she might perk up after that."

Riley nodded. "I'll be right back. I'll show this to the doctors."

When Riley stepped into the treatment room, the doctors had inserted Holly's IV, and Doc Thad was adjusting the drip. Julie Rae paused her examination and raised her eyebrows as she looked at Riley.

"Holly ingested half a tub of gravy sometime last evening," Riley said. "It doesn't look like there's any plastic missing, and her last round of vomiting or diarrhea was an hour ago."

"That's good news," Doc Thad said.

"I'm fond of gravy myself, Holly," Doc Julie Rae said. "We'll rehydrate her and keep an eye on her the rest of the day."

"Pick up at four?" Riley asked.

Doc Julie Rae nodded.

Riley returned to the client. "Thanks for bringing the tub in. She didn't eat any plastic, which is really good. We'll rehydrate her with an IV and keep an eye on her for the rest of the day. You can pick her up at four. If there's any change at all, Amanda will call you. Let's get you checked out then you can go home." Riley smiled. "My grandma would tell you to have a bite to eat then take a nap."

On the way to Amanda's desk, the client said, "Y'all are wonderful, and I'll take your grandma's advice. Thank you." She hugged Riley before she hurried to the counter.

After she left, Amanda said, "I think you've found the perfect way to talk to clients. Quote your grandma. Nobody's going to argue with wisdom, but if they do, I'll charge them extra fees for not following good advice."

"I believe you will," Riley said. "Is Pia with a patient?"

Amanda nodded. "In room two. Our next patient has an appointment in twenty minutes. Do you mind watching the desk for me? The baby's dancing on my bladder this morning."

"Not at all. Anything special you want me to do?"

"No, but thank you."

CHAPTER EIGHT

Amanda rushed to the bathroom. When she returned, Riley said, "We need a signal so you can dash to the bathroom whenever you have to."

"If I yelled tsunami, would that work?"

"Yes, but maybe we should have a less descriptive word." Riley rolled her eyes.

"High tide?" Amanda asked.

"Sorry I brought it up." Riley walked away from the counter to room one.

Toby stayed with Amanda. "What do you think, Toby? Fire hydrant?"

Riley chuckled as she closed the examination room door. After she cleaned the room, she returned to Amanda's desk. "I meant to ask, what's the news on your cousin?"

"Almost forgot to tell you," Amanda said as Pia came out of the exam room she had cleaned. "My cousin is coming in this afternoon to talk to Dr. Julie Rae. I'm really excited, but he's worried he won't be accepted in a small town. Doc will probably have him talk to Dr. Thad too, and I'm sure y'all will get a chance to chat with him."

"Why is he worried he won't be accepted?" Riley asked.

"His grandparents immigrated with their three small children to the US in the nineteen seventies from South Vietnam. My mother told me Zach's grandparents were brokenhearted when their daughter married my uncle, but it didn't take long for them to appreciate him. He's an enthusiastic teacher and very patient with kids. Zach's just like his dad, except a little less exuberant. I knew Zach was smart, but his grades are stellar."

"Ah," Pia said. "Book smart. We'll fix that."

Amanda glared. "You have to be nice."

"You just took away all the fun, Amanda." Riley snickered as she peered over Amanda's shoulder at the day's schedule. "Two patients at the same time?"

"I'd tell you two vet techs and two docs, but I actually made a mistake and double booked." Amanda's face reddened.

The two clients came inside, and the phone rang. Amanda pointed and slid a file folder toward Riley and another one toward Pia. They picked up the files before they accompanied the clients and patients to exam rooms.

Amanda jingled a bell, and Riley slipped out of her exam room to the counter.

"I have to tinkle," Amanda whispered as she hurried to the bathroom.

Riley giggled. "She really led me on, didn't she, Toby?"

Toby grinned.

After Riley checked out Pia's client, Pia asked, "What was the bell?"

"Amanda's tinkle alert."

Amanda strolled to her desk. "Thanks, Riley. Doc Julie Rae gave me a bell for my alert. While I'm thinking about it, I won't be in tomorrow until ten or ten thirty. I've got a doctor appointment at eight thirty. Sometimes I get in and out fairly quickly, but there's no telling. I think they use wishful thinking in their scheduling."

When it was time for her lunch, Amanda asked, "Are you taking the receptionist's desk, Pia?"

"I'll take it again, if you like, Pia," Riley said.

"I need to get over my fear of scheduling appointments. If one comes up, I'll schedule it but write down the details so Amanda can check to be sure I did it right. But if I break down in tears, feel free to take over."

Amanda frowned. "Are you sure you'll be okay? I could eat at my desk while you—"

"Go, Amanda. You're hovering," Pia growled.

After Amanda stomped to the breakroom followed by Toby, Riley held up her hand; Pia chuckled and smacked it.

The scheduled client was late, the next scheduled client was early, and Pia's eyes widened.

"Don't worry. I'll juggle them. I'm a magician," Riley said.

Riley picked up both file folders and scanned each one quickly before she led the late-coming client and her cat to room one. A minute later, she led the early client and his cat to room two.

"Thanks for taking us early," the client said. "We're just here for a blood draw."

While Riley weighed the cat, she asked, "Do you have any other concerns? Anything else you'd like for us to check for you today?"

"No. We have an appointment next week for a follow up, but I appreciate that you asked."

Riley smiled. "It's what we do." She reviewed the file and drew up the blood. "Good to go."

She opened the door and led the client and cat to Pia's desk. Before Riley took the tubes to their lab for one of the docs to examine, she said, "They already have a scheduled appointment for next week."

Riley strode to room one and asked, "How's Hazel doing?"

When Riley lifted Hazel to the scale, the client said, "I'm worried about her weight. I've increased her food and her snacks, but she looks like she's still losing weight." Riley recorded Hazel's weight in the chart and frowned. "How is her activity?"

"She's not as active as she used to be. She doesn't even stalk our dog, Bruiser, any more."

Riley shook her head. "Sounds like she's not feeling up to par."

Hazel meowed, and Riley stroked her as she talked. "I'm so sorry, Hazel. We have a new veterinarian who has joined us. Is it okay if I ask Dr. Thad to look at her? Dr. Julie Rae will follow up with him and you after he's completed his exam."

"As long as Dr. Julie Rae sees Hazel, that's fine."

"She will. Dr. Thad will be here in just a few minutes."

Riley strode to the breakroom. "Hazel and her person are here. Hazel's stomach hurts too much to eat. Here's her file. They're in room one."

Dr. Thad reached for the file. "I'll examine her. I've finished my lunch."

"I'll be there in a few minutes," Dr. Julie Rae said. After Dr. Thad left she asked, "Did Hazel tell you her stomach hurt?"

"Yes," Riley said.

"Thanks. That's a new finding for us," Dr. Julie said.

"Glad I could help," Riley said before she hurried to the receptionist's desk.

"How are we doing?" Riley asked.

"Phone has been quiet. Agent Reeves is on his phone out front. By the way, it was brilliant of you to read the files. I'm afraid I would have rushed to take care of both patients at once. Unsuccessfully, of course. I think I just learned my first magician's trick. I can't wait to see what else you have up those sleeves." Pia wiggled her eyebrows, and Riley smiled.

"Are you two ready for lunch?" Amanda peered at the parking lot. "Who's going to tell Agent Reeves it's lunchtime?"

"Too cold out there," Pia said. "He'll figure it out."

"How much time do we have before the next appointment?" Riley asked.

"Thirty-five minutes—I checked," Pia said as they headed to the breakroom with Jordy bringing up the rear.

"Well done."

While Riley unwrapped her sandwich, Pia heated her lunch in the microwave.

"Coffee?" Pia asked. "Doc must have made a fresh pot."

"Not for me."

Agent Reeves strode into the breakroom. "I wouldn't mind a cup."

Pia poured two cups, and Eli carried his to the table.

"What did you bring me?" Pia asked.

Eli laughed. "Lunch before the bribe."

"What about Amanda? Is she okay with waiting?" Pia narrowed her eyes.

"I have the dessert sack. Eat your lunch and come join me," Amanda called out from her desk.

Pia grabbed her lunch out of the microwave and hurried back to the table. "Pretty sneaky," she mumbled.

Riley asked, "How is Jordy doing? I'm not seeing any limp at all."

"He and Jackson are best buds," Pia said. "It used to be a battle to get Jackson to do his homework while I fix supper, but Jordy nudges him to stay on task, so they can play in the backyard.

My husband thought about putting in a dog door for Jordy but decided against it. It would be too convenient for Jackson."

Pia finished her lunch and left the breakroom before Riley had eaten half her sandwich.

After Eli and Riley ate, he said, "The team investigating the Trumans have a few questions they wanted me to ask you." He pulled out his notebook and thumbed through the pages. "Here we go. Were there any drug irregularities while you worked at the Allen Truman clinic?"

Riley frowned. "The first month I was there, Marcy and I did a quarterly audit of the controlled substances and found an invoice of a large shipment of ketamine that was not logged into the inventory. Ketamine is used for pain and anesthesia, especially in surgeries, but our clinic didn't do many surgeries and had no reason to have much on hand. We were worried because ketamine is also a street drug and reported the discrepancy to Dr. Truman, Junior. Before the next quarter, he assigned Dotty to be responsible for the audits, and as far as I know, there were no more discrepancies."

"Is that unusual for a bookkeeper to audit the records?"

"I don't know because I never worked anywhere else, but Marcy told me it was like asking a cashier to audit her own register. The other girls said we did the audit wrong because we were supposed to count the inventory on hand and the inventory used. After that, Marcy and I ate our packed sandwiches alone in the breakroom because the others went out together for lunch. Later,

Marcy told me we were excluded, and we laughed because we didn't care."

Eli smiled. "Marcy sounds like she was a good friend. You keep in touch with her?"

Riley nodded. "That's how I knew about Dotty's death."

Eli poured himself more coffee. "You said Dr. Truman, Senior's, office was always locked. Did you ever notice anything else out of the ordinary?"

"Not really. His office must have been cleaned almost every night though because first thing in the morning, the hallway smelled of ammonia. One of the girls complained it aggravated her asthma, and Dr. Truman, Junior, laughed and told her she should stay away from the hallway if it bothered her. She finally resigned because the building sometimes had a chemical, rotten egg odor from a nearby plant, according to Dotty." Riley rose to throw away her trash.

"Anything else?"

"Marcy told me on our last day at work there that Doc Junior always said I was his favorite vet tech and that the other girls claimed he had a crush on me."

Eli raised his eyebrows. "Really? Why did they say that?"

"I don't know. I never got any special treatment or preference in time off, approved training, or anything like that, and I certainly never saw him outside the office."

Eli handed his lunch sack to Riley. "I gave Amanda the sack of two dozen cookies. Hopefully, that's enough to keep me out of trouble. Here's special treatment: the last two Italian crème cupcakes from the bakery."

Riley peeled away the paper from her cupcake and bit into it. "Mmm."

Eli took a bite and nodded. After he finished his cupcake, he asked, "What does Dr. Julie Rae use to clean the clinic? It always smells fresh."

"Amanda has a spray bottle of sanitizing cleaner she uses on the counter. That's what you smell when you come in. We clean the exam rooms after every patient. A janitorial service comes in every evening to sweep and dust then once a week they mop with a dishwashing liquid and vinegar solution, and that's the same solution we use if there are any floor messes during the day."

"That seems certainly more than adequate."

Riley nodded as she took another bite.

"Thanks for the help." Eli threw away his trash. "Sheriff and I have a meeting with one of Dr. Witmer's vet techs at the sheriff's office. You've given me some ideas for questions."

Julie Rae stopped by the breakroom before she hurried to her office. "Thank you for the cookies."

"You're welcome. It's nice to have people to eat lunch with when I'm in town."

Riley rose. "I really enjoyed the cupcake. You didn't have to bring dessert, you know."

"Yes, he did," Amanda called out from her desk, and Riley rolled her eyes.

"You've been overruled." Eli headed to the front.

As Riley straightened the breakroom, her phone buzzed a text from Ben.

"You okay?"

Riley replied, "All good. You?"

"Same."

"Who was the text from?" Pia asked as she came into the breakroom to throw away more trash. "You can tell me it's none of my business, but you don't want to hurt my feelings, do you?"

Riley raised an eyebrow. "It was Ben. He was checking up on me."

"Normally, I'd worry that a man who checked up on his girlfriend in the middle of the day was a control freak, but in this case, it's completely understandable."

Riley frowned. "He's not my boyfriend."

"Oh, sure. My mistake." Pia snickered as she hurried to the front to greet their next patient.

After Riley pushed the chairs against the table, she strolled to the receptionist's desk where a slender young man with black hair chatted with Amanda.

Amanda beamed. "Riley, this is my cousin Zachary."

"Zach," he smiled as he held out his fist.

Riley returned his smile and his fist bump as her next patient, an elderly border collie, came inside with her person.

"Come with me, Zach; I'll introduce you to Dr. Julie Rae," Amanda said as Riley picked up the file folder on the counter.

Toby joined Riley as she led the way to the exam room. "Can you step up on the scale?" Riley asked the old girl. Toby whined, and the border collie gingerly stepped on the two-inch high platform scale.

"Thanks, Toby," Riley said as she recorded the weight. "Okay, girl. Thank you."

The collie eased off the scale. "How's her medicine working?"

"She's sleeping all night instead of pacing like she had been. She's still having her leakages and accidents during the day though."

Riley checked the file. "She's at a low dose. How's her energy?"

"Much better. I think she was exhausted from her lack of sleep."

Riley crouched near the collie. "I hope you'll excuse me, but I have to take your temperature."

Riley cooed then slipped in the thermometer. "That's it. Thank you."

She rose and read the thermometer. "Good news. Normal temperature."

The border collie yipped, and Riley nodded.

The client's eyes were wide. "I talk to Josie all the time."

Riley nodded. "Josie's a smart old girl. We have a new vet. Dr. Thad will check Josie if that's okay."

Josie yipped, and the woman said, "We're fine with your new vet. I'm sure he's good if Dr. Julie Rae hired him."

After Riley examined three more patients, Amanda said, "Zach and Pia are in the breakroom."

When Riley strolled into the breakroom, Pia and Zach were laughing.

"Riley, a few of Zach's instructors were ones that I had, and they haven't changed."

"And neither have their stories," Zach added.

"Right," Pia wiped her eyes. "It's going to be hard to pull any pranks on Zach though. He has three sisters."

"That means you're in trouble, Zach. Pia never walked away from a challenge," Riley said. "Tell us about what you learned from your clinicals."

Zach nodded and talked about the different techniques, styles, and overall paces he observed. "I learned my technical skills in a laboratory are stellar, but in practice, there's a balance between performing perfectly for a grade and performing efficiently for the patient and for the patient load."

Riley nodded. "That's a hard one to learn. One or two of our new graduates at my previous job couldn't adjust to that balance and left after a week."

"Mostly perfect and mostly efficient—you're right—it's a balance. I had trouble with that on my first job too," Pia said. "So, where are you?"

"I'm afraid I'm still at the A plus in knowledge and skills in the school lab phase and peeking over the fence at the A plus efficiency on the job," Zach said. "But I'm not afraid to learn."

"Pia and I have different styles. Neither one is right or wrong. If you work with me for a week then Pia for another week, I'll bet you develop your own style," Riley said.

"Brilliant," Pia said.

"That's awesome," Zach said. "I have an idea it will be just as hard for you as it will be for me because I'll slow you down."

"You will at first then you better get up to speed fast." Pia's eyes twinkled.

"Yes, ma'am." Zach's eyes widened.

"If you call us *ma'am*, Zach, we'll have to call you *sir*. Your choice," Riley said.

"Okay. Got it," he said.

Dr. Julie Rae stood at the doorway of the breakroom. "Still here, Zach? That's a good sign. I'll meet you in my office."

"Yes—" Zach glanced at Riley. "Okay, Doc."

After he left, Julie Rae asked, "What do you think?"

"We think he should work with Riley first for a week then me for a week. We think he'll survive," Pia said, and Riley nodded.

"Okay then," Julie Rae said. "That's what we're looking for, right? I'll see when he wants to start."

"Good," Riley said as she and Pia left to check in with Amanda.

"We're planning on Zach staying at our house until he decides he's ready for a place of his own. We've got a spare bedroom," Amanda said. "What did you think?"

"We like him. He's not full of himself like a lot of new grads," Pia said.

"I don't think he's afraid to learn," Riley said. "That's not as common as people think."

"I lost track. Who's next?" Amanda asked.

"I am," Riley said.

"Good. You've got the desk, Pia." Amanda jingled her bell then hurried to the bathroom.

"She knew," Pia grumbled as the client pulled up, and she handed Riley the file folder.

Riley nodded as she accepted the file and scanned it before she opened the door for the client and the patient, an old French bulldog. The bulldog snuffled and snorted as she waddled into the office.

"You feeling okay, Collette?" Riley asked as she led the way to examination room three. The patient whined, and Riley nodded.

"She hasn't been herself," the man said.

"Her feet are bothering her?" Riley asked as they went into the room, and she led the old girl to the scale. Riley recorded the weight then the bulldog eased off the scale.

"I don't think so. I think she has another ear infection."

"I need to take your temperature," Riley said, and the bulldog whimpered.

"It just takes a second." Riley took the bulldog's temperature and peered at the thermometer. "No fever, that's good. We have a new doctor. Are you okay if Dr. Thad checks her?"

"That's fine. Dr. Julie Rae's not going anywhere, is she?" the man asked.

"No, sir. The business has grown to a point where we need a second veterinarian to be able to get through the day."

"That makes sense," he said.

Riley went to Dr. Thad's office. "Room three. French bulldog, Collette, no temp; her feet are bothering her. The client thinks it's another ear infection."

"Thank you, Riley." He read over the file then followed Riley into exam room three.

Dr. Thad asked, "Is it okay if Riley puts you up on the table, so I can examine you?"

The dog whimpered, and Riley said, "Thanks," as she lifted the old girl to the table.

Dr. Thad peered into her ears and listened to her chest before he checked her skin and feet. "Her heart's good, and her ears are fine. I don't see anything on her chart that indicates she's taking anything for her stopped up nose. She can take an over-the-counter antihistamine. The skin on her back is irritated, but the bottoms of her feet are bright red. Have you noticed her biting her feet?"

"I thought she was just bored, and got her a new bone to chew on, but she hasn't been very interested in it."

"Has she been anywhere new? Have you made any changes to your yard?"

"We stick pretty close to home, but I do have a new landscaper, and he's done wonders with my grass."

Dr. Thad nodded. "Does he know Collette spends time in the yard?"

"Probably not. I keep the yard picked up, and she stays inside when he's here. She doesn't bark; she sleeps."

Dr. Thad nodded. "He may be using a chemical that isn't dog friendly. The antihistamine will help with her stopped up nose and the skin irritation on her back, but I'd like to check her feet again next week. Wipe off her feet with a damp cloth after she's been outside."

Riley picked up the bulldog and placed her on the floor as Dr. Thad wrote on a pad he carried in his pocket. "This is the brand name, but generic is just fine. Bring her back on Monday, so we can check her feet. I'd like to be sure they clear up. Amanda will make the appointment for you"

"Great. Thanks, Doc," the man said.

"I'll walk with you to Amanda's desk," Riley said.

After Amanda made the appointment, the man and the French bulldog left.

"Zach starts on Monday," Amanda said. "He's really excited to start. He was worried he wouldn't get any on-the-job training. I had tried to tell him all of us started as new grads. I don't think it sunk in until today because he told me you and Pia understood what it was like for him. He called it Imposter Syndrome—afraid somebody might find out he's not a real vet tech." She tittered. "Whatever that is."

"None here." Riley rolled her eyes.

Dr. Thad met her at the exam room when Riley returned to clean. "I don't know how you did it, but you and Collette communicated very clearly to each other. I might have just focused on her breathing and missed checking her skin and feet. You make me look good. Thank you."

"We're a team." Riley nodded.

Near the end of the day, Dr. Julie Rae said, "It's been a good day. Amanda you can go home early if you like."

"Thanks. Running to the bathroom has worn me out. Remember, I have a doctor appointment tomorrow."

"We will," Riley said. "I'll take the desk. Move. You're in my chair."

"Fine. I'm gone." Amanda smiled as she pulled her purse out of the bottom drawer then headed to the breakroom to grab her lunch bag.

At a quarter until five, a car sped down the street then swerved into the parking lot before it slammed to a stop on the sidewalk in front of the door. A man jumped out with a baby in his arms and ran into the office. "My baby's not breathing," he said.

Riley snatched the gray baby away from the man and listened for breathing before she flipped the child upside down and smacked it sharply on its back. After the third blow, a button flew out of the baby's mouth onto the floor, and the baby coughed and sputtered. Pia brought out a bottle of oxygen with the tubing attached and held the end of the tubing near the baby's face; the baby's color pinked up.

"The ambulance will be here in a few minutes," Dr. Julie Rae said.

The man dropped onto a chair and sobbed. "I didn't know what to do or where to go. We just moved and our moving van showed up yesterday two days late. I don't even know where I thought I was going until I saw you were here."

Dr. Thad sat next to the man and spoke softly. "Slow breaths. The baby's okay. You did the right thing."

When the man settled down, Riley handed him the screaming child, and after he comforted his baby, she quieted.

"I'm Dylan Price." He rocked the baby and patted her back. "My wife is unpacking at our apartment, and I was on my way to the grocery store. I can't thank you enough."

The ambulance pulled in front of the door, and the paramedic examined the baby in her father's arms. "Baby's breathing, and her lungs are clear, but we'd like for a doctor to examine her to be sure there's no tissue injuries."

"We have an appointment with her new doctor tomorrow morning. Can he examine her in the morning?"

"That's up to you," the paramedic said. "What did she choke on?"

Pia handed the button to the paramedic. "It's smooth. No rough edges. Do you know where it came from?"

"It was the nose on her stuffed dog. I didn't think about it coming off." His face reddened. "She had it with her in her car seat."

"Is it okay if we get it and look at the toy?" the paramedic asked.

The man nodded, and the ambulance driver went to the car and returned with the stuffed toy and handed it to the paramedic, who examined it. "Nothing else here an ambitious little one can remove," she said.

The baby whimpered and reached for her toy, and the paramedic smiled as she handed it to the baby.

"We have a form then we'll be out of your way." She reviewed the form with the father and after he signed it, the ambulance crew left.

"Thank you. Pretty weak words, but I'm grateful." Mr. Price carried the baby to his car and secured her in her car seat before he waved and left.

"We are an awesome team. Let's go home," Dr. Julie Rae said.

On the way home, Riley stopped at the grocery store. "I won't be long. I'm going to pick up a sandwich I can warm up at home."

Toby lay down on the back seat and closed his eyes. When Riley returned, she said, "The store was a zoo—I overheard a lady say it's supposed to snow—wouldn't that be something? I grabbed a sandwich from the deli and some ice cream in case it really does snow. "

Toby yipped.

"It made sense when I thought about it. Don't be judgy."

After they were home, Riley stuck the ice cream into the freezer before she fed Toby. Her phone buzzed a text. *Ben.*

"You home?"

Riley called him.

Ben chuckled when he answered. "I was going to call you, but I didn't want to call if you were driving home or something. Are you okay?"

"I'm fine. Tell me about your day."

"I have sunglasses. Life is good. How was your day?"

Toby yipped, and Riley strolled to the back porch to sit while Toby investigated his yard. "Just a normal day. Doc hired Amanda's cousin. He's a vet tech—fresh out of school, but smart enough to know there's a difference between school and practical experience. I think he'll work out great. Right before we closed for the day, a man ran inside with his baby who wasn't breathing. I smacked the baby on the back a few times, and a button popped out. I can't tell you how terrified I was."

"Oh, man. Where did you learn to do that?"

"I took a first aid class my first year in high school to avoid taking another physical education class."

Ben laughed. "That's hilarious and brilliant."

Riley shrugged. "I thought so, but my mother was not amused. She was always worried about my weight and said I needed the exercise."

"I'll bet she's proud of you now," Ben said.

"I don't know. She left Dad and me the following year. I'm not sure where she is."

"I'm sorry to hear that. It must have been a blow."

"I felt bad because Dad was so hurt. She kept to herself. I was always close to Dad."

"Where is he?"

"He was a chemical engineer in Germany, and the plant he worked in exploded my second year of college. He didn't make it out. I don't know what I would have done without Aunt Millie. She's always come through for me. So, tell me what you and your sunglasses did today."

"I spent the morning on radar and met a lot of ill-mannered people. None of them said thank you. I helped a man change the tire on his camper trailer on the interstate while another deputy slowed traffic. The man was as scared as I was that someone was going to hit us. He said thank you, so my day ended on a positive note too. How's your new vet working out?"

"He's going to be fine. I think word will get out that he's good. A client did ask today if Dr. Julie Rae was going to be leaving."

"Have you heard from your friend, Marcy?"

"I don't expect to hear from her until later in the week, but we should plan on going Sunday afternoon after you get off work whether she goes or not. I think it will be fun."

"I've been trying to come up with a way I could pick you up, so you don't have to drive by yourself, and I haven't come up with anything so far, but if we meet at my apartment, we'll only have one vehicle to park there. I hear they're really packed on Sunday."

"That might work."

After they hung up, Riley went to the door. "You coming, Toby?"

Toby flopped down on the grass while Riley went inside. She set her Cuban sandwich on a cast iron skillet and placed another skillet on top of it. While it heated and browned on one side, she poured herself a glass of iced tea before she flipped her sandwich to brown on the other side. When Toby scratched on the door, she opened it, and he pranced inside.

She ate her sandwich while she read through her grandma's cookbook. "Nice to read, but I don't have the energy for all the prep. My sandwich-making is stellar though."

After she picked out a book, she flipped on the fireplace and put up her feet to read with Toby by her side. When the wind rose to a howl, she shivered, and Toby whimpered in his sleep.

She froze at the sound of scratching. She pulled out her pistol and ran to the back door as Toby scrambled to follow her. When she opened the door to peer outside, Toby dashed into the yard and growled as he stood near the fence on the side of the house. She shook her head. *I have to find a better way to check the backyard.*

When the wind slid one of Toby's sticks the rest of the way off the porch, she exhaled and reholstered her pistol. "I'm jumpy. Ready to go back inside, Toby?"

Toby barked at the fence before he loped to the door.

CHAPTER NINE

The next morning, Riley hurried to her car in the early light of dawn, but Toby growled as he rushed ahead of her and sniffed the tires.

"I don't usually check the tires before we leave, but I will if you insist." Riley frowned when she reached the driver's side and peered at the front tire. "You're right, Toby, it's a little low. We might have a slow leak. Let's walk."

Toby yipped as he trotted alongside her while she jogged then changed to a fast walk.

"Thanks for the encouragement. Maybe I'll try for two blocks when we go home."

As the sky lightened, the birds chirped and sang as Riley and Toby passed the homes with rose bushes, small, neatly trimmed yards, and old pecan trees. As Toby marked trees along their way and stirred up the neighborhood dogs, Riley said, "We should walk more often. I never smelled wood smoke from the fireplaces when we drove through here and never realized there were so many pecan trees in town."

When they reached the office, Julie Rae's truck was already in the parking lot. "Wonder what time she gets here?"

As Riley stowed her lunch in the refrigerator, Thad strode into the breakroom. "Oh. I didn't see your car out back."

"One of my tires looked low, so Toby and I walked to work."

"Low tire?" Julie Rae stood in the doorway. "I'll ask Charlie and the boys to check it for you. Charlie will enjoy an excuse to get the boys out of the house."

Riley went to the receptionist's desk to list the morning's appointments, and Toby flopped down next to her feet. "Amanda's smart, Toby. She arranged the appointments so the patients can be managed by one vet tech." Riley chuckled. "The patient at eight o'clock is *Walk In*."

Riley set up exam room one for the unknown eight o'clock patient and room two for the eight thirty patient. When Pia rushed in at ten minutes until eight, she hurried to Riley's side at the desk.

"Who's our eight o'clock patient?" Pia asked.

"Amanda took care of us." Riley leaned so Pia could see the screen, and Pia exhaled.

"Thank you. I'll put my lunch away and bring you a cup of coffee. Have you been a martyr sitting here with no caffeine?"

Riley's eyes widened. "I forgot."

"You forgot coffee? Are you sick?" Pia shook her head as she walked to the breakroom.

When Pia returned with two cups, Riley rose to drink her coffee. "If I were the receptionist, I'd want a standing desk. The hardest thing for me about school was sitting still."

Pia nodded. "I agree. The hardest class for me was literature. I want to read a book, not analyze it."

Julie Rae and Thad joined them at the desk.

"I heard back from Zach," Julie Rae said. "He's packed and moving his things to Amanda's house today and could start tomorrow."

"You could tell him we think he's a slacker if he isn't here today by lunchtime," Pia said.

"That young man has a strong competitive streak," Thad said. "He'd be here before our first patient arrived if he heard that."

"If we told him to wait until Monday, I think he'd stalk the office," Riley said.

Julie Rae chuckled. "You three certainly have unique perspectives. I already told him tomorrow was great."

"See? Doc is the nice one," Pia said.

When the eight thirty patient and client arrived, Pia picked up the file folder Riley set out for her then led them to room two.

The next two hours were a steady rhythm of patients for routine examinations and injections. Amanda rushed in from the back at ten thirty. "How did everything go? Are you okay? Are we backed up?"

"Slow down, Amanda. Everything's under control," Riley said. "Pia and Dr. Thad are in room one with a patient. New clients called for appointments, and I scheduled them for Friday and next week, but I made a list for you to check. How was your appointment?"

"All good. Baby's fine, and I have a prescription. I'll put my lunch away. I knew everything would be okay here."

"Of course," Riley said.

After Amanda returned to her desk, she glanced at Riley's list as Dr. Julie Rae joined them. "Doc, our new appointments are all for former patients of Dr. Witmer," Amanda said. "Would it be okay if I called his sister and asked for their records? Do we have her number?"

"Call the clients and ask if they received the records first. If not, I may have his sister's number somewhere. Riley, can we talk a minute?"

Julie Rae and Riley stepped away from the public area to the hallway.

"Charlie called me. He's going to come by and pick up your keys so he can change your tire. Kenny found three screws in it. Charlie said with all the new construction going on around here, it's no surprise. He'll take the tire to the gas station to see if they can repair it."

"I appreciate everything Charlie's doing. That's awesome that Kenny found the screws. Am I taking too much of their time?" Riley asked.

"Charlie takes every opportunity to give the boys a new experience. He said it was a teachable moment, and they'll hang out at the gas station to watch and learn. I'll give you and Toby a ride home at the end of the day." Julie Rae smiled.

"Thank you, but we don't mind the walk. It's not that far."

"We've got a cold front headed our way later today. If you don't have your warm coat, it might be too cold and blowing too hard for a walk when we get ready to leave. You can see what you think," Julie Rae said.

When Pia led the client and patient out of room one to Amanda's desk, she asked, "All good?"

Amanda nodded then turned her attention to the client.

When it was time for Amanda's lunch break, Pia said, "I'll take the desk, Riley."

"Next appointment is running ten or fifteen minutes late," Amanda said. "Here's the file."

Amanda left the desk for the breakroom, and Toby followed her as Jordy took the prime spot under the desk.

Riley picked up the file and frowned as she read. "This is the fifth time the client has brought in our patient for scratching in the past four weeks. I'll show the file to Dr. Julie Rae."

Dr. Julie Rae was on her way to the breakroom when Riley approached her with the file.

"Read this, Doc. Doesn't seem like a simple environmental allergy to me."

After Julie Rae read the file, she asked, "We've changed the antihistamines several times, and it appears not one of them worked. What are you thinking?"

"I'm suspicious of a food allergy."

"Are you okay with asking about daily foods?"

"I'll do that," Riley said.

After she weighed the overweight pug, Riley led the way to room three. "Laverne's weight is down a bit from last year. That's great. Have you made a change in her diet that's helping her?"

"Oh, yes. My friends told me Laverne was too chubby, and I was overfeeding her, so I cut her food in half. She was very hungry after her meals, though. My friends said she needed more protein, so last month I started scrambling an egg for her to eat with her breakfast and dinner every day, and she gobbles them right up."

"I'll bet she does," Riley said. "Do you enjoy your eggs, Laverne?"

Laverne whimpered.

"I'm sorry," Riley said.

The woman's eyes were wide. "What did she say?"

"She loves the eggs, but they hurt her tummy. She might have an allergy to eggs."

"You poor girl." The woman hugged Laverne. "I'm so sorry."

Laverne kissed the woman's face. The woman tittered then asked, "But what do I do about Laverne's weight?"

"Let's ask Doc," Riley said.

The client smiled. "Thank you, Riley. They say you have a way with animals. We appreciate your help, don't we, Laverne?"

Laverne barked, and the woman beamed.

Riley smiled. "You're welcome. I'll get Doc. She'll be right in."

When Riley stepped outside the room, Doc waited for her in the hallway.

"I eavesdropped," Doc said. "You suspected a food allergy, and Laverne confirmed it. The client cut poor Laverne's portions too much. I'll give our client a gradual schedule to decrease Laverne's servings to normal portions for her size and age; she can tell her friends Laverne's doctor recommended a special diet."

As Riley entered the breakroom, Pia unwrapped her sandwich while Doc Thad dropped his crumpled trash into his lunch sack. "One comes in; one goes out," Thad said. "I joined Amanda after Julie Rae went to see your patient then Amanda left, and Pia came in as I finished my lunch."

"Tag team lunch crowd." Pia snickered as Doc Thad left. "Seems strange not to have Agent Reeves pop in. That must mean you didn't get into any trouble since yesterday except I meant to ask you about your car—it wasn't in the parking lot when I came to work. I thought Jordy and I beat you in."

"I had a slight leak in my tire, so Toby and I walked. I jogged part of the way, but it sounds more impressive than it probably looked."

"I'm impressed that you walked. My family wants me to walk with them in the evenings. Maybe I will. If it's not too cold. Or too hot." Pia chuckled. "Who am I kidding? This is Georgia. It's always too hot or too cold."

"Don't forget too windy or too wet." Riley grinned.

"Right. Or too humid. Because, you know, my hair."

As they giggled, Julie Rae came into the breakroom.

"Sounds suspicious. Laughing at work. Is that allowed?" Julie Rae's eyes crinkled.

"Don't say anything to Amanda. She'll create a schedule of fines for laughing."

"Will not," Amanda called from her desk.

"Do you think Amanda has this room bugged?" Pia whispered.

Julie Rae snort-laughed. When Pia and Riley shushed her, she giggled and carried her lunch to the table.

"My turn to leave." Pia tossed her trash and hurried to Amanda's desk to check on the next expected patient. Jordy trotted along behind her.

"Our client is happy," Dr. Julie Rae said. "I gave her our sheet of the suggested ingredients in dog food and the recommended serving size for senior dogs that are in Laverne's weight range and age, and we talked about decreasing the old portion size each week until she reaches the recommended serving. She's going to check the ingredients of their current dog food. Amanda made her an appointment for next month for us to check Laverne's progress. Good call."

Julie Rae joined Riley at the table. "I heard back from Charlie. He put your spare tire on your SUV, but the gas station said your tire was not repairable. They've ordered a new tire for you. Charlie said they'll probably have it by Friday."

"Thanks, Doc. It's really strange that I picked up three screws together in one tire." Riley furrowed her brow. "I drove past the new building, but I didn't pull onto the property."

"Yes, strange. Why don't I give you a ride home, and you can take your car over to the gas station to make sure none of your other tires have screws in them."

While Riley ate, she received a text. *Marcy.*

"Saturday afternoon? Sunday doesn't work."

Riley frowned as she replied. "Saturday conflict. Only Sunday works for me. Sorry."

"Problem?" Julie Rae asked.

"Just a weekend scheduling conflict. My friend Marcy from my old job and I had planned to get together, but it didn't work out."

Julie Rae furrowed her brow. "Is there something we can do to make it work for you?"

Riley smiled. "The conflict isn't mine. Only Saturday works for Marcy, and only Sunday works for Ben."

"I vote Sunday," Julie Rae said. "Best part of working in a nosy office is you have no private life."

"I vote Sunday too," Amanda called from the front, and Pia and Doc Thad laughed.

At the end of the day, after the front door was locked, everyone gathered at the receptionist's desk to review files and return file folders.

Amanda said, "I called all the Dr. Witmer clients who scheduled appointments, and they all had records. We had four more Witmer clients call for appointments, and I verified they had records too."

"That's unexpected, but a real relief," Doc said.

"We'll be sure to ask any new clients about records when we schedule appointments," Pia said.

"I added it to our guide on how to schedule new patients," Amanda said. "It will be useful to have all our documentation updated when Zach starts, but just having him here will help us to find any holes, won't it?"

"We have documentation?" Riley asked.

"Not quite. Almost." Amanda growled. "Fine—it's in my head. I haven't written it down yet."

Pia opened her mouth to speak, and Riley grabbed her hand to pull her toward the exam rooms. "Let's make sure the rooms are ready for tomorrow."

"Do we have a guide for that?" Pia asked.

After the rooms were cleaned, and everyone else had left, Riley and Toby followed Julie Rae to her truck.

"I'll follow you to the gas station in case you run into any problems," Julie Rae said when she stopped at Riley's house.

After they arrived at the gas station, Riley and Toby waited in the service office and watched while the mechanic raised the SUV on the lift to check all the tires.

"Ms. Riley, you've got three tires with nails. Your spare was fine. We'd like to take them off and check them, but we won't be able to get to it until tomorrow. It would be safer if you leave your car with us."

She frowned. "Is it normal for all the tires to have nails in them?"

"No, ma'am. Did you visit the new construction site?"

She shook her head.

"Only other thing I can suggest is to check the parking lot at Doc Julie Rae's place in case a construction truck took a shortcut or something and lost a box of nails. We'll give you a call tomorrow after we check your tires."

Riley and Toby returned to Julie Rae's truck, and Riley shivered and zipped up her thin sweatshirt as she stood next to Julie Rae's lowered window. "That wind just cuts right through you, doesn't it? We're leaving the SUV here. The other three tires have nails. The mechanic will check them tomorrow to see what needs to be done."

"Annoying," Julie Rae said. "Hop in. I'll pick you up in the morning. Six thirty okay with you? I can go in later if you like."

"Six thirty is fine with me. I wouldn't mind taking a quick inventory of our supplies. Pia and I don't seem to be able to get to it during business hours."

"That's a really good idea," Doc said. "Do you need anything at the grocery store? Drug store?"

"Can't think of anything. Thank you."

When Julie Rae dropped them off, Toby trotted to a small, empty box in the road between their house and the neighbor's. Riley frowned as she picked up the box and read the label, *3" screws*. When they went in the house, she set the torn box on the counter then texted the sheriff before she fed Toby.

After he ate, she scrubbed a potato then covered it with foil to bake in the oven before she brewed a cup of tea while Toby wandered in the back yard. Before her tea was ready, the sheriff pulled into her driveway.

"I'm here for the empty box. You didn't see anything else?" he asked.

"No. I wouldn't have noticed it, but Toby pointed it out."

Sheriff held out a plastic bag, and Riley dropped in the box.

"Thanks for calling." Sheriff sighed before he filled out the evidence tag and left.

She sipped her tea and read Grandma's cookbook more closely. *Tamale casserole. I can make this.* She listed the ingredients then rose to check the cupboard to see what she would need to pick up at the grocery store when her phone rang. *Ben.*

When she answered he said, "Are you okay?"

"I'm fine. My car's at the gas station though. I found a slow leak this morning in one of my tires. Charlie changed it for me while I was at work. He took the tire to the gas station, and it couldn't be repaired. They ordered a new tire for me."

"How did you get to work? Did Doc pick you up?"

"Toby and I walked. It was actually very pleasant. I saw my neighborhood with new eyes. The cold front blew in later this afternoon—not so pleasant."

"I know what you're talking about. I was on a traffic stop and thought I was going to freeze. What was wrong with your tire?"

Riley swallowed. *Kind of hoped to avoid that subject for a while.* "There were three construction screws in the tire. I took my car to the gas station for them to check the rest of the tires, and the other three had screws in them too. They'll check them more closely tomorrow. Doc gave us a ride home and will pick us up in the morning."

"That doesn't sound right." Riley heard the concern in Ben's voice.

"We'll know more tomorrow, but I agree with you; I found an empty screw box at the curb after Doc dropped us off."

"Does the sheriff know? What does he think?"

"I thought I'd wait to hear what the gas station says." Riley sighed. "I wasn't too worried about one tire, but now I wonder if it's time to panic. At least I didn't find another note, right?"

"Small consolation, I suppose. How about work? How was your day?"

Riley told Ben about Laverne, and he chuckled. "Ole Laverne was trying to keep it to herself because she was eating two eggs a day, even if they did hurt her stomach."

Riley giggled. "I think you're right. She was a hungry girl."

"I'm having second thoughts about my job. I talked to my trainer today, and he understood because he had the same problem."

"What's that?" Riley finished her tea.

Ben sighed. "My first speeder of the day was my eighth-grade teacher. He hinted that I should give him a break, but I wrote the ticket and told him to be safe. I know just about everyone in town, but for some reason, I'd never thought through what it would be like to ticket or arrest people I've known my entire life."

"What did your trainer do?"

"After a week on the job, he moved to a different county. He set me up with a meeting tomorrow to talk to the sergeant—he's lived in Carson his entire life."

"But you've worked in Carson for a while. Didn't you know the people you saw when you worked nights?"

"Most of them, but the circumstances were different. The ones who were my friends or people I admired called for help, and the people who abused alcohol and drugs were the same people they were in high school and not anyone I considered a friend. It's a generalization and not a hundred percent true, but does that make sense?"

"It does. I'll be interested in hearing what your sergeant has to say. Do you think you will be going to nights?"

"No, that isn't an option as far as I'm concerned. I was always an early riser, even as a kid. I didn't realize how hard it was on me to work nights until I shifted to days. I couldn't go back."

"I have more news—I heard back from Marcy. Saturday is the only day that works for her. I told her Sunday is the only day that works for me, and don't argue with me," Riley said.

"Not even to say something polite, like I don't want to keep you from seeing your friend?" Ben chuckled.

Toby scratched on the back door, and Riley rose to let him in. "Politeness duly noted, and no."

"Anything more about Amanda's cousin?"

"He told Doc he could start tomorrow, and she took him up on it. He's going to stay with Amanda for a while."

"What will your lunchtime schedule look like? Can you tell I don't have anything to think about while I'm on a traffic stop except your veterinary hospital?"

"It was pretty fluid today. Pia said we were the tag team lunch crowd. There weren't more than two of us in the breakroom at any one time, and I think all of us ate lunch with two different people. So, I guess I have no idea. That will drive Amanda crazy. She loves a schedule."

"I'm with Amanda. I don't mind a little flexibility, but it's nice to have a plan to fall back on."

The wind picked up outside, and Riley shivered. She hurried to the fireplace and flipped on the switch then watched as it flamed up. "I suspect the docs won't be having lunch together, and Pia and I probably won't either. I'm sad about that because I enjoy her company."

"I'll bet you haven't eaten yet. I was so anxious to talk to you that I called the second I got home. Speaking of nothing to think about except your veterinary hospital—I did some snooping and couldn't find an obituary for Allen Truman, Junior, and nothing about a murder. Dr. Truman, Senior, didn't give any details, did he?"

Riley frowned. "No, nothing. He said he didn't want to talk about it. If Dr. Truman, Junior, was murdered in another state or something would that explain why you couldn't find any record of his death?"

"Maybe. I'll have to ask my trainer." Ben chuckled. "He'll accuse me of studying for the detective exam."

After they hung up, Riley heated the water for another cup of tea then checked her potato. *Ten more minutes.* She opened the refrigerator. After she scanned the shelves, she removed the butter and grated cheese. She found a can of pinto beans and a jar of salsa in the cupboard. She chopped her onion and heated the beans while her tea steeped.

Riley piled her baked potato with beans, onions, cheese, and salsa. *Loaded baked potato.* Toby fell asleep under the table while she ate and read her grandma's cookbook. She turned the page, and a three by five-inch card was stuck between the pages. She read the card and smiled. *Grandma's secret spaghetti recipe. She used jarred spaghetti sauce.*

She rose to clear her dishes and put away her condiments and leftovers then made cinnamon rolls and placed them in the refrigerator before she moved to the sofa with grandma's cookbook.

At bedtime, she turned off the fireplace, and opened the back door for Toby while he went outside. When he returned to the porch, she opened the door. "Sorry I sent you out by yourself, but it's too cold for me."

She jumped when her phone rang. *Marcy.*

"I'm sorry to call you so late, but this is important. Were you in bed? I just got a call from one of the girls we worked with. Doc Senior is missing, and his lawyer is dead. She didn't have any details, but it really shook me up. It's like people associated with the clinic are dropping like flies. All the girls are nervous. One of them mentioned the accountant, but we laughed at her and told her to take off her aluminum foil woo-woo hat. Isn't that funny?" Marcy snickered. "My mom's going to want me to move home if she hears about this. I have to calm down before I can go to sleep, but I knew you'd want to know. Sorry we can't get together this weekend. Talk to you later."

Marcy hung up. Riley stared at the phone then ambled to the fireplace and turned it back on. "I'll go to bed soon, Toby. I'm a little wired by Marcy's news; I'm glad you're here."

After ten minutes, Riley turned off the fireplace. "I'm too tired to stress over Senior and the lawyer. I'll put them on my stress list first thing tomorrow."

* * *

Riley woke up before her alarm went off, and she padded to the kitchen to start her coffee and pop the cinnamon rolls into the oven. When she returned to her bedroom to dress, Toby raised his head. "Doc's picking us up this morning." After she was dressed in her gray scrub top, jeans, and green sweater, Toby followed her to the kitchen, and she opened the back door for him. When he was ready to come inside, she fed him and finished her grocery list.

A little before six thirty, Doc pulled into the driveway. Riley grabbed her foil-wrapped cinnamon rolls and warm coat, and Toby followed her to Doc's truck.

"Your famous cinnamon rolls?" Doc asked.

"For Zach's first day." Riley smiled as Toby hopped into the truck.

After they arrived at the veterinary hospital, Riley dropped off the cinnamon rolls and her lunch in the breakroom on her way to the supply closet; Doc brought a cup of coffee to Riley.

"How's it going?" Doc asked as she blew on her hot liquid.

"We're getting low, especially on gauze squares, bandaging, and medium-sized gloves." Riley set down her clipboard and held her hot cup with two hands to warm them before she sipped her coffee.

"I'm not surprised. The number of patients we're seeing each day is growing. After you give your list to Amanda, I'm sure she'll adjust the regular supply order. I don't know what I'd do without her and Charlie—they're geniuses at keeping track of the business side of the practice. After Pia arrives, would you two inventory our drugs? Charlie tracks our orders and asked if we'd done our physical inventory this month. He knows I don't think about it. That was his subtle reminder that he wants it by tomorrow," Doc said.

"We can do that. It won't take us more than ten minutes if I have everything ready when Pia comes in," Riley said.

Riley drained her cup then finished her inventory list. After she dropped off her list at Amanda's desk, she prepared the medication inventory sheet then hurried to the breakroom for a coffee refill.

When Pia and Jordy rushed in the back door, the cold wind blew in behind them. "It's cold," Pia said as she put her lunch in the refrigerator.

"Grab a cup of hot coffee. Doc wants us to do the medication inventory first thing. I set out the inventory sheet and the key for the controlled drug cabinet. You want to count or record?"

"You count. My coffee and I will record," Pia said.

After they finished with the inventory and initialed the sheet, Pia said, "I'll put it on Amanda's desk. After she scans the sheet, she'll email the scan to Charlie and file the paper copy here."

As they walked to Amanda's desk, Dr. Thad carried a plate of maple frosted donuts on his way to the breakroom.

"Those look delicious, Doc," Pia said.

Dr. Thad smiled. "My contribution to celebrate Zach's first day. I learned to make donuts in college. Maple frosted are my specialty."

"You must have been really popular," Riley said.

His smile widened. "It's how I got my wife."

"Smart man." Pia followed him to the breakroom.

"Bring one for me," Riley said as she hurried to the receptionist's desk to listen to the messages.

Pia brought three donuts and two napkins to the desk. "I'm going to want more than one, so you're going to save me from eating two."

Riley snorted as she noted the next patient's name, the client's name, and the phone number. When she finished, she picked up her donut and bit into it. "Mmm. This is really good, and it's still warm. I'm officially ruined from ever eating a room-temperature donut again."

Pia took a big bite and chewed her donut slowly with her eyes closed. "Wonder if we can convince Doc to hire somebody every week?"

"We'd have to buy all new clothes," Riley said, "but wouldn't it be worth it?"

Amanda and Zach came in the back door. "I'm frozen." Amanda kept her coat on as she sat at her desk. Toby flopped down on her feet, and Amanda smiled as she rubbed his ear. "I love you, Toby."

Toby nudged her other hand, and she rubbed both ears while he gazed at her.

"I'll make you a cup of hot tea, and we have sweet treats to celebrate Zach's first day. I'll bring you a plate while you look over the list and make your calls," Pia said.

"You're with me today, Zach, then starting next Thursday, you'll work with Pia, unless of course, plans change. Let's begin with coffee and pastries to get you started right before we check the first examination room and the trauma room, if we have time. Do you drink coffee?"

"I sure do," Zach said.

"You'll learn all their bad habits," Amanda said as they headed to the breakroom. "After that, you can develop your own."

Riley refilled her cup and poured a cup for Zach. While Zach ate a donut, she started another pot of coffee, and Julie Rae carried her empty cup into the breakroom. "Welcome, Zach. I see Riley has started your training off right."

Thad joined Julie Rae with his empty cup as she peered at the gurgling coffee maker. "We might need another coffee machine."

"Welcome, Zach. We're all glad you're here," Thad said.

Zach finished his donut and reached for a cinnamon roll. "Thank you. Amanda told me this is a sweet place to work. I didn't realize she meant literally."

Thad smiled. "Didn't think about that, but it's true."

After Riley and Zach finished their coffee, Riley led the way to exam room one. "I could tell you where everything is, but why don't you open drawers to see if they have what you expected in them. We can go from there."

Zach beamed. "Thanks."

After he examined each drawer and cabinet, Amanda called out, "Patient on the way in."

Zach followed Riley to the counter. Riley quickly reviewed the file before she handed it to Zach. "This will give you an idea of the patient's history. We'll go over it together after Doc examines her."

Riley smiled when the client came inside with a three-month-old German shepherd puppy on a leash. When the puppy raced around her person's legs, the client chuckled as she unsnapped the leash from the puppy's collar and disentangled herself. "We're working on the leash."

The puppy made a dash for the hallway, but Zach blocked her path, and she flopped onto the floor for a belly rub.

Riley smiled. "Good maneuver, girl."

The puppy yipped her thanks as the client clipped the leash onto her collar.

As Riley led the way to room one, she said, "I'm Riley, and this is Zach. He's a vet tech and started today."

When they reached the room, Riley added, "We also have a new veterinarian, Dr. Thad, who started on Monday. She's here for her boosters; any concerns?"

"No. She's doing fine; although, we've been doing puppy training, and I could use something for my nerves," the client said, and Riley chuckled.

"Does she relax in the evening? How is she sleeping?" Riley asked.

"She's restless in the evening and not sleeping through the night anymore." The woman frowned. "My friends said that's normal."

"You might want to take her for a long walk in the evening or throw a ball for her. It will be interesting to see if she returns the ball for you to throw again or if you two develop a different game. She might have some excess energy she needs to run off."

The client nodded while Zach weighed the puppy. "Hadn't thought about that," she said. "It wouldn't hurt either one of us."

After Riley administered the booster shots, she stroked the puppy's ears and neck, "Thank you. You did great."

After Doc Thad examined the puppy, Riley led the client to Amanda's desk then she and Zach went into the breakroom and sat at the table.

"Everything was routine," Zach said. "I was glad that we'd gone through the drawers. Why didn't you give the puppy a treat after the shots?"

Riley raised her eyebrows. "Good catch. Many vet techs do, I think. I prefer to reward with some attention."

"Is that why you thanked her?" he asked.

"I guess, and to be polite."

Zach nodded. "This is a good way for me to learn because I'm seeing things the books and instructors don't mention. My grandfather told me that classroom training keeps me from sounding like an idiot when I speak, but experience teaches me my skills. So, Pia took the next patient, right? What if an emergency patient came in while you and Pia are busy?"

"Glad you mentioned that. Amanda has a buzzer she uses if we have an emergency come in. We all drop whatever we're doing, assuming it's safe for our patient, and go to the reception area. From there, it depends on the situation."

When they returned the file folder to the receptionist's desk, Amanda said, "A package arrived for you, Riley." She pointed to the top of the file cabinet before she answered the phone.

"My tops I ordered. I was prepared to do laundry tonight if they didn't arrive today. I'll put them in the breakroom for now."

As Riley reached for the package, the sheriff came in the front door. "Can we talk a minute, Riley? Out in my car?"

"Sure. I'll grab my jacket first."

Riley left the package in the breakroom and threw on her jacket before she and the sheriff strolled outside.

"I know about Amanda's hearing," the sheriff said on the way to his cruiser. "It's phenomenal."

He opened the passenger door. "The wind's too bitter to stand outside."

After they were inside the cruiser, Sheriff turned on the engine. "Do you know of any connection between the Trumans and Dr. Witmer?"

Riley frowned. "I hadn't thought about it before, but when I interviewed the first time for the vet tech position at the Truman

Clinic, Doc Junior seemed really interested in who I knew in Barton when he asked where my family was from. He named four people he said he knew and asked if I knew them, but I didn't. I thought he was trying to find a common ground for a casual conversation to put me at ease."

Riley shifted in the passenger's seat to face the sheriff. "When I came to town, I passed Dr. Witmer's clinic and thought his name sounded familiar. At first, I thought he might be the vet that Aunt Millie said needed help, except she said the new vet, and Dr. Witmer's clinic didn't look like a new vet's. I realize now that he was one of the people Doc Junior mentioned, but I don't know how he knew Dr. Witmer."

"Was there any office gossip about either one of the Trumans?"

"Not that I know of except—I told Agent Reeves this—Marcy told me our last day at the clinic there was gossip that Truman Junior said I was his favorite, and he had a crush on me." Her eyes flashed. "Which was not true. I never received any favoritism treatment of any kind."

"What do you know about addict behavior? Did either of the doctors exhibit drug use?"

"We were taught that ketamine was highly addictive, and it was critical to maintain appropriate records and security for it as a controlled substances. I told Agent Reeves about the discrepancy between a large ketamine order and what we had on hand that Marcy and I found."

Sheriff nodded. "He told me about that."

"I thought there was potentially a drug dealer in the office, but since it never came up again, I decided it was a bookkeeping error."

The sheriff pulled a file folder off his dash and thumbed through it. "What about the ammonia smell and the rotten egg smell you told Agent Reeves about?"

"I don't see how that could have anything to do with ketamine, but I'm not an illicit drug expert."

Sheriff smiled. "You'll be okay with that one shortcoming." He closed the folder and frowned. "I got a call from the gas station about your tires. How are you doing?"

CHAPTER TEN

"I don't know whether to be angry or scared." She shuddered. "Correction. I'm scared."

"I understand."

"Would it make sense for me to leave? Return to Pomeroy?" Riley asked.

"That's a decision you'll have to make. I recommend you consider where you have the best support system—family or friends. How does Pomeroy compare to Barton?"

Riley furrowed her brow. "I've lived in Pomeroy my whole life, so it's familiar to me, and I've been here less than two weeks."

Sheriff nodded. "Would you feel safer in Pomeroy?"

"I was never afraid in Pomeroy, but I took my safety for granted." Riley gazed at the sheriff. "Marcy wants me to move back and work with her, so finding a job wouldn't be hard. I'd need an apartment that allows dogs, which is my number one requirement. I'll have two weeks to find one, not just three days, and a little more flexibility in price with a job under my belt."

"So, what are you thinking?" Sheriff asked.

"It seems logical for me to return to Pomeroy."

As the sheriff walked her to the door, he said, "I do appreciate that you feel comfortable enough to text me when you need me."

When Riley walked inside, Amanda was showing Zach their scheduling system.

"More later, but you have the general idea," Amanda said.

"It's straight forward," he said. "Here comes our next patient. I've already looked at the chart and room one is set up."

"You want to take the lead?" Riley glanced through the patient's file.

Zach swallowed. "Yeah, I'd like that. You'll be with me, right?"

"Sure will. I'll be your invisible sidekick," Riley said.

"Your conscience on your shoulder," Amanda said.

When the golden retriever and her person came inside, Zach said, "Hi, I'm Zach. Riley and I will be working together because I'm new. Is that okay with you, Gracie?"

The dog yipped, and the client smiled. "Gracie likes you."

"We have room one." Zach ushered the client and Gracie to the exam room, and Riley followed them.

When they were in the room, the client said, "Gracie's been scratching a lot lately, and she's been restless at night. We never skip a flea treatment, so I'm not sure why she's itchy."

Zach led Gracie to the scale. "I'll weigh you then take your temperature."

Gracie moaned after she stepped off the scale.

"I understand. Nobody really likes getting their temperature taken, but I'll be quick."

"And we'll check your ears too," Riley added.

Zach nodded while he took Gracie's temperature. "Done."

Riley removed the otoscope from a drawer and handed it to Zach. Zach peered into Gracie's ears. "Ears are red, and there might be some infection."

"We'll let the doc know," Riley said as Zach checked Gracie's legs and back.

"No other signs of scratching," Zach said.

When they stepped out of the exam room, Zach said, "We were taught to check the ears when the client complained about scratching, but Gracie told you about her ears, didn't she?"

"Yes, but you're right about always checking the ears."

"Ear infections would make it hard for anyone to sleep," Zach said.

Riley nodded toward Doc Thad who came out of his office. "Tell Doc."

When Doc checked Gracie's ears, he took a sample from each ear. Riley and Zach followed Doc to the treatment room to listen to his assessment as Doc peered through the microscope at the samples on the slides. "Interesting," he said as he stood to the side of the table. "Tell me what you see, Zach."

Zach inspected the samples. "Infection in one sample. The other sample looks normal, but Gracie was scratching both ears."

"The infection may not be enough to show up yet, or I may not have collected a good sample. The good news is that the antibiotic isn't location-specific." Thad entered the prescription into their system.

After Riley and Zach were in the medication room, she asked, "Did Amanda give you a logon?"

"Yes."

"Log onto the system, and we'll go from there."

Riley coached Zach through the process then they returned to the examination room.

"We have the antibiotic that Doc Thad prescribed. Let's go see Amanda," Zach said.

The client and Gracie followed Zach while Riley waited in the exam room. When Zach returned, she asked, "How was it?"

"Scary and easy. Thank you."

"Good. I was afraid I'd thrown you into the river to sink or swim, but you're a good swimmer. Let's clean the room for our next patient."

After they cleaned the room, they went to the receptionist's desk. Toby sat on Amanda's feet, and Jordy lay across the entrance to her desk from the reception area.

"You may have to go through the rooms to greet your patients," Amanda said. "The boys decided I needed bodyguards."

"Do we have a little bit of time? I'd like to call the gas station about my car," Riley said.

"Twenty minutes," she said.

"If they show up early, do you feel comfortable with starting without me, Zach?"

"No, but I can swim through it." Zach grinned.

As Riley walked to the breakroom, Amanda said, "Okay, Zach, explain."

Riley called the gas station.

After being on hold for five minutes, the mechanic picked up. "Hey, Riley. We just checked all the tires. We might be able to repair one. We'll work on it today, but we went ahead and ordered three more tires. I don't know when we can get them though. Want me to find you a car for the weekend?"

"No, I can catch a ride to work when it's too cold to walk."

"None of my business, but you shouldn't be out walking alone until the sheriff finds the vandal who put the screws in your tires."

"Thanks. I appreciate everything you've done."

After she hung up, Riley hurried to Amanda's desk. "Zach and the patient and client went into room one," Amanda said.

Riley sauntered to room one and slipped inside while Zach weighed the ten-year-old, black, tan, and white Pomeranian-Pekingese mix.

"Victoria has always been very active," the client said as Zach placed Victoria on the examination table to take her temperature. "Lately, though, she runs out of breath if she runs across the yard to chase a ball, and she wheezes sometimes. She used to be a real chow hound, but she only nibbles at her food. I've tried cooked chicken and scrambled eggs to get her to eat, but she just doesn't have any appetite."

"You don't feel like eating?" Zach asked, and Victoria whined.

Zach glanced at Riley who nodded.

"Sorry you don't feel well." Zach stroked Victoria. "I'm going to listen to your heart and lungs."

Zach listened then glanced at Riley.

"Okay if I listen too?" Riley asked, and Victoria whimpered.

"Thank you." Riley listened. "I hear those wheezes. Anything else?"

"She's having trouble sleeping. It's like she can't get comfortable," the client said.

"Doc will check her in a few minutes," Zach said.

After they left the exam room, Zach asked, "What did Victoria say?"

"She said the food doesn't taste good. So, what do you think?"

"Her feet were a little puffy, and her mouth was pale. I'm guessing maybe congestive heart failure?"

"I was thinking along the same lines. I lost track of docs. Which one's available?"

"Doc Julie Rae. I'll get her."

Doc Julie Rae examined Victoria. "This old girl has congestive heart failure, but we have medicine that can get her back to par."

She rubbed Victoria's ears, and Victoria relaxed. "For a week or so, offer her food she likes then return to her normal diet. She's not overweight and not diabetic. Big pluses in her favor."

Doc wrote the prescription, and Zach and Riley went to the medication room. Zach pulled up the prescription then filled it and completed the patient's record. They returned to Victoria's room, and Zach explained the prescription to their client while Riley cooed and stroked Victoria.

When the client and Zach were ready to go to Amanda's desk, the client whispered, "You've put her to sleep."

She carefully reached under Victoria to carry her, and Victoria raised her head and smiled then snuggled against her person's chest.

After Victoria and the client left, Zach asked, "How did you put her to sleep so quickly?"

"She was exhausted and relieved to get some medicine to help her feel better; she relaxed."

When it was time for lunch, Doc Julie Rae said, "I'll take over your desk, Amanda, but if I do something wrong, you are not allowed to fire me."

Amanda rose to go to the breakroom. "You just took all the fun out of today for me."

"Take Pia and Doc Thad with you; Riley, Zach, and I will take our lunchbreak when you return."

"Good scheduling, Doc." Amanda disengaged her feet from Toby and strolled to the breakroom. Toby followed her, and when Jordy saw Pia go to the breakroom, he ambled along behind her.

After Amanda left, Doc Julie Rae said, "Anybody want a sneak peek at our afternoon?"

As Doc pulled up the schedule, a woman who carried a black cat strolled inside and smiled as she approached the desk.

"Hi, Doc. Were you promoted?" The woman tittered.

"Good morning, or is it good noon, Mrs. Hartway?" Doc smiled, and Riley opened the A through H file drawer and quickly found Hartway. *Good thing I started at the beginning. I would have started with H-E-A.*

Riley handed the file folder to Zach and nodded. He glanced at the file. "I'm Zach. I'm the new vet tech. Would you follow me, please? What are we covering today?"

"It's time for Archie's annual. Time goes so fast that sometimes I lose track, but this time I wrote a note about his appointment and stuck it on my refrigerator. Last year I forgot it, and Amanda had to reschedule us," Mrs. Hartway said.

After they went into exam room one, Doc said, "Thanks for pulling the file. Amanda always calls Mrs. Hartway before her appointment. You can check, but I could have sworn it hasn't been that long ago since Archie had his annual. Shall I go in and work with Zach?"

"That's a great idea, and thanks for the hint for her name. I'm glad we didn't embarrass her."

After Doc joined Zach in the exam room, Riley checked the previous month's appointments but couldn't find anything.

Doc Julie Rae strolled alongside Mrs. Hartway, and Zach whispered as he handed Riley the folder, "Wait."

"You be good, Archie," Doc said as Mrs. Hartway and Archie left.

"You two are amazing," Doc said. "Mrs. Hartway is in early dementia. We'll bill her daughter for Archie's visit. I'll call the daughter to let her know the bill will be on it way. I want to talk to her about her mother anyway."

Amanda returned to her desk. "Mrs. Hartway was here? Archie had his annual appointment three months ago. Is she getting worse?"

"Might be. I'll call her daughter after lunch," Doc said. "Okay, team, let's chase Pia and Thad out of the breakroom and have lunch."

When Riley pulled her lunch out of the refrigerator, she said, "Doc, I heard from the gas station, and they think they can get replacement tires by Monday. Can I catch a ride with you tomorrow and Saturday?"

"Of course, you can. Won't you need to do some grocery shopping too? We can throw that in any time."

"I'm pretty set on food. Aunt Millie and Ms. Helen filled my refrigerator and cabinets. Thanks, I appreciate it. I could walk to work then home, but it seems like we have two kinds of weather lately: cold and rainy and cold and windy."

As they ate lunch, Riley said, "On my first day here, Daphne asked if Alyse had said anything about her. Did Alyse say anything to you?"

"Not at all. I overheard Daphne when she was here and thought she was unhinged. I can't imagine Daphne's thought process to come into my business and spew racial slurs."

"I was shocked too. I thought Amanda did a wonderful job of staying calm. Have you ever talked to Alyse or met her?"

Doc furrowed her brow. "Never thought about it before, but I haven't. That's curious. You know who would have though?"

Riley's eyes widened. "If Alyse ever went into the grocery store—"

"I was going to say Mrs. Smythe ten minutes ago," Amanda called out.

"Nope," Doc said. "You can't call hindsight dibs."

"Hindsight dibs?" Zach whispered.

"We'll observe and learn while the masters duel," Riley whispered.

"You can't make up rules after the fact, Doc," Amanda said.

Doc Julie Rae smiled.

Pia stood in the doorway with her hands on her hips. "Are you two going to do this all day? Take it outside. The rest of us have work to do." She tossed her hair, and she and Jordy went out the back door.

"Awesome dramatic exit," Doc Thad said.

"You're smart, Doc." Riley dropped her crumpled trash into the garbage can. "You waited until she was outside."

Riley threw on her coat and strolled to Amanda's desk. "Come on, Toby. It wouldn't hurt for you and me to go outside too."

Toby lumbered to his feet then followed her outside. Riley and Toby jogged to catch up with Pia and Jordy who were a half-block away.

"Daphne made a crack about Alyse getting to Doc before she did, but I didn't know what she meant. Do you?" Riley asked as they power walked.

"Daphne had a knack for alienating people. There could have been any number of people who would have been willing to speak their minds about the performance of Ms. Daphne, but to answer your question, I don't think Alyse would bother."

"Have you ever met Alyse?"

"No, and I don't think many other people in town have either. She must be a little odd because she didn't attend the open house

Dr. Witmer held to celebrate their new partnership. I didn't go because I have this entire second job called home and family, and Doc and Amanda didn't go either for the same reason. Doc said we get our socializing done during the day with our patients."

"I love it here because we socialize with our patients." Riley quickened her pace to keep up with Pia's longer stride.

"It was a really fancy affair with food and champagne, and almost everyone else in town went. I heard that Dr. Witmer presented an eloquent speech about the colleague he trusted who was willing to manage the financial side of the business, so Dr. Witmer could concentrate on his wonderful clients and patients. Dr Witmer said he loved animals, not numbers."

"I can't imagine having to focus on the business side instead of on the patients either."

"You're really smart. I've been wondering why you never went to veterinary school."

"Too expensive, even with scholarships."

"That's too bad—you're a natural. We should turn around before we walk all the way to the state line," Pia said, and they headed back to the office.

"We've got another patient in ten minutes. How's Zach doing?" Doc asked after they'd hung up their coats.

"Great. He's smart and eager to learn," Riley said. "Good with the patients and good with the clients."

"That's too bad," Doc said. "I was looking forward to Amanda whipping him into shape."

At the end of the day, Julie Rae locked the building then Riley and Toby hopped into her truck.

"Are you sure you don't need to stop at the grocery store?" Doc asked. "Toby and I can wait for you if you want to pick something up."

Mrs. Smythe.

"Actually, I could run in and pick up a bag of romaine for a salad and maybe some ice cream. Grandma always said the best time to eat ice cream is when the weather's cold because ice cream jumpstarts your body into warm up mode."

"Your grandma was brilliant."

After Julie Rae and Toby dropped her off at the entrance, Riley hurried inside and headed for the floral section. As she examined the fresh flowers, a shelf of small potted plants caught her eye. *Fresh herbs—what a good idea.* As Riley considered her options, Mrs. Smythe appeared next to her.

"Hello, Riley Malloy. You're very smart to have fresh herbs in your kitchen. Start with the sweet basil. Chop up a few leaves, then drop them into any soup or tomato sauce for that subtle peppery flavor with a hint of mint. The aromatic herb adds a little pizzaz to your kitchen too. You'll impress your young man."

"Thank you, Mrs. Smythe." Riley placed the sweet basil plant inside her basket. "I was wondering, have you met Alyse? She was Dr. Witmer's business partner." Mrs. Smythe bowed her head when Riley said Dr. Witmer's name, and Riley automatically copied her. *Grandma used to bow her head too when she or a friend mentioned someone who died. I'd forgotten that.*

"I didn't really meet her," Mrs. Smythe said, "because she didn't introduce herself. She was in the fancy, expensive wine section, and I asked her if she was having a party. She jumped like I'd thrown a spider on her."

Mrs. Smythe tittered. "Maybe I'll buy some plastic spiders to shake up some of these uppity folks. She's a tall woman and large boned. She must be in the middle of her menopause because she had a bit of a moustache that she had tried to shave. I would have told her plucking worked better, but she was too standoffish. Her hair's probably thinning too because her brown wig was good quality. I have an eye for wigs because I might need one someday. I believe in planning ahead, don't you?"

"Yes, ma'am. I love a good plan."

"I knew you would." Mrs. Smythe smiled.

Riley beelined to the salad section and picked up a bag of mixed salad greens before she strode to the frozen food section and selected a box of chocolate covered ice cream bars. When she stepped outside with her purchases, Julie Rae rolled to the entrance, and Riley climbed into the truck.

"How'd you do?" Julie Rae asked.

"Alyse is tall, large boned, uppity, and in menopause." Riley chuckled, and Julie Rae joined her.

"You smell good," Julie Rae said.

"I bought a sweet basil plant. Mrs. Smythe said it would impress my young man. She knows everything that happens in town, doesn't she?"

After Doc dropped off Riley and Toby, Riley rushed into the house to get her ice cream bars into the freezer. She placed the greens in the refrigerator then checked the soil with her basil. *Needs a drink.* Riley watered her potted plant before she placed it on the dining room windowsill.

She sent a text to Marcy: "I may return to Pomeroy."

After Riley grabbed her coat, she dropped her phone into her pocket in case Marcy replied. When she strolled to the back door, Toby waited for her to open it before he ambled outside.

"That was very polite of you, or did you have a long day?"

When her phone rang, she smiled as she answered. "Hi, Ben. I'm outside on the porch, and I'm freezing. What are you doing?"

Ben chuckled. "Please tell me that's the most excitement you've had all day."

Riley rolled her eyes. "Okay. It's the most excitement I've had all day, and I just told you a lie."

"Oh, man." Ben moaned. "I started this conversation off wrong."

"Sorry. I shouldn't have teased you. I think I've reached either the pinnacle or the pits of stress. I hate that I'm always boring you with my problems."

"Excuse me? Last I heard, that's what friends are for. To share problems and be boring. That didn't come out right. Do you want me to call back when I'm not so awkward?"

Riley smirked. "I don't think I could wait that long to talk to you."

"You're right. Me neither. So, tell me about your day."

Riley told him about Doc Truman, Senior, the lawyer, the accountant, tires, the sheriff, Mrs. Smythe, and Pomeroy.

"Tell me more about the tires," Ben growled.

"Now that I think about it, Toby and I heard a sound Tuesday night, and when I cracked open the back door to see if—"

"You did what?"

Riley sighed. "I was trying to slip that past you. I need to find another way to check the backyard without opening the door. Anyway, Toby ran past me and growled and barked at the fence along the driveway side of the house. When the wind slid one of Toby's branches off the porch, the scratching sound was very similar to what I'd heard. I've been very jumpy and easily spooked the past couple of days. After I called him, he barked a few more times before we went inside."

Riley paused. *Wonder if Toby was telling me there was an intruder, but I wasn't paying attention?*

"And?" Ben asked.

"Sorry, I got lost in thought. When we were leaving for work yesterday morning, he sniffed the tires and told me to check them. The driver's side front tire was low, so we walked to work. There were screws in all the tires. If the gas station can repair any of the three tires they will; otherwise, my replacement tires should be here on Monday."

"What did the sheriff say about you moving back to Pomeroy?"

Riley frowned. "I'm not sure because I asked him if he thought I should, and he asked me what I thought. You people are sneaky."

Ben was silent as Riley thought back about what the sheriff said.

"I think I missed the sheriff's point," she said. "When he suggested that I consider where I have the best support system, I thought that would be Pomeroy because I lived there my whole life. I'm not sure I thought about what he really said."

"So, where do you have the best support system?"

"I've only been in Barton for two weeks, but it feels like home maybe because I visited Grandma every summer, or maybe I feel accepted. I've lived in Pomeroy most of my life, and Marcy was a good work friend, but I don't have any other friends in Pomeroy."

"The good news is you don't have to decide today."

"You're right and talking about Barton and Pomeroy reminded me that Dr. Truman, Senior, didn't know my address. He asked me and Marcy for it, but neither one of us told him or anyone else in Pomeroy where I am. When I interviewed for the job with Dr. Truman, Junior, however, he asked me where my family was from, and I told him Barton. He asked if I knew several people, and I didn't, but one of the names was Witmer. I'd forgotten about that."

"Let me get this straight. Bottom line is that Senior didn't know where you would go, but Junior, who is deceased, did," Ben said. "Didn't you say you were jumpy the past two days? No wonder—you had all this in your head, and it was trying to get out. It must be downright crowded in there."

Riley snickered. "That's exactly how my mind feels right now. Tell me about your day. Did you see the sergeant?"

"I'm glad I talked to him. My trainer implied that Sarge had been in the county his entire life and loved his job. Sarge gave me the full story. He told me he wanted to leave Carson his first year at the department, but his wife didn't want to leave her friends. He said they bought a house and some rental property for her to manage then after they'd been married seventeen years, she ran off with a middle school teacher. By then, he was in too much debt to start over and had too many responsibilities with managing his rental properties."

"Oh my gosh, that's a terrible story," Riley said.

"I thought so too. I asked him if he had a chance to do it over, would he have left the county that first year, and he reminded me about the time he caught me with a beer in my hand when I was fifteen. He said he would have stayed for me and all the other boys where he made a difference."

"So now your head's exploding too. What are you going to do?"

"Sarge said I'd be better off talking to a professional. I have an appointment with a career counselor tomorrow."

"Do people usually tell you their life's story?" Riley asked.

"I don't think it's all that unusual, but yes."

"I can't wait to hear the career counselor's story." She giggled.

Ben snorted. "So, what are we going to be doing about the festival?'

"I've been thinking about it. Would it be so bad if we skipped it? Why don't you come here, and we can go to the cabin. Toby can explore, and we can hike the property and look for signs of wildlife. I wouldn't mind some pointers on my shooting. Maybe you could help me with Grandma's rifle. What do you think?"

"Sure sounds like a lot more fun than being on the road most of Sunday and fighting traffic."

"Oh good. I was hoping it didn't sound too boring."

"I don't know about you, but I could use a little boring time," Ben said. "I'll bet you're hungry. What are you planning for supper?"

"I've been reading Grandma's cookbook and found some recipes to try."

"Sounds great, but what do you plan to eat tonight?"

Riley laughed. "I was trying to sound all gourmet-like. I do have a sweet basil plant in a pot in my dining room window. Mrs. Smythe said a plant impresses young men. Are you impressed?"

"I'm impressed with how well you're avoiding the question. Did you rob that bank today?"

Riley laughed even harder. "Fine. Your superior interrogating skills win. I'm planning a hot dog sandwich. I didn't think to buy buns at the store."

Ben joined her as she laughed. "I was going to warm up a pizza, but I'm inspired by your genius culinary skills and will have a hot dog sandwich with you."

After they hung up, Riley went inside and turned on the fireplace before she returned to the kitchen and hummed as she made her hot dog sandwich. She set her plate in front of the fireplace and held Toby back while she snapped a photo and sent it to Ben with the caption, *campfire supper.*

As she knelt next to the fireplace and ate her hot dog, Ben replied with a photo of a young boy who was roasting a marshmallow on a stick at a campfire and the caption, *How I see myself.*

Riley snorted. "Ben is so funny, Toby."

Toby grinned and wagged his tail.

Riley texted back: "Yep. That's you."

After she ate, Riley settled down on the sofa with Grandma's cookbook while Toby circled the rug then flopped down with a thud.

* * *

The next morning, Riley waited on the front porch for Julie Rae while Toby explored the front yard. When Julie Rae arrived, they dashed to her truck and jumped in. "Were you waiting long? Why were you outside? Wasn't it cold?" Julie Rae backed out of the driveway and headed to the veterinary hospital.

"We weren't waiting long at all. Toby got a little extra outside time, and I was dressed warm."

"Charlie always told me I needed to get out more, until I complained and told him I was too tired after working all day to go anywhere. He laughed at me." Julie Rae glanced at Riley. "Can't you hear his big laugh? I got really irritated because I thought he wasn't taking me and my important, hard work seriously, so I stomped outside and slammed the door behind me. He came out and said—this is a quote—See how much better it is when you get out?" Julie Rae laughed, and Riley giggled.

Julie Rae pulled into her parking spot, and they all went inside. Julie Rae rushed to the breakroom to make coffee while Riley hurried to Amanda's desk to listen to the overnight messages, and Toby claimed his spot. When she listened to the last message, she jotted down the phone number and called the client. "This is Riley at the veterinary hospital. Both Doc Julie Rae and I are here. Come on in. We'll be waiting."

"We're on our way now. Two minutes."

Riley hurried to the breakroom and found Julie Rae and Thad in deep conversation. "A German shepherd was hit by a construction truck. They're on the way in. Our patient is not conscious."

Julie Rae and Thad dashed to the front door while Riley hurried to ready the trauma room for a German shepherd with possible multiple injuries. Thad led two men in construction hard hats who carried the German shepherd on a makeshift blanket litter to the trauma room.

"Right here." Riley pointed to the trauma table, and the men set the dog and blanket on the table then left.

Doc Thad bent over the dog to examine it. "Get Julie Rae."

Riley hurried to the reception area and motioned to Julie Rae. "I'll take over here, Doc." Julie Rae rushed to the trauma room.

Riley sat next to the woman who grabbed her hands and sobbed. "He jumped out of the window. I've never had him do that before."

A construction truck roared up and stopped in front. When the driver jumped out of the truck, the two men hurried outside and talked to him. The driver walked into the clinic and stayed near the door. "I'm really sorry, ma'am."

"It's not your fault. You couldn't have seen Thor. He jumped out of the window when he saw an armadillo." Her smile was weak.

The man stepped closer to her and handed her a card. "If it's not too much trouble, my boss asked if you'd give him a call to let us know how he's doing. All of us are shook up."

The woman accepted the card as she met his gaze. "I'll do that. Thank you for your concern, and thanks to the men for all their help. I couldn't have managed without them."

The driver nodded and hurried outside then the three men climbed into the truck and left.

"Riley, would you mind calling them for me? I know Thor will be okay because Doc Julie Rae is the best."

When Amanda and Zach came to the front, Riley said, "Amanda's here. I'm going to see if the docs need my help."

Riley rose and motioned to Zach to join her. "Amanda, Thor was hit by a construction truck."

Riley and Zach hurried to the trauma room. When they entered the room, Riley whispered, "Blow-by oxygen. He's breathing on his own." Doc Julie Rae glanced up. "His lungs are clear, and his heart's strong. Broken rib or two and possible hip fracture. Your timing is superb. We need x-rays. Doc Thad will stay with you while I talk to his person. I couldn't remember his name."

"Thor."

"Thank you." Julie Rae left.

"How do we get him to x-ray?" Dr. Thad asked.

"This table rolls. We'll still need to transfer him to the x-ray table, but we can use the blanket litter that the men left under him.

As they rolled the table to the x-ray room, Thor opened his eyes and gazed at Riley then whined.

"I'm sorry it hurts, but the docs will patch you up, and I'm sorry the armadillo got away." Riley stroked his head. "Does your head hurt?"

Thor whimpered.

"That's good. I'm glad you have a hard head too."

"Does his head hurt?" Doc Thad asked.

"No." Riley parked the rolling table next to the x-ray table. "Ready to slide him over?"

"We'll do it." Thad took the position at Thor's head, and Zach hurried to the other side. After they slid Thor to the x-ray table, Riley asked, "What do you want, Doc?"

Thad wrote the order for the x-rays, and Riley read it then handed the order to Zach. "I'll do the first x-ray then talk you through the rest."

"I'll be back to help transfer him back to the exam table," Thad said as he left.

"We're going to take some x-rays, Thor. It doesn't hurt, but I'll have to position you a bit for each one, and you'll need you to stay real still. Okay?"

Thor raised his eyebrows and replied with a short yip.

"Good. You won't be able to see me because the controls are in a different room, but I'll be close."

Riley read the order one more time before she and Zach put on their protective aprons and stepped into the hallway. "We'll discuss the operation of the x-ray later," she said. "I'll position Thor so he doesn't get confused, but you select the next position and take the x-ray."

Zach nodded.

After the x-rays for the different views were completed, Zach left to notify Dr. Thad that Thor was ready to be shifted back to the exam table while Riley waited with Thor. "We'll slide you back then Dr. Thad and Dr. Julie Rae will work to make you comfortable."

Thor sighed as Zach and Dr. Thad returned.

After Thor was back in the trauma exam room, Dr. Julie Rae joined them. "Give Dr. Thad and me a minute to look over the x-rays."

After the docs left the room, Zach asked, "Was Dr. Julie Rae talking to Thor or us?"

Thor's smile was weak.

"Okay, Thor. I get it. You and us," Zach rolled his eyes.

When Dr. Julie Rae returned, she said, "Would you like to help me, Zach?"

Zach's eyes widened. "Yes, Doc. I would."

"I'll take the next patient while you're busy, Zach. Thank you, Dr. Julie Rae." As Riley walked to Amanda's desk, she noticed two young women had joined Thor's person, and she smiled.

"What's our schedule, Amanda?"

Amanda pointed to her screen. "We have an appointment at eight, and two at eight thirty."

"I'll be in the back with a cup of coffee, if you need me."

"Your first of the day? Oh, my." Amanda put her hand over her heart.

"Shocking, isn't it? I'll bring you a cup of tea."

Riley delivered the promised cup of tea to Amanda then returned to the breakroom and poured herself a cup of coffee.

As she sipped her coffee, her phone buzzed a text.

Ben: "Happy Friday."

She replied: "You too."

Riley stared at her text. *That was dull.*

She added: "IOU sparkling text."

Ben: "No fair."

Riley giggled. *Ben is so smart. It will be interesting to hear what he and the counselor come up with.*

CHAPTER ELEVEN

Zach came into the breakroom and joined Riley at the table. "Doc told me to take a break, and Amanda told me you were here. Doc and the client decided Thor could go home. They're going over his care then I'll help move him to their car. Doc Julie Rae is the best vet I've ever seen."

"I agree. So, how did you know what Thor said when you asked who Doc was talking to?"

"Are you kidding?" Zach snorted. "Didn't you see Thor's sneer? First time I've ever been insulted by a dog."

Riley chuckled. "I took it as a sign that he was not as badly injured as he looked, but you're right—he did sneer."

She drained her cup. "I need to call the construction manager before we tackle our paperwork."

Riley hurried to Amanda's desk. "I said I would call the construction manager to update him and his crew about Thor's condition."

Amanda rose from her chair. "Use the office phone. I'll brew a cup of tea and go to the bathroom, except maybe not in that order."

Amanda hurried to the hallway while Riley made her call. After Riley spoke to the construction manager and hung up, she glanced over the schedule as Pia and Jordy came into the receptionist's area.

"What are you doing at the desk? Did I miss something? Is Amanda okay?"

"Amanda's in the breakroom. She's fine, and you missed a trauma, but our patient will be going home soon."

"You get all the good stuff before I can get here," Pia glared at Riley before she shouted over her shoulder as she headed to the breakroom with Jordy trotting behind her. "It's not fair. You shut me out on purpose."

Riley watched Pia stomp down the hall. *I'd be mad too.*

Amanda returned with her tea. "Pia's cranky."

"She's mad that she missed the trauma." Riley rose from Amanda's chair and headed to the trauma room. "Do we have anything exciting on the schedule? Pia deserves a heart-racing patient."

"You're right. I'll divert the next one to her."

When Riley stepped into the trauma room, Thor was moaning, and she rolled her eyes.

"You're going home. We're not set up to scramble your morning egg for you."

Thor yipped, and she laughed. "You got that right. We're terrible hosts."

Zach tugged on Riley's sleeve, and they stepped into the back hallway.

"Thor's been crabbing at me since I walked in. I'm glad you knew what his problem was. I was afraid he was in pain—not being a pain," Zach said.

They returned to the trauma room, and Doc opened the door as the client hurried to Thor's side. "Are you starving? Doc said you can go home with me. Our neighbors are here to help load you into our car. Doc said you can have breakfast when we get home."

Two middle-aged men came to the door. "How do we do this, Doc?"

"Thor's on a blanket litter. You can lift the litter to carry him."

"Gotcha. I've got the head," one man said as the other man moved to Thor's feet.

The two men lifted Thor and left with the client in the lead.

"Good work, you two." Doc Julie Rae headed toward her office.

"Now, we clean up, right?" Zach asked.

"That's right. After we clean and straighten up, we'll replenish the supplies."

While they cleaned, Zach said, "I was surprised the exam table in the trauma room rolled to the x-ray room so easily."

"I never saw that either until I came here. Really smart, isn't it?"

Zach nodded. "I know Doc Thad hasn't been here a week, but he and Doc Julie Rae were a coordinated team like they'd worked together for years."

"That's really interesting. The vets I've worked with or observed when I was in school seemed to prefer to work alone. Kind of sets the tone for our office, doesn't it?" Riley asked.

"I have a feeling I've landed in the perfect place—there's nothing like learning from the best," Zach said.

After they cleaned and resupplied the trauma and x-ray rooms, Riley and Zach checked in with Amanda.

"Next patient is yours," Amanda said. "Pia and Doc Thad are in exam room one. Here's the folder."

Riley handed the folder to Zach, who read it over. "Overweight Persian cat with a history of arthritis. He's scratching a lot, which is new."

He handed the folder to Riley who read it too. "He's an inside cat, so we can't blame the neighbor's grass, can we?"

"Wonder if there's something new like a change of food, litter, or cleaning products the client uses."

"Where do we start?" Riley asked.

"Weigh the cat," Zach said.

"Exactly." Riley glanced at the parking lot, and her eyes widened as a woman struggled to carry a large cat carrier. "Our client may have back problems."

Zach turned to look. "Whoa. Two causes of overweight in cats: overfed and lack of exercise."

Riley nodded. "We've got a perfect opportunity for client education, haven't we?"

The woman was breathing heavily when she came inside the door. She stopped to set the carrier on the floor then scooted it with her foot to Amanda's desk, and the cat inside the carrier hissed.

Riley's eyes narrowed. "Cranky cat," she whispered.

The client leaned against the counter. "My Dexter has been scratching a lot lately. He sometimes scratches so vigorously that he draws blood, and it must hurt when I brush him because he bites me."

When Dexter growled, Riley shook her head. "I'm Riley, and this is Zach. Let's go to room three."

Zach lifted the carrier.

"Thank you so much, young man," the client said. "My friends told me to put Dexter on a leash, but it's just as hard to drag him as to carry him."

Zach set Dexter on the exam table then wrapped Dexter in a small blanket before he lifted him out of the carrier. Dexter instantly went limp. "I'm still going to weigh you, Dexter," Zach muttered.

"Why did the young man wrap Dexter in a blanket?" the woman asked after Zach left to weigh Dexter.

"Sometimes cats feel more secure when they're cocooned," Riley said. *Also, it was a smart way to keep Dexter from biting him.*

The woman nodded. "Dexter did seem to relax, didn't he?"

"Yes, ma'am. You brought Dexter in because he's scratching?"

"Oh, yes. He's obviously in a great deal of distress. He can barely make it to his dish to eat. I was worried he'd lost his strength from all the scratching, so I put his dish next to his cat bed."

"Most cats prefer a schedule. Does he go to a groomer?"

"You're brilliant. I'd forgotten how much Dexter loves a schedule. I just won't tell my friends we're not self-feeding any more. He used to go to the groomer, but he's gotten too heavy for me to take him. She offered to come to our house, but I didn't know if that was a good idea."

"We'll see what the doc says, but it would help Dexter's skin problem if is he's groomed regularly. You could probably set up a regular schedule, so Dexter will be happy."

"I can do that. She does an excellent job, and Dexter loves her; he must miss playing with her. She wanted me to get him a cat tower, but my friends said he'd get hurt."

"Sounds like you have a great groomer. Maybe she has a cat tower recommendation that would be appropriate for Dexter. He does need regular exercise because lying down is hard on his skin too."

Zach returned with a purring Dexter. "Dexter likes the base of his ears to be rubbed," Zach said.

"Really? That's amazing, Zach. My friend said Persian cats don't like to be touched."

"I'll let Doc know Dexter's here," Riley said.

Doc Julie Rae met Riley in the hallway. "What's up with Dexter?" Doc asked.

Riley told her about the scratching, groomer, Dexter's weight, the current feeding plan, and the friends.

"Sounds like we need the groomer to clean away all that dead hair and skin and get Dexter up and walking. Do you think a once-a-week appointment with the groomer is enough?"

"Maybe twice a week for two months with a follow up appointment here?"

"Yes. Good plan. I'll talk to her. What did Dexter say?"

"He's got a trash mouth. I think it's because he's in such bad shape."

"Or he's just a crabby cat."

Riley nodded. "There is that. Zach relaxed Dexter by rubbing his ears."

"You two are awesome." Doc Julie Rae went inside exam room three.

As Riley waited at Amanda's desk, her phone buzzed a text. *Eli.*

"In town. Lunch?"

Riley snickered, and Amanda said, "What?"

"Eli's coming for lunch."

"I'm glad I wore my stretchy pants." Amanda grinned.

Riley replied: "Amanda said yes."

Riley's phone rang, and she frowned as she hurried to the breakroom to answer.

"Hello, Marcy. Are you okay?"

"Got your text, Riley. That's really exciting. Do you have a job? My mother wanted me to move home and found me a job in Atlanta—really fancy place—like a boutique clinic for purebred dogs and cats. I'm excited because I start my new job on Monday. My boss is not happy with me, but the girls told me it's hard to find any vet tech jobs right now, and they hired someone right away to replace me, so I don't know what they were so angry about—they had their pick of the cream of the crop. Aren't you glad you found that job in Barton so fast? And now you have another one in Pomeroy? Did Doc Truman, Senior, pull strings for you? Do you know where he is? When I told the girls at work you were from Barton, no one knew where that is. Isn't that a stitch? Of course, I had to look it up myself. The girls said it probably suits you just fine. Isn't that funny? We all laughed."

I don't get the joke. Riley furrowed her brow. "Like I said, I may move to Pomeroy. I have a few details to work out first."

"Sounds good. I have to dash—I'm meeting the girls for drinks this evening. Kind of my farewell party. It's supposed to be a surprise, so don't tell anybody that I told you. Talk to you later."

After Marcy hung up, Riley stared at her phone. *Who would I tell?*

"What's wrong?" Doc Julie Rae stopped in the doorway.

"People move on," Riley said.

"A friend from your old job?" Doc asked. "Are you going to be okay?"

Riley nodded. "I've never had a lot of friends, and she's the only friend I've had since I got out of school."

Doc closed the door and sat at the table. "It's more than this one friend, isn't it? You're under a lot of stress."

Riley joined Doc. "Now I'm worried that everyone I know isn't a friend after all. Maybe I wouldn't feel like that if I weren't so stressed."

"Charlie, Kenny, Freddy, and I will always be your friends, and Pia and Amanda. Can't leave out the sheriff. Of course, Toby and Ben are your most important friends. I don't know about Thad and Zach yet. We'll see if they're worthy." Doc smiled.

Riley returned Doc's smile. "That's funny, and Amanda could give us a schedule to determine worthiness." She shook her head as she sighed. "I've known Marcy for a long time. We ate lunch together every day at work, but I realize now that we never did anything after work or on weekends because I was always busy with school. I guess we were work friends, if there is such a thing."

"I think there is. Sometimes work friends become lifelong friends, and sometimes work friends are just that, and I'm sorry," Julie Rae said. "It's natural to mourn a loss—even a minor one."

"Thanks, Doc."

After Doc Julie Rae left the breakroom, Toby padded to Riley, and she scratched his ears. "If nothing else, Marcy helped me to understand that we belong here, and we need to catch a killer, so I won't be stressed anymore. Now I just need a plan."

Zach hurried into the breakroom. "Amanda said we have an unscheduled patient on the way."

"Let's give it to Pia. I'll take her patient and send her to the front desk. Wait for her there to help her." Riley hurried to room two.

Pia was recording an English spaniel's weight when Riley stepped into the room. "May I speak to you a second, Pia?"

Pia stepped out of the room with Riley. "What's wrong?"

"Trauma coming in. I'm taking over your patient, and Zach's with you. Is that okay?"

"Thanks. You're the best." Pia raced to the front, and Riley went into the exam room. "Pia was called to another case. I'm Riley. Ear infection, I see. My specialty."

The English spaniel whimpered, and Riley frowned. "What about her teeth?"

The client said, "Her teeth are fine. What does that have to do with her ear infections? Princess gets them all the time. She doesn't eat well when she has ear infections either, although the past week she's eaten very little."

Riley nodded. "May I look?"

Princess yipped.

"Thank you," Riley said as she checked Princess's gums then Princess yawned to show Riley her back teeth.

"Your gums in the back are puffy. We'll have doc look. I'll check your ears."

Riley pulled out the otoscope from a drawer as Princess rolled onto her side.

"This one's clear."

Princess rolled over.

"This one's clear too." Riley smiled at the client. "It's really difficult to take proper care of a spaniel's ears. You've been working hard to be sure her ears stay dry, haven't you?"

The client blushed and returned Riley's smile. "Yes, I have."

"I'll take your temperature, Princess. We need to know if you have any fever." After she read the thermometer, Riley left to find one of the docs. Doc Julie Rae met Riley in the back hallway. "Zach told me you gave Pia our trauma patient. What do we have?"

Riley told her about Princess's slight fever, swollen gums, and decreased appetite.

Doc Julie Rae went into the room and examined Princess. "We'll start with an antibiotic for the infection. After that's cleared, we can see what's going on with that back tooth."

While Doc Julie Rae and the client discussed diet options, Riley filled Princess's prescription then met the client and Princess at Amanda's desk. "We'll want to see Princess again in two weeks," Doc said as Riley handed the antibiotic to the client. "Call us if the soft diet hasn't improved Princess's appetite by Monday."

While Amanda scheduled the follow up appointment, Riley hurried to the exam room to clean it for the next patient. While she cleaned, Pia came into the exam room and closed the door.

"Thank you for taking over Princess's care and sending me to the trauma patient. She's a miniature schnauzer who tangled with a possum. Not surprising for a feisty miniature schnauzer, but her lacerations bled freely, and she was covered in blood. I can see why her people were so panicked."

"No need—"

Pia held up her hand and interrupted Riley. "I do need to thank you. My mother is very sick, and I didn't realize how much worry and stress I've been carrying. I'm sorry I snapped at you."

"I understand."

Pia gazed at Riley. "I guess you do. You've been under a lot of stress lately too. The hardest part for me is that I'm frustrated that there's nothing I can do to help her. Zach's cleaning the trauma room. It's a mess, but I couldn't put off talking to you."

Before Pia left, Riley met her gaze. "It's what friends do."

After Riley cleaned the exam room, she strolled to the receptionist's desk to check the lunch schedule.

"Good, you're here," Amanda said. "I'm having lunch with Zach and Julie Rae; you, Pia, and Doc Thad have the second lunch. Can you take over the desk now?"

"Go right ahead," Riley said.

Amanda hurried to the bathroom while Julie Rae stopped at the desk to drop off a file. "Amanda decided we'd try different lunch combinations to give Thad and Zach a chance to get to know everyone. I wouldn't have thought of that. She's brilliant."

Riley checked the schedule before Pia came to the desk to drop off the trauma file. "Amanda's shifting everybody around. You, Doc Thad, and I have second lunch today. Oh, and Eli—he invited himself to lunch. Here's the file folder for the next patient."

Pia picked up the folder and read the file. "William Wallace is scheduled for his annual exam and immunizations. Change of pace after our battle-scarred schnauzer."

The old, chocolate Labrador retriever with the gray muzzle carried his leash to the door and waited for his person to open it.

Riley raised her eyebrows, and Pia chuckled. "He has carried his leash when he leaves home since he was a pup. The client's neighborhood used to have the rule that dogs were not allowed off their own property without a leash. The client's oldest son was eight when he taught his best friend, William Wallace, to carry his own leash. Eventually, the homeowners' association was dissolved, but the old lab still carries his leash."

Riley snickered. "I think there's a lesson there for all of us, but I'm not sure what it is."

"Maybe always follow the rules like William Wallace?" Pia giggled and greeted her patient. "Nice to see you, William Wallace. We're in room one." Riley had answered the phone and made three appointments before Pia, the client, and William Wallace came out of room one.

"Amanda will schedule our next annual appointment later, Riley, but you probably already knew that," the client said.

After the client left, Riley said, "I didn't know that."

Pia nodded. "She calls the clients three months in advance. I've never thought to ask her how she tracks them though. Now, you've got me wondering."

Eli parked in the lot close to the road and strode to the door with two large white sacks in one hand and his lunch sack in the other. He looked around as he came inside. "Where's Amanda?"

"In the breakroom, and hello to you too, Agent Reeves," Pia said, and Riley chuckled.

Eli rushed to the breakroom.

"I'll get room one cleaned and ready for the next patient before it's time for our lunch," Pia said.

When Amanda returned with one of Eli's white sacks, she waved it before she set it next to her keyboard and grinned. "Seniority."

"I always knew you were open to bribes," Pia said.

"And you aren't?" Amanda smirked.

"Tough room," Pia said. "The hecklers are on point today."

Amanda laughed as Riley and Pia left for the breakroom.

After they joined Doc Thad and Eli at the table, Jordy trotted in and sat at Pia's feet.

Eli said, "I'd like to ask you more questions about your tires and the screws, Riley, but lunch first, right?"

"Absolutely," Riley said. "And I'm assuming, dessert."

Eli nodded as he bit into his sandwich.

"You did a great job with our possum-hunter, Pia," Doc Thad said. "She was a mess until you cleaned her up. I don't think all of the blood was hers. Oh, sorry, Agent Reeves. Our trauma discussions might not be the type of lunchtime talk you usually hear."

Eli smiled. "Usually we have someone from the crime lab describing their latest case, and they feel obligated to add descriptions of smells."

"Speaking of which, possums sure do have a distinctive stink, don't they?" Riley asked.

"Don't tell me you're a possum-whisperer too." Pia snickered, and Eli choked on his sandwich.

"I was eight the first time I was close to a possum that played dead. My dog yelped and ran to the house, and I poked the possum to see if it was alive. You're right, Riley. I was afraid to go to school the next day because I could still smell that possum and thought everyone else could too," Doc Thad said.

While they were eating, Zach came to the breakroom and paused before he wheeled away.

Riley cocked her head. *Wonder what that was all about?* She glanced at Pia, who shrugged.

Pia ate her lunch in a rush. "Dessert?" she asked.

Eli handed her the sack. "Take your pick."

Pia smiled. "What a wonderful choice. Their cupcakes are so good. I'll take an Italian cream outside with me. I have a call to make."

Riley nodded. *Calling to check on her mother.*

Doc Thad and Eli finished eating before Riley did. Doc Thad said, "I need to catch up on my paperwork before my next patient." He took along a cup of coffee to his office.

Eli brushed his crumbs off the table and into his hand then strode to the trash can. "This is going to be on tonight's news, but I wanted to talk to you before you heard about it. The Trumans have been under investigation for quite a while for operating a methamphetamine laboratory, but there was no evidence of that after all, but there must have been a lab at one time because of the odors from his office you told me about."

Riley nodded. "It's been quite a while since the odors dissipated."

"During his investigation, our undercover guy found invoices for large volumes of ketamine that never made the inventory list, and Dr. Truman, Senior, was arrested yesterday on charges of selling ketamine and is also under investigation in the murder of his lawyer who appeared to be Senior's partner in selling the drugs. The team determined that Junior wasn't involved with the ketamine, and his death had nothing to do with Senior's lucrative side business. The team thinks Senior may have been the one who was harassing you. Are you sure he didn't know where you are now?"

"I was until this morning when Marcy called and told me she'd discussed where I'd moved with her new coworkers."

Eli shook his head. "That would have made it common knowledge in Pomeroy. At least we know there's a good possibility he heard it from someone."

"If he's under arrest then maybe I won't have any more incidents?" Riley placed her trash inside her lunch sack.

"Yes, and even after he posts bail, he'll be under tight surveillance, and he'll know it."

Eli passed the cupcakes to Riley. "Take your choice. There are plenty for the new staff and Doc Julie Rae."

"Is that another Italian cream?" she asked.

Eli peered into the sack. "Looks like it to me."

Riley reached in and pulled out the cupcake. "Good. My favorite."

As she took a big bite of her cupcake, Eli asked, "Do you have plans for the weekend?"

She raised her eyebrows and nodded as she chewed, and he chuckled. "I have good timing, don't I?"

She snickered as she swallowed, and he continued, "It's supposed to be a nice weekend."

"I know. I'm looking forward to it," Riley said.

Eli tapped his fingers on the table then rose. "Hopefully this is the end of the problems Truman was causing you. I'll still invite myself to lunch when I'm in town."

"You're always welcome." Riley smiled then bit into her cupcake as he left.

Zach stormed into the breakroom and crossed his arms. "How do you know him?" he growled.

Riley's eyes widened. "He has led the investigation into who has been harassing me."

"Oh, really. Is that all? I heard him fish to see whether you had plans for the weekend."

"Would you please sit down and talk to me? You're making me nervous. Why do you dislike Agent Reeves?"

Zach glared. "Later. Enjoy your lunch."

"Zach, what do I need to know?"

Zach sighed as he sat with her. "Eli Reeves might be a good investigator, but he's slimy. He was dating one of my classmates for almost two years. He gave her every reason to believe he was serious, but she learned he was dating several other girls in different towns. When she asked him about it, he claimed the other girls threw themselves at him. She chatted with two of the girls then dumped him, but she was heartbroken."

"I'm so sorry to hear that. Can I tell you something?"

Zach nodded.

"I haven't dated all that much because I've always been focused on doing my job the best I could in the daytime, and when I wasn't at work, I was focused on my classes. I finally earned my degree in animal biology last month, but the cost was no life outside of work and school. I never mentioned I was working on a college degree because I didn't think it was a big deal."

Zach snorted. "Are you sure you aren't telling me the story of my life?"

Riley chuckled. "What I'm trying to say is, I haven't had men throwing themselves at my feet. Or if they did, I stepped over them because I was too busy studying."

Zach laughed. "I can see a slew of fallen men in your wake."

Riley laughed with him. "I like the way you tell my life story. We'll go with your version. I met my friend, Ben, my third day of work here when he brought in two dogs and a cat that had been in a crash. He lives in Carson, and I talk to him every day. When I moved from my grandma's house to town last Saturday, Eli sent me a beautiful vase of flowers for a housewarming gift. Really lavish."

"I can imagine," Zach said. "That's his style."

"Ben helped me move, and his housewarming gifts were a gun locker for my grandma's long guns and a larger propane tank for my fireplace. Do you know what Ben said when he saw the flowers?"

"Who sent those?" Zach guessed.

"Nope."

Zach furrowed his brow. "Wish I'd thought of flowers?"

"Not even close. He said *nice flowers.*"

Zach chuckled. "I like Ben."

"See? Big difference, right? Ben's my friend; Eli's—"

"Fallen in your wake." Zach grinned.

Riley giggled as Pia rushed into the breakroom.

"You aren't having fun without me, are you? I need another cupcake before I go back to work, but I can't eat one by myself. Who wants to split one?"

"I will," Zach said. "I can cut a cupcake in half with surgical precision."

Pia narrowed her eyes. "Fine. You cut then I'll choose. I have brothers."

After Zach cut the cupcake, Pia stared then hovered her hand over one side as she watched Zach's face.

"Oh for goodness' sake, Pia. Just pick it up. This isn't gunslingers' poker." Riley headed to the door, and Zach laughed.

"We've got a busy afternoon," Amanda said when Riley checked in. "I've double-booked for one and two o'clock, and we're solid after that. The patients' folders are lined up on my desk by time."

The rest of the day was as busy as Amanda promised. At four o'clock, Doc Julie Rae leaned against the counter. "That was a marathon at sprint speed, Amanda, but a good test of what we might be able to do under ideal circumstances."

"If we'd had an emergency or a complicated patient come in, we'd have gotten behind," Amanda said. "I'm getting a feel for where it's best to add in slack. Tomorrow's back to our normal Saturday schedule. Pia, Zach, and Doc Thad have our last scheduled patient of the day now."

As Riley left the reception area to finish cleaning the last exam room that she and Doc Julie Rae had used, her phone buzzed a text.

Ben: "Call when you can. Not urgent."

Riley hurried back to Amanda's desk. "Can I take a little time for a personal call?"

Amanda nodded. "We don't have anyone else scheduled. You'll hear anyone who comes in."

Riley and Toby stepped outside, and she called Ben.

"I didn't expect you to call back so quick. It's not urgent."

"We don't have any more patients to see today. What's up?"

"I saw the counselor this morning. My supervisor gave me the weekend off to think about my options."

"Wow. Would it help if you got away and came here?"

"I was hoping you'd say that. I can reserve a room—"

"Wait on that. There might be other choices. Were you thinking about leaving in the morning? Are you packed?"

"All packed. I can leave any time."

"I'll call you back in thirty minutes or so. It'll be great to see you, but I'm sorry you're in such a bind."

"It'll work out," Ben said.

After they hung up, Riley went inside and found Julie Rae in her office.

"I need to talk to you," Riley said as she closed the office door. "Ben is at a crossroads as far as his career is concerned. He saw a career counselor, and his boss gave him the weekend off to consider his options. When I suggested he could come here, he said he was hoping I'd say that. He was going to reserve a room—"

"Well, we can't have that. Our house is always open to him or you, but he might want a little more solitude. Have you thought about your grandma's cabin?"

"I thought about it briefly but wasn't sure if it would be appropriate. Social stuff is not my forte, so I'm glad you think it a good idea. It's quiet and relaxing, and he could have as much time for himself as he needs. When he wants company, I'm only fifteen minutes away."

"I think it's the best option. It gives him some solitude, but he can spend time with you to bounce off ideas. When is he coming? Would you like to come to our house for dinner tomorrow night? Tell him he's welcome at our house, but I think he'll prefer the privacy at the cabin."

"I'll call him back, and dinner at your house tomorrow night sounds wonderful."

Toby followed Riley outside. "You're being protective. Any special reason?"

Toby yipped, and she frowned. "Not Doc Senior? Interesting. So, who?"

Toby yipped twice, and she giggled. "Okay, I get it. Not Doc Senior."

When Riley called Ben, he answered right away, and she smiled.

"You have more options. You ready?"

Ben chuckled. "Ready."

"You can stay with Charlie, Julie Rae, and the boys and be entertained all weekend, or you can stay at my grandma's cabin for some solitude and relaxation and come to my house when you want company. You can choose. We've been invited to Charlie and Julie Rae's for dinner tomorrow night. Next question—when do you want to come to Barton?"

"The cabin sounds perfect, and I'm ready to leave right now."

"Then leave and come to my house, and we'll figure out the rest from there."

Ben hung up, and Riley and Toby hurried inside. Julie Rae waited for her by the back door.

"Well?" Julie Rae asked.

"He's coming tonight and will stay at the cabin. I wouldn't have seriously considered it if you and I hadn't talked; we'll come to your house tomorrow for dinner."

"Perfect. I was hoping he'd want to stay at the cabin. Time to reflect may be exactly what he needs."

"I need to clean rooms to get rid of some of this excitement, or I'll bust." Riley hurried to her exam room and cleaned it in record time. She hurried to help Pia and Zach clean the rest of the rooms.

While Riley and Pia were cleaning, Pia's eyes widened as her phone rang. "I have to take this. Will you be okay?"

"Go," Riley said. After she finished cleaning, she found Zach in room three. The two of them cleaned and straightened the room then checked the trauma room supplies. While Riley counted, Zach jotted down the list. Pia came into the room, and tears ran down her cheeks. She swiped at the counter with a sanitizing wipe.

"Is it your mother?" Riley asked as Zach slipped out of the room with his list.

"She was admitted to the hospital in Orlando, and she's in the intensive care unit. I need to be with her and to help my sister with her children so she can visit Mom too. Tom works this weekend, but Jackson can stay with his other grandmother while his dad works. Tom will make arrangements at work so he can take Jackson to school and pick him up until I come home, but Tom's mother has uppity cats and can't keep Jordy. I can't take Jordy with me, and I don't want to put him into a kennel." Pia sobbed. "I don't know what to do."

Jordy padded into the room and leaned against Pia. She knelt and hugged him.

CHAPTER TWELVE

"Jordy can stay with me and Toby. He knows us, and he can come to work with us."

"But that's a big imposition." Pia's brow furrowed as she looked up at Riley.

"Is not. It's settled, and Jordy will be fine with us. Right, Jordy?"

Jordy yipped.

"Thank you, Jordy," Riley said. "He can go home with us."

"Okay, thank you. I need to talk to Dr. Julie Rae. I'm glad Zach is here. He'll be fine."

After Pia rushed out, Zach peeked in the trauma room. "I've got the supplies. I heard what Pia said."

Riley and Zach replenished the supplies then checked the rest of the exam rooms.

"Ben is coming here this weekend to take some time off work," Riley said as they checked the supplies in the rest of the rooms.

"Will he drop by tomorrow morning? I'd like to meet him," Zach said.

"You filling in for Pia already? Just kidding, I'd like for you to meet him too," Riley said.

When they returned to Amanda's desk, Riley said, "All the exam rooms are sanitized. What's our schedule look like for tomorrow?"

"First appointment is at eight thirty, and the morning is full until eleven. Doc Julie Rae told me to lock the front door after you were finished then we're having a meeting in the breakroom."

As Amanda rose, Riley and Zach strolled to the breakroom. Doc Julie Rae, Thad, and Pia were sitting at the table. Riley and Zach squeezed three more chairs around the table before Amanda came into the room then the three of them joined the others.

"Good, we're all here. I love that we might need a larger table for a staff meeting." Julie Rae smiled. "We have some adjustments to make. Pia's mother is ill, and Pia is going to Orlando to be with her. Zach, you're fully competent to have your own patients solo, and we really appreciate that you were able to start this week because we can continue to increase the number of patients we see with two vets and two vet techs. However, we have another gap that Amanda, Doc Thad, and I have been discussing, and we may have a solution. We need to prepare for Amanda to be out for a while with her new baby, and Amanda would like to return part time for a while. Any guesses?"

"We're going to clone Amanda." Zach grinned.

As everyone laughed, Julie Rae nodded. "You're kind of right, Zach. Doc Thad's wife, Claire, is on the substitute teacher's list, but there are very few opportunities. If Claire works with Amanda for the next three months, we'll have our Amanda clone, and it will be simpler as Amanda's appointments become more frequent."

"That's ingenious," Riley said. "Does Claire know what she's getting into?"

Doc Thad laughed. "We've talked, and I'm not sure she understands how unusual we are, but she said this is a perfect opportunity for her to become better acquainted with the community."

"When is Claire starting?" Zach asked. "I'm looking forward to not being the new guy."

Julie Rae laughed. "Our new guy, Claire, starts tomorrow."

"I know this is short notice, but I'm going to leave in the morning for Orlando, and Jordy's going home with Toby and Riley."

"That's great news. Jordy will still be here with us during the day," Doc Thad said.

"Safe travels, Pia, and let us know how you're doing and what we can do for you here," Julie Rae said. "Tell Tom that Charlie will deliver dinner for him and Jackson on Monday."

Julie Rae rose. "Let's go home."

After Toby and Jordy jumped into Julie Rae's truck, Riley said, "Eli told me Dr. Truman's been arrested for selling ketamine, and Eli thinks Dr. Truman was the source of the notes and the screws in my tires."

"I hate to hear that any veterinarian has become involved in drug dealing," Julie Rae said. "Did Eli say anything about Dr. Witmer or Daphne? Was he involved with their deaths?"

"He didn't say."

"Tomorrow morning, same time?"

"Same time," Riley said.

After Julie Rae dropped them off, Riley fed Toby and Jordy then let them out back for a romp while she hurried to her room to change out of her work clothes. She flipped one hanger after another on the closet bar and frowned. *I've got one long-sleeved shirt, and it's dirty. I need to go shopping sometime.* She chuckled. *Time for another pawn shop visit.*

She pulled on a short-sleeved T-shirt and threw on a sweatshirt over it before she carried her laundry to the kitchen and started a load of clothes. Before she went outside to check on the boys, she opened the refrigerator. *What do I do for our dinner?*

Toby yipped.

Ben's here.

Riley ran outside to the porch as Ben pulled into her driveway.

"I'm so glad you're here." Riley waved her hands in excitement, and Ben grinned as he strode to the porch, and she returned his hug before they went inside.

"What's the plan?"

"I thought we'd go to the cabin, so you could unload your things. Then after that, I have no idea. Pia had to go to Orlando because her mother is in the hospital, and Jordy came home with us."

"Cabin first is a good idea. What about dinner? I stopped at the gas station to fill up, and a couple of guys told me about a new Cuban restaurant north of town. We could call in an order on our way back and eat here."

"What a great idea. I just remembered there's coffee at the cabin but not much else. If you want anything else, we'll need to stop at the grocery store."

After they loaded into the truck, Ben drove north to find the new restaurant.

"Seems like I haven't talked to you in ages," Riley said. "Doc hired Doc Thad's wife to work with Amanda to fill in when Amanda has her baby, and Claire starts tomorrow. That reminds me, I'll have to make cinnamon rolls tonight. You could come to the clinic in the morning for a cinnamon roll. It's become a tradition for me to make cinnamon rolls when a new person starts at the clinic. The first time I took cinnamon rolls was on my first day. If you want to say anything, you might have to raise your hand because I'm really excited to see you. I need to take a breath."

Ben chuckled as he pulled into a parking spot at the restaurant. "I could listen to you all day."

After he lowered the windows for Toby and Jordy, they went inside the restaurant, and a young woman with a long, single braid that went to her hips greeted them.

"Are you dining in?" she asked.

"We'd like to call in an order later and pick it up," Riley said.

"That's fine," she handed each of them a take-out menu, "but you may want to order now and take it with you because it's Friday night, and we'll be swamped in the next half hour."

"We could eat at the cabin," Ben said. "That takes a lot of pressure off trying to hurry back later."

Riley smiled at their greeter. "It sounds good, except we don't know what we want."

"Perfect," she giggled. "I'll order for you. Empanadas for appetizers, two main dishes—one chicken and one beef, and flan for dessert. Do you need sweet tea?"

"Yes," Riley said. "Two sweet teas."

"I'll put in your order. It won't take long. Why don't you take a tour of our restaurant? We have artwork and crafts on the walls and on a table near the back meeting room that are for sale by local artists. You may see something that needs to go home with you."

Ben and Riley strolled around the restaurant and admired the items for sale. Riley picked up a wooden carving of a dog. "This looks just like Toby." Ben picked up the information card. "The carver is local. He collects wood from old barns and houses. The dog is carved from a barn rafter."

"Very smooth." Riley rubbed the dog's back with her fingers. She set the dog back on the table. "I need to move on."

"Horses." Ben pointed to a shelf between two tables.

"Do you miss working with animals?" Riley asked.

"All the time. I always wanted to be in law enforcement, and I love it, but I miss being around animals."

"I understand completely," Riley said. "It's a lot easier for me to talk to animals than to people."

Ben nodded. "I've never been awkward around any animal, although I don't know if I'd want to work in a zoo. What about you?"

"Maybe, if I could pick my animal, I'd pick a sloth. Then I wouldn't have to chase my patient."

Ben smiled. "Mom said I told her I wanted an elephant. She said she pretended I wanted a toy elephant and got me one for my fourth birthday, but she knew better."

"Your poor mom," Riley snickered.

The greeter called out, "Mr. Ben, and Ms. Riley, I have your dinners for you."

"My treat," Ben said as Riley reached for her wallet.

"Thank you." Riley felt her cheeks warm. *Why did that feel awkward? It's not like we're on a date or anything.*

After they were back in the truck and on the road south of town, Riley said, "Remember we're burning your gas."

"If you feed Toby and Jordy when we get to the cabin, I'll carry in our supper and my backpack. I'm officially excited about spending the weekend at the cabin."

"I love being in the country. If you want to talk, I'd be happy to listen, but I won't push you," Riley said.

"I know that, thanks," Ben said. "Is our turn coming up soon? Or do we go past three more cotton fields and a peanut field?"

Riley chuckled. "We turn left in about a half mile after we pass the white house with a red barn first."

Ben snorted. "If you'd said to turn left at the white house that burned down twenty years ago, I would have known for sure I was in the country."

Riley jumped out and opened the gate. "We'll close it after the weekend."

"I've got options," Ben said. "I had a phone interview today for a deputy sheriff position not in my county. Of course, I always have the option of staying where I am, or I could go to veterinary school. I talked to Mom and Dad about school last year because I wondered if I'd regret not even trying to be accepted at school twenty years from now. Mom encouraged me to apply, and I did. Dad reminded me there were volunteer opportunities to work with kids in trouble, and he nailed it—that's why I had wanted to go into law enforcement."

Riley pointed to the right when they neared the lane to the cabin. "Not to mention the limited opportunity to work with elephants as a deputy sheriff."

Ben chuckled. "True."

"Here we are. Park along the side."

Riley hurried to the door and unlocked it while Ben opened the truck door for Toby and Jordy. Toby and Jordy toured the yard then went inside with Ben.

Riley placed the food dishes on the kitchen floor. When Toby sat in front of his, Jordy did the same. Riley twirled her finger then pointed. "Okay."

While Toby and Jordy gobbled their food, Riley filled the water dish then set the table. Before Riley joined Ben at the table, she opened the front door for the dogs. "Now, don't you run off."

Ben had set their food on the table. "Shall we do this family style?"

"Works for me." Riley read the sheet the greeter had included with their food then gave the list to Ben before she served herself shredded beef in creole sauce—ropa vieja; white rice, black beans, pan-fried, breaded boneless chicken breast—pollo empanizado; an empanada, and two fried sweet plantains.

"Bon Appetit." Riley lifted her large cup of sweet tea, and Ben tapped her cup with his.

"Bon Appetit." Before they finished eating, Toby scratched at the front door, and Riley let them inside.

After they finished eating, Riley said, "There's enough left for lunch tomorrow. I'll pack it up."

As Ben cleared the dishes, he asked, "Did you save room for dessert?"

"Always," Riley smiled. "I'll wash the dishes if you'll get the fire going."

"Deal."

As they sat on the sofa with their flan, Riley asked, "Can I hear more about your options?"

"Three options, so far, right? Stay where I am, transfer to a new county department, or veterinary school."

"I thought of a fourth option," Riley said. "You have a degree in biochemistry. The Georgia Bureau of Investigation Division of Forensic Sciences might be an option if research and analysis interest you."

Ben raised his eyebrows. "That's another good option."

"The other point is that you aren't under a timeline, right? You can take your time."

Ben frowned as he added another log to the fire. Toby jumped up to Ben's seat on the sofa, and Ben chuckled as he motioned with his hand. "Down, Toby. No fair stealing my seat."

Toby whimpered, and Riley said, "You are not crippled. You can get down."

Toby whimpered again, and Jordy jumped onto the sofa between Toby and Riley and grinned.

Riley glared. "Down."

Jordy jumped down, and Toby moaned then slid off the sofa.

Ben sat in the middle of the sofa next to Riley and patted the empty space next to him. "Here you go, gentlemen."

Toby yipped, and Riley raised her eyebrows.

"What did he say?" Ben asked.

"He said his plan worked. Old stinker."

"Thanks, Toby," Ben mumbled.

"Back to options." Riley sat on the sofa sideways tailor-fashion with her hands resting on her ankles, so she could see Ben. He shifted and put his arm across the back of the sofa as he watched her face.

"Which one is your favorite?" he asked.

Riley furrowed her brow and rubbed her hands. *My personal favorite isn't on the list.*

She reached for his free hand and held it between hers as she gazed at his face. "The thing is, the decision has to be yours. I can listen and make comments, but I don't know what's in your head."

Ben put his hand on top of one of her hands, and Riley smiled as she placed her other hand on top of his.

"You win." His eyes crinkled with his smile.

"Yay, me," Riley said. "Want to wrap up warm and take a walk? The sky's clear, and the moon's bright."

"Maybe it will clear the cobwebs in my head." Ben rose.

As they strolled to the end of the lane, Riley pulled up her hands into her sleeves as the strong north wind chilled her. "Brr. Cold. I need to have gloves in all my coat pockets, but it's worth it to be away from the city lights to see the sky so clearly."

"The supermoon gives the countryside a whole different look, doesn't it?"

Riley stuck her hands into her armpits for warmth as she stepped closer to Ben, and he put his arm around her shoulders.

"Much warmer, and you're blocking the wind." Riley snuggled closer. *This is nice. Ben's nice.*

Toby and Jordy dashed ahead and disappeared around the corner that headed to the hunting stand.

When Riley and Ben turned to go back to the cabin, Riley called, "We're going back."

Toby and Jordy raced past them before Riley and Ben were halfway back.

The four of them went inside, and Ben stoked the fire before Riley sat on the hearth to warm her back. The dogs flopped onto the rug near the sofa, and Ben sat on the rug near Riley

"I thought more about what you've said. If the reason you wanted to go into law enforcement was to make a difference with kids, it seems to make more sense to work directly with them rather than have the occasional chance encounter," Riley said.

"So, if I put aside working with kids, why law enforcement for a career?"

"Exactly." Riley rose to get away from the heat. "I think the back of my shirt was about to catch on fire."

After she climbed over the dogs to sit on the sofa, Ben rose and gazed at the bookcase. "The books sure cover a lot of different topics." He frowned as he strode closer and pulled out a book. "There's an envelope in this one. I use receipts from the gas station."

Riley's eyes widened. "I've been looking for an envelope."

"This one?" Ben handed it to her.

Riley smiled. "I thought I'd thrown this away. When Aunt Millie gave me directions to the cabin, I scribbled them down on it. See this? *White house red barn.* Do you know how many white houses with red barns there are in Charles County? I'd tell you, but I lost count—too many."

Ben chuckled.

"My paycheck and so-called reference letter the lawyer wrote were in there. I pulled out my paycheck and deposited it right away. We were sure all of us in the office got the same reference letter, and I never bothered to look at it."

She opened the envelope and shook it before she pulled out the sheet. "No key—just thought I'd check." When her smile turned to a frown as she peered at the page, Ben joined her on the sofa.

"You're right. The reference is so generic, it's meaningless, but what's that at the bottom?" Ben asked.

"A note from Dotty," Riley said as she read it aloud. "Riley, There's no hope for me, but I have hope for you. Get away. Watch out for Doc Junior. Thank you for being nice to me. I'm sorry we weren't friends. Dotty."

"This is almost sad, isn't it? Did Dotty have any friends? But wasn't Doc Junior dead?" Ben asked.

"I think the saddest part is that she thanked me for being nice. Many of the girls at work were a clique and kind of snippy and sometimes downright mean, but I don't know what I did. Dotty kept to herself." A tear slipped down Riley's cheek, and Ben brushed it away with his thumb.

"I suspect Dotty appreciated that you were a nice person and not mean. Too many people fall into the trap of trying to be part of the crowd."

Riley continued. "She gave this to me after we'd been told that Doc Junior was dead. If she wrote it before our meeting, wouldn't she have said something when she gave it to me?"

"Did she have a chance to write it after Doc Senior said Junior was dead?" Ben asked.

"Actually, she did. Doc Senior, the lawyer, accountant, and deputy were in the breakroom while I gathered Toby's things before I dropped off my key and picked up the envelope. She dropped the yellow note, but before I could tell her, she told me to go far away as fast as I could. I still don't know why she said that."

"I have a yellow note theory. The first few notes you found were not intended for you, but the last ones were because of your connection to the people who received the yellow notes. No one else has that same connection. That still doesn't explain who or why, though. So, what do you think?"

"Your theory makes sense, but the whole thing is really a tangle, isn't it?" Riley shook her head then covered her mouth as she yawned. "Excuse me, I think I'm tired."

"I'll take you home. I'll be able to find my way back here. Easy, right? Red house, white barn." Ben chuckled, and Riley snorted.

When Ben pulled into the driveway, he said, "I'd like to check around the house before you get out."

He strolled around the house then returned and opened the door for Toby and Jordy.

"I'd like to go into the house first just to be sure it's clear," Ben said.

Riley handed him the house key then climbed out of the truck while he went inside. He met her at the porch and grinned. "Welcome, it's nice to see you."

"You are so funny." Riley giggled.

"Now, I know you're tired. That was pretty lame, wasn't it?"

After Ben left, Riley said, "I'll mix the dough for cinnamon rolls and let it rise while I catch up on laundry. It's still a little early to go to bed."

While the dough rose, the dogs went outside, and Riley tossed a load of clothes into the washer then cleaned the kitchen. As she carried a dry load of clothes to her bedroom, her phone rang. *Aunt Millie.*

"How are you doing in your new house, Riley?"

"I love it. It's nice to be so close to work and the grocery store, but I loved the quiet at Grandma's cabin too."

"I'm so glad to hear that. Your diploma came in the mail today, and I'm having it framed. All my friends in Barton tell me you're an awesome veterinary tech, and they're asking me when you're going to veterinary school. Are you interested? And don't tell me you don't have the money like you did before because I still have the education money that Grandma saved for you set aside."

"I'm not ready to start up school again. Maybe later," Riley said. *Why did I have my diploma go to Aunt Millie's?*

"I knew you'd say that. You can apply. You won't hear back for a while anyway, and if you're admitted, you don't have to go."

Riley smiled. *Same way you talked me into going to college in the first place.* "I might do that."

"Glad to hear it. Do you need anything? Anything I can help you with?"

"I'm actually pretty set. Thank you for everything you've already done for me. I love Barton and my job, and I'm making friends."

"Of course, you are. You're a beautiful, smart young woman, and the nicest person I know. Love you, Riley. You're my favorite niece." Aunt Millie snickered.

"Love you, and you're my favorite aunt." Riley chuckled. *Our family joke.*

After they hung up, Riley opened the back door. "Ready to come inside yet?" Toby and Jordy trotted inside.

After Riley folded her clothes and put them away, the timer beeped, and Riley hurried to roll out her dough. After she cut the cinnamon rolls, she set them in a pan and covered them before she put them in the refrigerator.

After she flipped on her fireplace and brewed a cup of tea, her phone rang. *Ben.*

"Were you asleep? I'm sorry if I woke you."

"No. I just put a pan of cinnamon rolls in the refrigerator to bake in the morning. Is everything okay?"

"I've been thinking. The cabin's the best place in the world for thinking, isn't it? Did you see an obituary or anything? Did Eli Reeves say anything about Doc Junior?"

"No obituary, and Eli Reeves never said anything, but I don't see why he would. What do you think?"

"I'll drop by the sheriff's office tomorrow, and I think I'll always be a cop."

"Good. Now, you're down to three options."

"Or one. See you at the office in the morning. Good night. Call me if you need me."

After they hung up, Riley said, "Toby, Ben said he was down to one option. I wonder what that means?"

Toby yipped.

"You're right," Riley said. "He'll tell us tomorrow."

* * *

Riley woke early the next morning when her alarm sounded. When she bounded out of bed, Toby jumped up and growled. "It's okay, Toby. I'm just excited."

Toby flopped down on the floor and went back to sleep while Riley dressed. When she hurried into the kitchen, Jordy was asleep on the sofa.

She pulled out the cinnamon rolls, preheated the oven, and put on a pot of coffee. The oven and coffee were ready at the same time. After she poured her coffee and popped the rolls into the oven, Toby padded out of her bedroom, and Jordy jumped off the sofa. They met her at the back door and dashed outside.

When Toby and Jordy came inside, Riley fed them as her phone buzzed a text from Julie Rae.

"Do I still pick you up this morning?"

"Yes." Riley smiled. *No, Ben's not here.*

After Riley, Toby, and Jordy jumped into the truck, Julie Rae said, "I was just double-checking. I was trying not to embarrass myself, but I embarrassed myself."

Riley said, "That's exactly like something I would do. Is my social awkwardness catching?"

"Maybe it's a requirement for a successful veterinary career." Julie Rae wiggled her eyebrows as she parked at the veterinary hospital.

After they were inside the building, Julie Rae and Riley hurried to their early morning tasks. After Riley listened to the messages, she joined Julie Rae in the breakroom while Toby and Jordy slept at the receptionist's desk.

"I didn't hear anything that required an appointment today," Riley said as Julie Rae poured her a cup of coffee.

"That's out of our norm. Are we allowed to have a cinnamon roll before the rest of them show up?"

"We should probably test them because I made them a little differently this time."

While Riley plated their cinnamon rolls, Julie Rae asked, "Do you usually make them the same every time?"

"Never." Riley bit into her cinnamon roll while Julie Rae chuckled as she took a bite.

"I'll have to have one later for a quality check. I may like this batch the best. It has the perfect blend of cinnamon and butter," Julie Rae said.

Riley rolled her eyes. "Only a veterinarian who is well-acquainted with a chef has such a discerning palate."

"Speaking of which, if I didn't tell you, come to our house at five. The boys loved Toby and will be excited about Jordy. Pia called me last night. She's glad she's with her mom, and she and her sister have already had a fight. It sounded like that's normal for them."

The back door opened. "Thad and Claire," Doc said. "I'm used to Pia breezing in."

"I'll feel better when she gets back. It doesn't feel right," Riley said.

Thad and Claire strolled into the breakroom.

"Welcome, Claire," Julie Rae said. "Riley made cinnamon rolls to celebrate your first day. It's a tradition in our office."

"We're happy you're here," Riley said.

As Thad poured two cups of coffee, Claire said, "Thank you. I'm excited to be here."

Doc Thad gave Claire her cup and set his cup on the table before he plated two cinnamon rolls.

"It's going to be strange without Pia here. I think Zach is doing great, and that's saying quite a bit because you all are an intimidating force. I was terrified my first day," Thad said.

"As you should have been." Julie Rae drained her cup and refilled it.

Riley's phone buzzed a text. *Ben.*

"I'm in the back next to Julie Rae's truck."

"Ben's out back." Riley hurried to the back door, and when she opened it, Ben grinned. "Hi."

"Hi. I'm glad to see you." Riley gazed at his hazel eyes.

"I'll just stand here for a while." Ben returned her gaze.

Riley grabbed his arm. "Oh, come in. We're so silly." She looped her arm with Ben's.

"Hi, Ben," Julie Rae said. "This is Thad, he's our newest vet, and Claire, our newest receptionist."

Thad put out his hand, and the two men shook. "Nice to meet you, Ben."

Julie Rae poured Ben a cup of coffee while Riley plated a cinnamon roll.

Ben took a bite. "These are really good."

Amanda and Zach came inside.

"Hi, Claire, bring your coffee and cinnamon roll, and we'll get started," Amanda said.

Claire followed Amanda to the front.

"That's my cue to brew Amanda's tea and plate her cinnamon roll," Julie Rae said.

"That's become my job, Doc. Sorry we forgot to tell you," Riley said.

"As long as there's no cut in my paycheck, I can deal with it," Julie Rae said.

"I'm Zach." He held out his hand.

"Ben." The two men shook.

Riley took Amanda the cup of tea and the cinnamon roll.

"I feel like I should pull up a chair. Must be a party here."

Claire smiled. "I've never worked with warm feet before. I could get used to the fuzzy slippers."

"Our fuzzy slippers are superheroes that will turn into guard dogs if anyone bothers us," Amanda said.

"Riley, Amanda and I listened to the phone messages, and I tried to catch the client names, phone numbers, patient names, and why they called. Just to let you know, I failed miserably," Claire said. "I did fine on the names and phone numbers, but I had trouble discerning whether the clients called to give a patient history, dictate a memoir, or chat with Amanda. I can't criticize them, though, because I have a hard time leaving a voice mail message myself."

"It's a special skill that I don't have either. I'll show you how to review the messages, but I'm terrible at it. You save me a ton of time, Riley," Amanda said. "Our first appointment this morning is at eight, and I left nine o'clock open, but otherwise, we have appointments every fifteen minutes because I planned on Pia being here. Just a heads up that y'all better put on your running shoes."

"Glad I can help, Amanda, and I'll spread the word." Riley returned to the breakroom.

When Riley walked into the breakroom, Ben, Julie Rae, and Thad were laughing while Zach beamed.

Zach is funny? Riley refilled her cup. "I have news from Amanda. Our first appointment is at eight, and she has appointments scheduled every fifteen minutes except for nine o'clock, which she reserved for any fifteen-minute emergency. She recommended running shoes."

"We'll definitely get a workout. Zach, would you like to work with me? Everybody have another cinnamon roll. We'll need the extra energy."

Thad had already served himself a cinnamon roll as he joined the table. "My exact thought, Julie Rae, when Riley said every fifteen minutes. We'll take the first patient. Is that okay with you, Riley? It will give Julie Rae and Zach a chance to see how the masters do it."

"Challenge accepted, Bud." Julie Rae rose and grabbed another cinnamon roll.

"Tough crowd," Ben chuckled as he rose. "I'll check for survivors later."

Riley accompanied Ben to the back door.

"What do you have planned for your morning?" Riley asked.

"Nothing as exciting as yours. I'll drop by to see the sheriff, and I might stop by the gas station. See you later." Ben kissed Riley on the forehead then left.

She stared at the closed door. *Kiss and run? That wasn't fair.*

"Patient," Claire called out from the front.

"Well done," Amanda said.

Thad followed Riley as she hurried to the front, and Claire handed a folder to Riley. After Riley scanned the file, she handed it to Thad who read it and nodded.

"Okay if we go in together?" Thad asked.

"I think it's great," Riley said. "So, I'll weigh, interview, summarize, you observe, examine, prescribe?"

"Sounds organized. I like it. We can tweak as we go."

Julie Rae and Zach stood in the hallway.

"We like your plan too," Julie Rae said. "Right, Zach?"

"Yeah, except we'll tweak faster."

Thad snorted. "Game on."

CHAPTER THIRTEEN

The client opened the door for a four-year-old girl who wore a long, gauzy, red princess dress and carried a cat carrier. The girl set the carrier at Riley's feet. "My name is Allison, and Sir Cedwick doesn't feel good." Sir Cedwick yowled.

"I am so sorry. I'm Riley, and this is Doctor Thad. Come with us, and we'll help Sir Cedwick feel better." Riley picked up the carrier and cooed as she led the way to exam room one. "Sorry your foot hurts."

When they reached the exam room, Riley set the carrier on the exam table. "I need to help you out of the carrier and weigh you. Is that okay?" Sir Cedwick mewed, and she lifted him out. As she weighed the orange tabby, Riley asked, "How long has he been sick, Allison?"

"He told me his foot hurt the other day," Allison said.

"Thursday morning," the client added.

"Then Mommy called for a doctor appointment so we could come today."

"I'm off only on weekends, and Amanda said she'd squeeze us in. We really appreciate it," Allison's mother said.

"I'm going to take your temperature, Sir Cedwick, then Doc Thad will check your feet." After Riley took her temperature, she showed the thermometer to Doc Thad.

"A little elevated," he said, and Riley nodded.

Doc stepped closer to Sir Cedwick. "His right front paw looks swollen. Is that his foot that hurts, Allison?"

Sir Cedwick meowed, and Allison said, "Sir Cedwick said yes."

Doc Thad glanced at Riley, who nodded.

"I need to touch your foot; I apologize if I hurt you because I'll try hard to be as careful as I can."

Sir Cedwick meowed, and Allison said, "He said, okay."

As Doc Thad examined his foot, Sir Cedwick moaned. "Sorry, old fella," Doc Thad said. "Here we go. You have an ingrown nail."

Riley handed Doc Thad the clippers, and he raised his eyebrows. "Thanks."

After he snipped the offending nail, he said, "Riley will trim the rest of your nails while I write you a prescription for the infection."

Sir Cedwick purred as Riley examined the rest of his nails then trimmed them.

"He feels much better already," Allison said.

"Yes, he does." Riley lifted Sir Cedwick back into his carrier. "I'll meet you at Ms. Amanda's desk with his prescription."

Allison nodded. "Mommy, would you carry Sir Cedwick? I don't want to bump him."

After Riley gave the client Sir Cedwick's medicine, she met Doc Thad in exam room one. "If you'd like to finish your documentation and close your file, I'll clean the room and probably be done before you are. Not a challenge."

Before he left, Doc Thad said, "You and Allison understood everything Sir Cedwick said. Is that unusual?"

"Not at all. Most kids are tuned to animals."

"I think I was when I was a kid. Why didn't you outgrow being able to understand animals?"

"Guess I didn't want to." Riley shrugged as she changed the paper on the exam table.

After she cleaned the room, Riley checked in with Claire and Amanda. "Doc's finishing up his documentation."

"Doc Julie Rae and Zach are in exam room three." Claire glanced at the clock. "Your next is in ten minutes."

After Riley refilled her coffee cup, Thad joined her in the breakroom and sat at the table with his coffee. "How long have you and Ben been together?"

Riley smiled. "He brought in two dogs and a cat that were in a crash a week and a half ago, but it seems like I've known him forever. What about you and Claire?"

"I've known Claire since fourth grade. Our class was walking up the stairs to the second floor when the boy behind her lifted her skirt. She slammed him in the nose with her elbow, and he fell down the stairs. She was suspended for two days for fighting. When she returned to our classroom, I asked her to marry me, but I didn't get too close in case she decided to slug me. She tells it a different way, by the way."

Riley laughed. "I don't believe a word of it because Claire's so sweet."

"You'd think so, wouldn't you?" Thad wiggled his eyebrows, and Riley laughed harder.

"We can hear you," Claire called from the front desk. "And I'm the sweetest thug you'll ever meet."

Thad raised his eyebrows. "See?" he whispered, and Riley put her hand over her mouth to stifle her giggle.

After Thad and Riley saw their next patient, Claire came into the exam room while Riley cleaned.

"Ms. Riley, you have a very important visitor." Claire's eyes crinkled as she smiled.

Riley cocked her head and furrowed her brow then followed Claire to the front. Dylan Price stood at the receptionist's desk with a five-year-old girl who struggled to balance the large men's shoebox that she held with both hands. She wore a green tutu over her jeans and a sparkly, red headband to hold her long, red hair out of her face.

The girl's face brightened, and her dimples deepened when she saw Riley. "Ms. Riley, I'm Mini-me."

Dylan laughed. "We were at the gas station, and Maddie told everyone she had a surprise for Ms. Riley. One lady said she was Ms. Riley's mini-me. On the way here, Maddie told me to call her Mini-me."

"Mommy and I made special cookies for you, Ms. Riley, because you helped my baby sister, and she isn't sick." Maddie looked around. "Where can I put your cookies?"

Claire cleared a spot on the receptionist's desk. "You can put them here, Maddie."

Maddie looked at the ceiling.

Claire cleared her throat. "I'm sorry, I meant to say Mini-me. You can put them here, Mini-me."

Maddie beamed as she set the box on the desk then lifted the lid. "They are fancy."

Riley raised her eyebrows at the dog bone-shaped cookies iced with red frosting. "They certainly are fancy. Did you make these yourself, Mini-me?"

"Mommy helped. I'm not allowed to touch the oven because it is hot. I picked red because it's my favorite color. I like your red shirt."

"Thank you, Mini-me. I like your red shirt and headband and your green tutu. Is it okay if I eat a cookie now?"

Maddie turned to her dad. "Daddy?"

He smiled as he opened a small envelope and pulled out a pair of small garden gloves.

"Mommy washed my gloves for me." Maddie put on her gloves before she picked up a cookie and handed it to Riley.

Riley held up her cookie and examined it. "I never thought about a dog bone cookie before." She bit off one tip of the bone. "Mmm. This is really good. It's as tasty as it is beautiful, and I love red."

Maddie handed a cookie to Amanda and one to Claire. When Thad strolled to the desk, Maddie handed him a cookie. "Me and Mommy made these for Ms. Riley, but Daddy said Ms. Riley likes to share."

"Thank you." Thad bit into the cookie. "This is the best cookie I've ever had."

Maddie flopped down on the floor next to Amanda's chair and Toby and giggled when Toby gave her fingers a quick kiss. Jordy stretched across Amanda's feet to put his head close to Maddie. "You got good doggies here," she said.

"Yes, we do," Amanda said. "Toby and Jordy like you."

Dylan stepped away from the counter as he set his backpack on a chair. "Riley, when I was offered the Operations Manager position at the new distribution center, my wife, Tamara, and I had a long discussion because my sister still lived in Barton. Daphne had never been easy to get along with, and she never liked my wife, but Tamara told me family was still family. I don't think you knew Daphne, but we were surprised that she wasn't as negative about the move as we expected."

He opened his backpack. "We've been cleaning out my sister's apartment, and I found some papers that are vet notes and records, as far as I can tell. Daphne's journal is in the envelope too. It looked like more vet clinic notes to me. If nothing is useful to you, toss it." Dylan handed Riley a large manila envelope.

"Thanks, Dylan. I'll check to see if Daphne had any patient records that we'd want to include in our records."

"How's the baby doing?" Amanda asked.

"She's fine. My wife took her to our doctor, and he didn't find any tissue injury or swelling. Tamara and Riley's mini-me wanted to do something for you all."

"I thought stickers was best then Mommy and I thought you'd like cookies. I like stickers and cookies."

"Would you like to have a cookie with us?" Riley asked.

Maddie looked at her dad, and he nodded. She took two and gave one to her dad.

As she nibbled on her cookie, Maddie said, "I have a dance for you, Ms. Riley."

"I'd love to see it, but give your cookie to your dad so it won't break," Riley said.

Maddie bowed her head as she handed her cookie and gloves to her father who returned her head bow. She raised her hands with a flair then twirled and skipped across the room before she slid into a crumpled pose face down on the floor with her arms outstretched, and everyone applauded. Maddie jumped up and bowed. "Mommy said this is my Swan Lake dance."

"It's perfect," Riley said. "Just like a ballerina on stage. Thank you for the cookies and the dance." Dylan handed Maddie her cookie then took her hand.

"We need to go to the grocery store," Dylan said. "Thanks again for being here."

As Doc Julie Rae accompanied Dylan and Maddie to their car, Claire put her hand over her heart. "I'm a Mini-me fan."

"Aren't we all?" Amanda sighed as their next client arrived, and Doc Julie Rae returned from the parking lot then carried the box of cookies to the breakroom. Riley followed Doc to put the manila folder with the rest of her things.

"You don't expect to find anything useful in Daphne's papers, do you?" Doc asked.

"No, but if I can take some of the burden off Dylan, I don't mind taking the papers. I can't imagine how he and his wife deal with all the stress of moving to a new job in a new town with a baby and my mini-me then he has even more on his shoulders when his sister dies suddenly."

"I offered to deliver a meal on Sunday or Monday, and Dylan's going to let me know which day works best. Charlie loves to welcome new people to town with a meal."

"Riley, you're up," Claire said.

"What a great way to help them." Riley hurried to the front.

At eleven forty-five, Riley and Zach had sanitized and resupplied all the exam rooms for Monday and were in the trauma room when Doc Julie Rae stopped by. "When you've ready, we're meeting in the breakroom."

"Am I in trouble?" Zach asked after Doc left.

"Of course, you are," Riley said. "It's not my turn."

Zach rolled his eyes. "That makes as much sense as my question did."

Riley nodded. "If Doc had a problem with one of us, we'd have known it long before now."

When they walked into the breakroom, Julie Rae said, "We almost started without you. We need to make a decision about Riley's cookies. Do we divide them equally?"

"I vote we let Amanda take them all home," Zach said, and everyone laughed.

"Aren't you the gentleman," Riley said. "I think the people with kids at home take what they want, as long as I get two, I'm fine."

Claire said, "Let's do what Riley's doing. Take what we want then put the rest in the freezer for next week."

"Or we could fuss about it for a while then do what Claire said." Amanda rose and stretched her back.

"Logical solution, Claire," Julie Rae said. "I heard from Pia. She's hoping to be home next week sometime. Her mother is improving, and she and her sister have a truce."

"Zach and I can drop off a few cookies at Pia's house," Amanda said.

Julie Rae nodded. "Thad and Riley, tell us about how you managed your patients today. Zach and I tried to copy you, but I don't think we were that successful. I kept forgetting to go in with Zach."

Thad gave a quick explanation. "It worked well today with the patients we had."

Riley nodded. "We might have to be flexible on occasion, but I suggest we try it for at least a week or two."

"Agreed," Julie Rae said. "Everybody have a great weekend."

Riley's phone buzzed a text from Ben.

"Here. No rush."

She replied, "Okay."

After everyone took a few cookies and left, Riley wrapped the rest for the freezer while Julie Rae turned off lights and checked the front door lock.

Toby and Jordy dashed outside past Riley and Julie Rae.

Julie Rae waved at Ben as he opened the door for the dogs then hurried to her truck. "See you at six."

When Riley climbed into Ben's truck, he asked, "How was work?"

"It was great. Doc Thad and I tried out his idea to cut back on the amount of time the client and patient spent in an exam room.

We went in together to avoid the amount of time he spent asking the client the same questions I'd asked and the amount of time I spent looking for him and giving him a quick summary."

When Ben reached the intersection to the road, Riley said. "I'd like to stop by the house to grab a change of clothes before we head to the cabin for lunch. We're having leftovers, right?"

"I was hoping we would," Ben said as he turned to go to the house.

Riley continued, "We cut maybe five minutes off the total time. I was surprised. Doc Julie Rae like the idea too. We're all going to practice it next week, and Doc Rae said Pia may be back next week. Might be a good excuse for cinnamon rolls."

When Ben pulled into the driveway, Riley turned and gazed at him. "Can you tell I'm excited to spend the weekend with you?" He smiled as he met her gaze.

She hopped out of the truck. "Won't be long."

Riley returned with a tote bag. As Ben backed out of the driveway, she asked, "What about you? Did you sleep okay at the cabin? How was your morning?"

Ben smiled. "I slept better at the cabin than I've slept since I was on the farm. I think I need country air to thrive."

"That's it," she said. "That's exactly why I feel at home here. What did you do all morning?"

"I stopped at the gas station to check on your SUV. I met the mechanic, Isaac, nice guy. One tire came in late yesterday, but he's waiting for the other two, so he can put all three on at once. If he gets the other two today, he'll let us know. He told me some people are hinting Doctor Witmer was into some illegal activity, but he knew it wasn't true because Doctor Witmer has been a youth pastor at his church since Isaac was a kid. Another interesting tidbit is he told me Doc Witmer met his business partner at the gas station once, and the doc left Jordy in his truck because Jordy kept growling and barking at her. Isaac thought that was strange because he said Jordy likes everybody."

Ben drove up the driveway to the cabin then parked. "More after lunch, okay?"

Toby and Jordy jumped out of the truck and raced around the cabin while Riley climbed out with her backpack and tote.

"I had a second key made while I was out," Ben said. "I hope that's okay."

"Smart idea. I'm not sure Aunt Millie carries a key. I got the impression she used the key under the mat," Riley said.

"I'll pull out the food from the refrigerator and preheat the oven," Ben said as Riley hurried to the bathroom to change.

Riley changed into clean jeans and a red plaid shirt and brushed her hair. When she went into the kitchen she said, "I need a red sparkly headband." While she placed the food into the oven to warm, she told Ben about her mini-me.

Ben laughed. "Well, that sure explains what Isaac meant when he told me I'd just missed your mini-me at the gas station."

After they ate and cleaned the kitchen, Ben asked, "Ready for a walk? I'll tell you about the rest of my day."

As they strolled to the hunting stand, the dogs ran ahead of them.

"I had a job interview," Ben said.

"Another phone interview?"

"No. I interviewed with Sheriff Dunn," he said.

"My Sheriff Dunn?" Riley stopped. "You interviewed with Sheriff Samuel Dunn? Why am I just now hearing about this?"

"Sheriff asked me to keep it quiet until he and I had a chance to talk."

"Even from me?" Riley narrowed her eyes.

"Not answering that. I think this might be a slippery slope straight into a deadly trap. Should I stop talking?"

"No. I want to hear more, but I'm mad at you."

Ben nodded his head. "My counselor told me to talk to my sheriff about my concerns and interests, and I did. My sheriff knew Sheriff Dunn was in the search process for two deputies and contacted him for me. Sheriff Dunn and I had a couple of phone interviews before he invited me to come to his office today for an interview."

"Still mad inside, but that's really exciting." Riley giggled. "How did the interview go? Is the sheriff someone you could work for? Did he offer you the job on the spot? He should have. I'm sorry my mini-me isn't here—we'd do the happy dance for you."

"Is it okay if I make this dramatic?" Ben widened his eyes.

"Quit looking innocent, and the answer is no." Riley pressed her lips together to keep from smiling.

Ben chuckled. "You're fun."

When Riley elbowed him, he said, "Okay, okay. So, Sheriff Dunn has two positions—one night shift, and the other day shift. Drumroll, please. He offered me the day position. I told him I'd think about it, and I did for two seconds then accepted the position. I'll give two weeks' notice on Monday and start with Sheriff Dunn in two weeks and two days."

"That's awesome!" Riley hugged him, and Ben put his cheek on the top of her head. "Mmm. You smell good."

When she released him, he said, "Tell me again how awesome I am."

Riley laughed. "Aren't you full of yourself?"

Ben nodded. "Yep."

"The hunting stand is ahead," Riley said.

When they reached it, Ben examined it. "Okay if we go up?"

"Go ahead. I'll stay down here with the boys."

After he climbed to the top, he called down. "Can you get up here? The rungs are fairly far apart."

Ben's smart. "I climbed up there, but it was a struggle," Riley said.

"I'll bet." Ben climbed back down.

On their walk back to the cabin, Ben said, "I did tell Sheriff Dunn that I asked you about Dr. Truman, Junior, and you said you hadn't seen an obituary. He's going to look into it." Ben smiled. "He also said I'd be a good investigator for his team. I was so shocked that I couldn't breathe for a minute or two after that."

"You really are smart; you absolutely belong in law enforcement." Riley quickened her pace to keep up with Ben's long stride. "Slow down. Did you know you walk faster when you're thinking?"

"Sorry." Ben slowed his steps.

"Anything special you'd like to do before we go to Julie Rae's?" Riley asked.

"I need to find an apartment. Maybe we could drive around to see what's available," Ben said as they strolled toward the cabin.

"Why don't you stay at the cabin? I'll check with Aunt Millie."

"Don't bother," Ben said as she pulled out her phone and raised her eyebrows.

"Why not? I thought you liked it."

"I do, and it's a perfect place for the weekend, but I'd like to be closer to town."

"Makes sense. If you don't find anything available right away, you can stay at the cabin until you find something. I'll make sure Aunt Millie doesn't have other plans for it any time soon." After Riley sent a quick text, she dropped her phone back into her pocket. "What else would you like to do this weekend?"

"Split and stack wood. I've missed that."

"I'd enjoy that. You split, and I'll stack. I'll show you the shed then we can drive around before we go to the Sorensens'."

Riley opened the shed door, and her phone buzzed a text while Ben examined the tools.

"Aunt Millie said there's no conflict because the cabin is mine. I didn't know that, but maybe she didn't mean literally. Anyway, no conflict."

After Ben locked the shed, and Riley grabbed her work clothes, they loaded up and headed to town.

"Something else that Isaac told me is that Dr. Witmer's business partner is in town. He thinks Termaine and Witmer

Research will open soon, but he didn't know what their product is," Ben said. "A customer came into the shop while we were talking, and he said TWR probably has a government contract for a satellite part or something. Another customer said that Alyse Termaine bought out Doc Witmer's interest from his sister for a song. I don't know how much is conjecture, but the gas station is a great place to get ideas, isn't it?"

When they reached the outskirts of town, Riley asked, "What kind of apartment do you want?"

"They have to allow dogs so Toby and Jordy can visit. I'd like a washer and dryer in the apartment, but the rent has to be reasonable."

"Should be easy to find," Riley said.

"I have simple tastes. I don't need anything fancy—no pool, gym, or clubhouse, but it would be nice if it had a fireplace, a place to stack wood, a pistol range, and a hunting stand."

Riley choked then giggled. "I'm so glad I wasn't drinking coffee. Simple tastes—you are hilarious."

Ben smiled. "It's great that you think so; not everybody gets my humor."

Riley nodded. "Same."

Ben drove through the neighborhoods of new apartments and townhouses. "Can't really tell much, can you?"

"Not as far as the inside is concerned, but the work trucks in the parking lot and outside toys in the yards indicated young families."

"You're right, and there was no trash blowing around or litter along the street."

After they drove through a few more neighborhoods, Ben said, "It was easy for me to find an apartment in Conrad because I was familiar with the neighborhoods and the reputations of the landlords. I probably need some recommendations."

"We should ask Ms. Helen. I'll bet she'd have some ideas for us."

"Great idea," Ben said.

"Let's go to the house; we can take notes and maybe make some calls while Toby and Jordy get some outside time and rest before we go to Julie Rae's."

After Toby and Jordy were in the backyard, Riley picked up her phone. "I don't think I'll call. I'll send her a text because if I call she'll think something's wrong and dash over without answering."

"My mother's like that," Ben said. "I send her a text when I need to talk, so I don't scare her. I asked her a long time ago why phone calls scare her, and she told me that kidnappers use the victim's phone to call about the ransom. I didn't understand for a long time, but I'm starting to get it since I met you."

"I always text Aunt Millie unless it's an emergency because she spends most of her days in meetings or traveling, but I have a vague sense that she said something similar: she'd have a ticket in hand to fly home before she finished dialing. If she did, that was a long time ago, wasn't it?"

Riley's phone buzzed a text from Ms. Helen. After she read the text, Riley said, "Ms. Helen has a friend with two two-bedroom houses to rent. She sent me the addresses so we could drive by. If they don't look right or if you'd prefer an apartment, she has another friend. We have plenty of time to run by then come back here to feed the dogs before we leave for dinner."

Ben called the dogs inside then the four of them headed to the truck. When they drove by the first house, Riley said, "This is cute."

Ben pulled into the driveway and lowered his window. Riley tilted her head in puzzlement then lowered hers. When Ben turned off the engine, Riley's eyes widened. "Traffic noise from the by-pass. This is a no unless you would adjust to the sound of speeding trucks all night."

Ben started the engine. "You nailed it. I'd stay awake and fume about the speeding trucks."

They raised their windows. "That's too bad. That was a cute little house. How did you know to check for noise?"

Ben backed out and headed to the next address. "I knew I'd be working nights at the sheriff's department in Pomeroy. Dad told me to look for toys around the buildings when I looked for an apartment because children meant noise in the day while I slept. Most of the residents in my current apartment building are retired. There are still children around occasionally, but one or two children can't match the noise of a building full of kids." Ben smiled. "That was when I realized Dad was the wisest man I knew after my teenage years when I thought he didn't know anything."

Riley laughed. "I remember that feeling. Aunt Millie went from an embarrassment to an extraordinary woman that I adored."

When they drove past the next house, Ben nodded. "It has possibilities." He drove down the street then around the neighborhood before he returned to the house. "The backyard is fenced, and the house has blinds. The neighborhood is well-kept but not at the level of a professional landscaper, which is good."

"I'll let Ms. Helen know this house has possibilities and ask her how much the rent is," Riley said.

While Riley texted, Ben drove back to her house. After Toby and Jordy ate and romped in the backyard, Ms. Helen returned Riley's text.

"Ms. Helen isn't sure about the price, but we could meet the owner at the house tomorrow. What do you think?"

"Sounds good. Pick a time."

Riley sent her text. "I told her ten o'clock."

When they reached Julie Rae's, Ben said, "I see Kenny and Freddy peeking out the window. I think they're wearing cowboy hats. Wonder how long they've been there?"

"No telling, but I'm kind of excited myself. I can't wait to see them with Toby and Jordy."

Before they climbed out of the truck, Riley's phone buzzed a text from Ms. Helen, and she read it. "We're set for ten o'clock. We can meet Richard, he's the owner, at the house."

After Julie Rae opened the door, the dogs dashed past her toward the boys' squeals in the kitchen.

"Welcome to the Wild West, folks." Julie Rae had tied a pink bandana around her neck with the knot to the side, cowgirl style. "Come on in, and set a spell."

On their way to the kitchen, she said, "That's about it for cowboy talk from me. Charlie and the boys have been studying the old West this week."

When they reached the kitchen, Charlie stood at the sink as he pulled corn husks down and away from the cobs. He wore a chuck wagon-style white apron and a blue bandana around his neck with the knot tied in back, cowboy style.

"Howdy, pardners. Welcome to the cookhouse. Your menu tonight is courtesy of them thieving rustlers, the Sorensen brothers, out yonder." He motioned toward the sliding glass door as the two boys raced around the yard with Toby and Jordy. The boys wore dark brown cowboy hats, brown vests, and black bandanas tied around their thighs.

Julie Rae smiled. "Your bandanas are on the bar if you don't want to be mistaken for city slickers."

Ben selected a blue bandana and tied it on with the knot tied in front. "This is how the frontier marshals wore their bandanas."

"Here's your badge, Marshal." Charlie set a costume badge on the bar for Ben.

Riley folded a red bandana into a wide headband then tied it on top of her head with a bow. "This is how cowgirls wore their bandanas."

Ben stuck his thumbs in his belt and swaggered to the backyard. "I was looking for them thieving cattle rustlers. You boys see any?"

"Nobody around here except us cowboys." Kenny giggled.

"You cowboys let me know if you see any trouble." Ben saluted the boys and returned to the kitchen.

Charlie said, "The boys are having hot dogs and macaroni and cheese from a box, and we're having charcoaled burgers, potato salad, and smoked corn on the cob. The rustlers set their own menu and let me have a hand in ours." Charlie set the boys' pinwheels on the table. "Honey, you want to get those two yahoos cleaned up to eat? I'll dish up their supper."

"Shall I pour their milk?" Riley asked.

Charlie placed two blue campfire coffee cups on the counter. "That'd be great and grab the ketchup for the table."

Riley poured their milk and set the cups and ketchup on the table while Ben set the pinwheels near the boys' placemats. After Charlie dished up the macaroni and cheese and assembled the buns and boiled hot dogs, he set the food on the counter to cool then tied the corn husks in ponytails with kitchen string to hold them away from the corn. Riley watched in fascination as Charlie mixed chopped jalapeno and cilantro into slightly softened butter then spread the butter on the ears of corn.

The boys rushed to the kitchen and bowed to Riley and saluted Ben with two fingers like he had saluted them outside. Ben returned the salute before he placed their plates on the table.

"Cowboys were polite, even cattle rustlers," Kenny said. "They bowed to cowgirls."

Freddy added, "So nobody would know they were cattle rustlers."

"Smart move," Riley said.

"I have cold apple cider, coffee, and wine for us to take outside while I grill," Charlie said.

Julie Rae came into the room. "I'll take care of the drinks. I'm having wine. Riley?"

"Sounds good."

"Chuck wagon coffee for me," Ben said.

"And me," Charlie added.

Julie Rae poured two glasses of wine then two cups of coffee. Ben carried his coffee and the basket of tortilla chips as he followed Charlie, who carried his cup and the platter of corn to be roasted. Julie Rae carried the large bowl of salsa and her glass of wine while Riley carried the four individual salsa bowls and her glass.

Charlie set the corn on the unlit side of the grill then closed the lid.

"Is that mesquite?" Ben asked.

"Sure is."

Julie Rae sipped her wine and asked, "What's new?"

Riley smiled. "Ben has news."

"Good parry, Riley." Charlie grinned.

"It was, wasn't it? I start a new job in two weeks." Ben said.

"Is that good?" Julie Rae asked.

"Yes, Sheriff Dunn hired me for the day shift. I'm moving to Barton."

Julie Rae's eyes widened, and Charlie held out his hand and the men shook. "Congratulations, Ben."

"That's a huge, wonderful surprise." Julie Rae hugged Ben. "Will we have cinnamon rolls on your first day?"

"That's a good idea, Doc," Riley said. "Ben can take a batch to work, and we'll celebrate in our breakroom."

"And one for the cook." Charlie raised an eyebrow. "It's a tradition."

"I need details. Do you have a place to live? Are you moving yourself? What else do I want to ask?" Julie Rae asked.

Ben chuckled. "Ms. Helen arranged for us to look at a house tomorrow. It belongs to her friend, Richard."

"Mr. Richard takes good care of his properties, and his rent is reasonable," Julie Rae said. "His houses aren't often available. It's not the one near the by-pass, is it?"

"No, we drove past that one, but the traffic noise is too much, and it's probably worse at night."

"That's what I'd think too," Julie Rae said.

Charlie asked, "Do you have furniture to move? I'll help you move in. Julie Rae can wrangle the boys."

"That would be a vacation for you." Julie Rae giggled.

Charlie nodded. "I'm sure it will take us at least three days, right Ben?"

"Sure would." Ben grinned.

Freddy opened the sliding glass door. "We're finished. Can we play with Toby and Jordy now?"

"I'll check your plates first," Julie Rae said.

"Five minutes." Freddy closed the door.

Ben chuckled. "I could never get away with that either."

CHAPTER FOURTEEN

Charlie opened his grill and pressed the steaming corn with two fingers. "If you all want to pull together the fixings, I'll throw the burgers on the grill. Cheese for everyone?"

Riley and Ben nodded then Riley picked up the empty chip basket, and Ben stacked the salsa bowls as Julie Rae opened the sliding door for them.

"We're finished now, Mommy," Freddy said.

Julie Rae inspected their plates and glanced around the area under their chairs. "Okay, you can clear your plates and go outside with Toby and Jordy." The boys rushed their plates to the sink then ran outside.

When Charlie brought their burgers on toasted hamburger buns inside and plated them, Riley squinted at hers.

Julie Rae smiled. "Does your slice of cheddar cheese look a little lumpy? Charlie puts jalapeno on the burger then the cheese."

"Sounds good," Riley piled onion, tomato, pickles, and lettuce on hers before she cut the burger in half. When she bit into her oversized burger, juice ran down her fingers. "Now I see why we put extra napkins on the table, and this totally ruins me from ever ordering a fast-food burger, Charlie."

"My goal in life." Charlie beamed. "You need a burger, you come see us."

While they ate, Ben watched as the boys and dogs ran past the glass door from one direction then the other. "I love the entertainment that goes along with dinner here. Toby and Jordy are certainly going to sleep well tonight, and I'll bet the boys will too."

Julie Rae smiled. "We're going to the county animal shelter tomorrow. They are holding their semi-annual Go Home with Your Best Friend event, complete with prizes, a local band, and of course, cats and dogs to adopt."

"Kenny and Freddy would be out in the truck waiting if they knew, wouldn't they?" Riley asked.

"You know it," Julie Rae said.

"Have you heard any more about the note that my Julie Rae found?" Charlie asked.

"No, I sent it to the sheriff and Eli Reeves, who works with the GBI, but they are very neglectful and forget to update me on their investigations," Riley said.

Ben chuckled. "Pure oversight, I'm sure."

Julie Rae smiled. "Do you think Jordy will miss Toby when Pia comes back?"

"Maybe a little," Riley said, "but I think they are trying to outdo each other and have a feeling those two old guys are looking forward to taking it easy. We might have to arrange an occasional play date, for old times' sake."

"Ready for dessert?" Charlie asked after everyone had eaten.

Riley and Ben groaned then Riley said, "I can't turn down dessert."

Charlie opened the refrigerator. "The boys and I bought pecans from a local farmer this week then the boys learned how to use our pecan nutcracker. It was a perfect rainy day activity. They took turns using the nutcracker and the pick." Charlie pulled out the pecan-topped cheesecake. "The boys voted for pecan cheesecake over pecan pie."

Julie Rae called the boys in, and they dashed to their seats. She raised her eyebrows, and they hurried to wash their hands.

After everyone had finished dessert, the boys cleared the dishes then Julie Rae herded them to the bathroom for their baths, and Charlie loaded the dishwasher.

Riley stood at the sliding glass door and watched the orange deepen to red on the horizon as Ben stood behind her with his hands on her shoulders. When Riley sighed, Ben asked, "Are you having any second thoughts?"

"I'm happy you're moving to Barton," she said. "I can't help but wonder what Jordy would have to say about Dr. Witmer's partner."

"I hadn't thought about that. I'm not surprised when you understand Toby, but I had forgotten you understand Jordy too."

When Julie Rae returned from bathing the boys, she had changed her shirt. "I should get credit for a bath too as soaked as my shirt gets sometimes. The boys are reading in their rooms."

"Sounds good to me," Riley said. "We need to take the old dogs home, so they can rest too."

"And me," Ben said. "Thank you so much for dinner."

Charlie packaged extra slices of pecan cheesecake for them to take home.

"This is awesome, Charlie, thank you," Riley said. "I loved our chuck wagon meal."

On their way to Riley's house, Ben asked, "Do we hang around the gas station tomorrow in case Alyse Termaine shows up?"

Riley giggled. "Sounds like a wonderful idea, but we have an appointment to look at a house, and you owe me a shooting lesson."

"True, and I wouldn't mind working on the hunting stand to make it easier for you to get up to the platform."

"We planned to split and stack wood too. I'm glad your apartment is only an hour away, so you can spend the whole day here, but I'll be excited when you're down the street or around the corner. Of course, we could also do nothing except look at your house then go to the animal shelter party."

Before they turned to go into Riley's neighborhood, Jordy's shackles rose, and he growled as a car passed them.

"Can we follow that car without looking like we're following that car?" Riley asked.

"Sure can." Ben lightly accelerated as he passed their turn. "Any special reason? What did Jordy say?"

"Jordy said *bad man*, but I didn't see the driver, did you?"

"No, I was watching for my turn." Ben frowned as the car passed the grocery store. "I was hoping his destination is one where any other car would logically go too."

When the car pulled into the gas station, Ben said, "Good. We need milk and dog treats."

"No we don't." Riley's eyebrows raised. "Oh, I get it."

Ben parked in the shadows near the store while Jordy kept up his low growl as he stared at the car.

Riley squinted to see the driver, but the angle of her view was bad, and she could only see that a tall figure stood near the pump in front of another car that had pulled in at the one behind it. She raised on her knees after she moved to Ben's seat for a better look, but a post obstructed her view. Jordy's growl grew in intensity.

"I understand," Riley said. "Maybe Ben can tell us what the driver looks like."

After he finished refueling, the driver climbed into the car and drove away while the man at the other pump went inside the store. Jordy huffed a final growl then lay down on the seat with Toby. Riley peered at the store, and Ben was in conversation with a customer as they walked out. Ben strode to the truck and climbed into the driver's seat.

"That was informative," Ben said. "What did Jordy say?"

"Stay away, bad man. What was informative?"

"The driver wasn't a man. According to the guy behind me in line, who filled up at the pump behind her, it was Alyse Termaine, and the ugliest woman he'd ever seen in his entire life. Wonder why Jordy called her *bad man*?"

Riley shrugged. "I may have misinterpreted or maybe Jordy calls all people men."

"I could see how he might, especially a tall woman. What did you see?" Ben turned to glance at the pumps. "I guess you couldn't see much. I wanted to park here so the driver couldn't see you in the truck, but I guess I did too good a job."

"If nothing else, we verified that Jordy doesn't like Alyse Termaine, but I don't know if that's significant."

As Ben waited for traffic before he left the parking lot, Riley stared at a car that pulled up to the store. "Go back. I need gum or something."

"What? Okay." Ben circled the parking lot then parked in front of the store.

Riley jumped out of the truck and strolled into the store behind the man with the thick arms and muscular build who had just parked. As she wandered the aisles, she glanced at the man's broken nose then picked up a jar of baby food and read the label. *Yep, it's the accountant.* She set down the jar then stood in line behind him. She glanced at his shoes and coughed into her elbow to hide her smirk. *Cowboy boots that match.*

While she waited, she pulled out her phone and scrolled then sent a text to Ben: "Check out guy who leaves in front of me."

When her phone buzzed a reply text, she yawned then glanced at Ben's reply. "Okay."

After the accountant paid and while the clerk sacked the bottle of water and bag of chips, Riley asked the clerk, "Do you have any almond milk?"

"No, Miss. Sorry."

She strolled out the door behind the man and headed to Ben's truck.

Ben's eyes narrowed. "Who was the man?"

"Doc Truman introduced him as the accountant my last day at the clinic in Pomeroy."

"I see what you mean. He didn't look like an accountant to me either. What's he doing here?"

"Did either of the dogs say anything?" Riley asked.

Ben frowned. "Toby growled as you walked out of the store, but I didn't realize he might have been growling at the man in front of you."

"Good boy, Toby." Riley rubbed his ears. "Did you see that man before?"

Toby yipped, and Riley said, "Thanks."

"And?" Ben asked. "I hate that you and Toby can have private conversations in front of me, by the way."

"The man had been at the Truman vet clinic more than once."

"Other than the fact that we are suspicious of everything and everyone, there's nothing suspicious about him if he was the Trumans' accountant," Ben said.

"Do you suppose he's also the accountant for TWR?"

"It's hard to believe he's an accountant at all." Ben turned to return to Riley's house. After Ben parked, and the dogs jumped out to explore the front yard, Riley asked, "Are you coming in?"

"I'd like to, but I probably need to head back."

Riley raised her eyebrows. "It's a fifteen-minute drive to the cabin. Have you been stressing about the drive back to Carson all day?"

Ben chuckled. "I think I have. I suppose there's no recovery from that boneheaded statement, is there?"

Riley smirked as she opened the truck door. "I can offer you a warm fire before your long trek up the hill."

"Okay, you talked me into it."

When they were inside, Ben strode to the fireplace and turned it on. "Just trying to redeem myself." He rushed to the sofa in an attempt to beat Toby who jumped up next to Riley and grinned.

"You need a bigger sofa," Ben said.

"Give me a minute." Riley rose and hurried to the kitchen, and Toby followed her. Ben sat in the middle of the sofa; when Riley returned, she sat next to him. Toby trotted toward the fireplace and flopped down next to Jordy.

Ben rested his arm across the back of the sofa. "Well done."

"It was devious but easier than convincing Toby to move."

Toby raised his head and yipped.

"I'm not sure I believe you, but well done," Riley said.

"I'm going to guess," Ben narrowed his eyes at Toby. "Part two of Toby's plan."

Riley giggled. "Something like that—not bad."

"I think I haven't been so much stressing about returning to Carson as wishing I could load up and move here. I seem to be ignoring the minor detail that I'd need a place to live, and I still haven't given my notice to the department. Want to go for a walk around the block then I'll be tired enough to go back to the cabin."

"I'd like that." Riley pulled on her warmest coat and pulled up the hood.

When they reached the door, Jordy slept, and Toby raised his head.

"Aren't you going?" Riley asked.

Toby closed his eyes, and she shrugged.

"One block or two?" Ben asked as they headed down the sidewalk.

"Let's go two."

As they walked, Ben told her about Sheriff Dunn's guidance on law enforcement in a small town where everyone knows everyone else. "He said it takes a certain personality, and I had it. I thought I didn't. We talked through a few scenarios, and he gave me some tips. This is exactly the type of training I needed."

When they turned the corner to head back, Riley said, "I've always lived in an apartment. Until I moved to Barton, I went to the park as much as I could to get away from the lifeless pavement and close to living, breathing trees. Sometimes I'd have trouble focusing on my classes because I hadn't been to the park in three days."

Ben nodded. "I asked my uncle why he traveled to provide veterinary services, and he said he thrived on being outside. Made sense to me. I felt the same."

When they reached the house, Ben said, "I'll go inside with you to be sure everything's okay then I'm going to the cabin. Shall I bring something for breakfast? I can stop by the grocery store on the way over."

"I'll have coffee ready if you'll text me before you leave. Pick up bagels, and I'll scramble some eggs."

"Sounds like a plan."

As they walked into the house, Toby raised his head, and Jordy trotted to the back door. When Riley opened the door for Jordy,

Toby lumbered outside and the two of them flopped down in the grass.

Ben wrapped his arms around Riley as he peered over her head. "You looked cold. Guess they need a little outside time too. I'll hang around until they're ready to come inside."

"It is cold," Riley said as Ben stepped away so she could close the door.

While Ben turned on the fireplace, Riley hurried to her bedroom for a sweatshirt. When she returned, Ben stood by the fire, and she put her arm around his waist as she joined him. He smiled and placed his arm around her shoulders.

"This is nice." Riley leaned against him.

Ben's phone buzzed a text, and he pulled out his phone. After he read the text, he placed his phone back into his pocket.

Riley glanced up at him with her eyebrows raised.

"It's nothing," he said.

Toby scratched at the back door, and Riley frowned as she let Toby and Jordy back inside. *Why do I think it's something?*

After the dogs bounded inside and rushed to the fireplace, Riley locked the back door. When she turned, Ben was at the open front door. "I'll text you before I leave in the morning."

Before he closed the door, he said, "Good night. Lock the door."

Riley strode to the door and locked and bolted it. After she picked up her book and sat on the chair nearest the fireplace, she frowned. *Abrupt departure.*

She kicked off her boots and sat cross-legged to read then slammed her book closed. Toby jerked away, and Jordy opened his eyes.

"I must be on edge, Toby. Everything bothers me."

She turned off the fireplace and the lights then padded off to bed.

* * *

Riley woke before daylight and padded to the kitchen. After she started a pot of coffee, Toby and Jordy trotted to the back door, and she opened it. She stood in front of the coffee machine and listened to the gurgles.

She opened the back door, and the dogs trotted inside. "Sorry I woke you up so early. I didn't sleep very well last night because I kept thinking about Ben and his private text."

After she fed them, she hurried to turn on the fireplace. "I'm officially freezing."

She glanced at her bare feet. "I officially have no sense." Toby grinned.

"I meant because I forgot to put any socks on," she growled as she dashed to the bedroom and dressed then hurried back to the fireplace.

After he ate, Toby joined her, and she rubbed the sleep out of his eyes then stroked his head. "I don't have any claims on Ben. He's entitled to his privacy. I need to chill. Bad choice of words. I need to back off. He's a nice guy and a good friend. That's enough. Right, Toby?"

Toby whined then yipped.

"You're entitled to your opinion, but you're wrong. I am not grouchy, and it's enough to have a nice friend."

Riley poured a cup of coffee before she sat close to the fireplace to read her book. After a few pages, she closed her book and stared at the dancing flames while she finished her coffee.

When she rose to refill her cup, she stared at the clock. "It's only five. I thought it was later."

Riley returned to her chair and book. After an hour of reading, she carried her empty cup to the kitchen and refilled it then sipped her lukewarm coffee.

"This is silly. Doing laundry and cleaning the house makes more sense than moping." She grabbed her broom and duster, and Toby and Jordy ambled to the back door. After they went outside, Riley gathered her laundry and tossed it into the washer before she made her bed and swept and dusted her bedroom. She stood in the doorway and put her hands on her hips. *Much better.*

After she tidied and scrubbed the bathroom, she moved on to sweep the hall and dust and sweep the living room. When Toby scratched on the back door, she let him and Jordy inside, and they trotted to their favorite spots near the fireplace.

Riley frowned. "I need a carpet sweeper or something for the rug."

After she swept the kitchen and scrubbed the sink, Riley emptied the laundry from the washer to the dryer and started a fresh pot of coffee.

Toby yipped.

"No, I don't really feel any better, but the house looks nice. Maybe I need to do something about my hair." She rummaged through a kitchen drawer and found a pair of scissors, and Toby's shackles raised as he howled, and Jordy joined in.

Riley held up her hand and grumbled, "Okay. I won't cut my hair. You don't have to get all huffy." She threw the scissors back into the drawer and slammed it. "Happy?"

Toby grinned, and she stuck her nose in the air as she turned her back on him to watch the coffee drip.

When her phone buzzed a text, she picked it up.

Ben: "Grocery store opens in twenty minutes."

Riley strode to the back door and opened the door for the dogs before she replied, "OK."

Toby stared at her before he strolled outside, and Riley crossed her arms. "Don't bother me. I'm trying to keep it low key."

While the dogs were outside, Riley hurried to the bathroom and brushed her hair then smoothed it back into a tight ponytail. When she raised her eyebrows to examine her severe hairstyle more closely, she grimaced. *Ouch. It's too tight.*

She sighed as she brushed out her hair. After she tousled it, she nodded. *Better.*

When she let Toby and Jordy back inside, she said, "I'll just be wild and free today with not a care in the world."

Toby snorted as Ben's truck pulled into the driveway.

Riley hurried to the door with Toby and Jordy on her heels, but when she paused to slow her pace, Toby and Jordy crashed into her, and she fell. Before she could get up, Toby and Jordy smothered her face with kisses while Ben knocked on the door.

"Just a minute." She giggled as she tried to push away the two large dogs who were comforting her.

Ben knocked again. "Are you okay?"

"Come on, guys. Let me up." Riley rolled away then after she pulled up on the doorknob enough to reach the deadbolt and unlock the door, she opened it.

Ben's eyes widened. "Have you and the dogs been wrestling?"

Riley frowned as she clung to the doorknob to keep from losing her balance. "Kind of."

Ben helped her to her feet then carried in a grocery sack and dropped it on the table. "Sesame bagels okay? I found jalapeno cream cheese. Sounded interesting—I've never had it before, have you?"

Riley breathed in as she strolled to the coffee pot and poured two cups. *Be cool.* "No."

Ben picked up his cup and headed to the fireplace. "How did you sleep?"

Awful. "Good."

Toby growled, and Riley glared at him.

Ben narrowed his eyes. "Oh, really."

Riley pulled out the eggs from the refrigerator. "Scrambled okay?" She asked.

"Sounds good. That's my specialty."

Riley nodded as she popped the bagels into the oven to warm and stirred the eggs.

"How's your morning going, Toby?" Ben asked as he sat at the table with his coffee.

Toby moaned, and Ben said, "Thought so."

Riley slammed down her spoon and whirled around. "You understood Toby?"

"Sure. He said it's been rough."

"He did not. He said I was cranky."

Riley narrowed her eyes before she turned back to the stove to cook the eggs. "You tricked me."

When she heard Ben try to stifle a snicker behind her back, she smiled. *Maybe I'm not so grumpy, after all.*

"Maybe I'm a little irritated," she said.

"So, how'd that happen?"

"Let's eat then we can talk." Riley plated the scrambled eggs and removed the bagels from the oven.

After she set the plates on the table, she refilled their coffee cups. She glanced at Ben and smiled as his hazel-green eyes warmed her heart. "You sure make it hard to maintain a good cranky streak, cowboy."

"That's my job, ma'am," Ben saluted with two fingers and grinned before he picked up his fork to eat.

Ben cleared the table while Riley washed her pan and utensils then the dishes.

Ben refilled their coffee and took his cup to stand near the fireplace while Riley finished up. When Riley sat at one end of the sofa, she raised her eyebrows as Toby trotted to the back door. After Ben let Toby and Jordy out, he stood in front of the sofa, and Riley pointed to the other end.

"What's going on?" Ben asked.

"Right question. Wrong person asking it. You got a text yesterday and told me it was *nothing*. Why did it feel like something to me? And then, you just left. Boom, gone."

Ben gazed at her. "It was—"

"You already said nothing, and that didn't cut it." She lifted her chin and met his gaze.

He broke his gaze and glanced at the back door. "Can I let Toby back in? Maybe he can save me."

Riley glared. "Waiting."

Ben furrowed his brow. "Are you sure you want to know?"

"You're stalling."

"This really is a discussion that would be easier if we were walking outside. I was kind of engaged—"

"What?" Riley rose and let the dogs in then crossed her arms and growled, "I think you're right about taking a walk. I'll grab my coat."

The dogs trotted ahead while Riley and Ben strode in the opposite direction of their last walk.

"Go ahead." Riley picked up her pace to stay alongside Ben.

"I was kind of engaged, but now I'm not. She wanted to know if I had an engagement ring, so I called her."

"So, did you buy a ring?"

"No, it didn't occur to me. She called because she wanted to know if I was going to return it or give it to her."

"It didn't occur to you? What else?"

"Not much else. She called me a bunch of names and told me how much I embarrassed her. I'm actually very sorry about that." Ben furrowed his brow then sighed. "Pamela Suzanne lives near Atlanta and first visited my cousin when we were all in the ninth grade. She came to all the holiday events and other family gatherings with my cousin—the three of us just kind of hung out. Over the years, the family always joked that Pamela Suzanne and I would wind up married, at least, I always assumed it was a joke and went along with it. I wasn't surprised when my cousin told me Pamela Suzanne was getting married until she added that Pamela Suzanne had told all her friends she was engaged to me. I thought that was funny until my cousin told me Pamela Suzanne was serious."

"You went along with it? That's kind of a mess. Are you in trouble with your family?" Riley asked.

Ben slowed his pace. "I guess, except for Mom, Dad, and my grandparents."

"Anything else the family would tell me that you haven't?"

"What kind of question is that? Since when are you an expert interrogator?" Ben growled.

"Did you just say ouch?" Riley asked.

The dogs waited for them at the next intersection. After she checked for traffic, Riley said, "Okay," and Toby and Jordy dashed across.

"My cousin told me about my so-called engagement to Pamela Suzanne a year ago. It was easy to avoid the subject because Pamela and I never saw each other except at family gatherings, and the three of us hung out just like we always did. I never said anything, and neither did she, but I'm not proud it took me this long to tell her we weren't engaged. I guess I hoped it was just gossip and would blow over," Ben said. "I called Pamela Suzanne the day after I brought Carlie, Bella, and Mr. P to Doc Julie Rae's to make sure she understood that we weren't engaged. I didn't expect her to take it so badly."

Riley frowned. "That was the first day I met you."

"Coincidence," Ben said, and Toby barked.

Riley snorted. "Toby and I don't believe you."

"It was worth a shot to save a smidgen of my dignity."

"What other secrets do you have that will make me irritable later?" Riley asked.

"I don't know. My family in Omaha, maybe?"

When Riley rolled her eyes, he said, "Oh, good. You knew I was kidding."

She shook her head. "You're really pushing the boundaries of my good nature for someone who just broke his fiancée's heart."

As they continued to Riley's house, Ben asked, "You're never going to let me forget it, are you?"

"Nope." Riley smirked.

"I'm glad you aren't cranky anymore," Ben said. "I'm really sorry you had a rough night. I should have told you right away what was going on."

"Darn tootin'."

When they reached the house, Riley said, "It's nine thirty. Want to scope out the neighborhood around the house we're going to see?"

"Good idea. Maybe I can stay out of trouble for a while."

As they neared the address, Ben said, "Looks like an established neighborhood similar to yours. That's encouraging."

At five minutes until ten, Ben parked in the driveway, and a van pulled up and parked at the curb. Before Ben hopped out, Riley said, "The dogs and I will wait in the truck until you check in with Mr. Richard."

After Mr. Richard stepped out of his van, he and Ben shook hands. As he strolled up the driveway, Ben stopped at his truck. "Mr. Richard said you and the dogs are welcome to come in."

Ben opened the door for the dogs, and they jumped out and nosed Mr. Richard's hand before they explored the yard.

When Riley climbed out of the truck, Mr. Richard beamed. "It's a pleasure to meet you, Riley. You've made quite a splash in our sleepy town of Barton—you're a knockout, just like your grandmother. I had a crush on her for years."

"I never knew I looked like Grandma," Riley said.

"Oh, but you do. Her hair was as fiery as her personality. She was the nicest woman I ever knew unless you crossed her then her flames would scorch your soul."

Ben nodded. "That's you—you're just like your grandmother, Riley."

Mr. Richard chuckled. "Let's look at this little house of mine. Living room with a woodburning fireplace, eat-in kitchen, two bedrooms, a bath, and all the usual appliances including a dishwasher, washer, and dryer. I put in the dishwasher last year because I love mine. Do you cook, Ben?"

"I sure do, at least enough to keep from starving or spending all my money on fast food."

"I'll unlock the door and give you the grand tour then you can look around as long as you like. When are you moving?"

"I'll join Sheriff Dunn's department two weeks from tomorrow. I wouldn't mind moving at least a few things this coming weekend though, if that's possible."

"The house isn't occupied, so it's your call," Mr. Richard said.

When they went inside, Mr. Richard said, "The layout is simple. Hardwood floors in the living room, hallway, and bedrooms, and tile in the bathroom, kitchen, and small utility room. No garage, but I'm sure you noticed that." He led the way down the hallway. "Combo tub and shower in the bathroom, and a small linen closet. You'll have to get a shower curtain. The front bedroom is a little larger than the back bedroom, but both of them have fairly nice-sized closets. Blinds on all the windows."

Mr. Richard led the way down the hall to the kitchen. "You can't see the kitchen sink from the front door. That used to be important to people, but it isn't so much anymore. Back door goes out to a small porch that I'm told catches enough breeze to ring wind chimes. I've got two patio chairs out there. Let me know if you have your own, and I'll get them out of your way. The yard is fenced. There's the dining area next to the front window. There's a small pantry and the utility room is more of a utility area because it has no door. The utility area also has a few shelves. I'll go relax in my van. Come get me when you're done looking."

"What do you think?" Ben asked.

"I think it's nice, and it has plenty of room for you, but it depends on how much the rent is."

Ben nodded. "I'll also ask what utilities are included, and what are the terms of the rental contract?"

"The dogs and I will check out the back porch and yard while you talk to Mr. Richard."

When Riley, Toby, and Jordy stepped outside, she said, "Wow. I love this porch. We'll get Ben wind chimes for a housewarming present."

Riley sat on the patio chair while Toby and Jordy explored the yard. She closed her eyes and soaked up the warmth of the sun.

Ben stepped out onto the porch. "It's nice out here. Mr. Richard took my check, and I signed the rental agreement. I officially have a place to live in Barton. Want to go shopping? I need a shower curtain, a rug for the living room, fireplace tools, and maybe a hearth rug."

CHAPTER FIFTEEN

After they were in the truck, Ben backed out of the driveway and headed to the hardware store. "Mr. Richard gave me a key and told me I could move my things in anytime, as long as I understood any renter's insurance I got wouldn't be effective until next Saturday. I never had renter's insurance before because I thought the apartment insurance would cover my stuff if there was a fire or something. Mr. Richard explained it to me and gave me the names of a couple of people to talk to. Do you have renter's insurance?"

"No. I'm like you. I never considered it. Want to give me the names, and I'll check for both of us?"

"That would be great. I was trying to figure out how I was going to be able to make the calls." Ben bit his lip then asked, "Does that mean you aren't mad at me anymore?"

"Not necessarily."

Toby and Jordy jumped out of the truck and waited while Riley clipped on their leashes before they went inside.

"It's just for show," she said.

After they picked out the shower curtain and the hearth rug, they stood in front of the area rugs.

"These are more expensive than I expected," Ben said.

"Why don't you wait to see whether you really need one," Riley said. "Where would the fireplace tools be?"

When they found the sets on a low shelf, Ben said, "All I need is a shovel, brush, and a poker. These all include tongs. I suppose that would be okay. I'll have to get a metal bucket."

Riley peered behind the sets. "Wait a minute. Here's one in the back with no tongs." She slid out the set. "Marked half off."

Ben examined it. "I didn't see it. This is perfect."

After he turned their cart around, he said, "I'll need a metal bucket for the ashes. Let's check the next aisle."

"This is fancy." Riley picked up a bucket with one side that looked like a scoop.

"It's a decorative hod and not substantive enough to be used as an ash bucket; it would be fine to hold kindling, but so would a basket. Here's a bucket with a double bottom and a lid."

"Here's the same thing in a copper color that's ten dollars cheaper," Riley said. "Do you care whether it's black or copper?"

"No, I don't care about color. You're a remarkably frugal shopper."

"Another trait from Grandma," Riley said. "We'd go into town to the stores when it rained to cruise the aisles and find bargains."

"Sounds like an expensive way to spend a rainy day."

Riley chuckled. "We didn't spend any money—we kept score. She was really proud of me when I was seven years old and beat her. We went back to the cabin and made cookies to celebrate, and she let me put them into the oven and pull them out."

"Big day for a seven-year-old," Ben grinned as he pushed their cart to the checkout.

Riley nodded. "I loved my summers at the cabin."

When they reached the checkout, Toby and Jordy sat for the cashier and she gave them their treats. After Ben paid, she handed him his receipt, and Toby and Jordy grinned and cocked their heads as they dropped into their best sit..

The cashier smiled as she handed them more treats. "You are the most charming dogs I've ever met. Good boys."

As Ben opened the back door for the dogs, he said, "I could probably take some lessons from you and Jordy, Toby. I've never been called charming."

Toby howled, and Jordy joined in.

After everyone was in the truck, Ben asked, "What were Toby and Jordy saying?"

Riley snickered. "You mean when they howled? They were laughing."

Ben narrowed his eyes. "Am I insulted?"

Toby yipped, and Riley said, "Yes."

Ben turned at the street that led to his new house. "I'm not doing very well today, am I? Except for the house—I have a place to live in Barton, and we all like it."

The dogs jumped out while Ben and Riley unloaded Ben's purchases. While Ben put up the shower curtain, Riley removed the price tags from everything else before she put them in their new places at their new home.

"I thought of something else we can get Ben for housewarming. Did you notice the bellows at the hardware store? Grandma taught me how to use the bellows, and I loved them."

When Ben came into the living room, he stopped as he gazed at the room. "We've got a nice start. I'm excited about moving."

"If you like, we could have lunch then you could leave, so you could pack today."

"I'd love to do that, but I'd like to stay too."

"Let's have lunch then you can decide," Riley said.

Ben backed out of the driveway then stopped as a car drove by. "What are we having for lunch. Do we need to pick something up?"

"If sandwiches and chips are okay, I have the fixings for lunch."

"Sandwiches it is. What about dessert? Shall we run by the store and pick up some ice cream? Maybe some chocolate covered ice cream bars?"

"That sounds good."

When they reached the grocery store, Riley said, "Drop me off, and I'll run in."

Riley bought the ice cream bars then hurried outside and spotted Ben, who had parked at a nearby spot.

After they reached Riley's house, Ben and the dogs ambled to the backyard while Riley dashed inside with the ice cream and pulled out sliced ham, swiss cheese, mayonnaise, and mustard then sliced a tomato. After she assembled their sandwiches and put the bag of chips on the table, she poured two large glasses of sweet tea then called Ben and the dogs inside.

While they ate lunch, Riley asked, "What all could you do this afternoon in Carson?"

"I could give the apartment notice and go to Mom and Dad's for dinner. I texted them to tell them I'd accepted the job here, but I'm sure they'd appreciate some time to talk. That might be the best reason for me to return earlier than I'd planned, now that I think about it. I could box up my books then it would be easy to load up my bookcase and boxes to bring next week. I could even load up my dining table and chairs; I could manage without them for a week. The more large and bulky items I bring next week, the more likely I'll be able to load everything else in my truck for the following week and not have to bother with renting a truck."

"Makes sense to me."

"How did you manage your move? Did you rent a truck?"

Riley chuckled. "I had what they called a partially furnished apartment. I think they meant sparsely, but it was good enough when I first started working after school then after that, I was used to it and didn't see any reason to change. Our move here was simple—I loaded my things into my SUV, and Toby rode on the front seat."

After they finished lunch, Riley pulled out the chocolate covered ice cream bars and handed one to Ben.

"What are you going to do after I leave?" he asked.

"Laundry. I've gotten behind."

"What about groceries? Are you getting low? Do you need to go anywhere before I leave?" Ben's brow furrowed as he gazed at Riley's face.

"I'll be fine. I'm set for lunches all week, and tonight's supper. I'll get my car back tomorrow, and can pick up groceries for the rest of the week."

Riley rose to let the dogs inside as Ben finished off his ice cream then dropped his stick in the trash. "Well, then. I'll go. Is it okay if I call you after I get back from Mom and Dad's? I'll text you if it looks like I'll be real late, so you won't have to wait up."

The dogs barreled inside and raced to the fireplace while Riley locked the back door. Jordy beat Toby to their favorite warm spot; Toby grumbled as he jumped up on the sofa.

"Sounds good," Riley said. "Talk to you later."

When Ben remained in the kitchen, Riley joined him, and he put his arm around her shoulders as they strolled to the door. He faced her and put his hands on her shoulders and gazed at her. "Be safe."

"You took my line." Riley smiled. "Safe travels."

He returned her smile and hugged her. "So, guess I'll get going."

Riley nodded, and he hugged her again then left.

After she locked the door behind him, Toby yipped.

"I agree, he is a nice guy. Time for laundry."

After Riley started the laundry, she said, "The house is clean, the washer's going, Ben won't be calling me until tonight, and I'm restless. Anybody care to take a walk to the park?"

When Toby jumped up, Jordy eased to his feet and lumbered to the door.

"Were you asleep, Jordy?" Riley asked as she threw on her coat and grabbed the leashes.

Riley strolled to the park while Toby and Jordy raced ahead then waited for her at each intersection. As they neared the park, Riley slowed and called Toby and Jordy to her side. "Somebody's at the park. Looks like a mother with a small child and a stroller. We'll take it slow to give them a chance to see us. If the mother's nervous, we'll leave."

Riley led the way down the path through the park, when the child squealed, "It's Ms. Riley, Mommy."

Maddie ran toward Riley and the dogs, and Riley waved. "Hey there, Mini-me. It's nice to see you. Do you remember Toby? And this is Jordy."

"Come see my mommy and my baby sister." Maddie grabbed Riley's hand and pulled her along. Riley's eyes widened at Maddie's mother's silver hair that was streaked with red.

Maddie's mother smiled as they approached. "Hi Riley. I see what Dylan meant when he told me Maddie was your Mini-me. I'm Tamara. It's so nice to meet you."

"You too. This is Toby, and Jordy is spending a few days with us." Riley nodded toward the dogs then matched Tamara's smile. "Mini-me may have my hair color, but she certainly has your dimples." Riley grinned.

Tamara giggled. "My hair started turning gray when I was eighteen. When I complained to my mother, she told me her hair turned gray almost overnight when she was seventeen. I'd hoped for more sympathy. I was really excited when my dull gray turned to silver like Mom's when I was twenty. The streaks of red are courtesy of my hairdresser."

Wonder if Tamara is who Daphne meant when she said I was just like her.

"Welcome to Barton, although I've only been here a few weeks too, so welcome to us," Riley grinned.

"Join me." Tamara scooted to make room on the bench. "The baby falls asleep when we roll out of the house. We're here for her naptime."

Maddie waved as she climbed the slide's ladder, and Tamara and Riley returned her wave.

"Sometimes other kids show up, and sometimes they don't," Tamara said. "Maddie's observation point for friends is on top of the slide. When Dylan was here with us yesterday, he said I'd find my observation point too."

When Maddie pulled out an empty toilet paper tube from her pocket and used it as a spyglass, Tamara said, "I love to watch her creativity in action."

"Friend ahoy," Maddie pointed to the edge of a park as a boy held the hand of a man while they crossed the road. After they crossed the road, Maddie slid down and raced to the teeter totter and sat on one side.

Riley smiled. "Should we stand on the bench?"

Tamara laughed. "Do you suppose we'd draw new friends or more redheads?"

Riley laughed along with her. "Hard to say. The park does seem like an excellent place to find friends."

Tamara nodded. "Did you know Dylan's sister? Daphne?"

"Not really. I only met her once, but all of us in the office were saddened by the news of her death."

"She was a bitter woman. Her best skill was pushing people away, so I was shocked when she came to the hotel and talked to me a day or two before she died."

Riley nodded. "She did strike me as angry at the world."

Tamara shielded her eyes with her arm as she watched the boy climb onto the other side of the see-saw with the man's help.

"Daphne was crying and almost inconsolable. She said she was in trouble because she knew Alyse wrote the yellow notes. I had no idea what she was talking about, and still don't."

Riley's eyes widened then she cleared her throat. "It does seem like something strange to say."

Tamara nodded. "She also said I was the only one she could talk to then something about cooking drugs, but I decided later I misunderstood her. It was really unsettling. I didn't tell Dylan because he has enough on his mind. He still feels so guilty about the baby choking. You are his and Maddie's hero. Mine too."

"I cannot tell you how much I admire Dylan for having the presence of mind to stop at the clinic."

"I'll have to remind him of that. I don't think he realizes what he called his one fleeting thought saved the baby's life."

Toby yipped.

"Toby's my timer. I'm in the middle of doing laundry. I enjoyed talking with you. We'll see you again, I'm sure, probably right here because Toby and I thrive on our walks in the park."

On the way home, Riley said, "What do you think, Toby? Was Daphne telling the truth or weaving another lie?"

Toby whined.

"I asked you first," Riley said as they turned onto their street.

After they went inside, Riley's phone rang. *Julie Rae?*

"Riley, I hate to intrude. Is Ben there?"

"No, he's on his way back to Carson to pack. Did you need to talk to him?"

"No, I should have asked if you're available."

"I am. How can I help?"

"I got a call about a horse down. Can I pick you up? Charlie said we need to take Toby and Jordy along. He's worried about us."

"Sure. What do you need for me to take?"

"Heavy gloves and a warm jacket you don't mind getting dirty. Do you have muck boots? I'll bring two pairs. Charlie is packing water for us and the dogs and snacks for us. Maybe pack snacks for the dogs and water bowls for them. Do you have a flashlight? I have all our medical supplies. I'll be there in five minutes."

After Riley and the dogs jumped inside Julie Rae's truck, she headed north on the highway. "One of my favorite clients gives rescued horses a home until they can be fostered and isn't afraid to call for a phone consultation, but when Lindsey calls me to come check a horse, I rush right out. She's had Ruby for about two weeks. Ruby was horsehide over bones, as Lindsey says, when she came to Lindsey's shelter. Lindsey has a volunteer who has bonded with Ruby, and she called him too. Lindsey's going to assess Ruby then call me back. Answer my phone when she calls." Julie Rae placed her phone on the console between their seats as she sped north.

When Julie Rae's phone rang, Riley answered then put it on speaker phone so Julie Rae could hear.

"Hey, Doc. I have a little more information for you. Ruby was in a fenced-in area to socialize with other horses when something spooked one of the larger horses, and he broke through the gate. Ruby might have been spooked because he was, but for whatever reason, she chased after him before anyone could reseat the gate. She dashed into a low-lying area and is trapped in the swampy muck. We aren't sure if she stumbled and fell, but she appears to have an injured front leg and won't even try to get up. We've got a sling and the crane ready, but we'd like you here to assess her leg before we do much more. Park at the horse barn, and I'll walk you down."

"We're about ten minutes out," Julie Rae said. "See you there."

After the call ended, Doc frowned. "Troubling news. Ruby's still fragile and hasn't had a chance to build up her muscles yet. She's been on full portions of alfalfa twice a day for only a couple of days. Some horses might be able to survive a broken leg, but Ruby's not in good enough shape to be one of them. My least favorite thing in the entire world is to put down any animal."

Riley nodded as she stared at the passing countryside. *Doc's trying to prepare me, but that is the worst part of veterinary medicine.*

After Doc parked, she pointed to the muck boots. "Your feet may be smaller than mine. Make sure you can walk without falling."

When Riley tried on the boots, her feet slid around, and Doc chuckled. "Thought so. I brought a pair of thick socks for you. You'll have the bonus of warm feet."

Riley put on the extra sox, and the boots snugged up around her feet. "Good to go."

A wizened, weather-beaten woman who wore a black bandana over escaping wisps of gray hair strode their way. "Thanks for getting here so quickly, Doc. I'm glad you brought Riley. I've been looking forward to meeting Millie's niece. Leave your stuff here. I've got runners who can fetch whatever you need." Lindsey peered into the truck. "If the dogs aren't afraid of horses, the horses aren't afraid of them. I've found dogs help calm horses too."

Even though Lindsey was much older than Doc or Riley, they had trouble keeping up with her as Toby and Jordy trotted alongside the old woman.

When they reached the edge of the swampy area, Doc whispered, "I'm thoroughly embarrassed about getting my tail run off by a woman twice my age."

Riley nodded. "And probably half my weight."

"I'd like for you to go first and talk to her, Riley. I'll follow you after you give me the signal that Ruby won't freak," Doc said.

Riley nodded and eased toward Ruby. "Hello, girl. I'll bet that was scary. Are you okay?"

Ruby blew through her nose with her mouth closed.

"I'm Riley. Nice to meet you, and I'm glad you're okay."

Riley continued her slow approach. "Do you remember Doc? She's going to check your leg. Does it hurt?"

Ruby lifted her ears and sighed.

"I like Doc too."

Riley maintained her soft, calming voice. "Doc, Ruby said you can check her leg. It's a little sore."

When Riley reached Ruby, the edge of the muddy, dank water seeped over the tops of her boots, and she shivered. "This water is cold, Ruby. Could you stand on your sore leg if Ms. Lindsey can help you up?"

Ruby nickered, and Riley smiled. "I agree, Ms. Lindsey is kind, and I trust her too."

Riley stooped when she reached Ruby's head, and she stroked her and cooed while Doc made her way to check Ruby's leg.

"Left leg?" Doc asked.

"Yes." Riley hummed, and Ruby relaxed as Doc palpated her leg.

Doc smiled. "Good news. I feel the swelling, but the bones are intact. When you're ready, Lindsey, I think we are too."

Lindsey barked orders to her crew, and Ruby nickered at her voice.

"Ms. Lindsey is a force in action," Riley said.

As she made her way to make room for the crew to apply the sling, Doc slipped and sank deeper into the swampy muck when she tried to get up. One of Ms. Lindsey's crew members lifted her out and set her on firm ground. Ms. Lindsey threw a horse blanket around Doc's shoulders, and Julie Rae growled, "We shall never speak of this again."

When Ruby snorted, everyone laughed, and Julie Rae glowered.

"How was your swim?" Mr. Richard stood next to Lindsey. "I'm a volunteer, and Lindsey told me Ruby needed a friend, but I see she already has two of the best."

Lindsey guffawed and slapped Mr. Richard on the back as Julie Rae put her nose in the air and pulled the blanket tighter around her shoulders.

"Everybody's in trouble now," Riley whispered, and Ruby nickered.

After the crew lifted Ruby out of the swamp, Riley climbed out to dry land. She breathed a sigh of relief. *Didn't fall.*

Doc checked Ruby's leg again then Lindsey directed the crew. "Move Ruby to the barn, real slow like. We'll set her down there to see if her foot can hold her weight."

As the crew transported Ruby to the barn, Riley walked alongside and stroked Ruby's neck as she hummed her tune. A crew member walked along with his hand on Ruby's side to keep the sling from swinging while Mr. Richard walked along Ruby's other side with Lindsey steadying Ruby and the sling.

When they reached the barn, Ruby snorted, and Riley said, "Ruby's ready to try out her leg."

Lindsey waved for the crane operator to lower Ruby and shouted orders to the operator and the surrounding crew members. As Ruby's feet neared the ground, she lifted her sore leg.

"It's okay, girl. They're going to take it easy. Ms. Lindsey's in charge," Riley said, and Ruby lowered her leg. When her leg touched the ground, Ruby's muscles tensed, and Riley said, "Easy, girl. They'll take it slow for you."

When the sling was slack, Ruby stood with her foot on the ground, and Riley said, "You did great."

"If y'all don't mind taking her up a little to relieve the weight on that foot, I'd like to put an ice boot on her leg," Doc said.

"Good idea, Doc," Lindsey said, and a stable hand ran for the ice boot with its inserts. After Lindsey and the stable hand applied the boot, Lindsey directed the sling to be lowered then released.

Mr. Richard patted and stroked Ruby's neck and helped her along as she limped to her stall.

As Riley, Doc, and Ms. Lindsey strolled to Doc's truck.

"Well, Ms. Riley, horse whisperer. Any time you want to give Doc a little competition, my friends and I will be happy to send you to veterinary school. You have a gift that needs to be used to its fullest," Lindsey said.

Riley's eyes widened. "Thank you."

"I'm serious," Lindsey said. "Doc will tell you I don't flatter folks or indulge in idle chatter. Think about it. Talk it over with Doc and that young man who's going to be our new deputy. Let me know when you're ready."

After they loaded the dogs and Doc headed to the highway, Riley asked, "Does everybody in town know about Ben?"

Doc snorted as she turned up the heater. "Pretty much. Just like everybody already knows how wet and cold we are. You're lucky—you're the short one. I'll be the clumsy vet as long as you're short."

Riley snickered. "I see what you mean."

"Thanks again for going with me. You made the day go much smoother than I expected, and I was thrilled that Ruby hadn't broken her leg. I have a talent of my own, by the way. I foresee hot showers beckoning us."

"Pretty much right after I hit that door."

"Want to join us for supper tonight?" Julie Rae asked.

"Always, but I've got laundry and other mundane tasks that dogs refuse to do. I'm really sorry about that."

When Doc parked in Riley's driveway, Riley and the dogs hopped out and hurried to the door. When they were inside, the dogs flopped in front of the fireplace, so she turned it on before she climbed into a hot shower.

After she dressed, she rushed to the fireplace and stood in front of it then turned when she decided her clothes were hot enough to catch fire. She brewed a cup of tea then fed the dogs.

"I'm not going outside with you." Riley opened the back door for Toby and Jordy after they ate.

While Toby and Jordy explored their territory, Riley stood in front of the opened refrigerator. *I already had a sandwich today.*

She closed the refrigerator and sipped her hot tea in front of the fireplace.

After she let the dogs inside, she said, "I could have a bowl of cereal with chips on the side and an ice cream bar for dessert."

Toby growled.

"Don't be such a nag. It's kind of balanced."

Toby snorted and jumped up on the sofa; Jordy padded to his spot on the rug near the fireplace.

While she ate her cereal and chips, Riley dumped out the manila envelope Dylan had given her. She organized the loose papers into invoices, spreadsheets of data, patient records, and patient notes then flipped through Daphne's journal.

"Most of Daphne's journal is whining. I think I'll have to read it to scour for any facts in the middle of all her complaining."

She organized each stack of papers into date order, with the latest date on top then pulled out her ice cream bar and stood by the fireplace while she ate her ice cream.

She threw her stick into the trash as her phone rang. *Ben.*

"I got a lot of packing done this afternoon. I'm going to leave in a few minutes for Mom and Dad's. What have you been doing?"

"Laundry," she said.

"And what else?"

Riley chuckled. "You're so suspicious."

"Listening," he said.

She told him about Ruby, Lindsey, Mr. Richard, the water seeping into her boots, and Doc falling.

"What a day. What would Doc tell me that you haven't told me?" Ben asked.

"You are so suspicious. Where did you learn that?"

When Ben snorted, Riley giggled. After she told him about Ms. Lindsey's offer to pay for veterinary school, Ben asked, "What do you think?"

"My initial thought is I'm not interested because I'm just now getting settled in Barton, but I suppose I could think about it later."

"Makes sense to me. I'll talk to you later this evening."

After they hung up, Riley dashed to the fireplace for more warmup then returned to the kitchen table.

As she compared the spreadsheet to the invoices, her eyes widened. "There are large volume purchases on the invoices that don't fit into a veterinary practice, Toby, and none of them appear on the spreadsheets: paint thinner, pool acid, ammonia, pseudoephedrine, road flares, brake fluid, lye, and drain cleaner." Riley frowned. "Quite an eclectic group of supplies, but if I remember my chemistry lab class correctly, this is a shopping list for a methamphetamine laboratory. Could that be why Daphne mentioned cooking drugs to Tamara?"

Riley snapped photos of all the pages of invoices and spreadsheets then texted the sheriff.

"Come by tomorrow? I have papers from Daphne's apt."

He replied immediately. "Will do."

After she glanced at the patient records and notes, she took pictures of them before she placed them back into the manila envelope then slipped the invoices and spreadsheets into her lunch bag. *Amanda can file the records tomorrow.*

She brewed another cup of tea before she joined Toby on the sofa to read Daphne's journal. After a half hour, she closed the journal and paced. "It's hard to read a journal that is so filled with hate. Daphne said that J.R. wrote the yellow note and put it on Daphne's car, but Daphne got even and put it on Fire Demon's car. I guess that's me. Why am I Fire Demon? I'd rather be Fire Pixie. Then later Daphne said F.D. needs to take the hint and leave town."

After another hour, Riley flipped back three pages and reread them. "What did she mean by the dogs cooked at night for Alyse Termaine? Then two pages later, she said phony A.T. wrote the yellow notes. I think she was saying that Alyse Termaine was a phony, and that gives me a new theory. I think she started off spewing complaints about people she knew but then became afraid and slipped into writing her true thoughts. Is that a stretch?"

Toby growled.

"I guess it is, but it's the only thing that explains the change in her focus. The last ten or so pages sound less spiteful and more factual, if that makes sense."

Toby yipped.

"Fresh air's a good idea. Let's go out back."

Toby and Jordy rushed out to the yard then joined Riley on the porch. The humidity hung in the air and Riley's shirt clung to her skin. The tree frogs sang, the cicadas buzzed a chorus from one backyard to the next while the chirping crickets forecasted rain. "Crazy how fast the weather changes. Guess we've got another cold front on the way," Riley said as they returned inside and she found a text from the sheriff: "Be there soon with friend."

Riley sent a quick "Ok" before she sat to read the next section in the journal. "This is interesting. Daphne said E.W. was a fool because he didn't know what was going on at the office after he went home at the end of each day. So, Dr. Witmer wasn't involved, at least according to Daphne. Here's something I don't understand—*A.T. has Fire Demon's tag ready.*"

"I don't want whatever tag that is." Riley frowned as she stared at the journal. "This last page is the most chilling, Toby. Daphne said phony A.T. wrote all the yellow notes and agreed to honor their agreement; Daphne would receive five hundred thousand dollars for her services."

Riley shuddered as she pointed at the page. "Then Daphne gloated and said nobody could get the best of her." Riley shook her head. "I think A.T. decided to save some money. What do you think?"

Toby whined.

"I wouldn't have believed a killer would pay up for anything either."

Riley snapped a picture of every page in the journal then dropped the journal into her lunch bag. When she carried her empty cup to the sink, she paused. *I need to look at the patient records and notes again.*

She laid the patients' records and notes out on the table and lined up the records and the notes. "I see it!" she slammed her hands on the table and rose. "I've seen so many patient records, I had rabies tag blindness."

Toby trotted over to her and nosed her hand as Riley scratched his ears.

"This is all too strange; there are ten patient records, and each record has exactly the same rabies tag number, 000000. Is that what Daphne meant by Fire Demon's tag? The patient names are common dog names, like Max and Rex, and they are all large breeds. Rex's tag has deceased written over the tag number." The tiny hairs on the back of Riley's neck rose, and a chill ran down her back. She hugged herself as she shuddered. "I don't like this at all."

Riley strode to the living room window and peered out then checked the front and back doors to be sure they were locked and bolted. After she took in a big breath then exhaled, she returned to the kitchen table and focused her attention on the patient records.

"The client names are either E. Witmer or A. Termaine." She shifted the notes around to match them up by patients' names. "This is even more bizarre because the patient notes are dates and weights in pounds. For example, here's a German shepherd named Killer at twenty pounds then two weeks later ten pounds, and three weeks later, twenty pounds. What do you think, Toby? Records of drug sales or something? I think I'm getting overly suspicious and seeing criminal activity everywhere. I need to give these to the sheriff too."

A loud knock at the door startled her. *I am jumpy. Sheriff said he'd be here.* She hurried to the door.

"Riley, it's Sheriff Dunn."

When she opened the door, Riley's eyes widened at the man who stood with the sheriff. *The accountant. How do I warn the sheriff?*

CHAPTER SIXTEEN

Sheriff smiled. "Marc said you'd probably recognize him. What do you have?"

Marc's dimples transformed his face when he smiled. "I thought you would recognize me from the meeting at the Trumans'. I am an accountant, but I primarily work undercover for the Georgia Bureau of Investigation. I've tried to stay out of your way in Barton, but I wasn't always successful. You're very observant."

"Come on in and sit. This will take a little time." After the men joined her at the kitchen table, Riley explained that the sample rabies tags caught her eye. Riley pointed out Rex's tag before they reviewed the patient records and notes.

"Was someone killed in the explosion at Dr. Witmer's?"

"Unofficially, that's a possibility," Sheriff said. "If so, my guess is the same as yours—his code name was Rex. What else?"

She showed him the invoices and spreadsheets, and Marc let out a long whistle. "They were cooking meth. Good find."

"Dr. Witmer didn't know about it though. Maybe." Riley showed them the notations in Daphne's journal. "Daphne said a lot of things in her journal that weren't true, but towards the end, she may have realized that she was in danger. I'm not positive that I'm right because I don't understand her thought process. Daphne claims Alyse Termaine wrote the yellow notes and owed Daphne a lot of money."

Riley flipped to the last page in the journal.

"Five hundred thousand dollars?" Sheriff raised his eyebrows.

Marc's eyes widened. "You don't have anything else? Like a signed and notarized confession?"

When Riley snorted, Sheriff smiled. "Cop humor."

Marc rolled his eyes. "It was funnier in my head. Is there somewhere you can stay until this is over?"

"I've got Toby and Jordy; I don't want to go where I might endanger anyone else." Riley crossed her arms and glowered.

The sheriff narrowed his eyes. "I could take you into protective custody—"

Toby growled, and Jordy's hackles raised.

"Okay, boys. I get it," Sheriff said as he and Marc rose after Riley placed all the documents into a grocery sack then handed it to the sheriff.

"Just remember, it's on you to keep her safe." Sheriff narrowed his eyes at Toby and Jordy.

After the sheriff and the accountant left, Riley locked and bolted the front door then smiled at Toby and Jordy. "Thanks for having my back. I guess it showed that the accountant was a total surprise. At least the sheriff picked up all those documents, but I'm still worried about Daphne's statement that A.T. has Fire Demon's tag ready. Reading that journal was like wandering through a fire ant hill dragging a stick." She shuddered.

Riley sat on the sofa with her gardening book on her lap and read the chapter about bugs and slugs. When she finished the chapter, she stretched. "I just learned there are a lot of beneficial insects that will take down the pests and neem oil is my friend. So if I'm a broccoli plant—"

Toby yipped and grinned.

"What? I like broccoli—as I was about to say, I need my beneficial insects. You and Jordy are my spined soldier bugs. I never heard of them before, but doesn't that sound cool? And I need neem oil soap because it kills or repels the bad bugs. So, what's my neem oil?"

Riley stared at her gardening book. "Oh wait, I think I know. It's—"

Riley was interrupted when her phone rang, and she grinned. *Ben.*

"Is it too late to call? I forgot to text you that I was leaving Mom and Dad's," he said.

"It's not too late at all. How was dinner?"

"It was great. Mom and Dad were excited to hear about the new deputy position. Mom said she was worried because she's known I haven't been happy here, and she was worried I'd go to Atlanta; she's glad I'll only be an hour away." Ben snorted. "Dad said she wouldn't listen to him, but he knew the city's not for me. I talked to them about Pamela Suzanne. Dad said the family will give me grief just because that's what they do, but their hearts won't really be in it because nobody really cares for Pamela Suzanne. Mom said Pamela Suzanne is an attractive woman and will find the right man. Mom never says anything bad about anybody. When Dad said looks aren't everything, Mom said then he could tell her one other nice thing to say about Pamela Suzanne."

"I think I'll like your mom."

"I think you will too. Mom wanted to know when I'll bring you for a visit. We'll have to schedule a weekend soon. You'll love the farm. What have you been doing?"

Riley frowned. *Do I bother him with this? How mad will he be later?* "Daphne's brother gave me some documents he found in her apartment because they looked like veterinary records to him. I looked over them then gave them to the sheriff because they looked more like financial records."

"And what else?"

Riley rolled her eyes. "The papers included her journal, and I gave that to the sheriff too. Amanda told me that Daphne spouted off all the time, and sometimes what she said was true, and that's exactly what her journal was like. Most of it was raving nonsense, but there might have been some truth hidden here and there. I couldn't tell. The sheriff plans to turn over the whole mess of papers and her journal to the GBI."

"So does that mean that Agent Reeves will be coming to see you this next week?" Ben growled.

Now why is he so grumpy all of a sudden? "Hadn't thought about it, but maybe so. Amanda will be glad because he always brings dessert."

"What about you? Will you be glad to see him?"

That's it. "I need to tell you what Zach said about Agent Reeves." Riley told Ben about Eli and Zach's friend.

"That's too bad," Ben said.

Riley snorted. *Right.* "That's not the sincerest thing I've ever heard you say."

"It is too bad for Zach's friend," Ben grumbled.

When Toby yawned, Jordy did too then Riley yawned. "I'm so sorry. Toby yawned and started a chain reaction."

"I heard him and yawned when you did. He's right—it's late. I'll call you tomorrow. Be safe."

After they hung up, Riley said, "Back to my neem oil. I think I know who the Alyse Termaine that Daphne called phony is. I just need a little proof. You two may be able to help me except I'm not exactly sure how yet. Outside then bed?"

Toby and Jordy trotted to the back door. While they roamed the backyard, Riley looked at the sky. *Clouds have already rolled in. We'll have rain tonight.*

Riley and the dogs came inside and trooped off to bed.

* * *

A loud clap then a rumble of thunder woke Riley. She rolled over to check the time, but the room was dark. She pulled out her flashlight from the bedside table drawer then padded into the kitchen to check the battery-operated clock, and Toby and Jordy followed her.

"It's three thirty. Let's go outside before the rain hits."

As she stood on the porch, lightning lit up the sky. *Beautiful in a kind of scary way.*

After they returned inside, Riley sat in the middle of the sofa with a dog on each side. She leaned back and closed her eyes with her arms around the dogs. When she woke, the clock on the stove was flashing. She flipped on the light. "Five o'clock. Ready for breakfast?"

Riley started the coffee machine then fed the dogs and set the clocks. After she dressed, her coffee was ready, and the dogs had eaten. She poured a cup then opened the door for the dogs.

"It's foggy," She made her lunch while she sipped her coffee.

When Julie Rae pulled into the driveway, Riley and the dogs splashed through the puddles then jumped into the truck.

"Fog's getting thicker," Doc Julie Rae said. "Thanks again for going with me to Lindsey's, Riley. You know she was serious about veterinary school. I'm selfish—I would love to bring you in as a partner. You really are a natural, and I'm in awe of your skills. You just need the shingle."

"It's so strange because Ben was struggling with this very same decision a week ago. He spent summers working with his uncle who is a veterinarian, and the family always thought he'd be one too."

"He decided against it because he wanted to be close to you," Doc said.

Riley frowned. "Do you think so? That doesn't seem like a good reason to me."

Doc nodded. "So why don't you want to take Lindsey's offer? So you can stay here close to Ben?"

"That's different," Riley growled.

Doc rolled her eyes. "Of course, it is."

On their way to the veterinary hospital, Riley's phone rang.

"I'll be there as soon as I can," Riley said.

"What's up?" Doc asked.

"My car's ready."

Doc made a sharp turn to go to the gas station, and Toby and Jordy slid on the leather bench seat to one side with unlucky Jordy on the bottom of the pile.

"Sorry, guys," Doc said. "I'm not anxious to lose my commuting partners, Riley, but I know you'll be excited to have your SUV back."

"I sure am. I thought of a million places to go and things to do that required wheels this entire time. I'm really grateful for the rides to and from work, but I did miss the freedom to go and come as I please."

Toby and Jordy jumped out of the truck with Riley and trotted along to the office. She paid for the tires and labor while Julie Rae waited in the parking lot. The thick fog gave the gas station lights an eerie glow. *Fog is sometimes spooky.* Riley trembled before she hurried to the truck, and Julie Rae lowered her window.

"Anything wrong?" Julie Rae asked.

"No, they're going to pull it around. You can go ahead. I forgot my lunch. We'll swing back by the house then I'll be at work in a few minutes."

"See you soon. Be careful in this soupy fog," Julie Rae said.

As Riley and the dogs made their way to the gas station bays, Jordy gave a low growl.

Riley asked, "Where is the bad man?"

A car pulled away from the gas station pumps, and Jordy yipped.

"No, I didn't get a good look."

The mechanic said, "Keys are in the ignition. Alyse Termaine was asking when you were going to be picking up your SUV, but the clerk was busy and didn't see your ticket was paid. He told her you'd be picking it up pretty soon because it's ready. I guess she wanted to talk to you about something."

"I guess so," Riley said. "She'll probably come to Julie Rae's later."

After she parked in her driveway, Riley dashed inside and picked up her lunch then crept to the veterinary hospital. "I can barely see the hood. I'm glad we weren't at the cabin trying to drive to town in this."

When she parked in the employee lot, Jordy growled, and Riley peered across the street at the empty car that looked like a ghost ship on the high seas.

"Thanks for pointing out the bad man's car, Jordy." Before she climbed out of her SUV, Riley pulled out her pistol from its holster and dropped it into her pocket. When she opened the back door for the dogs, they went into an attack stance, and Toby growled at the shadowy figure that stole through the dense fog toward them.

"Thanks, Toby," she whispered. *Doc Junior. I thought so.*

"Hey, I got lost in the fog. Can you direct me to Pomeroy?" Doc Junior called out in a raspy falsetto voice.

"Sorry, Doc. Can't help you at all," Riley eased her pistol out of her pocket when she saw the flash of metal in his hand.

When Jordy and Toby rushed toward Doc, the sound of a shot ripped through the muffled sounds of nearby traffic. Jordy yelped and fell to the ground, and Riley shouted, "Down!"

Toby dropped down next to Jordy and Riley inhaled, aimed, then exhaled before she squeezed the trigger.

After her shot rang out, his gun fell from his hand before Doc Junior collapsed, and Toby dashed to Riley.

"We need to help Jordy," Riley said as Doc Julie Rae ran outside with a shotgun.

Doc set her shotgun aside and rushed to Jordy while Riley called nine-one-one and hurried to Doc Junior. When she reached him, she kicked away his pistol then spoke so fast that the dispatcher asked, "Where are you, Riley? I can't understand you."

Riley took a breath. "Doc Julie Rae's hospital in the back. We'll need an ambulance too."

"On the way. Is this where the shots fired came from? Are you hit?"

"Yes, shots. No, I'm fine."

Riley knelt near Doc Junior while she spoke. "One canine gunshot patient. Doc Rae is tending to him. The second patient is a man with a chest wound. His breathing is a little ragged." She heard nearby sirens and glanced up at the vehicle with flashing blue lights that was followed by another vehicle with flashing red lights before she moved closer to Doc Julie Rae.

The sheriff and the fire chief beat the ambulance to the parking lot. The sheriff hurried to Riley and Doc Julie Rae and glanced at the fallen man while the fire chief directed the ambulance to Doc Junior.

"You okay? Do you need help getting Jordy inside?" Sheriff asked.

"We're okay, and yes, I need help with Jordy," Doc Julie Rae said. "We'll need x-rays, Riley."

"On it." Riley and Toby dashed inside, and Riley set up the trauma room and the x-ray room then rushed with the trauma table to the back door in time for Doc and the Sheriff to load Jordy onto it.

Riley wheeled Jordy into x-ray. "I'm so proud of you, Jordy. You did an outstanding job of saving me from the bad man. Dr. Witmer would be proud of you too. You are so brave."

Jordy whimpered.

"Yes, I shot the bad man, and he's going to spend a very long time in prison."

After the x-rays, Riley rolled Jordy to the trauma room and Julie Rae studied the x-rays.

Doc Thad rushed into the trauma room. "Sheriff told me you all would need me in here. Riley, when you can break away, Sheriff wants to talk to you."

"No bones broken; no vital organs hit. I have a feeling Jordy's guardian angel worked overtime," Doc Julie Rae said.

Riley stroked Jordy's face. "Good news, Jordy, you're going to be okay. Sheriff wants to talk to me while Doc Julie Rae and Doc Thad patch you up."

Jordy whined.

"Thanks, and you're right. They'll take good care of you."

After Riley left the trauma room, she hugged Toby. "You made a big difference, Toby. I couldn't have shot Doc Junior before he shot you or me if you hadn't understood why I needed for you to drop down. You are awesome. Let's talk to the sheriff."

Before she reached the back door, the sheriff came inside. "Let's go to the breakroom; I need some coffee, and Doc Thad said he'd start a pot."

Riley and Toby followed the sheriff down the hallway. After the sheriff entered the breakroom, he paused, and his face softened as he smiled. "When the sheriff in Carson and I talked last week, I asked him to release Ben earlier than two weeks because I needed help with our crime spree. Ben won't know that until he gives notice."

Riley nodded and wavered before she grabbed onto a chair to keep from losing her balance.

"Please sit because you look like you're going to drop." Sheriff pointed to a chair then poured two cups of coffee.

After he joined Riley at the table, he said, "Now, tell me what happened, but take it slow because I'm turning into an old man faster than I planned, thanks to you and the dogs."

Sheriff leaned back in his chair as he sipped his coffee and listened. She told him about picking up her car, forgetting her lunch, Jordy recognizing Alyse Termaine, and Toby recognizing Doc Junior.

"Take a breath and sip your coffee." Sheriff drained his cup.

Riley shivered. "It was foggy, but when Doc Junior got close, we saw the pistol in his hand. The dogs rushed him, and he shot Jordy. I shouted for Toby to get down, and he did so I could stop Doc Junior before he shot Toby or me. The wound in Doc Junior's chest looked like I hit him where I aimed—in the midline of his upper chest. I kicked his pistol away from him then attended to Jordy with Doc Julie Rae who ran out with her shotgun after she heard the shots."

A deputy motioned to the sheriff from the hallway, and the two men spoke in low voices. Sheriff returned and joined Riley. "Allen Truman, Junior, confessed to murdering Dr. Witmer, Dotty, and Daphne. His chest wound was not fatal, according to the emergency department doctor, but Truman's body was weakened by years of being a meth addict, and he expired."

"I'm so sorry," Riley said.

"I understand, but remember you shot him after he shot Jordy, and when he had aimed at you. You didn't kill him; you stopped him from killing you. The meth killed him."

When Riley's phone rang, Sheriff glanced at her phone and refilled Riley's cup before he left the room.

Riley picked up the phone. "Before you yell at me, I'd like to tell you about rabies tags and neem oil soap."

She held the phone away from her ear, as Ben shouted, "Why can't you just go to work like normal people and not have to shoot a killer before you go inside?"

"Are you done?" Riley asked.

Ben sighed. "For now. Tell me about rabies tags, neem oil soap, and killers."

ACKNOWLEDGMENTS

Huge thanks to my husband for his patience, support, talented technical expertise, and guidance, and to my editor for her ever-ready pocket of commas and magic word-slicing sword.

Thank you for reading. The greatest gift any author receives from a reader is a review. Readers read the reviews, reviews determine where a book ranks in comparison with other books, and more than once, a review has made my day.

WHAT'S NEXT?

RILEY MALLOY THRILLER, BOOK 2

DEFY DEATH

Riley, vet tech and dog whisperer, stands in the way of a desperate criminal. Easy fix. Kill Riley.

SUBSCRIBE to the newsletter!

FIND the Subscribe button on www.judithabarrett.com

ABOUT THE AUTHOR

Judith A. Barrett is an award-winning author of mystery, thriller, crime, and survival novels with action and adventure to spark the reader's imagination. Her unusual main characters are brilliant, talented, and down-to-earth folks who solve difficult cases and stop killers. Her novels take place in small towns and rural areas in the southern states of the US.

Judith lives in rural Georgia on a small farm with her husband and dogs. When she's not busy writing, Judith is busy with farm chores, walking with her husband while the dogs investigate the field, or watching the beautiful sunsets from her porch.

Website   www.judithabarrett.com

Newsletter   *Subscribe* to her eNewsletter via her Website

Let's keep in touch!

Made in the USA
Columbia, SC
09 April 2023

14458495R00241